Star Promise

G.J. Walker-Smith

Star Promise

Print Edition

© 2014 G.J. Walker-Smith

Cover by Scarlett Rugers, http://www.scarlettrugers.com
Formatting by Polgarus Studio, http://www.polgarusstudio.com

Other Books by G.J Walker-Smith
Saving Wishes (Book One, The Wishes Series)
Second Hearts (Book Two, The Wishes Series)
Sand Jewels (Book 2.5, The Wishes Series)
Storm Shells (Book Three, The Wishes Series)
Secret North (Book Four, The Wishes Series)
Silver Dawn (Book 4.5, The Wishes Series)

Contact the author:
https://www.facebook.com/gjwalkersmith
gjwalkersmith@gmail.com
gjwalkersmith.com

For Michaela,
the princess of gentle nudges and the queen of hard shoves.

Acknowledgements

To my family, thank you for affording me the opportunity to write when the mood hits, even at the expense of dinner and clean clothes. I love you very much.

To my friend, Sophia. Thank you for all that you do. When I grow up, I hope to be just as organised and brilliant as you are.

To my Gems. I am in awe of the unwavering support you all give, and I'm so very appreciative of the friendships I've made.

To my girlies in the NGs. Don't tell any one, but I love you all dearly. Thank you for making my days so much shinier.

CONTENTS

1. GREAT HEIGHTS

Charli

The Décarie men are no angels.

Adam can be regimented and stubborn, Ryan can be arrogant and cocky, and their father can be downright tyrannical. I'd been at war with all of them at one time or another, but tonight's battle was with Jean-Luc.

Attending Ryan's birthday dinner was a chore made more difficult by the fact that Adam didn't show up. The king's smugness when explaining why was almost harder to bear than the abominable food. "You must understand, Charli," he said. "Work comes first. It's the way of the world."

"Not our world," I shot back.

He smirked. "Your world must be a wondrous place."

Most of the time it was, just not when I was left to defend myself against Jean-Luc's invisible blows.

I didn't blame Adam for not showing up. Thanks to his father, his workload was impossible. Accepting a job at Décarie, Fontaine and Associates was a mistake, but the only one with the power to pull the pin was Adam. And as long as he felt the need to stand up to the king, that was never going to happen.

I wasn't sharing the same level of career dissatisfaction. I loved my job at the gallery. I was surrounded by beautiful art all day and the cushy hours I worked meant that I got to spend plenty of time with my little girl.

Bridget had made the switch from the Apple Isle to the Big Apple without fuss, swapping days at the beach for days in the park. The change hadn't hurt her. Her imagination was still perfectly in focus, which meant that as far as parenting goes, we were doing a good job.

While she was occupied playing under the coffee table, I slipped out to call her dad. Standing in the big empty foyer near the front door wasn't going to buy me any privacy. I knew from past experience that even whispered words echoed off the marble floor, so I retreated to the downstairs bathroom.

Adam answered straight away. "Hey, I'm sorry." I hadn't even said a word yet. It proved that he knew what an ordeal dinner with his parents was when he wasn't there. "I'll make it up to you."

"I'm not mad," I insisted.

"No?"

"No. Your dad is being a jerk but I escaped." I sat on the edge of the bath. "I'm hiding out in the bathroom. I wish you were here."

"That could be dangerous – or productive, depending on how you look at it." His low laugh sounded positively sinister, with good reason. We were ninety-nine percent sure that our daughter was conceived in that bathroom.

"Wise guy. What time do you think you'll leave work?"

He sighed, and I could hear him shuffling papers around. "Late, I think. I've got so much to do."

It was a reply I was expecting, but it still disappointed me. "Okay, well you know where I'll be when you're done."

"In the bathroom?"

"No, in bed," I laughed, "waiting for you to make it up to me for blowing off dinner."

"Challenge accepted, Charlotte," he replied. "I'll see you later."

***

I returned to the lounge room feeling slightly more optimistic about making it through the evening until my father-in-law took one more shot at pulling me into line.

"I don't enjoy tension, Charli. I hope you've calmed down."

That was a lie. Jean-Luc thrived on tension. I didn't bother answering. I sat next to Ryan and tried my hand at silent combat instead. I could've stared him down indefinitely, but the battle was cut short when Bridget and Fiona walked in. I'd been so focused on the king that I hadn't even noticed they were gone.

Fiona kept a firm hold on Bridget's hand as she paraded her around the room. My little girl looked thoroughly miffed, which was understandable considering she was sporting a heavy tweed coat in July.

I was annoyed for a different reason. Fiona constantly took it upon herself to rain expensive gifts on Bridget. Absolutely nothing was off limits and I resented it, but like most Décarie related gripes, I kept it to myself.

I managed to force an insincere thank you just before Bridget broke free and landed in my lap.

"I don't like it, Mummy," she whispered.

"Shush," I replied, determined to keep the peace.

We made it through dinner and got out of there as quickly as we could.

I probably would've taken Ryan up on his offer of walking us home if we'd been heading that way, but I had bigger plans. If Adam couldn't come to us, we were going to go to him.

***

The massive foyer of the office building looked even bigger than usual when it was all lit up and empty. I knew the front doors would be locked but was hopeful that someone would be there to let us in. I was prepared to bribe security with cake if necessary, but I didn't get the chance. There wasn't a soul in sight. Our surprise was totally ruined, leaving me with no choice but to call Adam to come downstairs to get us.

"You're here?" he asked.

"We're outside," I explained. "But we're locked out."

"We brought you cake, Daddy," yelled Bridget.

Adam told me to stay put. "I'm coming down now anyway."

It seemed to take forever for him to get there. Bridget – ramped up on an excess of chocolate cake – killed time by jumping around on the front steps.

"Slow your roll, Bridge," I ordered. "You're going to hurt yourself."

"Mummy, I hate Mamie's coat," she said.

I didn't give her declaration too much credence. There were no shades of grey with Bridget. She either loved something or she hated it. She also changed her mind at the drop of a hat. There was a fair chance that it would become her favourite piece by winter.

My opinion, on the other hand, was firm. I hated the bloody coat.

"We'll talk about it another day," I said, unwilling to discuss it with her.

"I love paper money," she said randomly.

"Do you?"

"Papy gave me paper money." She reached into the front pocket of her dress and pulled out a fifty-dollar bill. "See?"

I fought the urge to snatch it from her. "You're a lucky girl," I said falsely. "Put it back in your pocket, baby."

"Why?"

I pointed at the glass behind her. "Because your daddy is here."

As Adam ambled across the empty lobby, a security guard appeared out of nowhere and let him out. Finally he was free – at least until morning when he'd don his pretentious suit and go back again.

"Hey, little girl," he crowed, scooping Bridget off her feet.

She leaned back and took his face in her hands. It was Bridget's most powerful move, one she made when commanding total attention. "Ry's very old today," she announced making him laugh. "We happy-dayed him."

"Awesome." Adam leaned across and kissed me. "Sorry I missed dinner."

I shrugged. "Are you hungry?" I half heartedly waved the plate of cake at him.

I couldn't blame him for his look of distaste. The frosting had run and the chocolately mess was stuck to the Clingfilm.

"I made it," said Bridget proudly. "I let Ry help."

"How about we find a restaurant and get Daddy some real dinner before he has his cake?" I suggested.

"Yeah." Adam shifted his hold on Bridget to check his watch. "Let's go."

***

The balmy July night was perfect weather for walking, but Adam was tired and Bridget's slow wander was beginning to grate on him. She was tired too, scuffing her little boots along the pavement with each step she took – but she still insisted on walking.

Her father finally lost patience and picked her up. Bridget didn't complain, which meant she truly was ready to drop at any second. When she buried her head in his shoulder, I used the opportunity to dump the cake in a nearby bin while she wasn't looking.

We ended up at the first restaurant we came across, a little Chinese place hidden behind scaffolding on Broadway. Adam ate, I drank tea and Bridget embarked on a one-girl sword fight with a pair of chopsticks. It was a short war. She climbed onto Adam's lap a few minutes later and crashed, still holding her weapons.

Adam somehow managed to keep eating with the dead weight of a sleeping child in his arms. "Are you sure you don't want anything?" he asked. "I'll share."

"No thank you." I huffed out a long breath. "Your mum cooked tonight. I won't be able to eat again until Wednesday."

"I'm sorry I missed it."

It had to be the fiftieth time he'd apologised in as many minutes, and judging by the grimace on his face, he was beginning to annoy even himself. I moved quickly to change the subject. "You look tired."

He abandoned the frown in favour of a sly smile. "Not too tired."

I smiled back. "How was work?"

"I don't want to talk about work." The frown set in again. "How was your day?"

Adam never talked about his job. I wasn't even sure what he did during the long hours he spent at the office. I never pushed for an explanation. I knew he was unhappy there, and I also knew that as long as we were in New York he was never going to admit it to me. As a result, we had a lot of conversations that danced around the subject.

"It was okay. We spent the morning at Ryan's making cake, had a quiet afternoon and then headed to the palace for dinner."

Adam pushed food around his plate. "Dad gave you a hard time?"

I shrugged. "Nothing I couldn't handle."

I could see the tension in his jaw. "I don't know what his problem is."

"I do," I volunteered. "You married her."

Tired as he was, his dark blue eyes shone as he smiled across at me. "A mistake, you think?"

"A massive error in judgement," I confirmed. "You'll never amount to anything now."

Adam reached for me. "You're wrong, Charlotte." He kissed my hand and then kissed the top of Bridget's head. "I'm pretty sure I've reached great heights."

2. GIRAFFE STOCK

Adam

After eight months of taking care of Bridget during the week, Mrs Brown was starting to become unreliable – and always at the last minute. Keeping up with Bridget was hard, and it was becoming more and more obvious that sweet old Mrs Brown just wasn't up to the task any more.

"We need to find someone else, Charli." I slipped my phone into my pocket. "Mrs Brown isn't working out."

"I know," she agreed, kissing the top of Bridget's head as she passed. "We'll sort it out."

If Charli had a plan, she wasn't sharing. She was heading for the door as if our childcare problem didn't exist.

"Stop right there, blondie," I ordered.

She dropped her grip on the door handle and turned back. "I'm going to be late."

"I'm already late," I replied.

"Me too," added Bridget.

Both of us looked across at the scruffy girl at the table eating breakfast. Some mornings we were organised, and some mornings we weren't – like today. There was a puddle of milk on the table, Bridget was still wearing pyjamas, and even from a distance I could see oatmeal in her hair.

"One of us has to stay home."

"I would love to." Charli's smooth tone would've sounded completely believable to Bridget, but I knew better. "But I have a meeting at nine."

I didn't even need to put my argument forward. There was no way I could swing a day off.

"He owes you a day, Adam," she added. "You've worked late all week." I shook my head but didn't reply, mindful of little ears. "Fine," Charli huffed, changing tack. "We'll resolve this like adults."

Scissors, paper, rock probably wasn't the most adult way to settle who'd stay home, but that's how we decided. Charlotte won because Charlotte always wins, but Bridget was confused by the result. "Who's the winner?"

"Your daddy is," she replied, grinning at me. "You've got him for the whole day, Bridge."

"I just love that winner!" she squealed, whacking her spoon on the edge of the table.

Bridget scored the first kiss. I got one in the dying seconds as Charli was leaving. Even in heels, she had to stretch to kiss me. She wasn't the least bit apologetic so I stood tall, making access difficult. "I love you both," she said, straightening my tie.

As the front door closed, I looked across at my newly acquired sidekick, wondering how the heck I was going to tie the day together. I had a mountain of work waiting for me at the office, and not getting it done would mean another night of working back late.

"Bridge, what experience do you have in drafting stock purchase agreements?" I asked.

She shrugged. "I like giraffe stock."

I smiled. "Perfect. You're hired. Let's go." She clambered off the chair before asking where we were headed. "You can come to work with me today."

She took off down the hall, heading for the bathroom. If her excitement had anything to do with spending the day with giraffes, she was out of luck. The only animals working at my office were lions and the odd snake.

***

I usually spent the long elevator ride up to the office in silence, daydreaming of all the ways I could tell my dad to shove his stupid job.

This morning was a little different. There's nothing silent about a little girl protesting at having her hair brushed. "Stand still," I demanded.

"I can't stand still," Bridget replied. "My feet need to move."

I shoved her hairbrush into her backpack, admitting defeat. "You look like a street urchin, Bridge."

I watched her through the mirror, sweeping her messy hair from her eyes. "Yes, I do," she proudly agreed.

A bell chimed and the doors opened onto the forty-third floor, home of the law offices of Décarie, Fontaine and Associates.

I firmly held Bridget's hand as we walked through the reception area, successfully ignoring Tennille's disapproving stare as we passed her desk.

"In here, baby," I said, leading Bridget through my office door.

I had no clue how I was going to occupy her for the day. Bribery was my best bet. "If you're a good girl I'll take you out for lunch," I offered, closing the door. "Anywhere you want to go." I was prepared to endure a meal of chicken nuggets if necessary.

Bridget was loud and fidgety and had no place in a law office, but she did look the part as she dumped her little backpack down on my desk and took up residence on my chair. Perhaps her outfit had something to do with it. After getting her showered, dressed and semi presentable, she had made me wait ten minutes while she raided my closet for a tie, settling on a blue silk number that she claimed matched her pink boots nicely.

She grabbed one end of her tie and flapped it at me. "Can you tie it better, please?"

I spun the chair so she was facing me. "Is a Windsor knot okay?"

"No, I need a girl knot."

I looped the tie around her neck. "A girl knot it is."

There must've been something wrong with my technique. She asked me to redo it, and I obliged as if I had nothing better to do with my time. My father stormed my office a moment later to remind me otherwise.

I wasn't worried about bearing his wrath. As long as Bridget was in the room, I was untouchable. She scrambled off the chair and ran to greet him. "*Bonjour*, Papy!"

Dad scooped her up at the last second, saving them both from certain collision. I reclaimed my chair.

"Why are you here today, my love?" He sounded calm and cheerful, but wasn't. "Little girls don't belong here."

Bridget picked up the end of her tie and waved it at him. "Yes I do. I have a tie."

Dad glared at me. "Your mother could watch her if you're in a bind," he suggested. "Call her."

"She's fine, Dad," I muttered. "She brought plenty of toys to keep herself occupied."

The mention of toys reminded Bridget of her backpack. She wriggled free of her grandfather, rushed back to my desk and upended the whole lot, scattering severed doll parts everywhere.

For Dad, it was the last straw. "Call your mother," he demanded, exiting the room.

"Poor Papy," said Bridget, piling onto my lap. "He's too busy to play with us today."

***

It would've been logical to call my mother to babysit. I just couldn't bring myself to do it. Any time spent with my daughter was precious, even if it was spent trying to stop her rifling through my desk.

I pulled her hand free of the drawer and closed it – for the third time in as many minutes.

"I need something in there," she insisted.

"What do you need?"

Bridget replied as if it was a silly question. "All the things that are in there."

It should've been a conversation that annoyed me, but it wasn't. I was more pissed at the prospect of having to do some actual work. I leaned back in my chair, resting my hands behind my head while I plotted my next move.

"Look," I said finally. "I'll make you a deal."

"I love deals!" She bounced on the spot. "I just love them."

"You're in luck then." Her bright blue eyes widened as I pulled open the top drawer of my desk. "You can have one thing in here – anything you like." I glanced inside and instantly regretted the offer – she was likely to choose the stapler. I continued negotiations anyway. "All you have to do in return is sit quietly and let me get some work done."

I breathed a sigh of relief when she made a grab for the calculator.

"Do we have a deal, Bridge?"

She nodded too many times to be believable. "Yes, a lovely deal."

***

With the exception of the quiet chatter directed at the pile of dolls spread out on the floor in front of her, Bridget kept to our arrangement.

She was still distracting me, but it wasn't her fault. Hearing her narrate emails to Ryan as she typed them up on her calculator was far more entertaining than anything I had going on.

"I love today, Daddy," she said out of the blue.

"Me too." I meant it.

"Can we go home now?"

I glanced at my watch. Skipping out early would earn me a two-hour lecture from the king the next day. On the plus side, he might fire me at the end of it.

"Yeah," I replied, closing my laptop. "Let's get out of here. We'll go to the park."

Playing in the park and chicken nugget lunches were always going to trump mind-numbing hours in the office, but that hadn't always been my mindset. Having Bridget changed everything. I'd learned to find joy in small things, and my daughter was the ultimate small thing.

Her take on the world was just as left of centre as her mama's, only louder. She was bright, sweet and unintentionally funny – and by far the greatest gift Charlotte had ever given me.

***

11

We slipped out of the office stealthily, turned onto Broadway and just kept walking. I had no idea where we were heading, and Bridget didn't seem to care. Her focus was on more important things, namely her plans for the rest of the day. "We need to go shopping," she told me.

I tightened my hold on her hand as we waited for the crosswalk light. "Why, Bridge?"

"I have too much money."

Spoken like a true Décarie, I didn't reply.

"My bag is full of paper money," she added.

The light turned green but I stood firm, much to Bridget's annoyance. "We can go now," she said, tugging on my hand.

"Wait." I slipped her backpack off her shoulders. "Show me where the money is."

She pointed at the front pocket. I nearly choked when I unzipped it. It was stuffed to the brim with fifty dollar bills. Working hard to keep the alarm out of my voice, I questioned her about it.

"Papy gave them to me," she explained.

"When?"

She shrugged. "All the time."

I was livid. Charli and I went to great lengths to keep Bridget grounded and unspoiled, which wasn't easy to do while living in Manhattan. Having her grandparents undermine us didn't help. Mom did it in the form of toys and clothes. I had no idea Dad was corrupting her with cold hard cash.

I wanted rid of it, and I didn't care what she spent it on. As far as I was concerned, it would serve my father right to find out that his money had been blown on frivolous junk.

I zipped the bag closed and reached for Bridget's hand. "Let's go."

Anger determined my pace as we crossed the road, which was unfair. The second I realised that Bridget was skipping to keep up with me I stopped walking. Ignoring the fact that I was loading my daughter up with hundreds of dollars on a public street, I hooked her bag over her shoulder and picked her up.

"What do you want to buy, Bridge?" I asked.

Her eyes bored into mine while she thought it through. "A treasure map," she finally replied. "One that squirrels can't read."

Every ounce of anger I felt dissolved in an instant. It was going to take more than a pile of money to taint her. No matter how much Décarie my kid had in her, the Blake part of her always shone through.

3. ART ADVENTURES

Charli

Art is subjective. What some consider sheer perfection is unappealing to others. My boss, Bronson Merriman, was subjective too.

Many people disliked him. He was loud, animated and insulted someone every time he opened his mouth. I, however, adored him. He was kind, generous and extremely supportive of up-and-coming photographers and artists. Those traits explained why he hired me to do a job that I was nowhere near qualified to do.

"Passion for art cannot be taught," he told me during our first meeting in Melbourne. "You have it here," he put his hand to his heart, "and here," he added tapping his temple.

Not all his words of wisdom were as insightful, but all were memorable. He once told Adam that his mother should've cut out his eyes and bottled them at birth. "Cobalt blue is my favourite Wedgwood colour. They should be kept in a gallery and admired by all."

Adam hid his horror well, but he did make me promise never to let him near Bridget. He'd also never been back to the gallery since.

Bronson knew his people skills were zilch. As a result, I handled most of the sales and had recently been entrusted with the task of buying new pieces for the gallery. It was a very big deal, and I always gave my best – a far cry from the girl I used to be. There's a certain confidence that comes with knowing you're on the right path. I was headed in the right direction. The tricky part nowadays was keeping Adam from wandering off course.

***

After meeting with a prospective buyer over brunch at a midtown café, I rushed back to the gallery so Bronson could leave. He met me at the door, almost complimenting me on my shoes as he left. "I love them, darling." He kissed both my cheeks. "Being three feet tall is challenging. It's nice that they make pretty heels for you."

The rest of the morning passed fairly slowly. In between cataloguing, I had time to embark on a gossipy text message session with Bente. The gossip was extra juicy that morning. Years after having her heart stomped on by Ryan, she was gearing up for round two.

A chance meeting the day before had paved the way for Ryan to make amends. I truly believed he regretted the way he had treated her in the past. I just wasn't sure he was beyond doing it again.

– Want me to lay down the law and tell him to behave?

Her reply was almost instant.

– No. I like him better when he's bad.

I smiled down at my phone. If they could survive the date without killing each other, it might just work out for them. I was midway through telling her so when the front door opened.

I abandoned the texting in an instant, dropped my phone into my drawer and neatened my hair. Then I looked up and wished I hadn't bothered.

I knew Jean-Luc would be upset that Adam hadn't shown at work that day. What I didn't realise was that he'd be angry enough to seek me out and take me to task over it.

"Good morning, Charli."

"Hi," I replied warily. "What are you doing here?"

Jean-Luc ignored me, wandering away to check the pictures lining the side wall.

I stayed put.

"I wondered if you might like to go to lunch with me," he finally replied. "We haven't had a chance to talk much lately."

The king and I didn't do lunch. Snarky comments and impolite banter was more our speed.

"I can't." I tried to sound regretful, but failed. "I'm the only one here for the day."

"It's a terrible thing to be left in the lurch." He slowly turned to face me, arms folded and bulletproof. "I'm sure your boss is grateful to have someone so diligent working for him."

"I'm sure he is."

"I appreciate the same level of dedication from my employees, especially my son."

My heels clicked on the wooden floor as I marched over to him. "Cut him some slack for once," I said boldly. "Bridget needed him today."

I wasn't remotely scared of the king, but every now and then I'd say something that truly pissed him off – and today, this was it. If I said it didn't rattle me, I'd be lying.

"You're detrimental to Adam's career," he snapped. "Do you understand that?"

"He's spending the day with his daughter," I returned, matching his angry tone. "I didn't steal him away."

Jean-Luc turned his back on me and resumed studying the pictures. "I understand that you need this little art adventure." The rage was gone, paving the way for condescension. "But you need to manage your time better. Stop being selfish and take care of my granddaughter properly."

I didn't know whether to be insulted or hurt. I went with royally pissed off. "What exactly are you accusing me of?"

The king took it up a notch. He turned around, gearing up to quietly yell at me. "You lumber him with the child as if his time is secondary," he hissed. "Adam put everything on hold for you four years ago. Enough is enough."

Jean-Luc had a cruel habit of making me second-guess my whole life in just a few sentences. It was pure artistry. I never got used to it and I never got over it, but I always fought back.

"Adam put everything on hold for you his whole life," I bitterly replied. "He knows better now."

Jean-Luc shook his head. "Adam put his heart and soul into –"

"I am his heart," I cut him off. "And Bridget is his soul. He's not yours any more."

I might as well have slapped his face. The king pulled in a long breath through his nose and straightened his pose. He pointed to a photograph to the right of me. "I want this picture for my home office."

He'd thrown me. It was as if the last nasty two minutes of conversation hadn't happened. I took a long minute to study the picture, trying to pull myself together. The black and white photograph of a derelict old yacht didn't seem his style, though it was gorgeous.

"Have it delivered to the house," he added.

"Say please."

"Please, Charlotte," he sarcastically amended.

I cocked my head and focused on the picture. "Why do you like it?"

I wasn't trying to rattle his cage. I was always curious to know what compelled people when choosing art for their homes.

"It's black and white," he replied. "It will suit the room."

"Half the pictures in this place are black and white. Why choose this one?"

He glanced at the picture. "You have terrible business acumen, Charli," he chided. "Appalling, in fact."

I quickly reined in the smile incited by his mediocre dig. "I'll add that to my list of shortfalls."

"I'm serious," he replied. "If you were selling me a car, would it be appropriate to ask me why I was buying it?"

I looked him straight in the eye, and let my smile break free. "I don't sell cars. I'm on an art adventure."

The king smirked at me. "You have a smart mouth."

I focused back on the photograph. "Maybe this picture chose you," I suggested. "Did you consider that?"

"Stop with the nonsense," he snapped. "Have it delivered tomorrow."

"It's four thousand dollars."

"Fine. I want it framed too."

I locked eyes with him. "That's an extra two thousand dollars."

"Fine."

"I'll get back to you about the delivery charges," I added.

The corner of his mouth lifted. "If you're trying to punish me, Charli, let it be known that it would take more than one lifetime to do it financially."

4. THE LITTLE BAD WOLF

Adam

Sourcing a treasure map in downtown Manhattan is no mean feat, especially one that challenges the literary skills of squirrels. I was just about to call the mission off and suggest Bridget find something else to buy when we stumbled across a military surplus store.

We spent a long time staring into the small window display. Everything in it was thick with dust and looked like it had been there for years. Old cigarette tins, yellowing decks of novelty playing cards and a stack of ancient newspapers held my attention. Bridget was fascinated by something else.

"I love that hat, Daddy."

I followed her pointed finger. "It's not a hat, baby. It's a gas mask."

"Can I buy it?"

I could deal with the quirk of her wearing galoshes every day of her life, but I'd struggle if she took to wearing a war-issue gas mask. "I don't think so," I said gently. "I have a better idea."

The antique brass compass I spotted at the back of the cramped display was the perfect alternative to a treasure map – and even better, the hefty price tag chewed up Bridget's loot. I didn't try beating the shop owner down on price, which should've made for a short transaction. Instead I found myself giving Bridget a long lesson in the value of a dollar. She was perfectly willing to buy the compass until it came time to hand over the money.

Then she wanted both.

I excused us from the counter and pulled her aside. "One or the other, Bridget," I explained. "You can't have both."

Bridget leaned to the side, sneaking a quick glimpse at the man behind the counter. "Ask him nicely," she said, getting upset. "Say please."

"It doesn't work that way." I swept her hair off her face. "If you want the compass, you have to pay for it."

The tears that followed weren't entirely her fault. She was used to sweet-talking people to get her own way. She did it to Ryan all the time, and had never once been told no by either of my parents. Parting with her money was new to her, and she wasn't handling it well.

There's nothing discreet about a little girl melting down in a small store, but my efforts at pulling her into line were. I bought us a little privacy by speaking to her in French. "Make a decision, Bridget," I demanded.

"*Les deux,*" she whimpered.

"You can't have both."

She fell forward, clung to my legs and began wailing as if her world was ending. The easy option would've been to cave and give her what she wanted. After a nanosecond of deliberation I went with the hard option and gave her what she needed instead.

Slightly embarrassed by my feral kid, I scooped her up, apologised to the man behind the counter, and for the first time in her short life carried her out of a place kicking and screaming.

***

It was a long cab ride home. Bridget spent the whole ride switching between calmly begging me to go back to the store and wailing about how mean I was when I refused. How we weren't thrown out mid-journey is beyond me.

Bridget didn't notice that Charli was home when we got there, mainly because she refused to come inside. She parked her butt on the floor of the foyer and told me she wasn't moving.

"Okay," I replied cheerily. "I guess I'll see you later then."

Before she had a chance to sass me again, I closed the door.

"What the heck is going on?" Charli rushed toward me. "You just locked our kid out?"

"Today she's your kid," I clarified. "And she's fine."

Charli couldn't seem to find words. It was an understandable reaction. She'd missed all the drama. The only thing she saw was me locking our daughter out of the apartment.

"She's fine, Charlotte," I mumbled, leaning against the door as if there was a chance the little bad wolf was about to bust her way in. "Trust me on this one."

After a long moment of focusing on Charli's worried face, self-doubt began to niggle. I was just about to open the door when a tiny little knock came from the other side.

I slowly opened it. "Yes, miss?" I asked. "Can I help you?"

"I'm home now, Daddy."

Bridget was calm, collected and marginally contrite. She also looked exhausted. Tantrums take a lot out of a girl. I stepped to the side and waved my arm as if royalty was entering. "Welcome back, Bridge," I announced. "We missed you."

***

There's no rest for the wicked, which is unfortunate because despite the fact that she needed a ten-hour nap, Bridget had dinner plans for the evening.

I thought Ryan's scheme of using her to win his date over was stupid, but Charli had already agreed to let her go. I didn't argue because with Bridget gone, I'd have her mother to myself for a few hours.

"It's not a real date," explained Charli. "He's going out with Bente."

"And he needs Bridget to referee?"

"Don't be cynical," she scolded. "He's really looking forward to it."

So was his niece. She came bounding down the hallway with an armful of clothes. It must've been a heavy load. She stopped short and hurled them the rest of the way.

"Which one are you wearing, Bridge?" asked Charli, stooping to pick them up.

"All of them," she replied matter-of-factly.

"Pick one dress," instructed Charli. "You can't wear them all."

Perhaps confused by the déjà vu moment she was having, Bridget frowned. "Do I have to give you my money?"

Charli thrust a yellow dress at her. "Bring it back undamaged and there's no charge."

Satisfied with her answer, Bridget took off to her room dragging the dress behind her. Charli dumped the reject outfits on the couch. "Your dad gave her fifty dollars last night," she explained.

That would've been a good time to let her know that he'd actually given her ten times that amount, but I kept quiet. I was hoping for a peaceful evening making love, not war. I snaked my arm around her waist and pulled her against me.

"Do you think I should say something to him or just let it go?" she asked.

I swept her hair over her shoulder and kissed her neck.

"Adam?"

"What?"

She tightened her grip on my forearm. "I'm talking to you."

"Sorry," I murmured against her skin. "I couldn't hear you over all the imaginary sex we were having in my head."

Her quiet laugh was as warm as she was. "Was it good?"

"I'll let you know in about half an hour when it plays out for real."

5. CREEPY BABIES

Charli

Ryan Décarie had undergone some changes of late. No one seemed to notice that he'd slowly been changing his ways, but I did. I couldn't remember the last time he went out on a date, which probably explained his slightly nervous demeanour when he turned up at our door.

I felt the sudden urge to give him a pep talk. "It'll be fine, Ryan," I encouraged. "Just be yourself."

"Don't tell him that," Adam teased. "Bente knows him. The only hope he's got is if he pretends to be someone else."

The nerves must've really been getting to him. Ryan didn't have a comeback. In fact, he ignored his brother completely. "Where's Bridget?"

"She's just getting ready."

Ryan glanced at his watch. "Please Charli, no sparkly crowns or weird outfits. I need normal tonight."

I was about to ask him for his definition of normal when Bridget stormed the room, made a beeline for her uncle and crashed into his legs. Ryan obviously approved of the dress she was wearing. He thanked me.

"The boots stay though," I warned. "It's as normal as we get."

"I can live with the boots."

It was Adam who wasn't pleased. He called Bridget over and asked her to hand over her backpack. "The bag stays here, baby," he told her.

Bridget stood in front of her dad, hand on hips. It was a move we didn't see often, for which I was grateful. There's nothing remotely cute about a four-year-old with attitude.

"I need it."

"No, you don't."

There had been major drama that day. I hadn't gotten around to asking what it was about so I didn't dare intervene.

"Please, Daddy," she said sweetly.

Adam stepped forward and took the bag off her back. Bridget didn't protest, perhaps because Adam had the good sense to explain why he was doing it. "If Ryan finds out you've got all that money in there, he's going to ask you to pay for dinner."

Bridget glanced back at her uncle. "True, Ry?"

"Probably. I'm cheap like that."

"Hide it somewhere," she urged her father in a very loud whisper. "Near my girls."

Adam nodded. "Understood."

Bridget returned to Ryan and grabbed his hand. "Ready, Ry?"

"Born ready." It was too bad if he wasn't. Bridget was already dragging him out the door.

I stood in the doorway until they reached the elevator, shamelessly eavesdropping on their conversation.

"You have to use your money for the dinner, Ry," Bridget instructed. "I don't have any."

"Maybe it's time you got a job then," he replied.

She didn't miss a beat. "I will when I'm six."

I closed the door, chuckling, but the moment was lost the second I turned around. Adam was on the couch pulling wads of screwed-up money out of Bridget's bag.

"Where the hell did that come from?" I asked, aghast.

He finished counting it before replying. "Apparently every time Dad sees Bridget he slips her fifty dollars," he explained, dropping the pile on the coffee table. "There's seven hundred bucks there."

"How dare he?" I was appalled. "She has no clue about money."

"I know," he replied. "That was evident today when I tried to get her to part with it."

I listened as Adam filled me in on the debacle. Hearing the details didn't make me feel any better. I was furious. "You have to tell your father that it's not okay to do that!" I stared at the stack of money. "I am so sick of being undermined all the time."

"Me too." Ire was noticeably absent from his tone. Maybe it was because he'd had all day to stew over it, or perhaps it was because he had other things on his mind. He leaned to the side, pushing me onto my back. My body sank into the cushions as he pressed against me.

I put my hands to his face in a futile effort to keep him at bay. "You're thinking about imaginary sex again, aren't you?"

When he grinned, my thumb moved to the dimple in his cheek. "It's getting closer to reality now," he replied, expertly unbuttoning my shirt with one hand.

It had been a long time since we'd had an evening alone together. Spending it in bed was a wonderful idea, but Adam seemed to think I needed convincing. His hand crept inside my shirt, trailing a gentle line across my body. In a very unsexy move, my stomach chose that moment to rumble.

He lifted his head. "Hungry, Charlotte?"

"Starving," I reluctantly admitted.

"Well that won't do." He got up, reached for my hands and pulled me to my feet. I stepped forward and pressed my body hard against him. "Dinner can wait."

"You need to keep your energy up." He gave a wily grin. "My imagination ran wild this afternoon. I have big plans for us."

***

I opened a bottle of wine while Adam stood mindlessly watching the plate turning in the microwave.

"There's something very wrong with this picture," he lamented. "Our daughter is probably enjoying filet mignon for dinner and we're having reheated leftovers."

I wrenched his folded arms apart and worked my way into his hold. "I'm hungry enough to eat it. I worked through lunch."

"I didn't," he replied. "I had to bribe Bridget with nuggets so she'd be quiet in the office."

I looked up at him but Adam didn't meet my eyes. "You went to work today?"

"Only for a few hours," he replied. "I had a few things that couldn't wait until tomorrow."

Jean-Luc's visit suddenly made sense. No wonder he was pissed. The only thing that would've infuriated him more than Adam being a no-show would've been Adam turning up with Bridget in tow.

I suddenly felt incredibly selfish. Taking Bridget to the office would have been a nightmare. I'd tried it once, and vowed to never let her set foot in the gallery again. How had Adam coped?

"What did Bridget do while you were there?" I asked.

He shrugged. "Played with her girls and typed emails on a calculator."

"And what did you do?"

He looked at me. "What do you mean?"

"I tell you about my job all the time. You never talk shop. I don't even know what it is that you actually do."

Adam kissed me, connecting with my lips at the exact time that the microwave dinged. "It's just not that interesting, Charli," he murmured, breaking our embrace. "To either of us."

I used the time it took him to plate up dinner to think his words through. I had always been under the impression that Adam was cagey about his job because it was complicated and stressful. The truth was much simpler: it bored him.

"I'm interested," I insisted. "Will you tell me?"

He turned around, a plate in each hand. "I'll tell you everything you want to know," he replied. "And then we're going to bed."

***

Adam Décarie was a corporate lawyer. That much I knew. What I didn't know was exactly what that meant. His explanation was an education and a half. Liaising between companies, negotiating mergers and drafting agreements sounded seriously hard-core. It also went a long way to explaining the ridiculous hours he worked.

"Did you always want to be a corporate lawyer?"

His dark blue eyes lit as he smiled. "Always."

"Why?"

"You ask a lot of questions, Mrs Décarie."

I took a sip of wine. "You're not usually this open with me," I told him. "I'm taking advantage of your candidness."

"My plan for tonight was to take advantage of you."

His grin was distracting, but I wasn't quite done. "Why corporate law?" I asked.

He let out a sigh. "Because it's less adversarial than other aspects of law," he explained. "I don't usually deal with wronged parties or criminals or people who've been ripped off. It's all about negotiating and closing amicable deals."

"So, you like your job?"

He grinned. He knew I was trying to garner some sort of confession out of him. "I like lots of things."

He pushed back his chair, making room for me on his lap. "Give me an example," I demanded.

"I like you," he murmured, slipping his arm around me. "I like you a lot."

"And?"

"And our kid," he added.

I smiled at him. "I like her too."

Adam dropped his head, whispering his next words into my ear. "Can we please go to bed and make another one?"

After toying with the idea for a year-and-a-half, the decision to have another baby had finally been made a month earlier. Meeting my little brother was the clincher. Convincing Adam that the time was right took no effort at all. If he'd had his way, we would've had a flock of free-range babies by now – and they probably wouldn't have been growing up in New York.

***

Running with the good cop, bad cop style of parenting only seemed to work for us some of the time. The biggest problem was, the little crook favoured the bad cop. Adam was much stricter with her than I, but Bridget relished the challenge.

The latest battle in the very long war played out over breakfast. Bridget was still keen to offload the small fortune her grandfather had given her, and Adam wasn't making it easy for her.

She wanted him to take her back to the store he'd carried her out of mid-tantrum the day before, and her pleas were falling on deaf ears.

"I will spend my money nicely," she assured him.

Adam stood and picked up his empty coffee mug. "Not happening, Bridge." He leaned down and kissed her as he passed her. "You chose to be a brat. You don't get two bites of the apple."

She twisted in her chair to look at him. "I love apples," she countered.

I laughed, but Bridget wasn't seeing the funny side. She was too busy plotting her next move. "I'll make a deal, Daddy." I wasn't surprised by her offer. Bridget and Adam liked to make deals. It was their thing.

Adam drew out her agony by making her wait for an answer. He poured another cup of coffee and sat back down at the table before uttering a word. "I'm listening," he said finally.

"I'll spend my money nicely and that's the deal."

Her smug tone was a little premature. Her father's stance didn't waver.

"Your negotiation skills need some work, Bridget," he replied. "Revise your offer and get back to me."

Bridget pointed her spoon at him. "I will," she declared.

As entertaining as breakfast wheeling and dealing was, it didn't last long. Adam left for work, Mrs Brown turned up to watch Bridget, and I made my way to a very familiar address on Fifth Avenue.

***

Fiona was expecting the delivery of the artwork Jean-Luc had bought, but she was not expecting me to deliver it. "Have you been demoted, darling?" She wasn't even kidding. She looked truly looked concerned.

"No." I huffed out the word in a laugh. "I just wanted to bring it over myself."

Her frown made way for a bright smile and open arms. "Come," she urged, waving me through the door. "It's lovely to see you."

I set the picture on the table in the foyer and offered to unwrap it. "Do you want to see it? He chose well."

Fiona grabbed my hand and spun me to face her. "No, darling," she replied looking me up and down. "I'd rather look at you. You always look so beautiful when you make an effort."

I dropped my head, glancing down at my outfit. I didn't think there was anything particularly special about the pale blue dress I was wearing until I remembered that she'd bought it for me. "It's one of my favourites," I lied.

Her face lit up. "I adore shopping for you – and for Bridget."

A braver woman might've taken the opportunity to air her grievances regarding excessive gift-giving, but I wasn't brave. I smiled and thanked her instead.

"Come," she said, leading me toward the stairs. "I have something to show you – a gift for my granddaughter."

A hundred excuses for not accepting it ran through my mind as I followed her, but none were polite enough to say out loud.

"She really doesn't need any more presents," I said gently. "Maybe you should keep it until her birthday."

The queen spun to face me. "Nonsense. Her birthday has only just passed."

"Which is exactly why you shouldn't be buying her gifts."

Fiona frowned, but wasn't angry. I'd hurt her feelings, which was ten times harder to deal with. "She's the only grandchild I have," she said pitifully. "Please don't taint that with rules."

"I won't," I mumbled. I'd let Adam do it.

Fiona led me into her bedroom and disappeared inside her massive walk-in closet. I remained near the doorway, unsure of what to do. The only thing that dulled the awkwardness was the fact that she kept talking.

"Bridget's going to love this," she predicted, from somewhere deep in the closet. "I've had it on order for weeks."

I felt like closing the door and locking her in; I could use the time alone to bounce on the massive four-poster bed. The thing was magnificent. Thankfully I managed to hold myself back.

"I'm sure she'll love it," I called distractedly.

The second she reappeared I wanted to rescind that statement. Whatever she was holding was oddly wrapped in a small pink blanket. The closer she got to me, the more I convinced myself that it was alive – or at least once was.

She was cradling it like a baby, and when she peeled the blanket back I understood why. I peered across, working hard to keep my expression straight as I studied the creepiest looking doll I'd ever seen.

"Isn't she exquisite?" asked Fiona.

"That's one word for it," I mumbled.

"She's handmade," she explained. "Very realistic."

Too realistic. I half expected it to start crying at any second. Perhaps Fiona did too – she was rocking it in her arms.

"Bridget's too young for something that precious," I reasoned. "She won't care for it properly."

"Nonsense," scoffed the queen. "It'll be good practice for her."

"For what?" My voice sounded as horrified as I felt.

"Well, I'm sure she'll have a little brother or sister one day," she hinted. "And there's Jack, of course."

I forced myself to have another look at the waxy corpse thing in her arms. "Jack looks nothing like that."

"Of course not," she replied, fussing with the blanket. "This one is a girl."

I couldn't think of a thing to say that would dissuade her from giving it to Bridget. All I could do was prepare her for the certain abuse it would receive in her care.

"Have you seen Bridget's doll collection?" I asked. "She pulls their arms and legs off so they're easier to dress."

Fiona glanced down at baby creepy. "You mustn't let her do that with this one," she warned. "It was hellishly expensive."

It was going from bad to worse. Not only was the hideous doll soon going to be living in my house – I was in charge of protecting it.

"I'll do my best," I promised listlessly.

The queen perked up in an instant. "Wonderful, darling," she crowed.

***

I was genuinely interested to see how Jean-Luc's new artwork would look in his home office, but after spending so long fussing with her fake grandkid, Fiona didn't have time to show me. "I've got an appointment downtown in an hour," she explained, checking the time on her watch. "You're welcome to stay and hang it yourself. Jean-Luc had a contractor in to put a hook in the wall yesterday."

She rushed over to the closet and I found myself in hot pursuit. "You paid someone to drive a hook into a wall?" I asked incredulously.

"Of course." She turned to face me, holding a pair of black heels in each hand. "Which ones, darling?"

I looked her up and down before pointing to the shoes in her left hand. As expected, she ignored me and went with the ones in her right. "Just lock the door when you leave," she instructed, slipping a foot into her shoe Cinderella-style. "Or stay, and we'll have a late lunch when I get back."

"I can't. I'm working."

"Of course you are, darling."

She was humouring me, but I let it go. Whether she believed me or not, I really did need to get back to the gallery so Bronson could make his mid-morning escape. I followed Fiona downstairs at her rushed pace, trying to pay attention to the list of demands she was throwing at me.

"I want you to come for dinner tomorrow night," she instructed. "I'll give Bridget her doll and make Adam his favourite meal."

"What's his favourite meal?" I asked curiously. There were a few contenders that I knew of, but nothing cooked by his mother.

Fiona stopped and turned so abruptly that I nearly knocked her down the winding stairs. "Darling, you know he loves venison."

I forced a smile while I told my lie. "Of course he does."

Fiona grabbed my hand and pulled me down a step. "I must go. I'll be late."

"Are you trying to take me with you?"

She released me and giggled her way to the door. "Have a lovely day, my darling."

I was bound to. I was alone in the castle without adult supervision.

***

No matter how many times I reminded myself that I had permission to be in Jean-Luc's home office, I couldn't stop the dreadful feeling that only comes when breaking rules. The office was a no-go zone. Until that moment, I'd never been further than the doorway. Realising it was probably my first and only visit, I spent some time looking around.

The furniture was exactly the same as the rest of the house – antique, wooden and huge. The view of the park from the big arched window was probably one of the best in the city, and in my cheekiest move of the day I sat at his desk to admire it.

Taking a selfie to prove I was there seemed juvenile but I did it anyway, then called Adam to brag.

"Hey," he answered. "I was just thinking about you."

"Really?" I asked, slowly spinning in the chair. "Was I naked?"

He laughed. "Almost."

"Guess where I am."

"I would love to play this game with you, Charlotte," he replied. "But I'm on my way to a meeting."

"Oh, that's too bad." I stopped spinning, got up and wandered over to the bookshelves lining the far wall. "It's a good game."

"Better than the one I'm playing, I'm sure." I could tell by his voice that he was on the move too. "I'm about to get hauled over the coals by my father."

"Because of yesterday?"

"I hope so," Adam replied. "I haven't prepared a defence for any other misdemeanours."

On a high shelf among the rows of perfectly aligned books was a small box. "Well," I said distractedly, "I wish you luck."

"That's it?" Adam sounded indignant. "I tell you I'm about to get slaughtered and you wish me luck?"

"I'm an old pro at being reprimanded," I reminded him. "Just agree with everything he says and promise to do better."

"Excellent advice, Coccinelle." I could hear the amusement in his voice. "It's good to see that your years of bad behaviour counted for something."

"I'm reformed now."

That was a lie. I was hanging off the library ladder, making a grab for the mystery box as I said it.

"I have to go," he told me.

I didn't answer. I was too preoccupied with the box, which I now knew contained a cache of Bridget's dolls. I had no idea what possessed her to hide them up there. I'd heard Jean-Luc warn her a hundred times not to go into his office.

I repositioned the box on the shelf and made my way down the ladder, managing to keep my grip on the phone. "Before you go Adam, can I ask you something?"

"Of course."

"When you were little, did you ever do anything naughty just to piss your dad off?"

33

"No," he admitted. "I never did. I was good and respectful well behaved."

"Like your daughter?"

"Yes." He laughed again. "Just like my daughter."

I stepped off the ladder and looked up at the box, marvelling at just how high Bridget had climbed to stash it. "It's never too late to change your ways, Adam," I told him, smiling. "A little illegal activity is good for the soul. Even Bridget knows that."

6. APRON STRINGS

Adam

By the time I walked into my father's office, the pound of flesh he planned to strip from me had grown to two. I could tell he was pissed before he even spoke.

"Take a seat," he ordered.

I did, but with attitude. "I'm fine thanks, Dad. How are you?"

"If you wanted pleasantries, Adam, you should've arrived on time."

I wasn't overly concerned by the cool reception. He had a right to be upset. Bringing Bridget to the office was unprofessional and bailing on my working day two hours later was irresponsible.

"I'm sorry about yesterday," I said. "It won't happen again."

I didn't even come close to winning him over. His sour expression remained. "I can't fault your work, son," he admitted. "What I can't understand is your lack of enthusiasm."

I wondered if he expected me to explain. Accepting his job offer had been a mistake from the get-go. My heart wasn't in it, and never had been.

"I'm here," I reminded. "I work hard for you every single day. Yesterday was a one-off, not a lack of enthusiasm."

"I trust that you'll make up the hours," he said curtly.

"I always do, Dad." I stood, gearing up to escape. "If you've no problem with my work, perhaps we should leave it at that."

"Sit down, Adam."

I slumped back down as if I'd been socked with a brick. The performance appraisal was over. He was about to attack the way I managed the rest of my life, starting with Bridget.

"I think you need to consider alternate child care," he began. "The current arrangement isn't working."

I suppressed the urge to let loose and really speak my mind. "Mrs Brown is –"

He cut me off. "Nothing to do with Mrs Brown. It's time Bridget became more independent."

I was livid. I'd spent years of living under the king's rule, and now he was pulling my daughter through the castle gates.

I leaned forward, drumming my finger on his desk with every word. "I decide Bridget's path, not you," I said. "And a four-year-old girl doesn't need independence."

Dad gathered the stack of papers on his desk and neatened them, avoiding looking at me. "She's smart, Adam," he said calmly.

"I know she is."

"She reminds me of you at the same age."

Aware of where the conversation was headed, I got in first. "She's not ready for school or tutoring or whatever it is you're about to suggest."

His eyes locked mine from across the desk. "I was going to suggest mainstream day care."

Of all the things I expected to hear from him, that was not one of them. "She's not ready for day care," I muttered.

"Her parents are not ready," he corrected. "You can't keep Bridget all to yourselves and expect she's going to benefit. She needs friends her own age – or a sibling."

"We're working on it." The words tumbled out of my mouth and I broke out in a cold sweat at the realisation that I'd just given him leverage. "And if you could keep that to yourself, I'd appreciate it," I added.

My father looked everywhere but at me. "Of course," he muttered.

"She's only little, Dad," I added. "Let her be little."

"It will serve Bridget well to mix with others her own age."

Despite the fact that he'd made my daughter sound like a mongrel puppy, his intentions were probably good. Broadening Bridget's social horizons had never occurred to me, perhaps because we'd spent so much time doing it geographically.

I promised to think about it. He didn't object when I stood this time. "Is there anything else?" I asked.

"No."

"Good." I made my way to the door before he changed his mind.

Hearing him call my name at the last second wasn't unexpected. The last word was always my father's. "I only have her best interests at heart, son."

"I do too," I replied, walking out.

***

Being the son of the boss meant that I was practically a leper. Every single person was nice to me. That was the problem. There's nothing genuine about overly polite conversations and false smiles, which was all I seemed to get from my co-workers.

Grayson Daniels was the exception. He was an asshole – sarcastic, forthright and bolshie, which is why I liked him. He called out as I passed his office on the way back from the king's chambers.

"Hey, jerk."

I stuck my head through the doorway. "What?"

He grinned. "Are you in trouble with Daddy?"

"No more than usual."

"You're going to get fired one of these days."

A man can hope. "He has no reason to fire me."

"Well, he has reason to fire me," said Grayson waving a piece of paper. "Settlement on the Channing case isn't happening. I think it's going to get ugly."

Grayson was a career lawyer. He'd been working at Décarie, Fontaine and associates for three years, slowly moving up the ranks. He cared when deals began to unravel. He also cared about making a good impression on the senior partners. That's where we differed.

I slapped the arms of the chair. "Well, it'll be a chance to show them what you're made of."

I wasn't really interested in hearing the ins and outs of the case, but pretended to listen as if I was. I thought I was doing a good job of it until he called me out on it. "Are you even awake?"

I shook my head, trying to jolt my mind into focus. "Sorry. I was miles away."

"What's going on?" he asked.

I gave him a shortened version of the conversation with my father, and then asked for his take on it.

"Kids need kids. It might be good for her." He shrugged. "You've got to cut the apron strings some time."

I had to give credence to his opinion. Grayson had two boys, a house and a dog. He was the real deal. Most days it felt as if Charli and I were still only pretending to have it all together.

My father was right when he claimed that we kept Bridget to ourselves. We'd always worked better on our own, and when Bridget came along, nothing changed. We still preferred our own company, and for the first time ever I began to wonder if it was to Bridget's detriment.

"Does she like sport?" asked Grayson. "My boys started Little League at four."

"Maybe," I muttered. "I'll talk to Charli."

Grayson is a problem solver, even when there isn't one. He threw up fifteen ideas in as many seconds. Everything from archery to fencing rated a mention. "Or cricket," he added at the last minute. "She's Australian. Her people like cricket, right?"

I laughed. "I'll talk it over with her people and let you know."

"How about dancing? I could see if Ella has any spaces in her dance classes if you like."

I didn't know Grayson's wife Ella well, which explained why I'd forgotten she was a dance teacher. I had no idea what his excuse was. "You didn't think to mention that before fishing and archery?"

"I was hoping you'd go with archery," he replied, pretending to straighten his tie. "I'd love to see your kid get hold of a crossbow."

7. TREASURE

Charli

All Adam ever had to do to earn a celebrity greeting at the door was come home. If he turned up with a blue cake box from the patisserie on the corner, Bridget would go nuclear.

Tonight was one of those nights.

He made it into the kitchen and set the box on the counter, despite the little girl hanging off him. "Hello, love of my life," he crooned, leaning to kiss me. He picked Bridget up and held her over his head as if she was weightless. "Hello, life of my love."

Bridget could barely speak for giggling. "I love that box," she told him.

"What box?" he teased.

The power of the cake box was mightier than anything. Its mere presence worked like a magic wand. The kid would willingly have a bath, put on her pyjamas and eat everything on her plate – which was exactly her father's plan.

Adam's motives were usually simple. He'd either had a rough day at the office or was planning an early night. I left quizzing him about it until Bridget was tucked up in bed, but one look at him as he walked into the room had me leaning toward a rough day.

I carried the last of the plates to the sink. "Bad day?"

"No," he replied. "Why?"

"You brought us cupcakes."

Adam smiled, but didn't reply. He answered his ringing phone instead, an interruption I was used to. I went back to cleaning up cake crumbs and tried to pretend I wasn't eavesdropping.

As the one-sided conversation progressed, curiosity stabbed at me. I stopped my cleaning charade and unashamedly listened.

"That's great," he beamed, looking straight at me. "We'll make sure Bridget's there on the twelfth."

As soon as the phone went back in his pocket, I pounced. "It's too late to adopt her out, Adam," I teased. "Bridget knows where we live."

"That was Ella Daniels," he explained, still smiling. "Grayson's wife. She's a dance teacher."

I forced him to elaborate by staying silent and looking pissed off.

"I mentioned to Grayson that Bridge might like to –"

"You put her in dance class?"

He nodded.

"Without talking to me?"

"Are you mad?"

I wasn't sure. Bridget's last foray into the dance world hadn't ended well. I'd spent years hoping that I'd lose the shameful title of being Mrs O'Reilly's youngest expulsion. In fairness, it hadn't bothered Bridget one iota. Small children tend to move on quickly. It's their mothers who suffer the pain of wondering if they're really ready to step out of their comfort zone and try something new.

"We've never even discussed it," I said quietly.

Adam weaved his arm around my waist the second I was in reach. "She needs something, Charlotte," he reasoned. "An outlet to socialise and make friends."

I knew the point he was trying to make. Bridget's circle was small and tight knit because we kept it that way, but I had to concede that it wasn't a healthy long-term plan.

"And she starts on the twelfth?"

Adam swept my hair back. "That's her first vacancy. It's a small class – just twelve girls."

I nodded, feeling slightly relieved and unreasonably scared, which Adam picked up on immediately. He whispered, "She'll be fine, Charli. It's the other girls you need to worry about."

***

I had purposely held off telling Adam about our dinner plans with his parents until the very last minute. The last minute was during the elevator ride to their door.

"Why are you surprised?" I asked. "Your dad let you go home early. You know paying the piper doesn't come cheap."

Bridget wedged herself between the two of us and looked up at her dad. "I'll give you some money to pay," she offered. "I have so much."

Adam swept his hand across the top of her head. "No thank you, baby. I'm good."

"We could make a deal," she offered.

"No deal."

"A lovely deal."

"Absolutely no deals," he said strongly.

I studied Bridget's expression in the mirrored door of the elevator, marvelling at the determination on her face. Whether Adam realised it or not, the deal for the compass was going to go down. It was just a matter of when.

***

It was kisses all round when Fiona greeted us at the door, but that didn't distract me from the awful aroma of whatever she was attempting to cook.

"I have something for you, Bridget," she said, leading her away by the hand.

"A horse?" she asked hopefully.

The queen's quiet giggle echoed around the foyer. "Not today."

As soon as they were out of sight, Adam leaned down to whisper. "What is that smell?"

I patted his chest. "It's your favourite, darling."

He scowled. "If it was cooked by Mom, it's not my favourite."

I didn't dare tell him that she was cooking Bambi while he was standing so close to the front door. I didn't want to be left there to explain why Adam had done a runner. I took him by the hand instead, and pulled him into Décarie land.

**

Jean-Luc wasn't home yet and Fiona had enlisted Bridget's help with dinner, leaving us to rattle around in the museum-like lounge room by ourselves. It gave me a chance to take another look at the magnificent show of china and crystal in the display cabinets. Even after checking them out a hundred times, I always managed to find something new.

"Did you play in here when you were kids?" I asked curiously.

"No, never."

I turned around but couldn't see him.

"Where did you play?" I scanned the room.

"On the roof or at the park."

I followed his voice to the centre of the room. Adam was hidden from view, sprawled along the couch. As I leaned over the back he pulled me down on top of him.

"She'll skin you alive if she catches you abusing the furniture this way," I warned.

He pressed warm lips against my neck. "There are worse things she could catch me doing," he murmured.

I wanted to push him away and tell him to get his act together. The problem was that Adam's act was perfectly together. It made telling him off impossible.

"Adam, stop it," I whispered.

The line of kisses he was trailing across my skin was almost paralysing, and he wasn't even close to stopping. I gave in after just a minute, raking my hands through his dark hair as I pulled his mouth to mine.

Nothing on earth compared to being touched by him. My whole body sang to music that only we could hear. It didn't matter that we were making out on his parents' couch. Nothing mattered, which is why neither of us noticed our daughter wander into the room.

"Stop kissing," she demanded in a tiny voice.

I tried to move but Adam's arms remained locked around me. The best I could do was turn my head. "What's wrong, Bridge?"

She stood just inches away looking dangerously close to tears. "Mamie gave me a present," she whispered. "I don't like it."

It could only have been the creepy doll. I was almost glad that she didn't like it. I'd been dreading the thought of her proudly carting it around with her since I first laid eyes on it.

Adam freed me, allowing me to sit up. "Where is it?" I asked.

When she pointed toward the kitchen, Adam reached for her hand. "Are you okay?"

Bridget shook her head but didn't say a word. The poor little girl looked terrified. There was no need for her to explain why. Fiona came waltzing into the room a few seconds later cradling the doll from hell in her arms.

"Darling, you left your baby in the kitchen." She tried handing it to her, but Bridget was having none of it. She piled on top of her dad, who was still flat out on the couch.

I took it instead, trying to save the queen some hurt feelings. Adam wasn't as considerate. "Mom, that's awful," he told her.

Fiona ripped the doll from my grasp. "I'll have you know she's incredibly special."

She sounded truly offended. Even Bridget picked up on it. "She's nice, Mamie." Her little white lie backfired instantly. The queen gently positioned the doll in Bridget's lap as if she was placing a real baby. To her credit, Bridget didn't protest, but she clung to Adam's shirt as if depending on him to keep her safe.

"You must treasure her," Fiona instructed. "What's her name?"

Not much thought went into Bridget's reply. "Treasure," she blurted, making it sound like a question.

"Trashure," Adam murmured.

I slapped his leg. The queen scowled. And Bridget discreetly knocked the hideous doll off her lap, letting it fall to the floor.

***

Treasure didn't eat much. I know that because the queen insisted that she sit next to Bridget at the table. Every time my poor little girl edged closer to Adam, Fiona would push the doll's chair closer.

Freakish dinner companions were the least of our worries. I'd never eaten venison before but I was pretty sure that it wasn't meant to be grey. I tore my eyes from my plate in time to see Adam's reaction as Fiona set a plate in front of him. He looked a little grey too.

Dinner suddenly became a magic trick. The meal was spent shoving it around our plates and hiding it under vegetables. Bridget ate like a bird at the best of times, so no one took offense when she set her fork down and claimed to be full.

The only person without a game plan was Jean-Luc. If he thought it was awful, he wasn't letting on. "This is magnificent, my darling," he praised. Fiona beamed. "Outstanding," he added. "A touch of mustard would complement it nicely."

Jean-Luc had a game plan after all. It kicked in the second Fiona rushed to the kitchen to fetch his mustard. He shamelessly scraped most of his dinner on to Bridget's plate.

"No, Papy," she scolded. "I hate it."

"I know, my love," he replied sympathetically. "I advise you not to eat any more of it."

Bridget was unimpressed by the notion of being an accessory after the fact. She turned to Adam and asked to be excused.

"Of course," he replied, helping her off her chair. "Go play." She took off in a hurry.

"And then there were three," announced Jean-Luc, refilling my wineglass.

"Technically four," corrected Adam, giving Treasure a poke.

Jean-Luc laughed. "When I suggested that Bridget find some real friends, that's not quite what I meant."

I frowned across the table at Adam, but he wouldn't meet my eyes. The silent plea for an explanation didn't go unnoticed – nothing gets past the king. "Is everything alright?"

"We've enrolled Bridget in dance classes," replied Adam, refusing to look at me.

"That's wonderful news," he approved. "She'll learn discipline and dedication."

I rolled my wineglass between my fingers, fighting the urge to snap it off at the stem. "I thought it was about making friends," I reminded him. "That was the instruction, wasn't it?"

Adam muttered my name weakly. I ignored him, keeping my focus on the king.

"Instruction?" asked Jean-Luc.

"Yes," I replied.

"I give no instruction where my granddaughter is concerned," he replied. "I merely spoke with her father and suggested that you consider broadening her horizons."

"When?" I snapped.

He frowned. "As soon as possible."

"No," I clarified, "when did you discuss it with her father?"

"We spoke yesterday, Charlotte," admitted Adam.

I took a long moment to think things through. Bridget grew faster than we did, and push often came to shove when it came to moving to the next level. I just resented it when the shove came from the king. I wanted her to explore new things, find friends and be happy. We all did. It's what made this family so special.

I looked at Adam and quickly let him off the hook. "I'm not mad at you," I assured him. "I want to be, but I'm not."

It was important that we leave it at that. Adam knew it too, which is probably why he didn't reply. There wasn't opportunity to continue the conversation anyway. Fiona reappeared with a huge dish of mustard, stopping dead in her tracks when she saw the king's empty plate.

"I'm sorry, Fi," he said regretfully. "I couldn't wait. It was just too good."

Her confused look gave way to a smile. "Never mind, darling." She picked up his plate. "I'll get you some more."

8. JUVIE

Adam

Love must be invisible. No one ever sees it coming. It sneaks up behind you, bashes you over the head and leaves you in a state of stunned confusion for the rest of your life.

Ryan was its latest victim. After years of dodging anything more meaningful than a quick roll in the hay, he'd been bashed over the head by love.

I still couldn't quite believe the news that he'd moved Bente in, but Charli swore she'd heard it from Bente herself.

I was staying out of it on the off-chance that my mother didn't know. In my experience, clueless was the best position to be in when drama took hold, and there was no greater drama than having a woman lay claim to one of her sons.

Part of me envied him. For Ryan, everything was exciting and brand new. Walking into my office that morning was a reminder that I had nothing exciting or new going on. I was stuck in the monotony of a nine to five job that I was slowly growing to hate.

Mercifully, I was always busy. Once I stepped out of the elevator I didn't have time to dwell. I got on with what I needed to do, then went home to my girls.

Very occasionally, I'd catch a break, but never from my father, so it was hard to hide my surprise when he walked into my office and told me I needed to go home.

"Mrs Brown is feeling unwell," he explained. "You're needed at home."

I closed my laptop. "Why didn't she call me?"

I could see the tension in Dad's jaw. "She called Charli," he replied. "Charli called me."

In an extraordinary move, the king sat down in the chair opposite my desk. I'd never known him to come past the doorway.

"The girl thinks I'm an ogre," he added.

The best I could do was word my reply gently. "You're pretty hard on her, Dad."

"I'm fond of Charli," he insisted. "I just have a low tolerance for her nonsense."

Charli's so-called nonsense was the only thing that kept me going some days, but telling him that would start a conversation that I wasn't interested in having. "Why did she call you?"

Dad sighed as if explaining was a chore. "She said you haven't arrived home before nine every night this week."

"No, I haven't."

"Charli demanded that I send you home early today to relieve Mrs Brown so she doesn't have to."

I hated the way he twisted facts to make them fit his story. "Charli can't take any more time off," I said, setting him straight. "Mrs Brown bails a lot."

He stared at me, straight-faced. "I told her no."

Of course he did. "So why are you sending me home?"

"Your wife is persistent." Dad took his phone out of his shirt pocket. "She followed up with a text message."

My father needed reading glasses, but wouldn't admit it. He held the screen at a distance, squinting while he read Charli's message out loud. "I know where you live, old man."

I grinned across at him. "She's not the least bit intimidated by you, you know."

Dad's expression was odd. He wasn't annoyed. He was fighting a smile of his own. "That may be," he agreed. "But I am marginally afraid of her at times." He handed me the phone. "Look at the picture she sent."

Charlotte Décarie is fearless. She had texted him a picture of herself in his precious private office. She was leaning back in the chair with her feet on the desk as if she owned the joint.

Even Dad was impressed. "I like her tenacity," he told me. "If the girl was capable of knuckling down and getting a law degree, I'd hire her in a second."

I handed back his phone, grinning. "I'll let her know."

"Say nothing," he demanded. "She'd probably do it to spite me."

***

I arrived home just after three. I barely made it in the door before I was met with a huge hug and shrieks of delight – and not from Bridget.

"Such a good boy," declared Mrs Brown, pinching my cheeks.

"I got here as soon as I could," I told her. "I hope you feel better soon."

She grabbed her bag and slung it over her shoulder. "Nothing a few days' rest won't fix," she replied, edging toward the door.

Mrs Brown didn't look ill. She looked fed up, and I was scared to find out why. I looked past her at the trash heap that used to be our living room. "Where's Bridget?"

Perhaps she was lost under the mountain of toys that were strewn in every direction.

"Playing in her room," she replied. "She ran out of space in here."

I held the door open and Mrs Brown made a dash for freedom. "I know this isn't working out," I said as she passed. "We'll make other arrangements for a while. Take a week or two off."

The first thing I noticed when she turned to face me was the look of relief on her face. The second was a tinge of sadness. "I have looked after Fiona's babies for twenty-nine years," she said proudly. "I want to do it for another twenty-nine, but I'm not a young woman any more, Adam."

I nodded. "I know."

When I kissed the back of her hand and thanked her for all she'd done for us, I was referencing much more than the time she'd spent with Bridget. Something about the shine in her eyes told me she knew it too. "I'm proud of you," she replied shakily. "More now than ever before."

***

Bridget nearly jumped out of her skin when I rounded the doorway to her bedroom. The kid was up to no good, and the speed in which she threw the doll in her hand under the bed proved it.

"Hi Daddy." Her voice was sickly sweet – more proof. "I love that you're home."

I folded my arms and leaned against the doorframe. "Me too. What are you doing?"

Her little shoulders lifted. "Just playing with Treasure."

She sounded casual but wasn't, and her terror amplified when I reached under her bed and grabbed the discarded doll. Bridget fell apart, with good reason. The ridiculously lifelike doll had had a makeover. Half of its face was covered in red scribble. "What did you do?"

She whimpered an answer. "She was too scary before."

Smudging my thumb across the inky stain did nothing. "And she's not scary now, Bridge?" I asked, waving it at her. "She's hideous."

"Don't tell Mamie," she begged.

I was at a loss. My eyes darted between my daughter and the Halloween prop in my hand. The easiest solution would be to throw the doll back under the bed and pretend nothing had happened, but Bridget would learn nothing and continue honing her skills in terrorism.

"I'm not going to tell Mamie," I told her. Pure relief washed over her, but it was brief. "You're going to tell her."

Her shoulders slumped. "I don't want to."

"And I don't want to visit you in juvie," I retorted. Bridget frowned, forcing me to elaborate. "Jail for little girls."

"Mamie will send me to jail for this?"

"Probably," I replied, walking out of her room. "That's where little crooks belong."

Bridget followed me, slamming into the back of me. "I'll tell Mamie," she assured me. "Take me there now, please."

I could understand her urgency. Like getting out of Dodge, confessions are best made quickly. I peeled her off my legs and sent her back to her room to bag up the evidence.

She reappeared a minute later, dragging Treasure behind her in a pillowcase. "She won't fit in my bag," she explained. "It's still got all the money in it."

I nodded, resigned to the notion that my world turned on a different axis to most. Some days were stranger than others, and this was one of them. My angelic little daughter looked like a serial killer gearing up to dump a body. "Let's do this, Daddy," she ordered. "I don't want to go to jail. I don't think they have good toys there."

***

If Bridget ever did end up on trial, I was confident she'd be able to defend herself. The child was a born defender. She sat her grandmother down, admitted to her crime, and then gave her shady version of why she'd done it.

"I'm sorry, Mamie, but it's a really scary baby," she said, slapping her hands down on her knees. "I had to make her pretty."

My mother's eyes drifted away from Bridget and locked on me. "How bad is it?"

Bridget answered for me. I almost thanked her. "It's bad, Mamie," she said seriously.

When Mom demanded to see for herself, Bridget whipped Treasure out of the pillowcase and waved her in the air.

My mother gasped but didn't say a word. I'd never seen her rendered speechless before. She looked so distraught that I wondered if she was about to cry.

"I coloured her mouth red," announced Bridget.

"And her cheeks, ears and eyes," added Mom, futilely trying to wipe it off with her fingertips.

"Bente has red lips and she's lovely," reasoned Bridget. "And now Treasure is too."

Mom dropped the doll in her lap and stared at her granddaughter. If Bridget found it unnerving, she did a good job of hiding it. She bounced around, swinging her little legs as if she didn't have a worry in the world.

"Do you still think Treasure is frightening?" Mom asked curiously.

"No." Bridget wildly shook her head. "I told you, Mamie. She's lovely now."

Mom stuffed Treasure back into the pillowcase, just as roughly as Bridget had pulled her out. "Well, darling, that's the main thing I suppose," she told her. "As long as you think she's lovely."

"That's it?" I asked incredulously.

"What am I supposed to say, Adam?" she snapped. "Charli warned me that she wasn't old enough to appreciate such a gift. It was my mistake."

Treasure looked like road kill and Bridget had gotten away with it. "I told her that she'd end up in juvie if she carried on like this." I stared at Bridget as I said it. "Jail for little girls."

Mom surprised me by backing me up. "It's true."

"And it's not nice to ruin toys."

"No, it's not," agreed Mom.

Bridget's bottom lip fell, which was magnificent. It gave me hope that I was back in control.

"I won't do it again," she promised.

Mom reached across and pulled her in close. "That's a good girl," she murmured, kissing the top of her head. "No more drawing on faces."

9. SEA DOGS

Charli

I wasn't a hundred per cent sure that the apartment was empty when I arrived home. It seemed perfectly plausible that Adam and Bridget might've perished in the toy explosion that had happened in the living room. I was just about to sift through it for bodies when they walked in the door.

Bridget ran to me and I scooped her up, kissing her. Adam moved slower. "Hey." He kissed my cheek.

I lowered Bridget and she took off to explore the mess. "We need a bigger apartment," I muttered.

Adam's arms slipped around me. "No, junior needs less toys." He rested his head on my shoulder. "But for now, we'll make her clean these up."

***

When Adam lays down the law, he sticks to his guns. He made Bridget cart every single one of her toys back to her room and put them away neatly. The only break she had was for dinner, which she dragged out for an hour before heading back to the rough conditions of the toy mine. She finished a little after eight.

"That was too much work," she complained. "I'm a very tired girl now."

"That's good news, princess," Adam replied, scooping her off her feet. "Because you're going to bed."

She wriggled in his hold to lean down and kiss me goodnight. "Love you so much, baby," I whispered.

"I'm not working tomorrow, okay?" she demanded.

"No," I agreed. "The day is yours."

They disappeared down the hall and the small room fell silent. I sat on the couch feeling slightly less agitated now that things were back in order. At that moment, Jean-Luc's concept of a private office didn't seem so arrogant. Small children infiltrate every part of a household. If we had a bigger home, I'd probably push for a room of my own too.

Staying in Gabi's apartment had originally been a temporary measure. We had planned to find something bigger once we arrived in New York, but life had got in the way and neither of us had time to find anything new.

If our plan of having another baby panned out, we were going to have to make some quick arrangements, but nothing about that worried me. That's how we worked best: our plans changed when our circumstances did.

Adam was gone for ages. I was just about to check why when he ambled back and flopped down beside me.

I shuffled closer, finding my way into his arms. "Is she asleep?" I whispered.

"Out for the count," he replied wearily. "Today was hard."

His rundown of the afternoon's events wasn't an explanation; it was more of a debriefing. Bridget had taken arts and crafts to a new level by giving Treasure a makeover.

"I warned Fiona not to give it to her," I grumbled. "I knew she'd maim her somehow."

Adam shifted slightly, sinking us further into the cushions. "I took her to Mom's and made her confess," he explained. "But it fell short."

I wasn't surprised to hear that Fiona forgave Bridget without question. She could do no wrong in either of her grandparents' eyes. It was a dangerous attitude that we constantly battled.

"So where is Treasure now?"

"She relinquished custody to Mom."

I patted his leg, laughing at his choice of words. "It's for the best."

Adam's head lolled back and he let out a sigh. "It's not funny, Charlotte," he chided. "She played Mom like a fiddle. The only time she looked remotely remorseful was when I threatened her with juvie."

My laugh got louder, which earned me the nicest kind of punishment. He stood and threw me over his shoulder. I gripped the back of his shirt as he marched down the hall. "Where are we going?" I asked, pretending not to know.

"To bed," he replied unapologetically. "I'm a glutton for punishment. I want to make another smart-mouthed, quick-witted little criminal."

He nudged the bedroom door open with his foot and abandoned the caveman act by lowering me to my feet.

"Damn," I grumbled, tugging the hem of my blouse. "I was just getting into it."

A smile crept across his face. "I haven't finished yet." His hand found my hip and pulled me forward. Even as it deepened, the kiss remained soft and tender. But I knew he wasn't completely with me. I broke away and leaned back. "What's the matter?" I asked, studying his sapphire eyes.

Adam shook his head infinitesimally. "You know those parents who say 'my child wouldn't do that' when their kid gets into trouble?"

"Yes." Meredith Tate and Carol Lawson came to mind.

"Let's not be those parents," he said. "We can't put anything past our kid. She's too smart."

Adam had a tendency to over-think things, especially where Bridget was concerned. Determined that her childhood would be different from his own, he encouraged her to make decisions without influence. The problem was that Bridget didn't always decide well, and it bugged the hell out of him.

The best way around it was to put things into perspective.

"You know those parents who wear matching sweat pants and sensible shoes?" I asked in return.

The dimple in his right cheek deepened. "Yeah."

I held his hands to steady myself as I stretched up and murmured against his mouth, "Let's not be those parents either."

He kissed me again. It wasn't slow and soft like before. It was hard and fast and over much too quickly.

"I love the way your mind works." He breathed the words against my neck, sending a hot rush of desire right through me.

"Forget my mind," I urged, tugging at the buttons on his shirt. "Concentrate on my body."

***

Our house was usually mayhem in the mornings, but for some reason I seemed to be the only one in a rush that day. When Adam's alarm went off, he hit the snooze button and turned over.

I took it as a win. I managed to get the first shower and dry my hair without interruption. Not even Bridget made an appearance.

I quickly worked out why when I returned to the bedroom. She was tucked up beside her dad having a very one-sided conversation about dogs that swim in the ocean. "They're called sea dogs," she explained. Adam grunted in reply, which wasn't good enough. "You have to listen, Dad."

"I am listening," he mumbled. "Sea dogs."

"That's right," she praised, patting his head.

"Bridge, please go and get dressed." He threw back her side of the covers. "We'll go and see Ryan."

The promise of visiting Ryan was as powerful as the cake box. She disappeared in a flash.

Adam's alarm started blaring again. I walked around the bed and thumped the off button. "Why are you going to Ryan's?" I asked. "Mrs Brown will be here shortly."

I took his hand when he reached out to me. "No she won't. I gave her a week off."

A hundred thoughts spun through my mind, namely how we were going to manage full time jobs with no childcare. "And you didn't think to tell me last night?"

His hand moved to my stomach. "I had other things on my mind."

I brushed him away and moved out of reach. "I can't take any more days off, Adam."

Bronson was very generous when it came to giving me time off when I needed it, but it didn't look good. I hated that I'd become so unreliable.

"I've got today covered," he insisted. "I'm going to see if Ryan can watch Bridget this morning. I have a meeting at eleven and that's it. I'll take the rest of the day off."

"And tomorrow?"

He leaned over and grabbed me. I stumbled as he pulled me forward and he took full advantage by pulling me down on top of him. "Tomorrow is a new day." He gently kissed my lips. "We'll figure it out."

"I hope you come up with a plan, Boy Wonder."

"Nope." He grinned at me. "I'm winging it."

10. FLYING STRAIGHT

Adam

The morning was bright and sunny. We weren't in any hurry so I decided that we'd walk to Ryan's. Bridget didn't complain. It gave her more talking time, and her topic of choice was still sea dogs.

"Why are they called sea dogs?" I asked. "Why aren't they just dogs who like to swim in the sea?"

Bridget tugged on my hand as she jumped over a crack in the sidewalk. "Because they make different noises," she explained. "They go 'squeep, squeep, squeep.'"

Even over the sound of the passing traffic, she sounded like a wounded cat. I laughed, which didn't impress her.

"It's true, Daddy," she huffed.

"I'm sure it is," I replied. "When we get back to the ocean, I'll be sure to check out the squeeping sea dogs."

Bridget looked up at me. "Are we going back to the ocean soon?"

I wanted to tell her yes, but that would've been a lie. For now, we were New Yorkers – but that felt like a lie too. We just didn't belong here any more.

"We're going to go back and visit at Christmas," I told her. "To hang out with Alex and Gabi and Jack."

"I have lots of big things to tell Jack," she crowed. "I hope he has nice ears for hearing."

I adored conversations with my daughter, even the confusing ones. It was the biggest reminder of all that it didn't matter where in the world we lived. Happiness wasn't geographical.

Before I knew it we were outside Ryan's building. I punched in the access code and held the door open for Bridget.

"I want to turn the key in Ry's door," she insisted.

It would've been good manners to knock, but I let her have her way – then wished I hadn't.

My brother wasn't expecting us – or anyone else, by the look of it. He stuffed something under a cushion and punched the remote, trying to turn the TV off. "Can't you people knock?" he snapped.

"I put the key in and turned it," chimed Bridget. "It's easy."

I wasn't listening to her. I was too busy being disgusted and horrified. "What did we just walk in on?"

"Nothing."

I didn't buy it. I grabbed the nearest cushion and whacked him with it. "What are you watching?"

Ryan looked utterly confused but I wasn't going to spell it out for him. There was no need to give him a reason why I'd just changed my mind about leaving Bridget in his care.

He eventually figured it out. "Oh my God," he growled, hurling the remote on the couch. "You think I'm watching porn?"

I shushed him but it was too late. He'd just increased his niece's vocabulary.

"What's porn?" asked Bridget.

I glared at my brother, furious. "Nothing, baby," I told her.

Ryan had the nerve to smirk. "Good parenting, idiot."

"Good uncl-ing, freak."

The juvenile exchange was cut short when the only grownup in the room ordered us to stop. "I'll tell Mamie and you'll both be in trouble," Bridget threatened.

I wasn't prepared to let it go. I reached under the cushion and grabbed the evidence. The *Dirty Dancing* DVD cover in my hand was not what I was expecting. "You've got to be kidding me."

Ryan whipped it out of my hand. "It's not mine."

"If you say so, princess."

Ryan couldn't even muster a reply. More proof that he'd been bashed over the head with the love stick. The career bachelor had been reduced to watching chick flicks in his spare time. Whether he'd admit it or not, he was whipped. And whether I'd admit it or not, I was happy for him.

**

My office was far nicer than I deserved, considering the lack of aptitude I showed when it came to working there. Sitting at the massive oak desk reminded me of a king holding court, but the moment was always fleeting. I was merely a prince. The real king's court was much more impressive.

My father insisted on monthly staff meetings. Everyone would file into the boardroom at eleven and spend twenty minutes waiting for him to arrive. Being purposefully late was tactical and obnoxious, but no one said so out loud. They were too busy making sure they had their game faces on in case he called on them to speak.

I wasn't quite so diligent. I used the spare time to text my wife or check my emails, which is exactly what I was doing when Ryan called me.

My phone sounded embarrassingly loud in the quiet room, and all twenty people sitting around the table stared at me. Fearing that their glares might burn a hole in my skull, I left the room to answer it.

"Please tell me you're not calling me to pick Bridget up," I said, wandering toward the viewing window at the end of the corridor. "I can't leave the office yet."

Ryan didn't need me to collect her. He needed cleaning instructions. My errant child had made the most of the few minutes Ryan spent in the shower by giving herself a makeover – less than twenty-four hours after promising me that her face painting career was over.

"She's covered in Bente's lipstick," he told me.

I should've been angry, or at the very least annoyed, but the panic in Ryan's voice amused me. "Lipstick?" I asked. "Did she steal it from your purse while you were watching *Dirty Dancing*?"

"She's your kid, Adam. I'm perfectly happy to leave it on her."

I didn't doubt him for a second. "Well, how bad is it?"

He likened her appearance to Sebastian from *The Little Mermaid*. We both knew Sebastian the crab well. *The Little Mermaid* was Bridget's favourite film, and we'd been forced to sit through it a million times. "She could now get a job as his stunt double."

It must've been bad. I thought back to the day before when I'd tried smudging the red ink off Treasure, and then imagined Ryan doing the same thing to Bridget. "What goes on must come off right?" I asked encouragingly. I wasn't exactly an expert when it came to makeup removal, and red lipstick seemed pretty heavy duty. "Look for anything that says 'remover' or 'antidote' or 'face cleaner'," I suggested. "It'll be there somewhere."

After complaining about the amount of crap now residing in his bathroom cabinet, he made the mistake of asking Bridget to look. I didn't have the heart to tell him that she'd use the opportunity to scope out her next arts and crafts project. I absently gazed out the window at the bustling city below while I waited for him to speak again.

"Eye makeup remover," he said finally.

"Good enough," I replied.

Ryan vowed to give it a shot and ended the call. I slipped my phone back into my pocket and continued the mindless window gazing as if I had nowhere else to be.

It didn't last long. My father called out from the boardroom. "When you're ready, Adam. We don't have all day."

I made my way back without a word. If I'd answered him, there was a danger I might've spoken truthfully: I wasn't ready. I would much rather have been at home with my little girl Sebastian.

***

Bridget wasn't up to the half-hour walk home from Ryan's apartment, which was a shame because we had a lot to talk about.

"We went to the park and my legs are tired," she complained. "I did lots of flying."

It took forever for her to pull the huge scarf out of the front pocket of her dress. It looked like a magic trick gone wrong. I took it from her, bundled it up and stuffed it into her backpack. "How about we walk some of the way and then pick up a cab?" I suggested.

Bridget wasn't happy, but kept walking. The heavy pedestrian traffic made it slow going. I asked her what she'd been up to and she gave me the complete rundown of her time at the park, including a longwinded story about a squirrel that yelled at her. The lipstick saga never rated a mention, so it was left to me to bring it up.

"You promised me you wouldn't draw on faces any more," I reminded her.

"It was just my face," she explained. "Nobody else's."

To Bridget, it was no big deal. I held her hand a little bit firmer as I prepared to inform her otherwise. "It was a really naughty thing to do," I chided.

"I know," she mumbled. "That's what Ry said."

I wasn't particularly upset with her. I was frustrated because I had no idea how to deal with her, and it was happening more and more often. My way wasn't working, so I changed tack and went the La La route.

"Crooked girls can't fly straight," I said casually. "You might want to think about that before you do something naughty again."

Even without looking, I could feel the stare of her bright blue eyes. "Am I crooked, Daddy?"

"You tell me, Bridge," I replied.

We walked in silence for a minute or two, but didn't cover much ground. Bridget's walk slowed to a crawl while she deliberated. She never did answer me. The only time she spoke was when she asked me to pick her up. Her arms linked around my neck, she buried her head in the curve of my shoulder and promptly fell asleep.

11. BURNED AT THE STAKE

Charli

Adam's plan of winging it was only good for one day. Neither of us was in a position to take any more time off, and we'd come up with no solution to our childcare problem over the weekend.

On Monday morning we resorted to playing scissors, paper, rock to decide who'd have the unenviable task of calling their boss.

I won because I always win.

"I'm sure you cheat," grumbled Adam, reaching for his phone.

"I'll call your dad if you want me to," I bravely offered.

"Brilliant idea, Charlotte," he mocked. "That's bound to end well."

Bridget wedged herself in between us. "I'll call Papy," she offered brightly. "He likes me."

Adam must've really been fed up. He tapped his father's name on the screen and handed the phone to Bridget. Despite the fact that it was on speaker, she held it to her ear. "Hello, Papy," she greeted. "It's Bridget Décarie."

Jean-Luc's chuckle filtered through the kitchen. "What can I do for you today, young lady?"

Bridget's hand moved to her hip as she paced the kitchen, holding the phone to her ear. "I want you to look after me today," she demanded. "My mum and dad have to go to work."

A frantic silent conversation took place between Adam and I in the form of frowns and raised eyebrows. The king had never spent the day with her before, and it was unimaginable to think he'd start now. I held my breath, waiting for the crotchety tyrant to shoot Bridget down in flames.

"I would love to spend the day with you," he replied, shocking me half to death.

"Can you please come and get me now?" she asked.

"Yes, of course," replied Jean-Luc. "Let your mother know I'll be there shortly."

Bridget spun around to look at me. I confirmed that I'd heard his instruction with an awkward smile. The deal was complete, and she'd carried it out with the arrogance and panache of a true Décarie.

***

I wasn't entirely convinced that Jean-Luc would show up. Adam didn't hang around to find out. He was shrugging on his jacket before Bridget ended the call. "See you later," he said, kissing me as he passed.

I grabbed his arm to slow him down. "Wait. What do I do if he doesn't show up?"

He kissed me again. "He'll be here."

I grabbed him again. "And what do I do if he *does* show up?"

"Just play it cool." He tucked my hair behind my ear. "And let Bridget do the talking."

I could count the number of times that Jean-Luc had visited our apartment on one hand. It was always awkward and uncomfortable, and that morning was no different. Bridget met him at the door with her trademark leg hug. All Décarie men were used to it, and strangely, none of them seemed to mind having a small child crash into them.

"You're here, Papy!" she squealed. "Mummy said you wouldn't come."

My mouth gaped open, which was as close as I came to defending myself. No words followed.

He smirked at me. "Did she now?"

I steered Bridget toward the hallway. "Go and get your bag, please." It might not have been my smartest move. Bridget took off at warp speed and I was left with the king.

65

He wasted no time in putting me in my place. "I'm a man of my word, Charli," he said pointedly. "If I say I'm going to do something, I do it."

"That's not entirely true," I slyly replied. "What about that time you told me you were going to have me tried as a witch and burned at the stake? That never happened."

He grinned, looking exactly like his sons. "I'm still working on it."

Bridget reappeared and declared that she was good to go. I hugged her. "Have fun today, and be good, okay?"

Her head nodded so swiftly that her blonde pigtails whipped her face. "Come, my love," urged Jean-Luc, nudging her toward the open door. "Press the elevator button. I'll be there in a moment."

"Was there something else?" I asked when she'd gone.

"I'm awaiting instructions," he replied. "I'm assuming you have some."

I wondered if there was any point in telling him what they were. I knew he'd probably ignore them, but I laid out my rules anyway. "Please don't give her any money," I said strongly. "She hasn't spent a single cent that you've given her so far."

His brown eyes widened in surprise. "Really?"

"None. I'm thinking of wallpapering her bedroom with it."

Jean-Luc huffed out a sharp laugh. "I didn't realise," he said. "I won't give her any more."

"Thank you," I replied. "I'd appreciate it."

"Perhaps I could take her shopping," he suggested. "I would like to see her spend it on something worthwhile."

I couldn't kill the smile that crossed my face, or the smartarse words that followed. "As opposed to seven hundred bucks worth of glitter and a cauldron?"

He dropped his head, smiling down at the floor. "And where might one buy a cauldron, Charlotte?"

"Bridget will show you," I replied. "She gets discounts on her frequent shopper card."

***

Despite my misgivings, I was happy that Bridget was spending the day with her grandfather. My concern was for him, not her. Jean-Luc wasn't used to dealing with small children, least of all Bridget.

I wasn't sure how I felt about her recently acquired shrewd streak. I couldn't find it in me to be appalled. She reminded me too much of myself, and every crafty act she carried out sent me straight back to all the years my father had spent trying to pull me into line. Just thinking about it made me want to call and apologise.

I wasn't intent on holding her feet to the fire like Adam was, but I certainly didn't encourage bad behaviour. Her latest misdeed had been an ill-gained Hermes scarf that she'd swindled from Bente a few days earlier. I found it stuffed in her backpack, completely trashed thanks to the red lipstick all over it. I hadn't been entirely sure who to direct my anger at. Bridget had wrecked it, but Ryan was the fool who'd given it to her in the first place. All I could do was replace it and apologise to Bente, which was how I spent my lunchbreak that day.

The rest passed in a blur. Most of the afternoon was spent dealing with pieces that had been delivered the day before. Three sold before they even went on display, and two buyers had shown interest in another. Bronson was over the moon. "Exceptional, darling." He clapped his hands together. "Find me more art. Buy me more art. More, more, more." He didn't give me a chance to reply. He was out the door before he'd finished his theatrical ramble.

I closed up shop soon after, managing to make it out on time for once. I wasn't the only punctual one. Adam beat me home, which had never happened before. He greeted me at the door with a huge hug that wasn't the least bit romantic.

"What's going on?" I wedged my elbows between us, trying to break free. Adam didn't release me until he'd walked us out into the foyer and pulled the front door closed.

"You're beautiful," he declared, lurching forward to kiss me.

I held him back. "Adam, what have you done?"

His tight smile led me to think it was nothing good. I didn't wait for him to string an answer together. I pushed past him and barged back into the apartment, stopping dead in my tracks at the edge of the living room.

"It'll only take a few days," he promised. "A week at the most."

I barely heard him. I was focused on the shabby green dresser taking up valuable space in the living room. "You have ten seconds to explain."

Adam couldn't tell the time in less than ten seconds. His long explanation wasn't that interesting. Bente's ugly drawers weren't to Ryan's snobbish taste, and he wanted Adam to fix them. The part that interested me was the pure excitement in his voice as he laid out his plan for restoring them. "It's Victorian – cherry wood, I think." He ran his hand along the top of the dresser, chipping off flecks of green paint in his wake. "It's solid and gorgeous – and they want me to paint it pink." He screwed up his handsome face as if the whole notion was ridiculous. "It should be lacquered and left alone."

It had been a long time since he'd talked carpentry, and I couldn't ever remember him doing it while wearing a tie. It threw me back to the cold winter afternoons we'd spent together in the shed in Pipers Cove. I could sit and watch for hours as he worked on boats. That was Adam at his very best, and seeing his joy while he talked about working on the drawers made me realise that I hadn't seen him at his best for a long time.

"You miss working on boats, don't you?"

"I can live without boats," he replied making his way back over to me. "I can't live without you."

I'd spent years being riled by the way he dodged my questions. I used to demand a straight answer. I didn't do that any more.

"I just want you to be happy," I mumbled.

"Seeing you find your feet in a job you love makes me happy," he replied, edging closer. "Having conversations with my kid about sea dogs makes me happy."

I wondered if that meant that the good outweighed the bad, then realised that he was the only one who could decide. "You thought it would be different, didn't you?" I asked.

His arm slipped around me. "New York never changes, Charli."

"No, I meant your job," I clarified. "It's not what you thought it would be."

It was impossible not to feel his angst, even though I wasn't supposed to. The be-all and end-all had always been a career in law. He'd studied for years to get his degree, then put his career on hold for a life in Australia with us. A great job in a prestigious law firm was supposed to be the reward, but for Adam, getting up every morning and going to the office had become a never-ending punishment.

He just wouldn't admit to it.

"We're okay, Charli." He smoothed his fingers through my hair. "For as long as you want to be here."

I bunched up the sides of his shirt in my fists, pulled him closer and kissed him hard in reply. I wasn't going to argue. Ryan had been the one to remind me that Adam was a grown man. When he was ready to call it quits, he would. But for now, he'd take a walk down memory lane and tear up some wood in our living room.

12. DEBT

Adam

My father was unapologetically hard, but there were two women who always managed to bring out a softer side. One of them was my mother. The other was just as feisty, only much shorter.

They arrived home in the early evening. Bridget was her usual amped-up self. My dad was much more reserved, but that might've had something to do with his outfit.

"Nice scarf," I told him.

"I do believe it's a feather boa," said Dad, flicking the string of green feathers. "My granddaughter says it suits me."

"It looks nice, Papy," insisted Bridget. "I picked it."

I glanced at my little girl and noticed she was rocking a few accessories of her own. Most notable was the little red stroller.

"What's in the stroller, Bridge?" I tried sneaking a peek, but was thwarted at the last second. "I'll show you," announced Bridget, forcing me back with a hands-up motion. "It's a lovely girl."

That was debatable. The lovely girl she dragged out headfirst was Treasure – and she was still heinous.

"Mamie couldn't get the red off her," she explained. "But she said I can have her back if I'm nice to her, so I will be nice."

It was hard to believe, mainly because she was clutching Treasure by the throat. The doll was already dead meat. Bridget roughly dumped her back in the stroller. "I got something else, Daddy," she announced. "Papy has it."

Dad pulled a small black box from his pocket. I flipped the lid and came face to face with the compass we'd nearly bought a few days earlier.

My heart sank. I'd been trying to prove a point to Bridget, and thought I was making headway. Bad behaviour shouldn't be rewarded, which meant the compass was off limits. I should've known that she'd pick her moment and con someone else into buying it for her.

Something in my expression let my father know I was pissed. "Many small lessons equal a large education, Adam," he told me.

There wasn't any point trying to make him understand, so I concentrated on the crooked little girl next to him. "I told you no."

She almost shrugged but thought better of it. "I paid the man all my money. I have no money left."

I shook my head, too furious to reply. She'd made it sound as if she was doing a good deed by offloading the cash.

Dad jumped in and quickly added to the story. "Bridget learned that impulse purchases aren't always a good idea."

I tore my eyes from my daughter to glower at him. "It's not an impulse purchase," I said roughly. "She's been plotting to get hold of it for days."

Dad pointed at the stroller. "Bridget bought the buggy first," he explained. "She didn't have enough money left to buy the compass."

I groaned out loud. It was going from bad to worse. "So you fronted her more cash?"

"Not exactly." He almost smiled. "I loaned her the money. Bridget owes me thirty-four dollars."

I had no idea what the implications of owing him money were. It was Bridget who spelled out the terms of the agreement. She grabbed the handle of the stroller and violently shook it. "I have to work now," she grumbled.

"Bridget is going to work off her debt," he told me. "I have some chores for her to do at home." He looked down at the disgruntled little girl. "You must learn to save first and spend afterwards, my love."

"Little girls can't work hard, Papy," she whined.

Dad dragged the feather boa off his neck and draped it around her. "That's not my issue, Bridget." He kissed the top of her head. "A deal is a deal."

***

Thanks to a well-timed phone call to Australia, Charli had conveniently missed Bridget's homecoming. She was ending the call when I walked into the bedroom.

"Is Bridget home?" she asked.

"Yeah," I replied. "She's getting Treasure reacquainted with the rest of the girls."

"Treasure's back too?" She sounded so revolted that I felt like apologising. "I thought we'd seen the last of that horror."

I sat beside her on the edge of the bed and handed her the small black box. "Dad took Bridget shopping," I said listlessly.

Charli flipped open the box and moaned as if I'd just given her diamonds. "It's lovely."

"It is a nice piece," I agreed. I would've been much more enthusiastic about it if it hadn't been so ruthlessly gained.

Charli took the compass out and held it in her hand, running her thumb across the glass front.

"Are you trying to turn it on, Charlotte?" I teased.

She bumped me with her shoulder. "What do you know about compasses, wise guy?"

"Only the basics," I admitted. "I was a boy scout for a while – until Ryan got us kicked out."

Her wonderful laugh instantly made me forget the pissed-off edge to my mood. I pushed her back on the bed and flopped my head down beside her.

"What did he do?" she asked, still giggling.

I stared up at the ceiling. "Broke a scout law," I said gravely.

"Scouts have laws?"

"Sure they do." I lazily turned my head to wiggle my eyebrows at her. "A scout is trustworthy, loyal, helpful, friendly, courteous, kind –"

Her laugh grew louder, but she still managed to cut me off. "You remember all that?"

"Of course." I rested my hand on her thigh. "I was a conscientious scout. Obedient, cheerful, thrifty, brave, clean and reverent."

"And Ryan lacked which attribute?"

I reached across and pulled her on top of me. "Three quarters of them," I murmured.

Charli softly kissed me. "I thought scout law was about being prepared."

"No, that's their motto; but for the record, I'm always very prepared."

"Good." She straightened up and held the compass out to me. "You'll be able to show Bridget how to find her way."

"I'm always trying to help her find her way," I muttered. "I don't think I'm succeeding at the moment."

It was an overly dramatic statement. A few naughty episodes in quick succession didn't necessarily mean she had the makings of a career criminal, but it weighed on me and Charli knew it.

She smoothed my frown with her fingertips. "Give the girl some magic and pull her back into line," she suggested.

I smiled enough to earn a thumb to the cheek. "You think it's that simple?"

Angling the lid open, Charli placed the compass on my chest as if setting a trap. "You have the makings of magic right here."

"Will you tell me about it, please?"

"I don't know a thing about orienteering."

I expected to hear that Alex had regaled her with all sorts of tales of being guided around the earth by bearings on a compass. It was almost impossible to believe otherwise. "Why not?" I asked.

"I had no use for a compass." Her shoulders lifted again. "I couldn't get lost in the Cove even when I wanted to. The sun rises in the east and sets in the west. The ocean was east. That was my compass."

For the first time ever, she had no story for me. That meant I was on my own when it came to sharing it with our daughter. "I'm disappointed," I said seriously. "I thought you'd know all about it."

"It just wasn't my thing," she replied. "What I really wanted was an astrolabe. That's where the real action is." I didn't even know what an astrolabe was. "Imagine a tool that can measure the altitude of stars. How cool would that be?" she asked wistfully.

"That would be cool," I agreed. "You never had one?"

Charli climbed off me. I made no attempt to move, hoping she'd come back.

"No, unfortunately." She scraped her hair into a messy knot and magically secured it with nothing. "Alex read up about them but couldn't figure it out. It was just too complicated."

My initial thought of surprising her with one went out the window. If Alex couldn't work it out, there was no hope for me. I snapped the compass shut. "I should stick with this then," I said, waving it at her.

"You do that, Boy Wonder, and your daughter will think you're the most amazing dad in the world."

I slipped the compass into the hip pocket of her skirt. "I can't tell stories like you do," I said quietly. "I don't know that I can bring her back into line with make-believe tales."

"You won't have to." She took my face in her hands. "Just plant the seed and the story will come from Bridget."

***

I'd been jogging the same four routes through Central Park for as long as I could remember. I much preferred running along the beach in Pipers Cove, but I made do. Jogging through the park wasn't as gruelling as loose beach sand, but I compensated by running harder and further.

I liked that it was a solo pursuit. It gave me time to think. To keep it a solo activity, I had to get out of the apartment before Bridget woke. Some mornings were more successful than others, and this wasn't one of them.

She cornered me at the door. "I'm coming too," she announced.

A tutu and galoshes didn't seem like appropriate running gear to me, but I had no reason to argue the point. I wasn't due in at the office until late that morning. We'd been playing childcare tag all week and it was my turn to show up at work late so Charli could make a meeting she'd had planned for weeks. "Wait here," I instructed, pointing as I passed. I let Charli know that I was taking Bridget with me and returned to the living room. Incredibly, Bridget was still in the same spot.

"You want to go to the park?" I asked.

"Yes I do," came the quick reply. "With this, please."

I didn't ask how she'd regained possession of the compass she was dangling in front of me because I knew I wouldn't enjoy her answer. I opened the front door instead. "After you, mademoiselle."

Her face lit up with pure cheekiness. "Okay," she beamed. "Let's go."

***

I took Charli's advice and let Bridget take the lead when it came to explaining the ins and outs of the compass. By the time we'd reached the Mall, I had a clear idea of what she was expecting to be able to do with it. I knew that her archenemies, the squirrels, couldn't read it and that she was going to eventually find treasure with it. All I had to do was work out how to make it happen.

My logical brain didn't wander too far off course as I explained the basics of orienteering. Bridget was a good student as long as she had the role of teacher's aide, and it wasn't long before she was making up her own rules.

She sat beside me on the park bench giving me her in-depth version of how it worked. "If you press the button on the side, you will fly up in the air."

Her expression was deadly serious, and she looked just like her mother.

"Baby, if you press that button, the lid opens."

"And then you fly," she insisted.

Excitement got the better of her then. She jumped up and stood in front of me, haphazardly waving the compass around.

I wasn't concerned that she might drop it. My focus was entirely on her – my little street urchin with the messy blonde hair, red tutu and pink galoshes.

"Don't ever change, Bridge."

"I won't," she promised, pointing her compass at me. "Don't you change too, Daddy."

I assured her I wouldn't, but that was a lie. I secretly hoped she'd never stop changing me.

13. SLIGHTED LOVE

Charli

Our apartment was beginning to resemble a woodworking factory.

Green flecks of paint peppered the floor, and despite the fact that Adam had last used it two days ago, there was still a faint whiff of paint stripper in the air. Considering the upheaval it caused, the favour of restoring the drawers was huge. In theory, Ryan should've owed him hugely, but in an odd turn of events, we were the ones indebted to him.

Our childcare problem was solved in an instant when he gallantly offered to watch Bridget four days a week. After a week off, Mrs Brown was back on board too, decidedly happier knowing that Ryan was relieving her in the afternoons. It wasn't an ideal arrangement, but for now the Décarie brood was back on track.

The only one with any troubles was Bridget. Treasure's shiny red pram hadn't come cheap. She'd taken the epic misstep of falling into debt to her grandfather to get it.

I thought Jean-Luc's plan of making her work it off was a good one. I wasn't sure how he was going to pull it off, but we didn't have to wait long to find out. Bridget was called to duty less than a week after the loan was made.

Jean-Luc had taken the extraordinary step of taking the morning off work to supervise her while she carried out his list of chores, and as expected Bridget tried her best to scheme her way out of it. We were standing outside the castle door when the theatrics began. "I'm very sick today," she began.

I put my hand to her forehead. "You seem fine to me."

"Why do I have to work?" asked Bridget. "I'm only a small girl."

I held her hand and headed for the elevator. "If you're not happy with the arrangement, you can always give the pram back," I suggested.

Bridget stretched up and pressed the elevator button. "Treasure needs a bed to sleep in," she grumbled.

"That's the problem with kids, Bridge." It took all I had not to smile. "They're demanding little creatures."

***

In my opinion, the foyer of the Décarie home was a huge waste of space. I'd always found it barren and unwelcoming. The only bright spot came from the colourful arrangement of flowers on the console table near the stairs. I'd never once seen the vase empty, which led me to think the lady of the manor thought the room was cold without flowers too.

Fiona was arranging a new bunch when we arrived, pointedly snipping at the stems and jamming them into the tall crystal vase. "I'm not happy with this at all," she said, taking a step back to study her handiwork.

"I like it, Mamie," announced Bridget. "I can help you do the rest."

Fiona glanced down and smiled. "Thank you, darling, but Papy has plans for you this morning."

Bridget's cheerful demeanour was replaced with a pout. "I might be busy," she replied.

Whatever she had in mind was abandoned the second Jean-Luc appeared at the top of the landing. It was my own fault that I didn't understand what he said to her – my attempts at broadening my French skills had slipped long ago, and laziness set in when my kid became old enough to translate for me.

Bridget held up her finger. "One day of work," she clarified. "Okay, Papy?"

His familiar laugh reminded me that for the most part his princes were carbon copies of him. "That was our agreement, yes."

Satisfied that she wasn't going to be worked to death, Bridget reluctantly trudged up the steps. Jean-Luc patiently waited. As soon as they were out of sight, I quizzed Fiona about Bridget's tasks for the morning.

"Oh, it's nonsense really," she replied, fussing with the flowers in front of her. "I think he mentioned getting her to dust the bookshelves in his office – as if she can reach higher than the third shelf."

I knew differently after finding her box of contraband girls, but kept that information to myself. "I can't stay long. I've got to be at the gallery by ten."

"Of course," she replied pityingly. "I heard all about your childcare issues – and that Ryan was your solution."

"He offered," I explained.

"I would've offered too," she snapped, "if you'd thought to mention it to me."

Clearly her feelings were hurt. Talking my way out of it wasn't going to be easy, or truthful. "You're always so busy with your charities and other commitments. We didn't want you to feel obliged."

A more honest explanation would've been that we didn't want our kid hanging out at the palace every day. Her grandparents spoiled her rotten, and we resented it.

"I adore spending time with Bridget," she replied.

"I know you do."

I brushed down the back of my skirt and sat down on a step, immediately earning myself a lecture. "Don't sit on the floor, darling."

"Why not?"

"We're not peasants."

"Will my dress get dirty?" I asked cheekily.

She huffed out a sharp laugh. "Not in my house, Charlotte."

We were quiet for a moment, but it wasn't uncomfortable. The days of sweating bullets in her company were long gone. "Why don't you just buy a plant instead of cut flowers?" I asked. "It would last much longer." Fiona frowned across at me as if I'd said something foolish. "It's wasteful," I added.

"How so?" she asked.

"Flowers are the ultimate replicas of human life," I explained. "They're planted, they grow, they bloom and eventually they wither and die. Cutting their lives short seems pointless to me. It's such a waste."

Fiona turned and began plucking at the arrangement. "I might agree with you in this instance," she replied. "If I can't make this look right, I'll have to throw them away and start again."

I stood up and wandered over to her. "You know why it doesn't look right?" Fiona tilted her head, studying the flowers while she pondered my question. I didn't wait for an answer. "It's a whole bunch of confusion in a vase," I told her.

She flapped her hands, motioning to the flowers. "Fix it, darling."

I started with the tall yellow asters, pulling them out of the vase one by one. "Asters are an open declaration of love," I explained. "It's bold and loud and only used when you're absolutely sure."

"I see no problem with that," she said, frowning. "There is much love in this home."

"I agree," I replied. "But you need to get your story straight." I plucked a few white gardenias from the mix. "Gardenias are also a declaration of love, but they're not bold and in your face. They're sent as a symbol of secret love – a private billet-doux."

Fiona pushed the gardenias to one side, as if putting distance between the two bunches was necessary. "Continue," she ordered.

I turned my attention back to the thinning display. "Well, carnations are a whole bag of ugliness."

Fiona jumped in and stripped every carnation from the arrangement before I had a chance to explain why. She waved a stem at me. "I quite like the striped ones."

I pulled a face, emphasizing my distaste. "They're the worst. They denote unrequited love, and the yellow ones signify disdain and rejection."

She gasped, looking horrified. "Oh, that will never do. Ryan and Bente are coming for dinner on Friday. I don't want to jinx them."

It was the first time she'd mentioned Ryan's budding new romance to me, and I wished she hadn't. The last thing I wanted was her grilling me for information. I turned the tables instead, bravely reminding her that she needed to play nice. "He likes Bente very much," I said strongly. "You'll make her feel welcome, won't you?"

The queen didn't attack. She didn't even show a hint of annoyance at my question. If anything, she seemed embarrassed that I'd asked. "Mistakes were made in the past," she said. "Lessons were learned."

It wasn't my intention to make her feel bad so I quickly smoothed things over. I plucked a white chrysanthemum from the vase and held it out to her. "In Australia, we call these chryssies. We give them to our mums on Mother's Day."

Fiona took the flower from me. "Thank you, my darling," she said quietly. She looked to the vase. "The yellow ones are lovely too."

"We're past yellow chrysanthemums, Fiona," I said seriously. "The yellow ones denote slighted love. I value the love you show me now. We're in a good place."

It was as close as I'd ever come to making the queen cry for a good reason. I didn't want to see her break down and blubber so I quickly got back to the task at hand. "So there you have it." I pointed at the now straggly looking floral display. "It didn't look right because it was a whole bunch of emotions and sentiments that don't gel."

The queen stared at the arrangement. "I just thought the colours were wrong."

I glanced at her. "Nothing to do with colour. The picture is always much deeper than the one we see with our eyes."

***

Bonding sessions with the queen tend to come on hard and fast, and disappear just as quickly. She returned to fixing her flowers and I escaped upstairs to check on Jean-Luc and his little workhorse.

The door to his office was open, which saved me the dilemma of deciding whether to knock. The king spotted me the instant I poked my head around the doorway. Bridget wasn't as observant. Her back was to me while she haphazardly scrubbed a cloth across one of the front windows.

"Come in, Charli," he invited, pointing at the chair opposite his desk. "Sit down, please."

Bridget spun around. "Mummy," she said desperately. "I can go now?"

I sat and looked to Jean-Luc for an answer. The king didn't bat an eyelid. He continued the monotonous task of signing his name on the stack of papers on his desk. "There are three windows, my love," he replied. "You've only cleaned one."

I looked past Bridget to the window she'd been scrubbing. Whatever she'd done to it wasn't really working for her. The glass at Bridget's height was cloudy, smudged and obscure. Above that was spotlessly clear.

"Are you sure you want her to continue?" I asked quietly.

Jean-Luc spun his chair and checked out her handiwork before turning back to me. "Of course." He winked at me. "She's doing a wonderful job."

Perhaps false praise was part of the lesson plan. Intentional or not, it worked for a while. Bridget went back to clouding up the windows until all three were a mess. When she was satisfied with her efforts, she turned and stood behind her grandfather's chair. "Now?" she asked hopefully.

Bridget couldn't see his sly smile, but I could. "Now what, child?" he teased.

My little girl looked down at the sodden cloth in her hand. I knew the wicked expression on her face well. It was like looking in a mirror. She had only a few seconds to decide if she'd take the Adam route and clarify her question, or the Charli route and sock him in the back of the head with the wet cloth.

All I could do was hold my breath and wait.

"Am I finished now?" she asked finally.

I felt my shoulders slump – one part relieved and one very secret part disappointed.

Jean-Luc spun his chair around to inspect his thirty-four dollars worth of child labour. "*Magnifique*, my love," he praised enthusiastically.

I had to give major kudos for his acting skills. Even from a distance it looked like a giant Labrador had spent an hour licking the glass.

"Don't you feel wonderfully accomplished?" he asked.

Bridget nodded as if she had half a clue what he meant. The king kissed the top of her head and sent her downstairs to find her grandmother. "Mamie will make you a snack," he told her.

Bridget handed me the cloth on her way out the door. "Don't touch those windows, Mummy," she instructed. "I just cleaned them."

"I won't," I promised.

Perhaps Bridget was aware of Jean-Luc's need to get the last word. She didn't walk out of the room – she ran.

I should've followed her but I was in the rare mood to engage the king in conversation. I started by asking what he thought of his new artwork.

Jean-Luc set his pen down and glanced at the picture. "It complements the room nicely, don't you think?"

His answer was banal, but not unexpected. "No one buys expensive art purely because it suits a room," I told him. "It has to call to you. It grabs you and sucks you in the very first second you lay eyes on it."

He chuckled blackly, the same way he always did when toying with me. "You have a flair for the bizarre, Charli."

"It wouldn't kill you to be honest with me," I retorted. "I'm just asking about the picture – not looking for chinks in your armour."

He surprised me by getting up and making his way over to the art in question. "I think it's a nice piece," he replied thoughtfully. "I like it very much."

"But why?"

Jean-Luc folded his arms, glancing at me only momentarily. "It calls to me. Is that what I'm supposed to say?"

I shook my head, warding off a bitter retort. "If you don't believe in magic, you'll never find it."

"Explain the magic in this." He pointed at the picture but looked only at me. "It is impossible to take you seriously when all you spout is nonsense. How Adam puts up with you is beyond me."

As harsh as his words were, I didn't get the impression that he was trying to hurt me. I frustrated him and confounded him. And that wasn't his fault.

"He likes me," I muttered.

I didn't need to look at him. His glare was burning a hole in the side of my head. I focused on the cloudy windows and waited for him to speak instead, which took forever.

Jean-Luc returned to his chair. "Bridget told me that there is a certain breed of dog that lives in the ocean," he began.

"Yes, I know," I replied. "Sea dogs."

"It's criminal to teach her such rubbish," he scoffed.

"I never taught her that," I snapped. "I have no idea what a sea dog is but I do know that my kid's imagination is perfectly in focus."

The king leaned back in his chair and let out a breath. "How far through this life do you think a good imagination is going to get her?"

"I have no idea," I admitted. "How much further do you think you'd be in life if your imagination was in good working order?" I walked to the picture on the wall. "You'd see everything so much clearer," I said wistfully.

"Nonsense."

Infuriating him was easy. Holding my ground until I was ready to end the conversation was trickier. I refused to lose this round. I was losing too often where he was concerned.

"Two fairies from Egypt," I announced, holding two fingers at him. "Habibah and Eshe."

"Stop it, Charlotte," he warned. "I'm not interested in the punch line."

I wandered back and sat down, making sure I had his full attention. "There is no punch line. It's not a joke. I'm telling you something very important." The king slouched and sighed. As far as I was concerned, it was permission to continue. "They were very talented seamstresses. The finer the threads, the more nimble their fingers."

"Move it along, please." He waved his hand in a circle.

"They sourced the finest cotton and crafted it into the most fabulous –"

"Sheets?" he asked, smugly cutting me off. "Or towels. Egyptian cotton is supposed to be the best."

"No." It was impossible not to smile. "Dresses. They made dresses."

"Fascinating," he drawled insincerely.

I shrugged. "It paid their bills."

His level of interest was low to begin with, but it was almost non-existent by that point. I got out the rest of the story as quickly as I could. Eshe fell in love with a boy with a wandering eye, so she hatched a plan to make keeping an eye on him a little easier.

"One night while he was sleeping, Eshe snuck into his room and sewed a thread of cotton to the cuff of his shirt," I explained. "Then she went all the way home, unrolling the spool as she went. The plan was to keep him tied to her so she'd know what he was up to at all times."

"Keeping a man on a leash is hardly a good plan," the king pointed out.

My heart skipped a little, secretly thrilled by his input. "It was a terrible plan," I agreed. "The boy, Ufa, woke up the next morning and saw the thread. He was furious."

Jean-Luc let out a chuckle. "Trust issues, I suspect."

I half-smiled. "She wasn't done. Eshe decided that essentially her plan was a good one – she just needed to conceal the thread better; so the next night, she sewed the finest string she could find."

"Silk?"

I shook my head. "Spider web."

Despite the fact that the story had strayed further than anything his closed mind could believe in, Jean-Luc allowed me to continue.

"It held up perfectly and from that day forward, every time Ufa strayed a little bit, Eshe tugged on the spider web and pulled him back to her side. They stayed together forever."

My time was up. The king whacked the edge of his desk with his hand. "Right, well that was an education," he teased. "Pointless, but –"

"I'm not done yet," I interrupted. "I was just getting to the good part."

He slumped back and stretched out his arms. "The floor is yours."

"Eshe's sister Habibah took it a step further," I continued.

"As if tying a man to herself against his will wasn't far enough?"

"Habibah sold the spider web thread to all and sundry. Any woman burdened with a man with a wandering eye bought it."

The king smirked. "A little entrepreneurism never hurt anyone."

"In this case it did," I said gravely. "Men far and wide were tied by invisible threads. Thousands and thousands of yards of tiny strings of fate. Everything was fine until the most powerful imp in the land, Pipui, caught wind of it."

Pipui was a stickler for rules. As soon as she found out that Eshe and Habibah were running amok with the fate of others for profit, she intervened.

"She conjured up a massive storm," I said theatrically. "The wild winds broke all the webs and sent them flying off in different directions."

"And the men were freed?" he asked.

"Not exactly." I shook my head. "Spider webs are sticky, right?" Unbelievably, he nodded. "When the weather calmed, each web attached itself to someone new. In one short storm, Pipui changed the fate of everybody in the whole world."

If Adam had been the recipient of the story, he would've been content to leave it at that. But Jean-Luc was no Adam. He hit me with a barrage of questions in quick succession, probably the same way he examined people in court.

"And what did that achieve?" he asked.

My shoulders lifted. "People who ordinarily would never have met were now destined to be together, bound by invisible strings of fate."

He straightened up. "One generation," he said holding a finger up. "At best, it would've been good for only one generation."

My smile was one of pure triumph. I'd won, and that never happened when Jean-Luc was my opponent.

"Have you never heard the term 'storm of the century'?" I asked smugly.

"Of course."

"Well, Pipui was so thrilled with the result that she now spends her days travelling the earth, conjuring up storms all over the place. Her invisible strings of fate have endured many generations. To this day, unlikely lovers from all over the world are finding each other."

Jean-Luc stared at me for a long time, deliberating. It wasn't uncomfortable. The mere gesture of thinking it through was good enough incentive to sit there and await his verdict.

"Spider webs," he mumbled finally. "You think they are the ties that bind?"

"Maybe," I shrugged. "I'm yet to hear a better explanation of why a boy from New York would find a girl from Tasmania."

Jean-Luc groaned as if he'd just sat through an ordeal. Far-fetched, totally implausible and incredibly ridiculous was his summation.

"But you listened," I reminded him. "There was a time that you wouldn't have. No one is immune to magic, Jean-Luc, not even the king."

14. LUCKY STARS

Adam

My days ended best when I escaped my office during daylight hours. Sometimes that was all it took to turn a bad day good. When Charli called and asked me to collect Bridget from Ryan's that afternoon, I didn't think twice.

They were watching a movie when I arrived. The only thing that hit me harder than the pang of jealousy when I walked in was Bridget crashing into me as she launched herself off the couch.

In a perfect world, I would've been the one suffering through *Little Mermaid* marathons, not Ryan. But our New York world wasn't perfect.

Making the most of the situation was the best I could do, and making the most of it that afternoon meant settling in and watching the rest of the movie. Bridget snuggled into my side, and before long I felt her little body relax against mine as she drifted to sleep.

Ryan and I continued watching Ariel as if it was our calling for the day. I enjoyed the downtime, and considering Ryan had spent the afternoon in the company of his niece, he probably did too – even if he did complain.

"The girls are on a bender and we're here watching cartoons," he said. "Do you see anything wrong with that picture?"

"No," I replied quietly. "The picture is good."

Charli never took time out. Cocktail bars in the afternoon weren't usually her scene, and I was glad she'd made an exception.

"You're so whipped, Adam," he teased. "You should call your wife and demand that she comes home."

I reached into my pocket for my phone, trying not to wake Bridget. "Call Bente," I urged. "Tell her to come home."

Ryan smirked. "I might."

"Yeah," I scoffed. "And after she tells you to go to hell, I'll help you box her stuff back up."

***

It turned out to be a late night. Bridget woke not long after Charli and Bente arrived. She was well rested and raring to go, which made getting her back to sleep when we arrived home almost impossible. Sweet-talking quickly gave way to threats – none of which she took seriously.

"I want to go back to Ry's house," she complained.

I tucked her in a little bit tighter than usual as if that was all it would take to keep her in her bed. "You'll see him tomorrow," I assured her.

"We're going to the park." She sounded much too excited, considering the late hour. "To look for Secret North."

I'd been enamoured by Charli's tales for years. She could hook me in with just a hint of the story to come. Bridget held the same power. I pushed a mountain of girls aside and sat on the edge of the bed. "Can you tell me about it or is it really a secret?"

"It's only a secret from Ryan," she replied. "I'm going to find it for him."

My curiosity was piqued in an instant. "How, Bridge?"

"If you listen nicely, I'll tell you," she whispered.

I couldn't tell if the longwinded story she told me about finding Ryan's secret place was the truth as she knew it, or a ploy to keep me in the room. Either way it was epic. I'd given Bridget nothing more inspiring than the basics when explaining how the compass worked. That was the seed. The story that grew from there was completely her own.

"There are flowers on the roof and it's very lovely," she explained.

I kissed her forehead. "I hope you find it, baby," I said sincerely.

89

"I will," she said. "I hope you find your place here too, Daddy."

At times her words were just too profound to be anything less than magic. She was her mother's daughter, and I thanked my lucky stars every day for gracing me with both of them.

"Me too, Bridge." I smiled. "But for now, I'm going to bed."

15. NOBILITY AND TITLE

Charli

Our room was never completely dark. The intrusive lights of night-time Manhattan bled through a crack at the edge of the blinds. It didn't bother Adam – he could sleep through a hurricane – but occasionally it kept me awake.

I wasn't blaming the light for keeping me awake that night. I was restless because the conversation I'd had with Bente was still playing on my mind.

The three fruity daiquiris we drank probably offered her more comfort than I did, but I saw no point in lying to her. I didn't envy the position she was in and I told her so.

Gaining acceptance into the Décarie fold would be a marathon process. Her plan of behaving and following the rules was a good one, and I didn't get the impression that it was dishonest. Bente was charmed by more than just Ryan. Despite the initial awkwardness, she liked his extravagant lifestyle. That didn't make her superficial and materialistic; it made her normal. I was the weirdo who couldn't adjust, even after seven years of exposure to it.

The Décarie fortune was massive, that much I knew. As to how massive, or how it came to be, I had no idea. It made me wonder. Too curious not to find out, I asked Adam if he was awake.

He tightened his hold on me. "Almost. What's wrong?" he mumbled.

"Nothing. Can I ask you something?"

"Uh huh."

He didn't sound the least bit interested, but I continued anyway. "How much money do you have?"

"What do you mean?"

He must've really been tired. It wasn't a complex question.

"Bente and I were talking about money today."

"Why?"

I turned over, resting my chin on his chest. It was just light enough to see that his eyes were closed.

"Because Ryan's been throwing his around again. She's a little freaked out by some very expensive presents he bought her."

Adam almost laughed. "He's good for it, Charlotte," he muttered. "It won't break the bank."

I turned his face toward me. "Can you please just answer my question?"

His blue eyes looked even darker in the low light. "I forgot your question."

"How much money do you have?"

"*We* have a lot of money."

"Where did it come from?"

"France," he mumbled, pulling up the covers. "A long time ago."

"How did the French Décaries get it?"

He groaned, a deep sound that did strange things to my insides. "How come you wait until midnight to start these conversations?"

"I'm just curious."

In a move I wasn't expecting, he shifted, pulling me on top of him. The corner of his mouth lifted and suddenly he didn't look sleepy any more. "Kiss me, then we'll talk."

It wasn't a bad trade-off. I lived to kiss this man. But I wanted him to talk to me, so the touch of my lips against his was intentionally short and uninspiring.

"That's it?" he asked. "That's all you're going to give me?"

"Tell me what I want to know and I'll give you everything."

The darkness of the room did nothing to hide his smile. His vision obviously wasn't impaired either. He reached for the thin strap of my top, pushing it off my shoulder as if he needed to busy his hands.

"The money started accruing in the seventeenth century," he began. "Back then, prestige and power was held by the nobility – upper-class people who owned lots of land."

"Seventeenth century?" I choked. "The 1600s?"

It was impossible to grasp that a family's history could be traced back centuries. My genealogy extended no further than Alex's mother.

"Yes." He slipped the strap off my other shoulder. "It's going to be a very long story if you keep interrupting."

"Okay." I grabbed his hands to stop them wandering. "I won't do it again."

"The Décaries didn't have land or title, but they had great business sense," he continued. "France was renowned for good agricultural production, but in order to get rich doing it, they needed land to farm."

I was expecting to hear that they formed their own army and pillaged the countryside, claiming land as they went. I was glad I held off saying it out loud. It wasn't even close to Adam's version of events.

"So agriculture wasn't for them. They needed to come up with something else. When trading agreements between countries came into play, the ports were opened up," he explained. "The Décaries saw a niche in the market. They set sail with an empty ship and travelled all over the place picking up exotic wares to sell in France."

As soon as I let go of his hands they settled on my hips, holding me exactly where he wanted me. The heat between us was palpable, and far more distracting than I let on. "They were wanderers," I murmured, walking my fingers down his bare chest. "Your people were wanderers."

"I guess so," he replied, catching my hand at the last moment. "Before long, their importing business was huge – many ships travelling the world. They did a roaring trade."

I wanted to hear more but I was having trouble concentrating. I dropped my head and kissed him, which did nothing to clear my thoughts.

"Are we done now?" he breathed.

"One more thing," I whispered. "When the Décaries became rich, did they achieve nobility or title?"

I had no idea what possessed me to ask. Perhaps it might've explained Jean-Luc's supercilious attitude toward the world.

"No, they never did," he breathed against my cheek. "You married a lowly commoner, Charlotte."

"It doesn't matter," I whispered in his ear. "You hail from a long line of wanderers."

The way it felt to be kissed by Adam was exactly how I always wanted to feel – not merely wanted, but desperately needed. I craned my neck, savouring the touch of his mouth against my skin.

"You're beautiful," he murmured.

I gripped his arms, feeling his biceps tense as he fought hard to keep things slow and gentle. His eyes never left mine, which made the next words out of my mouth easy to say.

"I am beautiful for the one who loves me."

16. MEAN GIRLS

Adam

We purposefully held off telling Bridget that we were releasing her into the wild via ballet lessons until the big day. It was one of our wiser parental decisions. She spent the whole morning bouncing off the walls, driven by the pure excitement of finally having a reason to wear a tutu.

A dance class full of ramped-up little girls wasn't exactly my scene, but it would make a nice change from Saturday mornings at the office. It was Bridget's day, and I was prepared to endure anything to make sure she enjoyed it.

I could ignore junior's skittish mood. Containing Charli was harder. I found her in the bathroom. At first it looked like she was fixing her hair, then I realised she was just trying to keep busy.

"What if she doesn't like it?" She fluffed her hands through her hair, giving her a reason to pick up the brush again. "The other girls will be way ahead of her."

I stooped down to rest my chin on her shoulder. "She'll be fine," I assured her. "No worries, okay?"

Charli nodded at me through the mirror. She looked calm but her body was tense. "I just want it to go well."

If it didn't, I got the impression that Charlotte was going to take it much harder than Bridget. I spun her around by the shoulders and forced her to look at me. "What's really the matter?"

She tried to shake her head but I held her firm. "You were never that kid, Adam," she said, poking me in the chest with the hairbrush.

"What kid?"

"The weird, awkward kid who never gave a damn about fitting in because she was too busy being weird."

I smiled. "Sounds like my kind of kid."

Charli pulled my hand away from her face. "What would you know about it?" she asked. "You were Mr Popular, probably from the very first day of kindergarten."

There wasn't a reply I could give that would make her feel better so I stayed quiet. If I'd been the most socially inept kid ever to set foot in the playground I still would've been popular. I was Ryan Décarie's younger brother.

The brush bounced into the sink as she dropped it down on the counter. "I was that kid," she said quietly. "And I don't want Bridget to go through the same torment. We're supposed to look after her heart. Not throw her to the wolves."

We'd done a great job of protecting her to that point, mainly because we'd kept her all to ourselves. I didn't need to explain that isolating her was just as harmful as any bite the wolves could deliver. Charli already knew it.

"I'm imagining a room full of miniature Beautifuls," she confessed.

"They were the weird ones, Coccinelle," I told her. "Not you."

"Adam, I carried a wooden box of wishes around with me until I was five."

I slipped my arm around her and hauled her in close. "That's endearing, not weird."

"I also went through a phase of planting feathers in the hope of growing ducks," she added. "Tell me that's endearing."

I still smiled. "Okay, a little weird."

She pulled away and groaned, slapping her palm against her forehead. "See what I mean?"

"Look, as far as I know, Bridget hasn't planted any feathers," I reasoned. "She loves dolls and sparkles and pretty dresses." I was rambling now, and couldn't seem to stop. "And princesses – all things pink and fluffy. She's a perfectly well-adjusted little girl who's going to fit right in."

I nearly had her. The crease on Charli's forehead disappeared and she almost nodded. Then our daughter appeared in the doorway of the bathroom and blew my pep talk to smithereens.

"Can we go to the dancing school now?" she asked.

Her sweet little voice didn't quite match her appearance. Bridget had decided to accessorise the simple but cute ballet outfit her mother had dressed her in. She was now sporting a flashing bunny ear headband, one of my ties and the gaudy blinged-up galoshes that Bente had made her the day before. Topping off the look was Treasure, looking every bit the murder victim as Bridget clutched her by the neck.

The moan that escaped Charlotte sounded like one of fear. "What do you know about ducks, Bridge?" she asked.

Bridget grabbed Treasure's hand, bending the doll's arm at an odd angle. "They go 'quack quack quack'," she sang.

I leaned close to Charli and whispered, "See? Endearing and sweet."

"And if you feed them lemonade, they blow up," said Bridget, adding a theatrical "kaboom" at the end that made us both jump.

"Great," drawled Charli. "Not weird at all," she grumbled.

***

Ella Daniels's dance studio was an unassuming little shopfront in the Garment District. Arriving on time, we followed the trail of little girls filing through the door and introduced ourselves to a young woman behind the reception desk.

"Oh, yes." She beamed at Bridget. "Miss Ella is expecting you."

Her tone was kind, but that didn't stop Bridget from wedging herself between Charli and me as if she needed protecting. Realistically, she was on her own at that point. With the exception of the boots, we had stripped her of all props before we left home. Toning down her outfit was the most protection we could offer.

"Are you shy?" asked the girl.

Bridget didn't reply.

"She'll be okay." Charli didn't sound the least bit believable.

"Of course she will," beamed the girl, trying to reassure Bridget with a stun gun smile and a hand on her shoulder. "Come. I'll show you around."

The first thing I noticed about the room she led us into was how big it seemed. I then noticed that the far wall was entirely covered with mirrors, and that the room really wasn't big at all. The second thing to catch my eye was Bente's sister, Ivy. In fairness she would've been impossible to miss, especially when she boomed out Charlotte's name and rushed toward us.

I mumbled from the corner of my mouth, "What's she doing here?"

"I don't know," she whispered. "Malibu must dance here."

I'd never met Malibu Denison before, but I knew she was a whole bag of trouble. She was Ryan's new archenemy, and after just a minute in her company, I understood why.

"I hate those dumb baby shoes," she barked, pointing at Bridget's boots. "You can't wear them to ballet."

My little girl shrank before my eyes, cowering behind me like a puppy.

"Shush," ordered Ivy, covering her wretched daughter's mouth with her hand. "She can wear whatever she wants to."

Malibu shrugged her away. "You're not dancing with my friends."

At least Ivy had the good manners to appear embarrassed. With a flick on the butt, she sent her kid off to join the girls that she'd forbidden Bridget from dancing with.

"I didn't know Bridget did ballet," she said.

"It's her first day today," replied Charli. "She's nervous."

"She'll settle in." Ivy smiled awkwardly at me. "The first day is always the hardest."

I tried to smile back but it wasn't easy. I had Bridget clinging onto my side for dear life, and her mother crushing the bones in my hand.

Then things got worse.

The studio's policy of no parents in the classroom wasn't something Charli was comfortable with. As much as I tried to convince her that Bridget would survive an hour without us, she wouldn't budge.

I wasn't going to win, but thankfully I didn't need to try. When Ella arrived, she introduced herself to Bridget and invited us to watch from the sidelines. "She'll be more confident with you here."

Charli shot me a triumphant smirk before thanking her.

***

Ella was nothing like her husband, Grayson. He was loud, rude and mouthy. She was a softly spoken ballerina with a pretty smile and impeccable manners. Maybe he'd won her in a raffle.

Charli crouched to Bridget's level. "Just have fun, okay?" She fussed with her hair. "And dance with whoever you want to."

Bridget nodded and took off to join Malibu and her posse.

I turned to Ella. "Are the boots going to be a problem?" I asked. "She's rather attached to them."

Ella let out a quiet giggle. "We're not the Bolshoi, Adam."

***

They were most definitely not the Bolshoi.

Ella's voice was small and totally lacking in authority. The problem was, her charges were also small and lacking in authority. None of them seemed to pay her a skerrick of attention when she gave instruction. It was pure anarchy.

"This isn't going to work, Charlotte," I murmured from the corner of my mouth.

For the first time all day, she agreed with me. "Malibu is running the show," she noted.

It was sad but true. Only a few girls were watching Ella's demonstrations at the front of the room. The rest were too busy down the back hanging off the little red-headed wretch's every word. "The dumb girl has baby boots," she teased, making her posse giggle. If Bridget heard, she didn't let on. For once in her life, she was behaving, twirling around at the front of the room with a couple of other girls.

I'd always considered my fuse to be longer than most, but it was coming dangerously close to being lit with every word out of Malibu's mouth. Charli sat beside me with her hand on my knee, as if holding me back. When the horrid child realised that Bridget wasn't reacting to her taunts, she moved her little gang closer.

"Eyes to the front, ladies," Ella pointlessly demanded. "I want to see dancing."

"You can't dance," spat Malibu.

Bridget didn't reply but she did turn around. Her blue eyes found mine and I instantly knew she was comforted by it. "Are you okay, baby?" I asked in French. "We can go if you want to."

"*Non*," she replied. "I want to stay."

"Ignore them."

"I will," she said remarkably strongly.

Monster Malibu took immediate offense to Bridget's foreign reply. "You can't talk fairy words," she barked. "I know fairy words. Ryan called some fairies on the phone and I talked to them."

I thought back to the ridiculous phone call we'd received from Ryan a few weeks earlier. Charli remembered too. "The sunflower conversation," she mumbled.

"You're not a fairy girl," she added. "Only Ryan knows them."

"Yeah," agreed the annoying little brunette standing next to her.

I'd had enough. My plan was to snatch my daughter and run. Charlotte had other ideas. As I tried to stand, she yanked me back down. "Wait," she told me. "Bridget's got this."

I don't know where her sudden change of heart had come from, but I had no choice but to trust it. Bridget was essentially a miniature version of Charli, and if she had a game plan, chances were Bridget did as well.

"Ry is my uncle," announced Bridget far too proudly.

"He's going to be my uncle too," Malibu retorted.

I made a mental note to call my brother and congratulate him. He'd surely be thrilled to know Malibu was laying claim.

The brunette minion put a hand on a hip. "Yeah," she concurred. "*Her* uncle."

Whether she realised it or not, Malibu Denison had just made a serious mistake. Bridget objected to Bente making the moves on Ryan. There was no way in hell she'd let Malibu muscle in.

The good ballerinas continued their uncoordinated twirling at the front while Ella sweetly complimented their technique. The bad ballerinas stood off to the side in a huddle, and my kid was right in the middle of them.

Gone was the shy little girl who'd walked in clinging to my side. In a surge of bravery, Bridget opened her mouth and let Malibu Denison know exactly what she thought of her, and every word of it was in French.

"Is that fairy words?" asked the brunette, puzzled.

Malibu played it cool. "Yeah," she conceded unwillingly. "She knows fairy words."

Perhaps impressed, a new little bully chimed in. "How do you say the teacher's name like a fairy?"

Bridget looked across at me before replying. I knew she was up to no good. She knew it too, which explained why I couldn't hold her gaze.

"*Tête de guimauve*," announced Bridget knowingly.

"*Tête de guimauve*, Miss Ella!" yelled Malibu. "That's fairy words."

"Lovely, Malibu," sang the oblivious teacher. "Keep dancing, please."

Despite the fact that they all botched the pronunciation, the rogue ballerinas took turns shouting it out. I wasn't the only one who noticed Bridget's triumphant expression every time they did it. Charli caught on in an instant. "What did she tell them to say?" she asked.

I leaned in close. "Your kid just trained her new pets to call the teacher a marshmallow head."

17. PILLOW TALK

Charli

I realised a long time ago that Adam and I had completely different burdens when it came to fretting about Bridget's wellbeing.

I worried about her heart being broken and whether or not she'd find friends and be happy. Adam's concerns were much more long-sighted. He wished that she'd grow up to be good and make wise choices – which is why having her slide off the rails the tiniest bit tended to send him into a blind panic.

Bridget was smart, and stunts like outsmarting Malibu Denison proved it. At an age when most kids would've run crying to their parents, or settled it with a good thumping, Bridget chose to bide her time. It wasn't a one off, and that's what bothered her father. We'd been home for hours before it rated a mention, which could only mean that he'd been stewing about it all afternoon.

Some of the best conversations we had took place while changing the sheets on our bed. It was our version of pillow talk.

"I don't think we've seen the last of Bridget versus Malibu," he told me. "I don't know what to do about that."

I tossed a pillow across the bed. "You don't have to do anything. She did a good job by herself."

"You know she's travelling way beyond the norm, right?" he asked, stretching his arm. "Completely off the charts."

I studied him for a moment, trying to work out if he was scared or annoyed by the notion. "Does it bother you?"

"She's four years old, Charli," he said, doing the Adam dodge. "What will she be like at fifteen?"

"Dangerous, I'd say."

He shook his head. "I don't want that for her."

I pointed toward the door. "You'd better go and pull her wings off now then, before it's too late."

He scooped the quilt off the floor and dumped it on the bed. "You know that's not what I meant," he grumbled. "Don't put words in my mouth."

Making assumptions was easy. The simple truth was that the future that he was determined to prevent was my past. When I'd been the unruly teenager he'd found it endearing, but the mere notion of Bridget acting out made him break into a cold sweat.

Being the dad of a headstrong, slightly bent little girl was a tough gig, and I knew from experience that tightening his grip on her would only make it harder. All I could do was keep reminding him of that.

"She didn't need you today," I said gently. "That's probably going to start happening a lot."

"You were the one who was intent on keeping her safe and shielded from the big bad world," he replied. "What changed?"

I couldn't adequately describe the feeling of seeing my daughter fearlessly and confidently shut her tormentor down, but I tried. "She made herself safe."

Adam held the corners of the quilt and threw it out across the bed. "I just want to do right by her, Charli," he complained. "Sometimes I feel like I get it wrong."

"Sometimes we both do," I replied. "But not today."

18. PERFORMANCE ANXIETY

Adam

Every now and then, the tie I wore to work started to feel like a noose around my neck. On days like that, just being in the office took effort.

Despite the fact that I'd forgone breakfast with my kid to make an early start, I'd hardly made a dent in the pile of paperwork on my desk. By mid morning I was fast losing the will to live, and could feel a headache coming on. Resting my elbows on my desk, I closed my eyes and kneaded my temples.

"Rough morning?"

When I looked up and saw Charli, the ache in my brain disappeared in an instant. I went a step further than asking her to close the door. I asked her to lock it.

"Why?" She flashed me her deadliest grin. "Are you trying to hide me?"

I walked over and cornered her against the door. "There's nothing wrong with wanting you all to myself." I slipped my hand behind her, turned the lock and kissed her – far more suggestively than I should have.

Charli eventually pulled away, which was for the best. My mind was getting creative, and so were my hands.

She held me tightly, presumably to stop my creeping hands. "Back to my original question," she said. "Are you having a rough day?"

I leaned down, brushing my next words across her lips. "Not any more."

Charlotte gave up holding me at bay. She linked her arms around my neck and pressed her body against mine before kissing me twice as dangerously as I'd just kissed her.

Without breaking the embrace, I walked her toward the window and lowered her onto the couch. "Glad you locked the door?" I whispered in her ear.

Her laugh combined with a breathy moan that made my head spin. I'd wanted her even before she arrived, and now that she was in my grasp, I decided that the couch in my office was the perfect place to have her.

Charli decided otherwise. The layers of her soft skirt got caught between us as she grabbed my hand. "Don't you want to know why I'm here?" she asked.

I slipped my other hand between her knees. "You mean this wasn't it?"

She wriggled out and pulled herself together, tugging her dress back into place. I straightened my tie, pretending to do the same thing. "I need to talk to you about something," she said.

Whatever it was had to be serious. She'd never left work and come all the way downtown to see me before. "Talk to me."

"I'm late," she said simply.

I'd heard those words only once before, when I was least ready to hear them. Things were different this time. First, I knew what it meant. Second, I wasn't scared. And third, I was excited. "Seriously?"

Her nod was cut short by my hug. "Ow! Adam, I need to breathe."

I leaned back to give her space. "I'm sorry," I told her, grinning like an idiot. "No, not really," I amended, lurching forward again.

"Don't get too excited," she warned. "I'm not sure." Just when I thought I was getting the hang of the whole girl-versus-boy dynamics, she upped the ante. Apparently late doesn't always equal pregnant.

"Well, can we find out, please?"

"That's why I'm here," she replied, grabbing her purse. After a long moment of rummaging, she pulled out a pregnancy test. "I thought we could find out together. I just need somewhere to pee."

I could feel the wry smile that crossed my face. "I know just the place."

***

Charlotte is nearly a foot shorter than me, which meant rushing down the corridor at my pace was practically a sprint for her. The reason for my urgency was a good one. Commandeering my father's office was only going to work if he wasn't in it, and I knew he was attending a board meeting that morning.

Slipping past Tennille at the reception desk was easier than expected. She was on the phone at the time, and judging by her giggle, it was a personal call.

I usually dreaded entering the double doors at the end of the hall, but at that moment nothing but excitement flowed through me.

Charli was excited too, but I suspect it had nothing to do with peeing on a white stick. When I ushered her inside, she headed straight for Dad's chair. "Nicely done, dauphin," she crowed.

"I can't be the dauphin," I replied, laughing. "The eldest son of the king is the dauphin, not the youngest."

"No worries," she said unperturbed. "We'll just have to do away with Ryan – poison his cologne or something." She followed up with a wicked smile that I desperately wanted to kiss.

I only held back because I knew it probably wouldn't stop there – even at the risk of being sprung by my father. I pointed to the dark oak panelled wall to her left. "Go," I ordered.

Charlotte looked at the wall. "Go where?"

I waved her over. As I pushed on a panel, a concealed door swung open, exposing the bathroom hidden behind it.

"A secret door?" she quizzed me. "Who are you people?"

"I don't know about the rest of them, but I'm yours." I took her face in my hands. "I'm the father of your babies," I announced with the reverence it deserved. "I'm also your partner in crime, so if you could please hurry up and do what you need to do, we won't go to jail."

Whether she believed it was a possibility or not, she did as I asked, slipping into the bathroom and closing the door behind her.

The only fault with the plan was that I was left alone in the king's chambers. Feeling anxious for two different reasons, I paced my dad's office, occasionally stopping to gaze out the windows that took up the whole length of the room.

I didn't need the view to remind me that New York is an enormous city. Being there can sometimes make you feel small, and on a bad day, insignificant. I never felt that way any more. As far as I was concerned, I was a giant. The life I'd created with my girls was a good one. It was the other things I had going on that were small and insignificant.

***

It seemed an eternity before the panelled door swung open again, and even longer before Charlotte spoke. "Performance anxiety," she explained. "It took a while."

"Now we wait?"

She nodded. "A couple of minutes."

The urgency to get out of Dad's office had all but disappeared. I took Charli by the hand and led her to the couch near the window.

"We should go," she mumbled. "I don't want you to get in trouble."

I directed my smile at the window. "I'm not worried," I replied. "If we have to wait, I'd rather we do it in style."

Charli shuffled closer. "You're my hero, Adam," she teased. "Brave and defiant. I'm glad you're my baby-daddy."

I whispered my next words against her hair. "That doesn't mean I won't blame you if he catches us, Coccinelle."

***

We were quiet for a while. Charli seemed engrossed in the view. I had trouble taking my eyes off her. The last seven years played out in my mind in less than a minute, trying to pinpoint the moment we grew up and became adults who were capable of raising a child and planning another.

We didn't even look like the same two love-struck kids we used to be. Charli wore heels to work and her hair was always neat. Vintage Charli was far more casual and blithe than the well put together woman sitting next to me. The change in me was almost the opposite. I'd started out wound far too tightly, determined to control every single aspect of my life. I didn't live that way any more, and the tie I wore to work was rarely straight because of it.

We'd found a happy medium, and as far as I was concerned, our struggles were over. Ballet lessons and making nonsensical deals with my four-year-old were always going to trump the life I used to think I wanted. And my heart thumped a little harder at the realisation that we might be on the edge of more magic.

19. DIRECTION

Charli

The view from Jean-Luc's office was as good as any in the city, and from the forty-third floor the streets below almost looked peaceful.

Adam was doing a good job of appearing calm, but I wasn't buying it. It was impossible not to compare this moment to the last time I peed on a stick. The circumstances were different, but the look in his eyes was the same.

I knew better than to question it. Adam had been ready for another baby since Bridget was a year old. He wasn't concerned about a positive result – that was exactly what he was hoping for. He was worried about a negative one.

"Boy or girl?" I asked out of the blue.

Adam frowned. "I'm not sure. Will the answer be written on the stick?"

"I'm just curious. Would you like a boy or another girl?"

"I don't have a preference."

I leaned closer, pinning his face beneath my hands while I studied his eyes. I didn't have a preference either. All I wished for was another healthy baby who shared her father's lovely cerulean eyes. I kept the thought to myself. "She might be twice as shady as Bridget," I warned. "Then what?"

I pressed my thumb into his dimpled cheek as his smile broadened. "Boarding school," he replied.

I could've taken five tests in the time we spent discussing the pitfalls of raising shady daughters. I put an end to it by reminding him that time was well and truly up.

As I reached for my bag, Adam grabbed my hand. "Wait," he said, squeezing my fingers. "I want to tell you something first."

I nodded. "Okay."

"We're good either way, alright?"

"Better than good." I smiled, trying to reassure him. "We're perfect."

I handed him the test without even looking at it. I was more focused on him and how incredibly nervous he'd suddenly become.

I knew the result before the words came. His shoulders sagged infinitesimally, telling me all I needed to know. "Negative," he said quietly. "I'm sorry."

I wasn't sure what he was apologising for, or what I should say in reply. The feeling of disappointment shouldn't have been this strong. We'd been trying to get pregnant for two months. Compared with the waiting game Alex and Gabi played, it was a miniscule amount of time.

"Next time," I said quietly. "It's early days."

Adam gave me a smile that I knew was false. "And we get to keep trying," he said. "Win–win."

I smiled back, just as fraudulently. "Always an upside."

He dropped the test back in my bag and pulled me into his arms. My body sagged against his.

"I love you, Charlotte," he whispered before kissing the top of my head. "And all the crooked babies we're going to have together when the time is right."

***

We got out of the king's office as stealthily as we arrived. Adam reluctantly let me go at the elevator. I headed back to the gallery feeling a strange tinge of sadness that hadn't been there earlier that morning.

I was dealing with a tinge, but jumping the gun had crushed Adam. It didn't feel good and I already knew it wouldn't happen again. Until I was absolutely sure I was pregnant, there would be no more peeing on sticks in his presence.

The rest of the morning passed in a blur of boring paperwork, an evil but necessary part of my job. Just when I thought the day couldn't get any less enjoyable, I received a blunt text from my father-in-law.

– **Lunch?**

If that was his idea of an invitation, it sucked.

– **I'm at work**

– **I'll come to you**

He was cruising for a snarky reply.

– **Great. You can bring me a sandwich.**

As expected, his reply took forever, and my eyes didn't leave my phone while I waited for it.

– **No sandwiches.**

– **Turkey on rye, please. No tomato.**

Jean-Luc didn't reply, which was the first indication that I'd won. The second came when he turned up an hour later carrying a bag of sandwiches.

"Oh," I crooned, taking the bag and peeking inside. "My favourite. How did you know?"

"No games today, Charli," he grumbled. "I am not in the mood."

His demeanour made me wonder if he knew I'd made use of the facilities in his office that morning. I tried to think of a quick defence, but he had other things on his mind.

"Where is Adam?" he demanded, following me to my desk.

"At work, as far as I know."

Jean-Luc momentarily forgot his line of questioning when he realised we were dining in. "Here?" he asked.

"I can't leave. I'm the only one here."

He looked seriously inconvenienced, but pulled up a chair and sat down. I didn't care. I already knew lunch was going to be miserable.

"He's not at the office," he told me.

I handed him a sandwich. I was at a loss. Maybe Adam was more disappointed by the morning's events than he'd let on. My first instinct was to find out where he was and go to him. My second was to stay and defend him against his father.

"I don't know where he is," I said strongly. "Maybe he just needed some time out."

"Adam doesn't have that luxury," he snapped. "I don't tolerate unreliability from any of my employees."

There was very little in life that Jean-Luc did tolerate.

I dropped my sandwich into the wrapper and brushed my hands. "Why don't you just call him and ask him where he is?"

"It's not up to me to chase him."

"You think that's my job?"

"No, Charli," he replied quietly. "I just want you to talk to him. He listens to you."

I stared at him, and was immediately struck by his worried expression. Adam looked exactly the same whenever he thought Bridget was running off the rails.

"You think he's off track," I said, thinking out loud.

Jean-Luc gazed at his still-wrapped sandwich. "My son has the potential to be a brilliant attorney," he told it, "but he's unfocused at the moment."

That's because his heart wasn't in it. It annoyed me that he couldn't see it.

He unwrapped his lunch and set it in front of him. "I want you to encourage him more," he demanded.

"Why would I ever do that, Jean-Luc?" I asked, appalled. "A career in law isn't for him."

"Nonsense," he barked. "His Ivy League education suggests otherwise."

I took a bite of my sandwich so I didn't have to reply. I had nothing remotely pleasant to say. The king didn't speak either, which made for an uncomfortable minute of silence.

"What more do you want from him?" I asked finally. "He gives you eighty-hour weeks all the time, which you never acknowledge. He more than makes up for any time he takes off."

"More than his presence is required, Charli," he replied. "He used to have dedication for his craft."

Working with wood was his craft. Law was his profession. How sad that his own father didn't recognise the difference.

"What do you want me to do, exactly?"

Jean-Luc paused before speaking – a sure-fire sign that his reply would be ugly. "Help him find direction again. He could return to study," he suggested. "Perhaps gain his masters degree."

The sound out of my mouth was almost a growl. "Do you know him at all?" I asked roughly. "Adam would never do that, never."

"I will not sit back and let him throw his career away, Charli." He hissed the words with forced restraint. "I am his father. It would be remiss of me to do that."

"Carry on, then," I shot back. "Tighten your hold and continue squeezing the life out of him."

I'd been holding my own until that point, but in one of the hardest blows he'd ever dished out, Jean-Luc called me an insolent, selfish witch. "Never before have I dealt with anyone as infuriating as you," he added exasperatedly. "Why must you continue to make things difficult?"

I probably looked calm, but in my mind I'd already thrown my sandwich at him. "All I've ever done is love your son," I replied. "Why can't you do the same?"

My harsh question hung between us with the weight of a brick. I took a sip of water I didn't need to stop myself saying anything more. Jean-Luc busied himself by picking apart his sandwich.

"I loathe cucumber," he finally volunteered, dropping a slice on his napkin. "When I started courting my wife, she worked at a cinema in London called the Odeon. Every day at one o'clock I'd meet her for lunch in the square. And every day she'd pack vile cucumber sandwiches." I managed a half smile, too beaten down to offer anything more. "I was trying so hard to woo her that I never let on that I hated them. We'd been married twenty years before I finally confessed."

"What were you doing in London?" I asked.

For the first time all day, he smiled. "Studying. I attended King's College," he explained. "I'd only been there a few weeks when I met Fi."

I liked hearing him shorten her name. It hinted toward a much kinder man.

"She was lovely," he continued. "Truly beautiful."

"She still is," I muttered.

His smile broadened. "I'm well aware of my good fortune in the romance stakes, Charli."

Fiona might've always been beautiful, but she hadn't always been high society. "You could've married anyone you wanted. Why did you choose Fiona?"

My question was so outrageously ballsy that I expected him to order me to mind my business. But he didn't.

"Because I adored her," he replied. "And thirty-two years later, I still adore her."

"True love always prevails," I mumbled.

"That's it?" he asked. "You're not going to give me a tale of magic to accompany my answer?"

I looked straight at him. "Magic is wasted on the non-believers."

His laugh echoed across the gallery floor. "Eat your lunch, Charlotte," he told me. "I've had enough nonsense for one day."

20. DISAPPOINTMENT

Adam

The morning hadn't panned out the way I hoped it would, but the rest of the day did. Less than half an hour after Charli left my office, I packed up my desk and bailed. The afternoon was mine, and I spent it working on Bente's drawers. By the time Charli arrived home, it was painted and dry to the touch. The pink paint was garish, but the finish was perfect.

"You're a genius, Boy Wonder," Charli declared. No one had the art of ego-boosting praise mastered as well as my wife.

"Thank you." I kissed her cheek. "Where's my kid?"

"Having dinner with her grandparents."

"Why?"

"Funny story," she quipped, patting my chest. "Your father came to see me at work today."

"Looking for me?"

"Of course."

"And?"

"And, long story short, he suggested that Bridget spend the evening with them," she replied. "So I could use the time alone with you to find out why you've become such a flake at work."

I cringed, imagining how the conversation would've gone down. "Was he awful to you?"

"Not too bad – He brought me lunch."

I apologised to her, but cowardly made light of the reason why. "I bailed after you left," I explained. "Spent the afternoon playing at home instead of working."

Her focus remained on the chest of pink drawers. "So I see."

"Are you mad?"

"No." She twisted in my arms to look at me. "I just want to understand what's going on. If you're unhappy at work, quit. I don't understand why you put yourself through it."

Neither did I. Rebellion was ingrained in Charli. It flowed through her veins like blood. Acts of mutiny only struck me in short bursts. Most of the time I was content to go through the motions of pretending to enjoy the job I'd spent years studying to do. On days when I couldn't, I'd flake, which was confusing to everyone.

"I just needed the day." My answer wasn't fair considering she'd probably been through an interrogation over lunch with my father. He would've demanded information that she couldn't give him. "There's nothing more to it."

"Nothing to do with this morning?" she hinted.

"No, of course not." I brushed the back of my hand across her cheek. "Is that what you've been worried about?"

"I know you're disappointed," she said seriously.

"Maybe a little," I conceded, smiling. "But I was disappointed long before that."

"Why?" she asked in a small voice.

"For so many reasons, Charlotte." I spun her around and pulled her back against me. "Bridget polished off the last of the milk this morning. That cut me to the quick." I leaned in and murmured against her ear. "And the queue at Starbucks on the way to work was horrendous – really disappointing."

When she giggled, she trembled against me. "You've been huffing too many paint fumes," she teased.

"Possibly," I agreed, kissing the side of her neck. "Maybe I need to lie down for a while."

***

Now that the drawers were finished, Charli understandably wanted them gone. I called Colin the delivery guy and arranged to have them sent to Ryan – at seven in the morning just to be a jerk.

I expected a scathing phone call. What I got instead was a short but heartfelt text message thanking me, which was a letdown considering the trouble I'd gone to to piss him off.

"He's found someone else to play with, Boy Wonder." Charli's soothing tone didn't match her grin. "And she's much prettier than you." I'd always thought Ryan would end up with a stewardess called Mindy or a fashion model with a secret cocaine habit. Seeing him land a girl as sweet and nice as Bente was almost anticlimactic, but he was smitten.

We hadn't spent much time together lately. I'd been putting in extra hours in an attempt at getting Dad off my back. It wasn't working. The more conscientious I became, the harder he pushed me. Sooner or later we were going to come to blows. I could feel it brewing, especially since he'd started mentioning the idea of me going back to school to gain my masters degree. But the inevitable showdown was not going to happen today.

In the nicest of surprises, Ryan showed up in my office with Bridget in tow.

I was on the phone at the time, which made no difference to my little wannabe fly-girl. She launched herself at me full force, giving me no recovery time before she threw her arms around my neck and squeezed me half to death. I managed to end the call on a polite note and prised myself free. "What are you doing here?" I asked, tickling her enough to make her giggle. "It's such a nice surprise."

"It's a good story of the day today."

"Indeed," I agreed.

Bridget had been taking note of the story of the day for a long time. Alex once told her that her day could be determined by the weather. It wasn't such a left-of-centre concept coming from a diehard surfer like him.

If he missed a morning in the water because of crappy weather, his day was ruined.

Ryan's story of the day was obviously a good one too. He sat opposite my desk and got straight to business, explaining that he'd stumbled across a building that would be the perfect site for a new restaurant.

"It's on West 52nd," he told me. "It'd be perfect, Adam."

We were always on the lookout, but hadn't come across anything since Billet-doux. I didn't even need to see it to know that he'd found something good. The reason for my hesitation had nothing to do with Ryan – I trusted his business nous implicitly. I just didn't have the time to commit to anything so involved.

Bridget picked up a pen and made a grab for the purchase agreement contract I'd been slaving over all afternoon. I snatched it away and handed her a notebook. "I don't have time to do this, Ryan," I said regretfully.

"You don't have to do anything," he assured me. "I just want to know if you want in on it."

Bridget pointed her pen at him like a wand. "We want in on it, Ry," she declared. "Just do it."

I ignored her. The kid made enough deals without encroaching on real estate negotiations. "I'll think about it," I told him. At the very least, I needed to talk to Charli about it. I had no idea what her take would be. Undertaking a renovation would chew into even more precious family time. I wondered if Ryan had already run it past her so I didn't have to. "Have you mentioned it to Charli?" I asked.

"No, that would involve dealing with your wife." He shuddered. "And I make it a habit never to deal with your wife."

"Daddy, can we go to the park?" interjected Bridget.

I looked at the mountain of work on my desk, quickly deciding that I'd been playing the part of diligent attorney for far too many hours that week. "Yes," I replied. "Let's get out of here for a while."

***

After stopping for coffee, we ended up at Battery Park. I couldn't ever remember taking Bridget there, which was criminal considering we'd been in town for nine months.

She took to the climbing frame as if she'd been there a hundred times. Ryan and I sat on a nearby bench and watched as she climbed up and down, performing stunts that would've made her mother a nervous wreck.

The conversation was strange. My brother wasn't renowned for deep and meaningful chats, but every now and then he'd surprise me. He had never claimed to love any woman before, and he'd had more than his fair share. When he told me that he loved Bente, I believed him. He was too confused and worried to be anything other than genuine.

"You're not locked in for a lifetime, Ryan," I pointed out. "It's not like you've married her."

"What if I do marry her?" he asked, looking terrified. "How do I know it won't happen again? I might fall in love again one day."

He might've been on his way, but he clearly wasn't all-in just yet. Falling in love is an inexplicable sensation deep within your soul. When it's right, it never goes away. It endures everything, no matter what the story of the day might be.

"I fall in love ten times a day, Ryan," I said with reverence. "But it's always with Charlotte."

It was too early to tell whether Bente was imbedded in his soul forever. I'd never had the misfortune of doubt. I knew from the minute I laid eyes on Charli that she'd stay in my heart forever. That made me the lucky one.

21. GOOD LAWYER, BAD LAWYER

Charli

News of the potential new restaurant site was good. As Adam explained the deal to me, I watched more than I listened. I didn't really need to know the details. All I needed to see was the spark of excitement in him that had been missing for a very long time.

When Ryan called a few days later and asked him to go and check it out after work, I all but demanded that he go. Then I crossed my fingers and wished hard that something would come of it.

Adam worked late so often that missing dinner didn't faze Bridget any more. We made the most of it, indulging in a girly night that was predominantly spent in the bathroom. Mutual makeovers were always more fun for her than me. Sitting on her little pink footstool for half an hour was almost as excruciating as scrubbing waterproof mascara off my cheeks when she was finished. I never complained, mainly because I was relieved that she never called me out for being clueless. Bridget was undoubtedly a prissy girl – poles apart from me at the same age. Wearing pretty dresses and getting my toenails painted hadn't rated highly when I was little. Truthfully, it hadn't rated highly until I reached my twenties.

Childhood makeovers were definitely not something I indulged in. The closest thing to makeup in Alex's house was sunscreen. I didn't feel disadvantaged by that. It was just a different way of life – a life my girl would never know purely because she was a Décarie.

Adam and I kept her grounded as best we could. He was much tougher than I was, but he had a better idea of what was coming. Our daughter was in line to inherit an obscene amount of money when she turned eighteen. How she handled that was going to depend on how we handled the eighteen years before it.

"I just love blue sparkles," she said, coming at me with a brush full of powder. "Do we have blue sparkles, Mummy?"

If I opened my mouth, I was going to eat the brush. "No one has blue sparkles, baby," I murmured from a corner of my mouth. "Except maybe Cheynie's mum."

Jasmine Davis had been wearing blue sparkly eyeshadow since primary school. It wasn't a good look, even back then.

"Oh, I love that lady," chimed Bridget.

"Who? Jasmine?"

She nodded, convincing me that she had no idea who I was talking about. Then she spoke again and changed my mind. "She has a wiggly butt."

I laughed harder than I had in weeks. Bridget giggled too, but probably had no clue why. I pulled my little girl in close. Thanks to my position on the pink footstool, we were eye to eye. "I love you Bridget Décarie," I told her. "So very much."

Her dark blue eyes sparkled under the bright bathroom light. Her lips curled into the most beautiful of smiles, revealing the deep dimple on her right cheek. And just when I thought she couldn't remind me any more of her father, she answered me in French. "*Je t'aime, maman.*"

***

By the time Adam arrived home, Bridget had been in bed for hours, and he looked like he wished he had been too.

"Well?" I asked, rushing him at the door. "How did it go?"

He shrugged off his jacket and draped it over a chair. "Interesting."

I groaned out loud, annoyed by the lack of information. "Did you buy it?"

Adam's smile was tired but his eyes were bright. "We did. I think we paid too much, and we only bought two thirds of it, but it'll work out okay."

I grabbed his tie and pressed myself up against him. "I see fire in your eyes, monsieur."

He rested his elbows on my shoulders. "I wish you'd seen it, Charli," he said quietly. "It hasn't been touched in years. Parquetry floors, pressed tin ceiling, decorative mouldings ..."

Architecture was Adam-porn. He would've seen things that his brother didn't notice. Ryan wouldn't have given a damn about the history or the charm. The only thing he would've cared about was whether he could install a mezzanine level, and how much it would cost to do it.

"The guy who owns it is a cranky old man," he added. "Tough to deal with."

"So Ryan did the wheeling and dealing?" I asked, heading for the fridge. "He's cranky and old too."

Adam pulled out a chair and sat down at the table. "It was a team effort," he replied. "Good lawyer, bad lawyer, baby."

***

I wasn't a good wife. It was one of the many reasons Jean-Luc thought his son was hard done by. My cooking skills were non-existent, but the salad I put together that night was a decent effort. The wine was better, offsetting any culinary disappointment Adam might've been feeling.

Shortly after dinner, a late night visitor put an end to our plans of a quiet night on the couch. Adam answered the door, which probably wasn't the outcome Bente was hoping for.

She didn't look good. She looked miserable and cold in the lightweight dress she was wearing, and it was obvious that she'd been crying.

"Are you alright?" he asked, stepping aside to let her in.

"No," she muttered. "Your brother is an asshole."

This wasn't exactly news to us so I couldn't blame him for laughing. But I could show a little more support. Bypassing my unsympathetic husband, I grabbed Bente's hand, led her to the couch and demanded that she talk to me. Adam bailed. "I'll leave you ladies to it," he offered, leaning down to kiss me. His parting words were reserved for our distraught friend. "Tomorrow's a new day, Bente. You'll be fine."

After hearing her teary breakdown of events, I was pretty convinced she'd be fine too. A silly misunderstanding ended with her going postal with a blueberry bagel. It was funny, and because Bente isn't a drama queen, she realised it. The conversation started with tears and ended with giggles, which was the best outcome possible.

Ryan wasn't calm like Adam. He was a short-tempered hothead, just like their father. I'd been on the receiving end of the wrath of both of them at one time or another. It wasn't frightening, but it was exhausting. Staying away from Ryan for a while was the best solution I could come up with.

"Do you want to stay here tonight?" I asked.

Her reply was small and sheepish. "Yeah, if you don't mind."

"As long as you don't mind crashing on the couch."

"It's fine." She reached forward and grabbed Treasure off the coffee table. "The girls will keep me company."

"Watch that one," I warned. "It's likely to come alive and murder you while you sleep."

22. DEAD FAIRY GUTS

Adam

Bridget and I were flying solo the next morning. So far Charli and I had put on a united front and endured ballet lessons together, but she'd been called into work early so the glitter duties were all mine.

After three lessons, relations between Bridget and the red-headed horror were no better. Malibu was relentless in her attempts at rattling her cage, and Bridget wasn't getting any better at grinning and bearing it.

My pep talk at the door was always the same. "Just ignore her, okay?" I ran my hand through her ponytail. "Do your own thing and pay attention to Miss Ella."

Bridget promised she would, then took off running. Ella's offer of sitting in on the class probably wasn't meant to be an indefinite arrangement, but as long as Malibu had my daughter in her sights, I wasn't going anywhere. I sat near the wall and watched her like a hawk. It took all of a minute before Malibu started. "Dumb girl," she baited.

Bridget's reaction was always the same. She'd spin around and look for me. Making eye contact with her had an instant effect. Her worried expression would dull, but there was no denying the hurt in her eyes.

I couldn't believe she was sticking it out. She had no reason to put herself through it, but I was so proud that she was.

Minutes ticked by like hours in that damned room.

After a few long and pointless twirling routines, Ella changed introduced something new. "We're going to do something really special this morning," she announced, inciting a round of high-pitched squeals that made me wince. She floated off to the side room, returning with a pink helium-filled balloon and a fairy wand. "Fairy dancing!" she announced, waving the props at the girls.

More squealing followed, this time accompanied by bouncing. Bridget was usually the first to lose the plot when presented with anything pink and glittery, but for some reason she wasn't moving.

"The balloons are very special. See how they float high in the air?" asked Ella.

Every girl in the room looked up as she did.

"I want a balloon!" demanded Malibu in her trademark obnoxious growl. "Give me one!"

Ella ignored her and continued her pitch. "Fairies live in these balloons," she said with a touch of theatre in her voice. "That's why they float so high, and if you look carefully, you can see them inside."

Twelve little girls took a step forward, craning their necks. One didn't move. Bridget stood cemented to the spot with her hands on her hips and a mighty pissed-off look on her face. I grabbed her attention by calling her name. She glanced at me for a second with a look of pure thunder.

La La Land is subjective – at least, it's supposed to be. Alex and Charli had been making up stories for years, and I'm sure Bridget's take on Sea dogs wasn't factual. But for some reason, Bridget seemed to deny Ella any creative licence.

"Fairies can't live in balloons," she stated. Every girl turned to stare, and Bridget didn't care. "There are no fairies in there, Miss Ella," she added.

"You don't know!" screeched Malibu.

"Enough, Malibu," chided Ella, weak as water. "Bridget, sweetie, fairies live in lots of places."

"Not in them." She pointed at the balloons. "Never, ever."

I wasn't sure what Ella's sideward glance at me was supposed to mean. If it was a plea for help, she was out of luck. My little girl was finally taking a stand. Ella was on her own.

"Girls, we're going to concentrate on gentle turns and pretty feet," she instructed. "Dance gently so we don't disturb the fairies."

Twelve little heads looked skyward. One didn't.

Bridget made her way over to me to air her grievances to someone who'd listen. She climbed onto my lap, threw her arms around my neck and whispered in my ear. "There are no fairies, Daddy."

"How do you know, Bridge?"

"They don't like being stuck," she explained. "They die when they get stuck in places."

"What do you think is in the balloons, then?" I asked curiously.

Ella had gone to great lengths to make her story believable. Even from a distance I could see the confetti in them, but Bridget wasn't buying it.

"*Que des confettis pourris,*" she grumbled.

She must've really been pissed. Never before had Bridget referred to sparkles as rotten.

Ella fetched the rest of the balloons and wands from the side room, rationing them out to each little hand that made a grab for them. When there was only one left, she wandered toward us. "How about you just dance with a wand, Bridget? Would you like that?" she asked gently.

The little La La aficionada didn't have a problem with the wand. She took it from Ella and thanked her.

"Come," encouraged Ella extending her hand. "Join your friends."

I liked Ella Daniels a lot. She was sweet and kind and got extra points for putting up with Grayson on a daily basis. What I didn't like was that she seemed totally oblivious when it came to reading the social workings of her dance class. She had no clue what was going on, which meant my kid was always going to be fair game.

Bridget returned to the group, but something about her mindset had changed. She even looked taller.

"You don't have a fairy balloon," Malibu taunted with a swing of her hips. "I've got the best one."

The little brunette next to her piped up. "Me too," she crowed.

Ignoring Malibu was no longer in Bridget's game plan. She turned around and growled at her. "There are no fairies in there, dumb girl."

Malibu was taken aback. The balloon she was holding wobbled a bit, but she recovered quickly. "Yes there are!"

As usual, the teacher's focus was only on those who were prepared to listen to her. She didn't see Bridget make a grab for the string Malibu was holding. The little redhead didn't stand a chance. Bridget was madder than I'd ever seen her.

Popping it was obviously her plan, but she wasn't having much luck. "*Pas de fées!*" she screamed, futilely trying to burst it with a one-armed hug to her chest.

Malibu took a big step back, hopefully in terror. Her posse followed suit. Ella finally tried diffusing the situation, but calling out Bridget's name and ordering her to stop didn't cut it. The balloon wrestling continued.

My kid was nothing if not resourceful. The wand in her other hand suddenly morphed into a weapon. With one stab of a pointed star, her mission was accomplished. The balloon popped, showering everyone with red and white confetti.

Bridget wasn't content. She grabbed the vapid brunette's balloon and did the same thing. "No fairies!" she yelled, in English this time.

Malibu dropped to her knees and began scooping up confetti. "You killed them," she wailed.

"All dead," whimpered the brunette.

My daughter the serial killer, stood firm. Actually, she didn't. She thumped around the floor, literally sinking her boot in.

"Now I have dead fairy guts on my boots," Bridget ruthlessly claimed. "That's why I have to wear boots."

I put my hands to my face, peeking at her through my fingers. I'd warned Charli that we couldn't put anything past her, and this was a prime example of why. Bridget Décarie was dangerous, and at that moment victorious, brilliant and strong.

Best of all, she was mine.

23. FLASHLIGHT FAIRIES

Charli

Something was wrong. I could feel it. I could also see it. Absolutely no good could come from having Adam and Bridget show up at the gallery at one in the afternoon.

I met them at the door. "What's happened?"

"Nothing," replied Adam, too fast to be convincing.

I looked at Bridget, hoping for a more honest answer. "I can't go to the dancing school any more," she confessed. "I got fired."

The horrified stare I directed at her father wasn't nearly strong enough. "She got kicked out?" I think I saw him nod. "Why?"

Again, it was left to Bridget to explain. "*C'est juste des histoires –*"

"English!" I demanded.

"Miss Ella didn't believe me," she amended. "Fairies can't live in the balloons."

I was none the wiser, and close to throttling both of them due to an acute lack of information.

Adam obviously knew it. "Have you had a lunch break yet?" he asked. "We can go somewhere and talk."

"No she hasn't," boomed Bronson, making a grand entrance. "Take her away." He flapped his hands at me, but spoke only to Adam. "Spoil her rotten and take her shopping."

Shopping wasn't high on my agenda, but I couldn't deny I was eager to get out of there. "Thank you," I mumbled.

"Of course, of course." He was walking away, still flapping his hands. "Begone with you and your Wedgwood blue-eyed beauties."

***

Central Park was where we ended up. It was one of the few places we could hang out with Bridget as well as have a private conversation. While she ran herself ragged on the playground, we sat on a nearby bench and talked. Well, Adam talked. My only input was the occasional moan as I listened to the story of how our daughter came to be expelled from another dance class.

"It wasn't her fault," assured Adam. "It was good to see her finally get one over on Malibu."

I agreed, but it didn't make me feel better. "What are we supposed to do now?" I slapped my hands down on my knees. "Wait another year and try again? We could put a sign around her neck." I drew invisible letters in the air. "Does not play well with others."

Adam chuckled, riling me even more. "I hope she never plays well with the likes of Malibu Denison."

I agreed with that, too. In fact, I agreed with everything he was telling me, which made staying angry impossible. "I just want her to be okay, Adam."

His eyes drifted toward the playground. Bridget was standing near the swings, deep in conversation with another little girl. "Look at her, Charlotte," he urged. "She's perfectly fine."

Mercifully, we never seemed to have panic attacks about our daughter's wellbeing at the same time. Adam was perfectly level-headed, optimistic even. "Ella gave me the number of another dance school," he said. "Apparently this one is a little more structured. She thinks Bridget would benefit."

"What do you think?" I asked.

He shrugged. "It can't hurt to check it out."

"You're willing to try again?"

Adam pulled my hand to his mouth and kissed my fingers. "I will try again and again and again for that little girl," he declared. "Sooner or later, she's going to find her place."

***

After a drama-fuelled day, it was good to get an early night. I crawled into bed at eight o'clock with the intention of sleeping for twelve hours straight. I probably would've managed it if Adam hadn't woken me when he came to bed at ten.

"I'm sorry," he whispered, quickly switching the light off again. "I thought you were awake."

I turned on the lamp. "I am now," I mumbled.

"Excellent." He peeled off his T-shirt and leapt on to the bed, somehow managing to land on me without killing me. He buried his head into the curve of my shoulder and kissed me. "I want to talk to you about something," he murmured.

The weight of him on my chest constricted my laugh. "Just talk?"

He lifted his head to look at me, wiggling his eyebrows like a vaudeville villain. "For now."

"Fine. Speak."

He gently swept my hair off my face. "Well, I've been thinking about the whole fairy-in-the-balloon thing," he began. "Bridget was adamant that Ella's story wasn't true. Do you know why?"

"I've been thinking about it too," I confessed. "There's a story about a witch that kept fairies in jars because they gave off light," I explained. "The witch liked to cast her spells in the forest at night."

"Flashlight fairies would've been handy then, I guess."

"Yeah, but they were like cheap batteries – not very long-lasting. They couldn't breathe and kept dying, and the heartless witch just kept replacing them."

"A horror story for a four-year-old, Charlotte," he chided.

"I never told her the story," I defended. "But my dad may have."

Alex's tales were always cautionary. If it served a purpose, he shared it – gruesome or not. I'd been told the story of the glowing fairies after he'd caught me trapping butterflies in a jar. It wasn't pretty, but I'd never trapped an animal since.

"I wish he'd censor them sometimes," murmured Adam.

"What's the point in that?" I asked. "If there's a story to be told, you've got to tell it all. Half a story never helped anyone."

A tiny smile ghosted across his face. "You don't even know how lovely you are."

"Sure I do," I teased. "I'm gorgeous, darling."

His head dropped, bouncing his warm laugh off my skin. "And humble."

"I don't need to be humble," I breathed. "My husband is drop-dead gorgeous too."

24. PUPPET

Adam

Almost a full week passed before we acted on Ella's recommendation of a new ballet class for Bridget. Charli hadn't been enthusiastic the first time round, and was less so now.

Ella had warned us that Minuet Dance School was hardcore. The classes were run with discipline, and diva shenanigans weren't tolerated. After dragging her feet for days, Charli finally called the school. A girl called Erin spoke to her. "We'd like to set up a meet and greet," she explained. "We need to know that Bridget will be comfortable attending classes here."

Charli liked that idea. I just liked that the studio name was French. I was reserving judgment on everything else. The fees they charged were exorbitant, but the money didn't bother me. I would've paid twice what they were asking if it meant my kid got to twirl her feet off in peace.

The Minuet Dance School was conveniently located a few blocks from my office. I had Mrs Brown deliver Bridget to me just before my lunch hour, and we headed off to check out her new dance school.

"No mean girls, Daddy." Bridget's rough demand made it sound as if I had a choice in the matter.

"I hope not, baby."

"It might be a nice place," she said hopefully.

"It is," I told her, coming to a stop. "This is it."

It really wasn't anything special from the outside. If not for the small sign at the door we might've missed it; but the inside was more impressive.

It was reminiscent of the club we'd just bought. It was of the same era, and the décor was similar. But unlike the club it was spotlessly clean, tastefully furnished, and didn't stink of stale cigar smoke.

We made our way through the foyer and approached the reception counter – a gorgeous ornate oak piece that didn't quite fit the theme of the building. "May I help you?" asked the receptionist.

I couldn't help running my hand along the grain of the wood. "Has this counter always been here?" I asked.

The girl frowned. "What do you mean?"

"I think it predates this building."

Her frown intensified.

"Never mind." I shook my head, feeling slightly stupid. "We have an appointment at twelve. Bridget Décarie."

"I've got this, Erin, thank you."

I turned to see a woman walking toward us. Instantly I knew she was a ballerina. She seemed to glide rather than walk.

"The counter was salvaged from the old Priory Hotel before it was torn down," she told me. "It's beautiful, don't you think?"

"Spectacular," I replied, extending my hand. "I'm Adam."

She shook my hand and then turned to Bridget. "And who do we have here?"

Surprisingly, Bridget didn't shy away. She actually introduced herself.

"Welcome. I'm Madame Kara."

We were off to a promising start.

Kara led us through to a room at the back. It was at least three times the size of Ella's studio, even without the wall of mirrors playing tricks on the eye. She gave us a rundown on what to expect in her class, told us her mammoth list of rules and gave us a lecture on attendance as if we'd already played hooky three times that week.

"Are you punctual, Adam?" she asked. "It's the height of importance."

"Very punctual," I replied.

Just don't ask my dad.

Bridget wasn't paying attention to Kara's list of demands, which wasn't a great first impression to make. She was standing in front of the mirrored wall making faces.

Madame Kara called her over. "Do you like to dance?" she asked, crouching to her level.

"Yes."

"Have you been in a dance class before, Bridget?"

No, no no! I silently chanted.

"I got fired," said Bridget casually. "But I'm going to be good now."

We were about to get booted out of ballet for a third time.

Kara's eyes drifted from Bridget's to mine, looking concerned. "Discipline is of the utmost importance in ballet."

I nodded, trying to work out whether another run at ballet was a good idea or a bad one. "Bridget is very keen to learn," I equivocated.

I didn't think Kara was as pretty as she should've been, even when she smiled. Her features were hard, but it was nothing a few extra pounds wouldn't fix. She looked frail, but wasn't – that became apparent when she invited Bridget to have a quick one-on-one session in front of the mirror. I wasn't sure what to do with myself. There was nowhere to sit so I stood by the door while Bridget followed Kara's moves with the grace of a three-legged puppy.

Erin from the reception desk appeared by my side a minute later, handing me a folder. "This is our prospectus," she told me. "Everything you need to know is inside."

I'm much better at reading paperwork than observing ballet moves, so I busied myself checking out the contents. Kara's credentials were outlined in a three-page résumé that was tucked into the front pocket. I thought it obnoxious but not unexpected. I didn't get as far as reading it. I tried, but the picture on the first page stole my attention.

My heart cottoned on before my head came close to figuring out what I was looking at. The caption read: Sydney School of Dance, aged sixteen.

My heart recognised the girl in the picture, but not as Kara. The young girl smiling for the camera was a dead ringer for Charli at the same age.

I was jumping to ridiculous conclusions.

I knew Charli's mother was from Sydney. I also knew she was a ballerina. For a moment my head was winning because I also knew that her mother's name was Olivia Fielding.

But then my heart told me to look up and take another look at the woman dancing beside my daughter. I'd detected a hint of an accent that was very similar to Bridget's – a hybrid mesh of Australian and American. Kara was a brunette, but that meant nothing. Women dye their hair all the time, or perhaps Charli just took after her dad, who was fair.

I almost groaned out loud then, berating myself for being an idiot. Research was part of my job – the job I hated but got paid for. I stopped making pointless comparisons and turned my attention back to the folder to see what else I could find.

The only affirmation I needed was pinned to the back cover. Her business card explained everything, and paved the way for the biggest can of worms in existence to be blown wide open.

"Olivia Kara," I muttered out loud. "Charli's mom."

***

I needed to know for sure, and there was no subtle way of finding out. My first inclination was to scream out the question – just put it all out there let the chips fall where they might.

My second was less likely to get me thrown out of the building. Once she'd finished with Bridget, I asked for a minute in private.

Her expression was odd, and for the briefest of moments I wondered if she knew what was coming. "Of course," she muttered. She put her hand on Bridget's back and started walking her toward the door. "Why don't you go and have a chat with Erin," she suggested. "She'd love to show you around, I'm sure."

Bridget turned back to me.

"It's fine, baby," I permitted. "I'll be out in a minute."

In the strangest twist of fate I'd ever experienced, I was alone with the woman I suspected was Charli's mother.

I had no clue how to ask the question, and the struggle of wording it actually made me sweat. "I've read your prospectus," I said, holding it out to her.

"I hope you found it satisfactory." Her smug tone was warranted. I knew nothing about ballet, but I could tell her credentials were stellar.

"You're Australian." It came out sounding like I was accusing her of something terrible. "My wife is Australian."

She shrugged, which was a casual gesture that didn't quite fit her refined stance. "Originally," she replied. "I haven't lived there in a long time."

"This is going to sound strange, but I need you to hear me out," I blurted. "I think you may know my wife."

As cringeworthy as it was, that was the absolute best I could come up with.

Olivia laughed, a sound as demure as the rest of her persona. "Australia is a big place, Adam."

"No, you don't understand." I cleared my throat, trying not to choke on my next words. "You had a child."

She was shaking her head before I'd even gotten the words out. "I have no children."

"A daughter, Olivia," I said. "She's twenty-four now."

Olivia folded her arms. Her calm demeanour was gone. She was pissed, which wasn't a good sign. "I have no children," she roughly repeated.

I'd come too far to back down; and couldn't find reason to. I knew she was lying. "Her name is Charlotte."

Nothing. Not a single pang of recognition hit her. Her neutral expression remained, and I was determined to break through it.

"She was born in Sydney."

Nothing.

"You relinquished custody to her dad."

Nothing.

"Her father's name is Alex Blake."

Her head whipped up. Finally I was getting somewhere; but the conversation was akin to walking on a knife blade. I had no idea how this was going to play out. Olivia wasn't exactly jumping for joy at the prospect of being reunited with the child she'd given up at birth.

I saw her swallow hard. "What do you want from me?" she asked bitterly.

"Absolutely nothing," I assured her. "I had no idea who you were until I read this." I waved the folder at her. "Charli hasn't been looking for you."

"Good," she snapped. "I have no desire to know her."

My heart fractured in at least three places, which wasn't fair. For all I knew, Charli might feel exactly the same way. I was playing God – attempting to align the stars in a stubborn pursuit that was none of my business in the first place.

"Please, just think about it," I urged. "I make no demands of you. I'm just letting you know that you have a beautiful daughter within your grasp."

She shook her head. "This conversation ends here," she ordered. "And if it doesn't, I'll sue you for everything you've got."

Her threat was almost laughable. Suing a filthy rich family of attorneys for everything they have would be no mean feat.

"Bridget is your granddaughter," I informed. "Flesh of your flesh."

Her reply was cold and definite. "It means nothing to me."

I believed she meant it. Her blue eyes were as hard as flint as she fought against the gift I was giving her.

I'd reached the end of the line. "I'm sorry for you," I quietly told her. "You're missing out on something wonderful."

"Leave," she said simply.

I reached for my wallet, grabbed two business cards and held them out. "This is my card, and this is Charli's," I told her. "Maybe you'll change your mind one day."

Olivia reluctantly took them. She paid no attention to Charli's, but studied mine closely. "Décarie?" she asked. "Any relation to Fiona?"

Her question beggared belief. I'd just given her access to the daughter she'd never known and she was more concerned with my family tree.

"She's my mother."

Olivia's focus remained on the card. "I know her," she said vaguely. "Our paths cross often."

I wasn't surprised. Manhattan could be a small place at times, especially the circles my mother moved in.

"Wonderful." Keeping my voice even was difficult, but I tried. "Next time you see her you'll have plenty to talk about."

Her head snapped up, her stare fierce. "I meant what I said," she said. "This conversation goes no further than you and I."

***

Bridget chattered the whole way back to my office, but I barely heard a word. My mind was a jumbled mess of thoughts, and working through them was impossible.

I'd put myself in a horrible position. Charli deserved to know her mother was in the city. I just couldn't protect her from the hurt that would follow when she found out she wanted nothing to do with her.

"I like that dance place, Daddy," declared Bridget, tugging on my hand as she skipped beside me.

"And Madame Kara? Do you like her?"

"She's a nice lady."

I wasn't convinced, but I wasn't about to share my misgivings with Bridget. "I'm glad you had fun, baby."

I tried to pay attention to her as we continued our walk. By the time we got back to my office, she'd all but talked my ear off.

Ryan was waiting in the lobby, unwilling to head upstairs in case he ran into Dad. Bridget pulled free of me and took off running. Ryan scooped her up before the inevitable crash.

"Ready to go?" he asked, giving her pigtail a playful tug.

"Yes!" She squashed his cheeks between her hands. "To the park, Ry. Okay?"

Her hands moved with him as he nodded. "Just for a change?"

She giggled, and it was by far the best sound I'd heard all day.

Ryan lowered Bridget to her feet. She slipped into her own world as she twirled on the marble floor, practicing the moves Olivia had shown her.

"Everything okay?" he asked.

"Yeah."

"How's the permit situation looking?"

I'd been dealing with paperwork pertaining to the club all week, and our business partnership was fairly one-sided because of it. I looked across to make sure Bridget was out of earshot before speaking. She was busting out her ballet moves for George, the security guard on duty.

"I've lodged most of them," I told him. "Which is more than you've done, I'm sure."

"I've been busy too, you know." Nothing about his tone was believable.

"Doing what?"

Ryan folded his arms. "I've been taking care of public relations."

I wanted to smack the smug look off his face, but laughed instead. "Is that what you're calling it, now?"

"Don't cheapen it, Adam," he mocked, feigning hurt.

Any thought I had of a witty reply escaped me when Bridget let out a shrill squeal that echoed around the vast space. Every person in the lobby turned to stare. "You're a lovely dancer, George," Bridget shouted, clapping her hands.

George the security guard, a stout man in his early sixties, stood with both arms above his head, clumsily pirouetting as if his life depended on it.

"Is the whole world her puppet?" asked Ryan incredulously.

"No," I replied. "Just the people in it."

25. THE PERFECT DRESS

Charli

I'd had more visits from my family that week than ever before. Fiona was the latest to cut in on my working day, appearing out of nowhere while I watered the display of begonias outside the front window of the gallery.

"Darling," she purred on approach, "don't they have people to do that?"

I emptied the small watering can into the planter box. "I am people," I replied.

She hesitantly leaned in and kissed me, keeping her distance as if I was covered in mud. "I have something to show you – a surprise."

I guessed whatever it was was concealed in the garment bag she had hooked over her arm. I pointed the watering can toward the door. "Come inside," I offered. "I'll make you some tea."

"You don't have people for that either?" she asked, making me laugh. "I thought you had a real job here."

***

It didn't take a genius to work out that her surprise was a dress. Bente had shown me the gorgeous gown she'd gifted her to wear to Trieste's upcoming wedding. I assumed she'd bought me one too.

Fiona laid the garment bag across my desk and unzipped it.

"Is it a dress for Trieste's wedding?" I asked.

She looked up. "No, darling." Her perfectly made-up eyes widened. "But leave it with me. I'll find you one."

There was no point saying no, so I thanked her.

"My pleasure," she replied. "The occasion for this dress is far more special than that strange girl's wedding."

Fiona never referred to Trieste by name. She was always 'that strange girl'. It was an honest but rude assessment that I'd given up scolding her for.

She lifted one of the prettiest dresses I'd ever seen out of the bag. I loved all things vintage, but this was vintage at an extreme level. It was positively medieval.

"The Sunkiss foundation is hosting a charity ball on Saturday night," she explained. "The theme is the French Revolution. I want you and Adam to attend."

Fiona's philanthropic ventures were always on a grand scale, raising thousands of dollars per event. I'd attended a few in my time – at her insistence – but nothing as formal as a grand ball. The notion made me a little nervous, until she flashed the dress at me.

I would've sold my firstborn for an excuse to wear it.

The patterned brocade gown was over-the-top in the best possible way – floor length with huge pagoda sleeves. Lappets of heavy lace decorated the bodice, and I could tell just by looking that it probably weighed a tonne.

"Why do you want us to go?"

She replied as if it was a silly question. "Because I found you the perfect dress, darling."

***

Talking Adam into attending was going to be hard, but I had all afternoon to plan. I beat him and Bridget home that afternoon, and in a purely tactical move, I used the head start to prepare dinner.

They arrived home just after six. Bridget dumped her backpack on my carefully set table, gifted me a quick kiss and headed for her pile of girls in the living room. Adam moved slower. He shrugged off his jacket, stripped off his tie and made his way over to me.

"Hey," he breathed, wrapping his arms around me. "You're cooking?" He let me go and lifted the lid off the pan that was bubbling away on the stove.

"Yes," I proudly replied. "Real food."

"You spoil us, Coccinelle," he teased.

"How did your meeting go today?" I'd tried not to put too much thought into it until now. I wasn't quite over the last debacle. Torturing myself with thoughts of round two wasn't good for my soul.

"It was okay," he said simply.

"When does she start?"

Adam grimaced. I had no idea what to make of it. "I'm not sure," he replied. "She didn't tell me."

"But it went well?"

He leaned against the counter and swiped his hands down his face. "Yes, Charlotte," he roughly replied. "It went well."

Being tired might've explained his pissy mood, except Adam was tired most nights. I didn't usually cop attitude because of it.

"I'm only asking."

He straightened up and pulled in a long breath. "And I'm only telling you. It went well. I have nothing else to report."

He walked away then, heading to the bedroom without another word. It wasn't Adam's usual MO when it came to avoiding conversations. He was usually much less abrasive about it, choosing to deflect with ambiguous answers or an artful change of subject. Something wasn't right, and I wasn't above grilling the little person in the next room to find out what it was.

***

Bridget has more dolls than most little girls could dream of, but the only one who had received any attention lately was Treasure, the reborn nightmare.

I sat on the floor beside her, trying not to look appalled as she wrenched Treasure's arms behind her back to get her dress off.

"Mamie gave her some new dresses," she told me, "but I can't get them on her."

"Can I help?"

She thrust the doll at me. "Yes, please."

I loosened Treasure's dress. "Did you have fun dancing today?"

Her longwinded answer went on forever, which was fine except for the fact that I didn't gain a whole lot of information from it. They met the teacher, she danced for a while, then Adam took her back to his office. Ryan picked her up and they spent the afternoon playing at the park with the compass.

The only thing that seemed to be troubling her was her teacher's demand that she ditch the boots. "I might not do it," she said in a tiny voice. "I just love boots."

I kissed the top of her head. "You do what you think is right, baby. Only you can decide."

26. HABIT À LA FRANÇAISE

Adam

It's hard to avoid someone in a twelve-hundred-square-foot apartment, but I gave it my best shot. Poor Charli didn't deserve it and I was too inept to explain why I was giving her the cold shoulder.

It was a hopeless situation, any way I looked at it. I didn't want to lie to her, but not telling her what I knew was essentially the same thing.

Avoiding her only took me so far. Once Bridget was in bed, she bailed me up in the bedroom and demanded an explanation. "You've been a jerk all night," she accused.

"I'm sorry," I inadequately replied.

"Have I done something to upset you?"

Her sad look crushed me, and at that moment I realised the poison of Madame Kara was already taking hold.

"Nothing." I trailed my hand down then length of her arm. "A tough afternoon, that's all." I touched my mouth to her ear and whispered, "Let me make it up to you."

I felt her swallow as my lips passed across her throat, and in another promising sign that I was on my way to making amends, the rhythm of her breathing changed.

"I can think of a better way," she murmured.

"Better than this?" I undid the first three buttons of her shirt and kissed a line to her heart. "There is no better way."

"What if I told you it involved dressing up like a dauphin?"

I straightened up, cocking my head. "Kinky."

"No." She giggled, swatting my chest. "Your mum wants us to go to a charity ball on Saturday," she explained. "The theme is the French Revolution."

My groan betrayed me, as did the plea that followed. "Anything but that, Charli."

She pulled me close. "Please, Adam," she said sweetly. "Your mum bought us costumes and everything. I have the prettiest dress you've ever seen."

"You always look beautiful. You don't need a dress to –"

"It has a corset," she said cutting me off. The only thing sexier than her tone of voice was the look she gave me. It was classic Charlotte – a perfect combination of fire and ice. "It's black and lacy and just wearing it is going to get me pregnant."

When my laugh dulled she changed tack, swapping the seductress pout for sad eyes and rapid blinking. Both were killer moves. I groaned again, looking to the ceiling to escape.

"What's my costume like?" It was a dangerous question. It gave her the impression that she was winning.

"Very, um ..." she faltered "... traditional."

I gave her a grin that she read perfectly. "*Habit à la française?*"

"Maybe," she shrugged. "Whatever that means."

"It's what they used to call men's formal attire in the eighteenth century," I explained. "And if you think I'm wearing a waistcoat and tight pants, you've got another thing coming."

She pressed herself hard against me. "You don't have to," she purred. "Say we can go and I'll let you wear my corset."

***

It wasn't Olivia who'd given me the don't-call-us-we'll-call-you line. It was Erin, her sidekick. Olivia gave me nothing other than an order to leave, which was perfectly clear and final – right up until she cashed my tuition cheque a few days later.

145

I had no idea what that meant. Given what she knew, it was madness to think Olivia could teach Bridget to dance, but my whole week seemed to have descended into madness.

The only time my father didn't complain about impromptu visits to the office was when they were carried out by my mother. When she turned up and demanded that I try her stupid period costume on, he did nothing to save me.

"I'm busy, Mom," I grumbled.

She sat opposite my desk and laid the suit bag across her lap. "Do what you need to do, darling," she said. "I'll wait."

Clearly, she wasn't going anywhere. I closed my laptop, leaned back and gave her my attention. "I'm not wearing pantaloons to your party."

"They're authentic for the period, Adam."

When she made a grab for the zipper on the bag, I told her not to waste her time. "I don't even want to go," I complained. "I'm only doing it to keep Charli happy."

She beamed at me. "You take such wonderful care of your girls, Adam."

My mother was resolutely of the opinion that neither of her sons could do any wrong. It'd probably screwed us both up in one way or another, but I couldn't deny that her unwarranted praise was sometimes good to hear.

"Bridget told me she's starting at a new ballet school soon."

"Yeah, it's run by someone you know, actually. Olivia Kara."

She smiled in a way that didn't work. "Lovely," she said tightly.

I leaned forward, resting my elbows on the desk. "What do you know about her, Mom? She said you were friends."

"We're not friends." Her denial came out fast. "I barely tolerate the woman. She's affiliated with some of the charities I work with. I find her values questionable and her motives disingenuous."

This was not what I wanted to hear, especially considering the speed with which Olivia had cashed my cheque.

"Do you think Bridget will be okay there?"

She shifted, making the bag on her lap crackle. "I didn't say she was a brute, darling. By all accounts she's a wonderful dancer. I just don't like her."

"She seemed to know what she was doing," I reasoned. "And Bridget liked her."

Mom's eyes narrowed, picking up on my angst. "But you didn't?"

Mindful of the dangers of giving her any information, I gave her half an answer. "I'm not sure yet. Time will tell, I guess."

"You'll have a chance to get to know her better on Saturday night," she replied. "She's attending the Sunkiss ball too."

Wearing tight pants and a waistcoat instantly became the least of my problems. The bigger issue now was going to be keeping my wife away from the past she'd never known.

My mind was still working its way through a game plan when the phone on my desk rang. "Mrs Kara on line two, Adam," announced Tennille.

Her ears must've been burning – probably an occupational hazard for witches.

I covered the speaker with my hand. "I have to take this, Ma," I said regretfully.

"Of course, darling." She draped the suit bag across the length of the couch. "I'll come back later."

I would've tried dissuading her if I hadn't been so eager to get her out of my office. As soon as she slipped out of the room, I punched the button on the phone and answered the call.

"I've put serious thought into this," announced Olivia without any greeting. "Bridget can start under one condition."

Her attitude was appalling, and I refused to overlook it. "You cashed my cheque. There are no conditions."

"I want your assurance that you'll make no mention of our earlier discussion."

She'd chosen her words carefully, making sure she made no reference to the dirty little secret she'd kept hidden for twenty-four years. There was no way of knowing what her motives were, and I didn't care to find out.

"Olivia, if you knew anything about Charli, you'd know that she deserves only the best from this world." My tone was calm, but it was impossible to hide my contempt. "I'm certain you're not it. Having you in her life would be of no benefit."

She didn't pause to ponder the cruelty of my words. Her reply was quick and cutting. "I suggest you keep your mouth shut then."

All my doubts about her were proved in a flash. As hard as it was to fathom, the woman who'd blessed me with the love of my life was a total and utter bitch.

"Bridget won't be attending your classes, Olivia," I said curtly. "Keep the tuition money."

"It was never refundable," she retorted.

I heard the click as she hung up on me. And at that point, the only thing I felt was utter relief.

***

Keen to get out before my mother came back, I called Ryan and asked him to meet me at the club. His phone rang out several times before he finally picked up. "Don't ever call me again," he barked. Clearly I'd interrupted a session in public relations.

I gathered up the plans on my desk. "I don't even want to know what you're doing right now."

"I'll bet it's a damn sight more fun than what you're doing," he snapped.

That was a given. Dealing with hateful ballerinas, sorting out building permits and trying to weasel my way out of wearing man-tights didn't even compare to a morning in bed.

Convincing Ryan to meet me wasn't as difficult as I'd expected. I left the office straight away, and we arrived at the club at exactly the same time.

I was glad we walked in together. It took two of us to deal with two octogenarians attempting to change a light bulb. Earl was hanging off the top of an eight-foot ladder. Tiger was supervising.

"You crazy old bastard," berated Ryan, looking up at Earl. "You're going to kill yourself."

I thought he was overreacting. My daughter was a big fan of climbing too, and her feats were usually much more terrifying. Bridget would've leapt from the top of the ladder. Mercifully, Earl took the slow route down. Once he was safely on the ground, I swapped places with him and changed the bulb myself.

"Job well done, Earl," crowed Tiger, smacking his friend on the back.

"Yes," he agreed, stumbling forward. "Time for a drink, eh?"

I stepped off the ladder and checked the time on my watch. "It's ten in the morning."

"That's right kid," replied Tiger. "We're late."

***

I liked being at the club without the constant scrutiny of Tiger. He wasn't coping well with the idea of us being part owners. It made me worry how he'd deal with Ryan's grandiose plans for overhauling it.

The only renovation that took place that morning was the changing of the light bulb. Everything else was on hold until we could sort out planning permission, which wasn't going to happen if we couldn't submit the correct blueprints.

Double-checking the measurements was my plan, but my brother is a dick. If I'd known that a task as simple as measuring up a room required an explanation, I would've asked Bridget to help me do it.

"So what happens if they differ from the plans?" he asked, clueless.

"We'll have to get new ones drafted." I handed him the end of the tape measure and ordered him to stay put.

"More delays," he muttered.

"We've got to do it right, Ryan."

He might've agreed, but my phone rang before he had a chance. I had to answer it – I was on my father's time, not mine. The measuring got put on hold while I undertook a complicated conversation with a client, doing my best to pretend that the contract in question was on a desk in front of me.

The next call came just a minute later. As soon as I saw Dad's number on the screen I hit the end button. It happened three times before Ryan questioned it.

"It's Dad," I explained. "He's hunting me down. He has no idea where I am."

Ryan had always considered my decision to take a job at our father's firm to be idiotic. He also knew that as far as told-you-so moments go, that one was off limits.

I read the measurement on the tape as he pulled it taut, then wrote it down. "How does Charli feel about you working for him?" asked Ryan.

"She knows he's a hard taskmaster," I replied. "She understands."

That was only half true. She knew better than anyone that he was hard to please, but she wasn't the least bit understanding when it came to my decision to keep working for him.

"She knows you're unhappy there, Adam."

I told him to drop the tape and began reeling it in. "Has she said something?"

Deep down, I already knew the answer. Ryan and Charli had a strange rapport built on sarcastic digs and snarky insults, but it worked. Charli often confided in him, and although he'd never admit it, she was sometimes his sounding board too.

His answer was vague but telling. "Once or twice." We met in the middle of the room. "You should look for something else," he added.

"It wouldn't matter what firm I worked at, Ryan. I hate the job. I hate everything about it," I muttered. "I might as well stay where I am." It was easy to admit my professional discontentment to Ryan. Perhaps it was because he understood what I was up against.

His suggestion that I quit and take on the project manager role at the club fell on deaf ears, despite the fact that it was his best sell. "You could quit your job, work the hours you want to, see more of Bridget and Charli —"

I cut him off. "Don't bring my girls into this."

"Just think about it, okay?"

"I don't want to commit to anything new." The excuse that followed was more wishful thinking than anything. I blamed it on the fact that Charli's contract at the gallery was up for renewal, and I wasn't sure if we'd be staying in New York.

The truth was, Charli had only mentioned going home in passing. My desire to escape my city was growing undeniably stronger, but if she made the call to stick it out for another year, I'd support her.

Falling head first over Charlotte happened hard, fast and without any permission. It was too much to deal with at twenty-two, and I hadn't played fair because of it. Giving her the time she needed to build her career in New York went a little way toward making it up to her, and even on my worst day it felt good.

I was now the man who could tell his wife that he'd go anywhere with her, do anything for her, and mean every single word of it.

27. RESEARCH

Charli

Most of the wicked deeds I carried out were planned, but occasionally I'd do something shady without realising it. Calling Adam at work with the promise of amazing news, and then making him stew all day before finding out what it was wasn't kind.

It hadn't occurred to me that he'd jump to baby-related conclusions, which made for an awkward conversation when he got home, mainly because my exciting news wasn't actually that exciting.

"Nothing to do with a baby," I said sheepishly. "I solved your man-tights problem."

He jingled his keys in his hand. "That's it?"

"Yeah. I thought you'd be pleased."

After a long moment of more jingling, Adam dropped his keys on the counter. "If by solved, you mean called Mom and told her we're not going, I'm very pleased."

I hadn't even come close to talking him around. "I won't force you," I said bleakly. "I'll call and cancel. We'll just make a donation or something."

He grabbed my arm and hauled me in close. "No, don't," he said quietly. "I know you're looking forward to it. You don't need to cancel."

I yanked the end of his tie, pulling him down to my level. "I offered to cancel your place, Boy Wonder, not mine," I teased. "I'm not giving up the opportunity to wear that dress."

I felt his laugh on my lips. "I'll go, Charli," he yielded, "depending on how you solved the man-tights problem."

I leaned back, wiggling my eyebrows at him. "Do you want to see?"

"What else would I want to see at ten o'clock on a Thursday night?"

The distance from the kitchen to the living room is ridiculously short, and if you're in a rush, you can get there in less than ten steps.

I grabbed the shopping bag off the couch and waved it at him. "You know what your dad always says to me?"

The corner of his mouth lifted and he puffed out his chest. "Stop talking nonsense, Charlotte." His French accent was faultless. "Stay home, raise my granddaughter and be a good wife to my son."

"Yes." I could barely speak for laughing. "He says all those things, but he also says that over-thinking ruins your mind."

He frowned, but his smile remained strong. "He does?"

"Yeah. The costume your mum bought is dead on for the period, absolutely perfect, but I think she over-thought it."

Adam screwed up his face, probably picturing the tight-fitting velvet waistcoat and white breeches in his mind. "It's ridiculous and I'm not wearing it."

"I know. That's why I did a bit of research."

"And what did you come up with?"

I took a pair of beige linen trousers out of the bag. "If you jump forward to 1820, Cossack trousers were all the rage," I explained. "They're long and manly," I added in a rumbly voice that made him laugh.

I held them out to him. "Ivy made them for you."

His verdict wasn't exactly heart-warming, "I'm still going to look like a dick, Charlotte."

I dropped the trousers, took the few steps necessary to reach him and slung my arms around his neck. "But you'll be the only dick in long pants, monsieur."

Adam kissed me. "I'll wear them for you," he said. "Then we'll burn them."

***

I hid the pants at the top of my closet, fearful he'd burn them before the ball. I dragged them out on Saturday night and refused to leave the bedroom until he was dressed.

I quickly decided that Adam Luc Décarie would've made a fabulous French nobleman back in the day – one who was constantly surly and antisocial.

"I feel stupid."

I turned him around. The tails of his coat ended at the back his knees. I had no idea what sort of insecurities men dealt with while wearing fitted pants, but from a woman's perspective the tails hid all.

"You look lovely, Daddy," came a little voice from the doorway.

His shoulders drooped. "Lovely" is not a good word when describing a man in period costume. "Thanks, baby," he muttered.

I turned to Bridget. "Daddy looks rugged and handsome, don't you think?"

She took a flying leap onto our bed. Her reply came mid-bounce. "Very drugged and handsome."

At least his discomfort wasn't physical. The sexy, lacy black corset was the unsexiest thing I'd ever worn in my life. Even the process of putting it on was a little off-putting. Both of us were clueless, but thanks to a five minute YouTube tutorial on his phone, Adam worked it out.

"Can you still breathe?" he sounded worried. "I might've done it wrong."

I stumbled back as he tugged on the laces. "I don't need to breathe," I wheezed. "I just need to look pretty."

Making sure the little girl trampolining on the bed didn't hear, he whispered in my ear, "You look prettier without it. I hope it's easier to get off."

My giggle was quiet, but Bridget didn't miss a trick. "Don't laugh at Dad's dumb baby pants," she scolded.

Adam threw his arms up. "That's it," he announced. "I'm not going."

28. UNCOOL

Adam

Leaving the house looking like an eighteenth century moron was not one of my finer moments, but I did it. On the plus side, the woman on my arm was the belle of the ball.

Charli looked tiny but huge all at the same time. The skirt on her dress had about a hundred layers to it, and I checked three times to make sure Bridget hadn't smuggled her way in underneath it. I knew it wasn't a likely scenario. She was holed up at Ryan's watching her mermaid movie, which would've been my dream night out at that point.

The ball was at the Parker Royale Hotel. The family of my former best friend owned it, and the foyer we stood in was the exact spot that our friendship had ended with a few punches to his face five years earlier.

I hadn't thought about Parker in a long time. The last I heard, he was practising in a big firm somewhere on the west coast. I hoped he was doing well. I wasn't interested in knowing him again, but the urge to punch his lights out was long gone.

"I remember this place," Charli said from the corner of her mouth.

"Fondly?" I teased.

She flashed her most wicked grin. "Not particularly."

I couldn't help glancing around as we made our way across the foyer, and the highly inappropriate smirk on my face was impossible to kill. There were at least twenty miserable looking men wearing emasculating knee-high breeches. As far as beige linen trousers went, mine were rocking.

"You're beautiful, Charlotte," I murmured. "And ten times smarter than any woman in this room who forced her man to wear tights."

She hooked her arm through mine. "You're mighty cocky, considering you're the odd man out," she teased. "If we were really back in the eighteenth century, they'd be mercilessly mocking you right now."

I stepped in front of her, forcing her to a stop. "Why, Charlotte?"

"I told you." She picked at the buttons on my coat. "I researched it. Cossack trousers were very uncool. I just talked them up so you'd wear them."

I squinted down at her, playing along. "How uncool?"

"They wrote poems about them." The rhyme that tumbled out of her mouth was effortless. The accent she used was not. She sounded like a drunken pirate. "Some folks in the street by the Lord make me stare, so comical droll is the dress that they wear. For the gentlemen's waist is a top of their back, and their large Cossack trousers that fit like a sack."

The world through Charli's eyes was phenomenal. I couldn't always live there, but I visited often.

"Arr, me hearties," I added.

Her head fell forward, burying her laugh in my chest. The casual hold I had on her was nothing out of the ordinary, but a quick look around the foyer reminded me that it probably wasn't appropriate considering the company we were in. I held her hands and took a step back.

Charli took no offense. "We should go inside."

I was seconds away from agreeing until I took one last look around the foyer. In a blow that I felt, I locked eyes with Olivia. I knew she'd be there, but it didn't making seeing her any less unpleasant.

She was travelling solo, sashaying across the marble foyer as elegantly as she always did, despite the big dress she was wearing. Judging by her expression, she wasn't thrilled to see me, either. I could feel the poison in her glare, but that wasn't the damaging part. The bigger picture was far more disturbing.

She had to look past her daughter to get to me, and she did it with absolute ease.

29. LA LA DEFICIENT

Charli

The foyer gave no hint of the extravagant event taking place in the ballroom. It looked nothing like the cheesy Christmas party we'd attended there years earlier. I knew Fiona must've had a hand in decorating the tables: there was an excess of cut flowers on all of them, and the settings were perfect.

Weaving through tables while wearing a wide dress was like navigating though a maze in the dark. Terrified of knocking something over, I impolitely clung to the tails of Adam's coat for direction. Fiona and Jean-Luc were already seated when we made it to our table. I was trussed up like a Christmas ham underneath my heavy dress, but the queen certainly wasn't wearing a corset. Her ivory chemise gown was free flowing and far more forgiving. Fiona should've been relaxed and cool, but she was flapping a paper fan in front of her face as if she was on fire.

Despite her odd conduct, it was Jean-Luc who stole my attention. His navy blue coat was velvet with a line of brass buttons down his chest and a ruffled shirt poking out at the top.

The king was undeniably handsome, and like Ryan, he knew it. Not a man in the room looked so much at ease, strengthening my theory that he truly was Lord Muck.

"Sit, my darlings," urged Fiona, almost whimpering.

Adam pulled out my chair and I sat, studying the queen the whole time. She didn't look good. "Are you alright?" I whispered.

"No, Charli," she miserably replied. "My wig itches and it's terribly hot in here."

Her hair should've had its own postcode. A huge arrangement of brunette curls was piled on top of her head. Another heap trailed down her back. Pulling it off would've brought her instant relief, but she was much too vain to do it.

I tried taking her mind off her discomfort. "You look beautiful," I said. "I love your dress."

She smiled. "Do you love yours?"

I looked down at my gown. "Yes. I'm going to wear it for the rest of the week."

Jean-Luc tutted as if I'd said something ridiculous enough to bring shame on the family. It was all the encouragement I needed to rattle his cage. "I like your tights, J-man," I quipped. "They suit you."

Adam's chuckle earned him a swat of his mother's fan. My punishment was far more brutal. Jean-Luc stood, extended his arm like he was checking the time on his watch, and then asked me to dance.

"I don't dance," I replied.

"I'll teach you," he shot back.

"Oh, fine," I grumbled, gathering my skirt as best I could. "Who am I to defy the king?"

"*Lèse-majesté* is probably one of your lesser crimes, Charli."

I looked to Adam for a translation.

"Treason against the king," he said simply.

There was no point denying it so I left it at that and begrudgingly accompanied him to the dance floor.

***

Jean-Luc was too polite to call me out on my dire lack of dancing skills, but he gave up trying to give me instruction after just a few minutes, content to let me concentrate all my efforts on not stepping on his feet.

"Do you like events like this?" I asked.

"They're important to Fiona," he replied. "Her charities do a lot of good work. It's important to show support."

"A bit different to the Odeon theatre days, eh?"

"Quite," he agreed, briefly dropping his head to smile at me.

Conversation lulled, but it wasn't weird. I suspect Jean-Luc enjoyed the peace. When we turned, I looked across at Adam and Fiona. Adam looked like he'd rather be at home with a good book and Fiona looked miserable, still flapping the fan to cool herself down.

I turned back to the king. "Jean-Luc, have you ever heard of Jean-Pierre Duvelleroy?"

"No. Should I have?"

"He was a fan-maker," I replied. "When he was twenty-five, he established his own fan house in Paris."

With a firm hand to my back, he spun us around. "Fascinating," he said, not very sincerely.

"I thought you appreciated ambition."

"Indeed I do," he agreed. "Tell me the story of our friend, Jean-Pierre."

Never before had my father-in-law shown a skerrick of interest in any of my tales. I tried to find reason for the change of heart. "Are you drunk?" I wondered.

"Not yet," he replied, spinning us around again.

"He started his business in the 1820s," I began. "The only problem was, fans had gone out of fashion after the French Revolution."

"Not a bright business venture then, was it?"

"He had vision," I told him. "Jean-Pierre was convinced that they'd come back into style. He struggled along for two years before he got his big break."

The music stopped and so did we, but the conversation kept going.

"A duchess friend threw a grand party to bring him luck. For the quadrille, all the women sported his fans," I explained. "And that's all it took. Fans came back into vogue, and Jean-Pierre was a huge success."

Another song started, and Jean-Luc reached for my hand again. If anything, my dancing was getting worse, but he didn't seem to notice. "I don't understand why you retain such mindless information, then choose to bring it up whenever the urge to be odd hits you," he said, frowning down at me.

"You'll never understand me," I grumbled. "You're La La deficient."

"Continue," he grunted. "Silly girl."

I squeezed his hand, mildly hopeful of breaking his fingers. It didn't work so I tortured him with my words instead. "Jean-Pierre developed a communication system – a secret fan language."

It was too much for the close-minded king to grasp. He threw his head back and laughed. "Of course he did."

"It's true," I insisted.

"Do you speak fan language, Charli?" he mocked.

"Luckily for you, I do," I replied smugly. "Some of the gestures are simple. If the woman rests her fan on her right cheek, that means yes. The left cheek means no."

"Ah," he crowed. "But what was the question?"

"It's simple body language," I replied. "There is no question."

After a few minutes of unrestricted shuffling, the dance floor suddenly became crowded with oversized dresses and man-tights. We were barely moving so I spoke quickly, determined to get to the end of the tale before Jean-Luc called it quits. "If she places the fan near her heart, it means you have won her love. If it's over her left ear, she wants you gone – you're done."

"It doesn't sound terribly accurate, Charli," he complained. "Lots of room for misinterpretation."

I smiled, enjoying the feeling of victory that came with making him think outside the box. "What do you think Fiona's fanning is saying right now?" I asked curiously.

He huffed. "I have no idea."

I craned my neck, looking up at him. "I dare you to turn around and look."

Never one to back down from a challenge, he turned both of us around to face the table. "She's scratching her head with it," he noted. "What does that mean?"

My reply came quickly. "It means she's totally miserable, her wig is itchy and she wants you to take her home."

Jean-Luc looked down at me, almost smiling. "You may be right."

"I'm always right," I said smugly. "But she won't leave unless you woo her away."

"Couldn't you have just suggested that in the first place?" he asked. "There was no need for theatrics."

"*Au contraire, monsieur.*" My accent was so appalling that both of us grimaced. "Because of my theatrics, you're now acquainted with Jean-Pierre Duvelleroy, the French fan maker."

***

I was Cupid in a big dress. Jean-Luc went back to the table, whispered a few sweet nothings in his wife's ear and helped her to her feet. After too many kisses on the cheek and orders to have a good time, they left.

I looked at Adam, who was clearly plotting the rest of our evening in his head. Judging by his smile, his plans didn't include Cossack trousers and a four-course meal. "We'll leave," he suggested. "I will take you anywhere you want to go."

"Adam, do you know your father paid ten thousand dollars for this table?"

He shrugged. "He wouldn't care about that. They bailed too, remember?"

I put my hand on his leg. "You'd really take me anywhere?"

"Anywhere." His voice was low and gorgeous.

"The bathroom?"

A sly grin crept across his face. "Wouldn't be the first time."

"To make a few adjustments," I clarified. "This corset is really tight."

30. GOOD ODDS

Adam

There were at least a hundred people seated in the ballroom. As far as I was concerned, these were good odds. I'd been on the lookout for Olivia all night, but hadn't seen her since the stare-down in the foyer. Even on the move, the chances of running into her were slim, and if by chance we did I was doubtful she'd give us the time of day anyway.

Breaking through the double doors into the vast foyer was as good as a receiving a rush of fresh air. Charli must've felt it too. Her walk slowed and she made a grab for my hand.

"This way, I think," I said, pointing toward a corridor to our left.

Figuring she'd need help adjusting her underwear, I offered to venture into the bathroom with her. "I could make a few bucks," I teased. "I could stand in there and be a professional corset loosener, for a price."

"Not in those pants, peasant."

With a cheeky grin she shoved the door open with her back and tried to make her way inside. A smooth entrance was never going to happen. Several layers of her skirt didn't make it through before the door closed, trapping her.

"Adam, help me," came her plea from the other side.

I leaned close to the door. "I would Charlotte, but I'm just a simple peasant."

"Excuse me," interrupted a horribly familiar voice from behind. "You're in the way."

If my brain planned for me to speak, it took too long. Olivia pushed her way past and bumped the door with her shoulder. The fabric of Charli's skirt disappeared as the door opened, and a second later Olivia did too.

Our charmed life was about to be ripped to pieces, and it was all going down in a hotel bathroom.

31. CONFUSION

Charli

It was ridiculous to think I was going to be able to loosen the laces down my back by myself, so I didn't bother trying. I did what I needed to and spent a long minute in front of the mirror. I couldn't be comfortable, but was marginally hopeful of making myself appear that way.

I didn't really pay much attention to the woman standing off to the side. I assumed she was waiting for someone, or for a chance to use the mirror I was hogging.

"I won't be a minute," I said, smiling at her.

"Take your time, Charli," she quietly replied. "I've already been waiting forever."

Surprised that she knew my name, I turned to look at her. Momentarily forgetting that I was wearing a big flouncy dress too, I was struck by how out of place she looked. Her black velvet gown was more Vivienne Leigh than Marie Antoinette, but she was impeccably put together. I tried hard to place her face, but couldn't. I had no clue who she was.

"Do I know you?" I asked.

I got no reply.

I was at the door when the woman made a move. She stepped in front of me, reached for the handle and twisted the lock. That was the moment I realised that no one else was in the room. I was alone with a potentially crazy lady.

"Open the door," I demanded. "My husband is right outside."

She lurched for the handle when I did. I contemplated screaming.

"Please Charli," she said. "Don't call Adam in. He won't be pleased."

"Who are you?" I snapped. "How do you know me?"

Crazy lady reached behind her neck and undid the clasp on her necklace. "I met Adam and Bridget last week," she explained, holding her locket out to me. "I teach ballet."

I kept my hands by my sides. "Minuet Ballet School?"

"Yes." She dropped her hand, and began winding the chain around her fingers. "Adam read the prospectus folder my receptionist gave him while I tutored Bridget."

"So?"

She stared at me, her blue eyes wide and worried. "All of my information is in there – my complete résumé," she continued. "He realised something very important, Charli." She held out the locket. "Please take it."

Curiosity was killing me and I'd never been good at playing it cool. I reached out, keeping my eyes on hers. "What is it?"

"Open it, please."

I took a second to study it first. It wasn't a pretty piece. The front was etched with a tacky floral pattern, and the thing was huge – about the size of a small makeup compact. Opening the stiff lid took effort. Holding onto it once I saw what was inside took even more. The photo was rough, and probably always had been. It was crudely cut to fit the inside frame, and faded with age.

"Is this you?" My voice was barely there.

"Yes."

The brunette girl in the picture was about fifteen, smiling, fresh faced and pretty as she posed with her arm around a handsome boy's shoulder. I didn't need to ask who he was. I would've recognised the shaggy blond surfer boy anywhere. It was my father.

"Alex gave me that necklace." She put her hand to the base of her throat as if she missed it being there. "I've worn it every day for twenty-six years."

I tore my gaze from the piece of history in my hand and forced myself to look at her. "You're Olivia?"

She nodded, looking as distraught by the notion as I felt. "I'm your mother, Charli. I've thought about you every day."

I couldn't return the sentiment. I rarely thought of her at all, and if I did it was only to wonder what she looked like. I didn't feel like I was getting a true picture at that point. It was likely that her hair wasn't usually coiffed into a foot tall mass of curls, and she probably didn't swan around in period costume either.

I snapped the locket shut and held it out to her.

"Keep it," she urged. "I want you to have it."

Probably wondering what was taking me so long, Adam knocked on the door and called my name. "I'm okay," I said through the door. "I'll be out in a minute."

As if confusion wasn't muddling me already, Olivia asked a question that made even less sense than finding my long lost mother in a hotel bathroom.

"Are you frightened of him, Charli?" she whispered.

"Who?" I gasped. "Adam?"

I couldn't quite place her expression. It was a cross between pity and fear. "He got quite nasty when he found out who I am," she said quietly. "He warned me to stay away from you." She glanced at the door as if she was worried Adam would bash it in. "I begged him to give me your contact details, but he refused," she added.

Adam's voice sounded distant, but his fist was loud. Maybe he *was* about to smash his way in. "Charlotte, open the door."

"Wait, Adam," I demanded, putting my hand on the door. "Please."

"He knows I'm in here talking to you," Olivia said morosely. "He saw me come in."

I shouldn't have been giving any credence to her words. I didn't know her from a bar of soap. She was a stranger who'd busted into my life claiming to be my mother. What she thought of my husband was inconsequential.

My eyes dropped to the locket. It was tangible proof of who she was, and a tiny glimpse of the beginning of me. The confusion that came with that realisation was crippling.

I ran my thumb over the gaudy etching. "I don't know what's going on," I mumbled.

"I loved your father, Charli," she declared with reverence. "Giving you up was the hardest thing I've ever done. I want us to know each other. It's everything I've dreamed of."

Another sentiment I couldn't return. "I'm not sure what I want," I muttered.

"Just promise you won't let Adam stand in the way," she begged. "He's gone out of his way to keep me from you for a week. It's been horrendous."

When Olivia took a step toward me, I took a giant step back. I wasn't just trying to get away from her. I was trying to escape the whole situation.

"Adam would never stop me from seeing you, if that's what I choose to do."

"He's made it impossible so far," she replied.

Everything darkened around that one sentence. It gutted me to think Adam had kept this secret from me. I had no idea why he would do it.

"He cancelled Bridget's ballet lessons," she added. "I begged him not to. He told me that having me in your life would be of no benefit."

When she burst into tears, I almost moved to comfort her. But I stayed put, because I needed comforting more.

Adam wasn't above lying to get his own way – he pulled it off for a whole year when we were first married. Perhaps New York brought out the worst in him. Or maybe he was just a jerk. I didn't care either way at that point. He'd stumbled across my mother and then dared to keep it a secret from me. It was controlling and nasty beyond measure.

"Please don't let me lose you a second time, Charli," sobbed Olivia. "I couldn't stand it."

"I need time to think," I said weakly.

Olivia reached into her purse, grabbing a couple of tissues and a business card. "Call me," she pleaded, thrusting the card at me. "Day or night."

I nodded, but wasn't sure I meant it.

Teary and upset, she unlocked the door and wandered out. Like the most powerful of hurricanes, Olivia Fielding had dropped in, torn up my whole world and then left.

32. ACCIDENTAL VILLAIN

Adam

I paced the corridor, doing all I could to stop myself from kicking down the bathroom door. When it finally opened, Olivia swaggered out. Charli was nowhere to be seen.

I stood and waited for her to pass me, fearful of what I might do if I approached her. I didn't get the baleful glare she'd hit me with earlier. I got an ingratiating grin that made my stomach turn.

"Such an emotional reunion," she exclaimed, dabbing her eyes with a tissue. "Poor Charlotte is a wreck."

Her tears were as bogus as the emotion in her voice, showcasing another of her talents. She was also an actress.

"What did you do?" I hissed through gritted teeth.

Olivia dropped the wounded mother ruse instantly. "Played my hand, Adam," she said slyly. "It's your move now."

***

The desperate need to get into the bathroom was all but gone. I stood at the door for a long time, dreading what I might find on the other side. When I called Charli's name and got no answer, I pushed myself to open the door.

Women's bathrooms are far better decked out than men's. It was no wonder they spend so much time in them. I found Charli in the lounge area, slumped on a chaise lounge in a puff of heavy pink fabric.

"You shouldn't be in here." Her voice was flat and empty. "Get out." Her head fell forward, shifting her focus to the oversized pendant in her hand.

I made my way over to her, pushed her dress aside as best I could and sat beside her. "I'm not going anywhere."

After a long moment of silence, Charli picked up the necklace and dangled it in front of us. "Do you know what this is, Adam?"

"No."

"There's a picture of my parents inside," she explained. "My mother just gave it to me. I just met my mother."

I didn't know how to acknowledge the news, so I didn't. I commented on the necklace instead, and even that wasn't honest. "It's pretty."

Charli huffed out a sharp breath. "That's all you've got to say?"

"I'm not sure what else to say, Charlotte."

"You knew about her a week ago." The disgust in her voice was clear. "You kept it from me. Why would you do that?"

"I tried to talk her into meeting with you, Charli." My voice took on a completely different tone as I pushed for understanding. "She was adamant that she didn't want to meet you. I didn't know what to do."

Charli jumped to her feet, furiously waving the necklace at me. "Olivia has worn this every day since before I was born. Why would she do that if she didn't care?"

I was beginning to realise that Olivia was more toxic than I had first thought. The ugly necklace was just an extension of her venom. She wasn't wearing it the day I met her. It was nothing more than a prop; but there was no way of explaining it without making the situation worse.

"I don't know," I muttered.

I did know, which made looking Charli in the eye nearly impossible. Her mother was evil. Plain and simple.

The necklace bounced off the cushion as she threw it down beside me. "Olivia said she begged you for my number." The words raged out of her. "How could you refuse?"

I exhaled, trying to keep my anger in check. Yelling back at her wasn't going to help. "I gave her your business card," I insisted. "Mine too."

She shook her head, making the wispy blonde curls at her shoulders bounce. "You're lying to me."

The accusation was a spear through my heart. I couldn't allow her to accept Olivia's version of events, but a simple denial wasn't going to cut it. It hurt that she believed her without question, and I developed a sudden ache in my chest because of it. I looked her dead in the eye. "I am telling you the absolute truth," I said firmly. "I have no reason to want to keep you from your mother."

"So you *didn't* refuse to let Bridget join her class?"

Every ounce of concentration I possessed went toward wording my answer. Before I even spoke I knew it was game over.

"I did refuse," I admitted. "I don't want Bridget in her class."

I hate the moment when anger suddenly turns to tears. It usually took a lot for Charli to reach that point, but not tonight. "Why, Adam?" Her fists thumped my chest as she answered her own question. "Because having my mother in my life would be of no benefit, right?"

Olivia had really pulled out all stops. Every single word I said had been twisted to make me look like the villain. It was impossible to deal with that level of malice, especially considering I had no idea why she was gunning for me in the first place. I grabbed Charli's wrists, mainly to stop her whaling on me. "You need to calm down," I told her. "There are two sides to this story, and for some reason you're only listening to one."

I felt her body go limp beneath my grasp. "Nothing you say will change the fact that you kept this from me," she said weakly. "I will never forgive you for that."

I tried to see further than her teary brown eyes. "I'm sorry."

She pulled her hands away. "Me too." She snatched up the pendant and made her way to the door. "Where are you going, Charlotte?"

She shrugged. "I don't want to be near you right now," she whimpered. "I need time to think."

"You can't just leave."

"Sure I can," she retorted. "I've done it before."

***

When everything falls apart, my first instinct is to pull those I love in close. Charli had put herself out of reach, but Bridget was well within my grasp.

The Parker Royale Hotel had to be cursed. I'd never experienced anything but conflict there. The long line of chauffeured town cars waiting on the street was one short. As inconvenient as it was, I was relieved to notice that ours had gone. Wherever Charli had run to, it wasn't on foot.

I walked down the street, hailed a cab and made my way to Ryan's apartment. My little girl was asleep on the couch when I got there, looking angelic and sweet. Heinous Treasure was by her side, looking … well, heinous.

After a few digs at my costume from Ryan, and a few half-hearted threats of violence from me, I gathered up my baby and headed to the door.

"Don't forget this beauty," called Ryan, rushing over with Treasure in hand.

"Thanks," I muttered.

"No problem." He grinned. "We'd be sleeping with one eye open with her here."

I grabbed the doll with my free hand and shook it, making her wonky eyes flutter. "Just like Treasure."

***

Bridget was wide awake by the time we got home, but still insisted that I carry her. "My legs don't work at night time," she explained.

The elevator door slid open and I slowly moved toward our door. "Lucky I'm here to carry you then, huh?"

"Yes," she replied. "Mummy can't carry me far."

172

It was the first time she'd mentioned Charli since I picked her up. The reason why became obvious the second we walked in the door. Bridget thought her mom would be there waiting for us.

"She'll be home later, baby." It wasn't the black kind of lie that Charli accused me of, but it wasn't quite white either. It was a grey lie, with room to move.

"But I need her." Bridget pouted. "Call her, Daddy."

"She's busy, Bridge," I soothed her. "Maybe later."

Her little mind wasn't entirely one-track. I diverted her attention with chocolate milk and coaxed her into her bed with the promise of an early morning trip to the park. It was lazy parenting at its best, but I was tired and drained and unhappy.

I hadn't spent a night alone in my bed since Charli went home when Jack was born. I didn't enjoy it then, and tonight was even worse. When Bridget appeared in the doorway, I didn't even try sending her back to bed. Neither of us coped well when her mama wasn't there. I threw back the covers on Charli's side.

The running jump from the doorway was a skill she'd mastered perfectly. Her little head thumped on the pillow beside me. "I really love this bed."

I turned off the lamp. "That's good, but you really need to go to sleep."

She was quiet, but not for long. "Are you awake, Dad?"

I didn't answer in time. She poked a finger into my eye to check.

"No, Bridge," I grumbled, rubbing my eye. "I'm sleeping."

33. STREET URCHIN

Charli

Staying out all night to punish Adam wasn't my style, and I'd made a promise a long time ago that if I ever felt the need to run away again, I'd take him with me.

I crept into our apartment at a little after one. All the lights were off, which led me to think he thought I wasn't coming home. Another hint was the little girl on my side of the bed.

I would've let Adam sleep, but I needed help. I trailed my fingers down his bare arm and whispered his name. His eyes fluttered open, and he reached out to me.

"I'm glad you're home." He kissed my hand. "Come to bed."

"I can't."

He let out a disapproving low groan. "I'm sorry, Charli. Truly," he said. "If I could go back and handle things differently, I would. I don't –"

I put my hand over his mouth to stop him talking. "I can't because Bridget's there," I whispered. "Also, I need help getting my dress off."

Adam pulled my hand away and got up. "I'll move the baby," he offered. "And then I'll gladly help you get naked."

***

We hadn't made it through the night unscathed. Something between us had shifted, and it didn't feel good. But I wasn't an idiot. Adam and I were ninety-nine per cent perfect. Because of that, we were more than capable of dealing with the one per cent that wasn't.

The introduction of my mother into my life hadn't brought me thoughts of joyous, happy endings. I was scared and apprehensive, and possibly even miffed at the disruption.

Once I left the hotel and really thought things through, I conceded it was probable that Adam felt the same way. He was fiercely protective of Bridget and I. He was the part of our souls that would never let anything bad happen to us. Looking back on the evening from hell, I realised I'd momentarily forgotten that.

***

My dress had no pockets. I reached into the tight space between corset and boobs and pulled out the locket I'd stashed earlier. I hid it in my underwear drawer, unsure if I'd ever look at it again.

By the time Adam returned to the bedroom, the only things I'd managed to take off were my shoes. I was hugely relieved when he turned me around and unzipped my dress. What felt like a hundred metres of brocade pooled at my feet, and then Adam made a start on the corset laces.

I used the time to try and set things right between us. "I know you'd never intentionally hurt me," I said quietly. "Tonight was awful."

I felt a tug at my back as he pulled at the laces. "What's going to happen now, Charli?" I could hear the apprehension in his voice.

"I'm probably going to meet her," I replied. "I think I owe it to myself to try and get to know her better." In a moment of pure bliss, the corset hit the floor.

"I hope you get to know her well," he replied, planting a kiss on my back. "I hope you figure out exactly what kind of person she is." He turned me around, pressing his next kiss against my collarbone. "Then you'll be able to decide whether you want her in your life or not."

"Do you really think it's that simple?"

His smile was tiny. "No, but it won't matter. I'm here."

***

I called Olivia the next morning, after a restless night and very little sleep. After telling me how thrilled she was to hear from me, she suggested we get together as soon as possible. "You could come to the studio," she said. "I'm here all day. Bring Bridget if you like. I'd love to see her too."

I agreed to meet her later that morning, but Bridget was off-limits. The last thing I wanted was Olivia confusing her with claims of being her grandmother.

I was nervous. Things might've been different if I'd spent my life pining for the mother I'd never known, but I hadn't. Alex had never been forthcoming about her, and I hadn't been curious enough to push the issue. I hardly knew anything about her except for the most important detail: Alex had once loved her with all his heart.

Time bends all ideas. Alex no longer loved Olivia. His heart now belonged to Gabrielle, and I had no intention of disturbing the happy life he was building with her and Jack. The news that Olivia was on the scene was not something he needed to deal with. At that point, she felt like a powder keg that we should all be steering clear of.

***

The Minuet Dance Studio was locked when I got there, so after alternating between checking the address and knocking on the door, I called Olivia.

"I'll be out in a just a minute," she said, and hung up.

It was a long minute – closer to ten by my reckoning. It wasn't a shining start to our relationship and I wouldn't usually have tolerated such jerk-like behaviour, but when she finally opened the door, I bit my tongue and plastered a smile on my face.

"Come in, come in," she beamed.

She looked different without her French Revolution garb. She was super slim and tiny but quite tall. Alex was tall too. It made me wonder how I'd ended up a disappointing five-four. She hooked her arm through mine and

176

we walked down a short corridor into her office. She sat at her desk and gestured to the chair opposite.

It was weird. Impersonal, awkward and weird.

"It's private in here," she explained. "We can spend some time getting to know each other."

From what I'd seen, we needed no privacy. It was eleven o'clock on a Sunday morning and I hadn't seen another soul since I arrived.

I sat on the white suede chair and nervously smoothed down my dress with both hands. "Do you work every day?" I asked. I didn't really care one way or the other. I was one sentence in and already grasping for conversation.

"Ballet is my life," she said strongly. "It's a craft of total dedication."

My eyes followed her hand as she pointed to a collection of photos along the far wall — no less than twenty pictures depicting a ballerina in various poses. A closer look revealed that Olivia was the ballerina in every single shot. At best it was conceited. At worst, it was creepy.

"Are you married, Olivia?" I asked curiously. "Do you have a family?"

Her eyes drifted to mine. "I was married for ten years, but I'm divorced now."

"Oh, I'm sorry."

Her soft laugh had a hard edge to it. "I'm not," she replied. "He was a fool." She stood up, wandered over to her picture wall and studied her photos as if looking at them for the first time. "As for a family, I was advised against having more children after you." She turned back, looking positively wounded. "There were complications. It's never easy having a child so young, as I'm sure you understand." She sat back at her desk. "You were merely a child when Bridget was born, too."

"No," I corrected. "I was twenty."

Olivia shook her head, tutting like she felt sorry for me. "Far too young."

I was so far out of my depth that breathing took effort. I would've preferred sparring with a hundred Décaries to having one conversation with this lady.

"I'm very happy with the path I've chosen. You needn't worry."

Olivia leaned across the desk, reaching for my hand. For some reason, I obliged. "I'm not worried, darling," she said gently. "You've landed on your feet. The Upper East Side is a world away from Tasmania – married to a Décarie, no less."

Her smile was absolutely genuine, which was troubling. "Tell me about Alex," she urged. "I often think about him."

The conversation felt uncomfortable, but answering questions about Alex was the ultimate no-go zone. I deflected the best way I knew how – I told a bold-faced lie. "I don't have a lot of contact with Alex," I admitted, feigning regret. "We're very distant these days."

Her blue eyes crinkled at the edges as she smiled. "Understandable," she said gently. "He could never have given you this life."

I wondered what sort of life she thought I'd led pre-Décarie. The pity in her tone suggested something underprivileged and lacking. I wanted to scream at her. I wanted to defend the man who loved me and raised me after she chose to walk away.

But I didn't. I stood up and made a quiet excuse to leave.

Olivia didn't see me to the door. She remained seated, calling out to me at the last moment. "You look like him," she said. "You have his eyes."

I nodded. "I know."

It was more obvious to me then than ever before, and I'd never been more proud to be my father's daughter than at that moment. I'd found nothing of Olivia in myself – no spark of kinship or shared physical trait. She wasn't even particularly likeable.

The meeting left a hole in my heart that hadn't been there the day before. It was unfair and undeserved; and worst of all, I had no idea how to fix it.

***

Despite the fact that the whole of New York was at our doorstep, we were creatures of habit. Any spare time was spent in the park. We'd made a loose arrangement to meet before I left home that morning, and Bridget and Adam were already there when I arrived.

My kid was atop a climbing frame that looked much too high, and from a distance, it looked like her dad was trying to coax her down. I sat on a bench and watched the battle of wills play out. The stand Bridget was making only lasted until she spotted me, and then she let Adam help her down.

As she ran toward me I studied her every move. Adam often likened Bridget to a street urchin. On days when we didn't fight to get a brush through her hair or demand that her clothes matched, she was free-range, just as I had been. Her personality was wild regardless of her presentation, but she had balance. Smoothing her rough and flighty edges were patience and wisdom that belied her years. These qualities came courtesy of her dad, meaning she was just the right combination of the two of us.

"Mum!" she yelled from fifty metres away. "Did you see me fly?"

I smiled, arms outstretched preparing for the inevitable crash. "I must've just missed it," I told her. "I only just got here."

After a quick hug, Bridget turned on her heels and took off back to the playground. "Watch this time, please," she ordered. "I might do it again."

Adam scored a high-five as she passed. Bridget scored a half-dimpled smile that matched her own and a warning to be careful.

I shuffled along the bench to make room for him. He draped an arm around my shoulder, and for the first time all day I felt comfortable and relaxed.

"How did it go?"

"It was hard," I admitted, keeping my focus on Bridget. "We don't have much in common except DNA."

He rubbed the back of my neck. "Are you going to see her again?"

His casual question was deceptively loaded. Adam had made no secret of his dislike for Olivia. He had no reason to persevere in the hope she'd turn things around and change his opinion, but I did. She was my mother. That alone meant I'd go back for more, and he knew it.

"Probably," I muttered. "You think I'm foolish, don't you?"

"No. I think you're looking for the good. I just hope it's there."

"I'm not sure it is," I admitted. "I have a sinking feeling that she's shady."

My focus never left our daughter, who was hanging upside down on the climbing frame with her belly on show. Adam's gaze was solely on me, and I could feel him silently demanding an explanation.

"She mentioned that I'd grown up in Tasmania," I explained. "I was born in Sydney. That means she knew where I was all along and never did anything about it." I turned to look at him. "I don't know why she suddenly wants to be in my life. I don't trust it."

Feeling cynical was unpleasant but I couldn't shake it. Olivia didn't act like she was thrilled by the idea of finding me, at least not in public. As I left the studio, she'd asked me to keep the news of our reunion a secret. "Just until we get to know each other better," she suggested.

My feelings weren't hurt by the request. I wasn't exactly shouting it from the rooftops either. From what I'd seen that day, long lost daughter wasn't a title I was in any hurry to claim.

34. SLOW POISON

Adam

I promised Charli I wouldn't interfere – that I'd leave it to her to decide how much of a part her mother played in our lives.

Olivia administered her poison in slow, controlled doses over the next couple of weeks. Charlotte probably would've taken a step back and let her slip out of her life but Olivia was relentless.

Her angle was simple. Olivia gave Charli something Alex never had – information. I didn't buy her idealistic tale of star-crossed lovers who met too soon, but Charli seemed to accept every word without question.

There's nothing remotely romantic about two seventeen-year-old kids having a baby. Olivia recalled that time with fondness and nothing but love for her baby daughter. Just hearing Charli retell the tale made me feel queasy. As her mother's stranglehold began to tighten, Charli seemed to forget that Alex was the hero of the story.

It was becoming impossible to keep quiet and let it play out, especially when Charli announced that Bridget was back on Olivia's list of dance pupils.

"No, Charli," I protested. "There are a hundred dance schools in this city. Find another one."

"Bridget is looking forward to it." For once, her ploy of cosying up to me on the couch wasn't working. She could've done it buck-naked and I still would've been immune.

"You knew I'd say no," I accused. "But you went ahead and told Bridget anyway. Not cool, Charlotte."

I'd been railroaded before, but never by my wife. I was furious. Promising not to interfere only applied to Charli. Sooner or later the whole debacle was going to end in tears, but they weren't going to be Bridget's.

Charli straightened up. "Are you really that upset?"

I bit the inside of my cheek, unwilling to let words escape.

"Say something, please."

"Olivia is in your head, Charli," I said gravely. "A week ago you'd never have agreed to this." I stood, then turned back to her. "And a week before that, you would never have gone behind my back."

***

Dishonesty was creeping in from all sides. It wasn't a new concept in my marriage; it was an old one that we hadn't visited in a long time.

Charli's decision to get Bridget ramped up about dance classes was purely tactical. I wasn't in the habit of breaking my daughter's heart, which is exactly what would happen if I overruled her mother.

Sneakiness tends to beget sneakiness. After two weeks of holding my tongue and trying to be supportive, it was time to put an end to it. Snooping was part of my job, only it wasn't called snooping. Reputable lawyers call it researching. Doing a background check on Olivia wasn't something I wanted to undertake myself. Perhaps a little fearful of what I'd discover, I delegated the task to Grayson.

Nothing about the request troubled him, even after hearing the details. I thumped Olivia's prospectus on his desk, signalling the end of my rather rambling speech. As plans went it was average at best, but it was all I had.

He rested his hands behind his head. "So let me break it down," he said. "You want me to snoop around and see what I can find out about her?"

If use of the word snoop made him less reputable, I didn't care. I wanted to nail Olivia, and if there was dirt to be dug, Grayson was the man to dig it.

"That's exactly what I want."

He took a notebook out of his desk drawer. I spent a long minute watching him fossick for a pen, then reached into my top pocket and handed him mine.

"Right," he announced. "What's her full name?"

I pushed the folder closer. "I told you. Everything you need is in this."

Grayson returned my pen. "You might be playing with fire, Adam," he warned.

"Thank you for your concern, but I'm actually trying to start one."

35. SOCIETY SOWS

Charli

Shopping wasn't something I was particularly good at, but neither was declining Olivia's invitations to spend time together. The pace she set when it came to getting to know one another was unyielding. I felt obliged to take her up on her requests to meet during my lunch hour, and if I didn't, she tended to show up at the gallery anyway.

Adam was under the false impression that I'd welcomed Olivia into my life with open arms, and from the outside looking in that's exactly how it would've seemed. The view from the inside was different. My mother wasn't remotely curious about me, or the twenty-four years of my life that she'd missed. She was self-absorbed, egotistical and conceited, even during the emotional speeches she constantly gave about loving the child she'd given up.

It made liking her difficult. I felt selfish for not trying harder. Perhaps that's why I had trouble saying no to her.

The row of exclusive boutiques just down the road from the gallery wasn't one of my usual haunts. As long as Fiona insisted on being my personal shopper, I didn't need to frequent them. Olivia's plan of a girly hour bonding over shoes and handbags was wasted on me, but I smiled politely and pretended to be happy to be there.

"I'm hosting a charity event in a few weeks," she explained, wandering around the small store. "I need something new to wear."

To hurry things along I pointed out several dresses that I thought would be good contenders, only to have her veto every one of them.

"I'm looking for something unique, Charli. These events are always overrun by spoiled society sows in similar dresses. Horrendous affairs."

Her cattiness didn't sit well with me, perhaps because one of the society sows was my mother-in-law. "Why do it then?"

Olivia turned to look at me, a graceful ballet move. "Because this one is for *my* charity," she replied. "I'm hoping to raise a lot of money."

I didn't need to ask what her cause was. She barely paused before launching into a spiel about how rewarded she felt being able to provide underprivileged wannabe ballerinas with tuition that they couldn't afford otherwise. It wasn't exactly cancer research or feeding the homeless, but it was a start.

"We supply them with costumes and transport and anything else they need to attend class," she continued. "I'm always looking for extra help if you're interested."

I wasn't interested at all, and had far too much on my plate already. For the first time since I met her, I managed to say no.

Olivia began raking through a rack of clothes. "Pity," she said wistfully. "Perhaps you could help out in a different capacity."

"I'll do what I can." Even to my own ears, it didn't sound believable.

"Fiona Décarie is a major player on the charity scene," said Olivia. "Perhaps you could convince her to support our cause. If she attends, all of her underlings are likely to follow suit."

"Do you know Fiona well?" I asked casually.

"Not well, but I'm sure that will change." Her smile looked more like a smirk, adding to my growing unease. "My daughter is married to her son. When that becomes public lots of things will change."

Adam couldn't mention Olivia's name without following up with a warning about her having a hidden agenda. Comments like that made me think he was right.

I picked up a red handbag and pretended to study the label, purely so I wouldn't have to look at her. Terror isn't an easy expression to hide. "This is pretty." I held the bag out. "It matches your shoes."

The strappy red heels in question tapped on the wooden floor as Olivia approached. "It's lovely," she agreed, studying the label. "You should buy it."

"Red isn't really me." Nor was the three thousand dollar price tag. "It suits you, though."

Without taking her eyes off me, Olivia rudely clicked her fingers at the sales assistant.

"Can I help you?" asked the meek girl.

"Yes." Olivia handed her the bag but kept her focus on me. "Are you sure about this, Charli?" she asked.

I shrugged, confused by the question. "Sure. It's a pretty bag."

"Yes it is," she crowed, clasping her hands together. She turned to face the sales girl, who now looked as bewildered as I felt. "I'll take it."

"Wonderful," replied the girl. "Cash or credit?"

Olivia cocked her head to the side. "Charli?"

My heart began thumping as I tried to get a grip on what had just gone down. Replaying the conversation in my head was no help. I still couldn't recall the part where I'd offered to fork out thousands of dollars on a handbag for a woman I barely knew.

"Credit." I choked out the word.

The smile Olivia directed me was unwavering, even when I frowned in return.

The girl disappeared to the counter with my credit card, the outrageously expensive bag, and any respect I'd ever felt for my mother.

36. DIRT

Adam

The only person beside my father who ever stormed my office without knocking was Grayson Daniels. It usually pissed me off, but when I linked the excited expression on his face with the folder in his hand I decided to keep my mouth shut.

"You're never going to guess," he announced.

In the time it took him to walk to my desk and sit, I tried. I'd been so hell-bent on shutting the hateful ballerina down that I hadn't put much thought into what I might be exposing by doing it. If Grayson had dug up something really incriminating, there was no telling how that might affect Charli, or how she'd handle me bringing it to her attention. I made a deal with myself. If he'd found anything too wretched, I'd say nothing and find another way to oust Olivia from our lives.

"Hit me with it," I demanded, sounding far surer than I felt.

He slapped the folder down on my desk. "Her name isn't Kara," he began. "It's Karabelas. She's Sam Karabelas' ex-wife."

I shrugged, none the wiser.

"Oh, dude. Come on."

Grayson was the only grown man I knew who used the word 'dude' on a regular basis. It was a quirk that actually suited him, much like the cartoon character ties and ridiculous bright socks he wore to individualise his stock standard suits.

"Karabelas was a prominent Greek shipping magnate," he explained.

"*Was?*" I asked. "Is he dead?"

"No." He threw his head back and laughed. "Although he's getting on a bit. He's pushing sixty – much older than his ex."

"My dad is fifty-four, Grayson," I said dryly. "Knock on his door and tell him he's old."

"Yeah," he scoffed. "Not likely."

"So what happened to him?" I asked.

"He lost his fortune in the GFC." He leaned back in his chair, hands behind his head. "The ballerina's charmed life hit the skids when his money disappeared in 2008."

"She's broke?"

"Stone, motherless broke," he confirmed. "All she got out of the divorce was a building over on –"

"I know where it is. I've been there. It's a dance studio."

Grayson cocked an eyebrow. It was a move as annoying as the bright green sock he flashed when he crossed his ankle on his knee. "Do you frequent dance studios often, Adam?"

"Yeah, we like to shop around." I grinned at him. "Especially since your wife booted my kid out of her class."

"From what I heard, your daughter is a little French menace," he replied with a laugh. "Ran rings around every other kid in the class."

Including the teacher, I didn't reply. "What else did you find?" I asked, getting back on subject.

Grayson motioned to the folder on my desk with a nod. "That résumé is nothing more than a fairy-tale," he told me. "None of it's true."

I hadn't paid much attention to it when her receptionist first gave it to me. Once I connected the dots and realised Olivia's connection to Charlotte, none of it mattered.

I snatched the folder up and pulled out the résumé. "The Imperial French Ballet Troupe?" I asked, reading off the page.

"Never worked for them."

I thumbed to the previous page. "The Australian International Dance Company?"

"She's originally from Sydney, but was never affiliated with that company." Grayson picked at an invisible piece of lint on his knee. "She made it through two months of a ballet scholarship after high school, but that's it."

I couldn't begin to imagine why, and was probably never going to know. I closed the folder. "Does she have any formal qualifications at all?"

"Amateur certificates and a few years in B-grade theatre productions."

I might've felt pity for a person who'd spent years concocting such an intricate façade, but this was Olivia. The only person I had to feel sorry for was my wife. The woman who'd pushed her way into Charli's life had done nothing but fill her head with lies from day one.

The fake résumé had nothing to do with duping Charli. Olivia had been peddling that crock long before it was handed to me. Clearly the woman was an opportunist. She likely married for money and social standing, and bailed when it ran out. I didn't even hold that against her. It wasn't a world I cared to know but she wasn't the first to do it, and would most certainly not be the last.

My concern was that she was searching for a new opportunity to bring her back into the fold of the Manhattan elite, and it didn't take a genius to work out that Charli was it.

***

Grayson's morning of snooping hadn't come cheap. In return, I agreed to complete a mountain of his mundane crap that should've been dealt with weeks ago. In fairness, he did stop by to thank me – on his way out the door at six o'clock. The next time I checked my watch was just after nine. I looked down, groaning at the sight of two more hours of work in front of me.

Any distraction would've been welcome at that point, but none more than the one I got when I looked up again. Charli was a vision, leaning against the doorframe, smiling as if I was truly the best thing she'd seen all day.

"Mrs Décarie," I drawled, leaning back in my chair. "Long time no see."

"I was just in the area," she teased. "Thought I'd stop by and say hi."

I knew this woman implicitly. Her smile was strong and her words were light, but something was going on. Her eyes gave her away.

"Everything okay?"

"Yep." She almost nodded before amending her answer. "No. Not really."

I tried to work out where the conversation was headed. Chances were, whatever was troubling her was nothing compared with what I planned to burden her with. My eyes drifted to the bogus prospectus on my desk. "Anything I can help you with?"

"Yeah," she said quietly. "Just come over here, take me far away, and make me forget everything."

As I stood, I dropped the file into my drawer. This wasn't the night for sharing what I knew. It was a night for remembering all the good we had going on before the bad crept in.

37. STAR PROMISES

Charli

I felt Adam's touch long before he reached me – it was that familiar. And the only thing better than the comfort of having his arms around me was the fact that he didn't press me to talk.

There was no immediate need to explain why I'd teed up Bente and Ryan to come over and watch our kid so I could trek downtown to see him so late at night. I didn't have to tell him why I felt totally duped by my so-called mother, or why I cared enough to be hurt by it.

My hands moved to his face, determined to hold his kiss as long as I could. Adam's hands moved everywhere, and when he gathered me up and carried me to the couch near the window, I really did forget everything.

***

An office on the forty-third floor of a high-rise building is an extraordinarily quiet place to be late at night. I lay completely still with my cheek against Adam's chest, concentrating on the sound of his heart.

"Far enough away, Charlotte?" he whispered, displacing me slightly as he shifted to kiss the top of my head.

I wriggled, forcing him back into the position I wanted him in. "Yes, but I'm back now."

"Do you want to talk about it?"

I picked up his hand and laced my fingers through his. "I don't really know where to start," I mumbled.

"The beginning is always good."

The ending was probably more relevant at that point. In a long and emotionless monologue, I explained the saga of the designer bag. Adam never said a word, but I could feel the tension in his body as the tale progressed.

I straightened out our fingers, pressing my palm flat against his. "She's never going to love me," I told him. "I could try and try and give and give, and still, Olivia will never love me."

I felt him groan, deep within his chest. "Is that what you were hoping for, Charli?" He sounded appalled, and rightfully so.

I hadn't explained myself well. What I should've told him was that I'd come to an important realisation. Olivia didn't have a maternal bone in her body. That meant she'd never feel guilty about screwing me over to get ahead. She was never going sound believable when telling me of her regret at giving me up. And I was never going to like her because of it.

"I don't care that she doesn't love me, Adam," I explained. "What I care about is that she probably never did."

"What do you mean?"

I exhaled. "When my baby was born, I took one look at her and knew that I'd feel her in my bones until the day I die," I explained. "I loved her that much."

Adam kissed my fingers. "Me too."

"Alex once told me that Olivia never even looked at me when I was born," I continued. "Never even held me. I can't fathom that." When said out loud, it didn't sound like a reason to be resentful. She'd made the decision to adopt me out months before I was born. Having no contact with me was probably a logical choice.

"Do you feel like you missed something because of it?" asked Adam.

"No," I replied strongly. "She did, and there's nothing she can do from here that's going to get it back." I wasn't convinced that she was trying to. From the day I met her, I'd had the sinking feeling that she was acting –

merely playing the part she thought I wanted to see. I still had no clear picture of who Olivia was or what she wanted, and after the stunt she pulled that day, my interest in finding out was gone.

"Are you done with her, Charlotte?" he whispered.

"I'm done, Adam."

***

Avoiding Olivia over the next few days was relatively simple. That weekend, my family caught the wedding bug.

It started with the long-awaited nuptials of Trieste and William Best. On the most perfect of August days we stood in the Conservatory Garden at Central Park and watched the quirkiest girl I'd ever known marry her prince. It was a simple but classy affair, especially when compared to the last wedding I attended. Trieste and William had a flautist. From memory, Jasmine and Wade had Ave Maria cranking out of a boom box.

The reception was just as tasteful, and very intimate thanks to the small guest list. I couldn't quite believe that Ryan's skittish mood was brought on by the stress of making sure Trieste's reception went off without a hitch, but that was the story he gave me when I cornered him at the podium and asked him about it.

"Are you sure that's all it is?" I put my hand to his forehead. "You're sweating."

He pushed my hand away. "I'm hot, Tinker bell," he snapped. "I've been telling you that for years."

He might not have been forthcoming with me, but Adam got the whole tale when his very panicked brother finally worked out that he'd found his chocolate cake girl.

In a move that no one could've seen coming, Ryan bit the bullet and proposed to Bente.

It wasn't supposed to be public knowledge, but ten minutes after promising that he wouldn't tell a soul, Adam came to me and sang like a bird. "I had my fingers crossed," he grinned, "so it didn't count."

I was excited, for more reasons than one. After a lifetime of sketchy behaviour, Ryan finally deserved Bente. Proposing to her meant that he realised it too.

Bente was one of the best people I knew. She was also strong and feisty and more than capable of holding her own, which meant that when it came to being a Décarie, I now had an ally. She'd already made it clear that she wasn't interested in rocking the boat. Bente would always be the good wife, but being the black sheep had never bothered me. If anything, I relished the challenge.

It wasn't until I was lying in bed that night, thinking everything through that I realised just how much of a sense of family I'd gained. They all annoyed me, and the urge to smack them had struck more than once in the past seven years, but I loved them. Annoying or not, they were mine.

***

After a particularly busy morning at the gallery, the afternoon dragged. Bronson skipped out early, taking his usual six-hour lunchbreak. My lunch consisted of three cups of tea and some crackers I found in the bottom of my bag. I sat at my desk while I ate, poring over the photos I'd taken at the wedding. I was proud of how they'd turned out, but was slightly bemused that I'd managed to take a whole series of photos that didn't have Bridget in them.

My daughter was probably the most photographed child on the planet. I'd captured thousands of her moments through a lens. I'd never grown out of being impressed by every move the kid made and I loved seeing her grow and change and dazzle me on a daily basis. If I could come up with a way of photographing the workings of her little mind, I would've done that too.

I was so engrossed by the pictures that I didn't hear the front door open – which wasn't good, considering I was the only person attending a gallery with hundreds of thousands of dollars worth of art displayed within its walls.

I looked up at hearing my name to be confronted by the person I'd been avoiding all week.

"Olivia, hi." I stood quickly, as if jumping to attention.

"Don't get up," she said loosely waving her hand.

I sat back down. "How have you been?" I asked, purely to be polite.

"Fine," she replied. "You?"

My answer came too quickly to sound anything other than rehearsed. I told her how busy we'd been, and then rambled about Trieste's wedding and Ryan's secret engagement. She cut in when I mentioned the pointless topic of Bridget's squirrel phobia that cut our morning walk through the park short.

"They're pesky creatures, that's for sure," she agreed.

I laughed, which sounded just as forced as the rest of the conversation.

Olivia turned around and wandered away, following the line of art on the wall. "You have some lovely pieces in here."

"We do," I agreed.

She briefly turned back. "Are they all for sale?"

"Yes."

"I'm thinking of getting something for the studio," she replied. "Perhaps when I'm ready, you can help me choose something."

I shrugged. "That's what I do."

It wasn't the most interesting discussion I'd ever had, but it was a welcome relief from the usual heavy topics she favoured – right up until she asked me why Bridget was a no-show at her dance class.

"I thought we agreed that she'd start yesterday." Olivia sounded hurt. "I was looking forward to seeing her."

My eyelids felt like tonne weights as I blinked. "We've been busy, that's all."

She began her aimless wander again. "I wondered if her father had put his foot down," she said. "Adam made his feelings perfectly clear. I understand that he calls the shots."

"Don't do that," I berated. "Don't make comments like that. You've no idea how my family works."

Olivia turned, looking wounded.

"I'm sorry," she replied. "I didn't mean anything by it."

I couldn't find words. I shouldn't have been giving her the time of day. If I'd kicked her out of the gallery it would've been in accordance with my own rules that I'd set less than a week ago.

But I couldn't bring myself to do it.

"I brought you something," she announced.

I lifted my head to see her reach into the three thousand dollar bag I'd unintentionally gifted her. She slowly ambled toward me as if she was scared to approach. When I was within reach, she handed me a small square wooden box. "Your father gave me this. I thought you'd like to have it."

I looked down at the box in my hand; quickly deciding it was far more Alex's speed than the gaudy locket.

"He didn't have a lot of money for presents, but he was forever giving me bits and pieces," she explained. "Alex's heart was big, and so were his dreams."

As hard as I fought against it, she'd struck a chord with me. The guilt that came with tying Alex down for so many years had crippled me in the past. "What did he want to do?" I asked.

If Olivia was to tell me that he once aspired to travel the world it might just have been the end of me.

Her smile was small. "He just wanted to be happy, Charli. Happy and free."

Gripping the box much too tightly, I demanded an explanation. Olivia's story was compelling, but I took it with a grain of salt. She didn't realise it, but we had believability issues.

According to her, Alex's home life was abominable. His mother was a hopeless, neglectful drunk. Every few months they'd move house when she stopped paying rent.

So far, so good, I thought. It was nothing Alex hadn't already told me.

"When we found out I was pregnant, he begged me to keep you," she revealed. "He was desperate for stability."

"Or perhaps he just wanted to do the right thing and raise his child," I suggested unsympathetically.

If my comment hurt her feelings, she did a good job of hiding it. She continued as if I hadn't spoken.

"We were just a couple of stupid kids," she said. "He used to make me promises. It was never things like houses and riches. Even Alex knew he'd probably never be able to deliver on that." Olivia smiled as if she'd said something funny. I remained stone-faced.

"We used to go to the beach a lot," she continued. "Does he still like the beach?" I shrugged as if I didn't know. "It was best at night – in the summer of course. I still remember how clear the sky was. Millions of stars on show."

There was something different about her that day. I wasn't getting the usual made up, overacted rubbish she'd tried to regale me with in the past. There was a small chance she was being honest, and I had no idea how to deal with it.

"Alex once told me that stars were little promises wrapped up in light," she continued. "And that shooting stars were broken promises falling from the sky."

It wasn't a tale that he'd ever told me, but I couldn't discount it. Plenty of legends are based on stars, and most are wildly different.

"We'd lie on the beach at night, and he'd point out star after star as he claimed them." She turned and wandered away, but kept talking. "'That one is my promise that I'll always look after you' he'd say. Or 'That star is my promise that I'll love you forever'." When she turned back to face me, her eyes were glazed with tears.

My hands began to tremble, reminding me that I was still holding the box. "What does it have to do with this?" I asked, holding it out to her.

Her smile was tiny but honest for a change. "He told me that star promises stay hung in the sky until they're fulfilled or broken. The broken ones fall, and the fulfilled ones just disappear. All the others just wait, twinkling in the sky," she explained. "One day I asked him how I'd know they were still there while I waited for them to be fulfilled." She pointed at the box in my hand "That's when he gave me the box."

I flipped open the lid to find a small card inside. "They're always close. All you have to do is look for them."

"That's it?" I asked, slightly disappointed. "It's not even a handwritten card."

Her laugh choked. "I know," she replied. "I think he typed it up on his mother's typewriter."

I placed the card back in the box and snapped the lid shut. "Thank you," I said. "I would like to keep it."

I half expected Olivia to ask me to shout her a free piece of artwork in return, but she didn't. She told me that she had to get back to the studio and made a quiet, fuss free exit.

After a minute alone with the box and my thoughts, I wondered if guilt was her ploy – and then totally confused myself by feeling guilty for thinking it. I eventually concluded that I wanted to believe her, but couldn't do it without proof. Ignoring the fact that it was three in the morning in Tasmania, I typed a ridiculously vague text message to my father.

– What are stars?

I wasn't expecting a reply for hours, but didn't get through too many more crackers before my phone chimed with a reply.

– They sit in the sky, serving a punishment for something that happened so long ago that no star now knows what it is.

It was probably the longest text Alex had ever sent me, but *Peter Pan* quotes aren't short.

– What else could they be?

He was probably cursing me for not accepting his first long one-finger typed reply, but he answered anyway.

– Promises wrapped up in light

There it was – cold hard proof that Olivia was telling the truth. I wondered what would change because of it.

I tapped out one final sentence to my dad.

– I love you.

No matter what happened, that would never change.

38. JUNIOR NEGOTIATOR

Adam

Things were back to normal, but deep down I knew it would only be a matter of time before the hateful ballerina sank her claws back into Charli. It took just under a week.

Using her usual routine of tugging at Charlotte's heart with mementos of her past, Olivia showed up at the gallery and weaselled her way back in. Within days, Charli was back to being irritable and uncertain, and my daughter was back on the list of Minuet Dance School pupils. There was no point protesting a second time. The first time hadn't worked out well, and I wasn't foolish enough to incite round two.

***

I answered directly to my father at work. Some days he was pleasant and encouraging. Today was not one of those days.

I was summoned to his office first thing in the morning. I usually spent the time it took me to walk from my office to his to work out my defence. The problem I faced that morning was that I had no clue what I'd done wrong. I hadn't been late to work in over a week, and as pitiful as it sounded, that was a good effort for me.

As it turned out, his foul mood had nothing to do with me. My mother had dropped a bombshell on him over breakfast and he was still seething.

"She thinks Ryan's about to propose to Bente," he said getting straight down to it. "Do you know anything about it?"

The level of panic in his voice wasn't unexpected. Men in this family didn't have the luxury of falling in love with a nice girl and marrying her without fuss. There were rules. We were expected to wrap our finances up and ensure our money was sufficiently protected in case our nice girls turned out to be not so nice.

"I think he's already done it," I admitted. "That's what dinner tomorrow night is all about, isn't it? They're going to announce it."

Dad's shoulders sagged. "I wish he had come to me first," he muttered. "It makes things infinitely harder in the long run."

What he really meant was that Ryan had removed the option of a sneak attack. The ring couldn't be held to ransom until Bente signed the pre-nup. It was a done deal.

"And they say romance is dead," I sighed.

My father pointed a finger at me. "The inclusion of romance in your life is the sole reason your judgement is so skewed," he chided.

"Let's not start," I begged. "I have enough trouble protecting Charli from other forces at the moment. I'd appreciate a break from you."

Speaking freely was costly. My father was like a dog with a bone at the first hint of information. A smarter man would've run for the door, but I wasn't feeling particularly bright that morning.

I spent the next few minutes filling him in on all the details instead. I had no clue how he'd take the news that Charli's mother was on the scene, especially after I voiced my concerns that she was after money.

He didn't fly off the handle and rant and rave. If anything, he seemed quietly concerned. "Her story doesn't sound credible, Adam." A deep crease appeared in his forehead. "She could've made contact long before now."

"I know," I agreed. "Nothing about her is credible. I struggle to believe anything she says. Even her résumé is a piece of fiction."

Dad wasn't overly outraged. "People embellish their credentials all the time," he said. "Especially in this profession."

"She's a ballet teacher, Dad. Who's she trying to impress?"

He smiled, but avoided my question. "Have you told Charli?"

"No, not yet."

It might've been his calm demeanour, or perhaps I'd completely lost my mind since walking into the room. They were the only two explanations for what came next. I asked my father what he thought I should do, then dropped my head so I wouldn't have to watch him keel over in shock.

"Divorce your wife and move on," he replied. "All your troubles will disappear."

I glowered at him, but the effort was wasted. He was grinning.

"Not funny."

"Oh, come now, Adam," he replied, walking to the window. "It was both witty and comical."

He stood at the window a long time, staring at the skyline. At first I thought he was stalling, but soon realised he was using the time to ponder my question.

"Charli's not a weak girl, Adam," he said finally. "She faces her adversaries head on. I greatly admire her for that." He kept his back to me, probably because it was a hard admission to make. "Chances are, she doesn't need you to do anything."

"So you think I should just keep what I know to myself?"

He slowly turned. "I think if this woman's intentions are less than honourable, Charli will work it out," he suggested. "If you try and rush the process, it may not end favourably for you."

As hard as it was to accept, he was right. Pushing Charli to cut her mother from her life would never work, especially with bullying tactics like digging up dirt. I'd end up coming out of it looking shadier than Olivia. The only option I had was to take a back seat and wait for the wretched woman to come unstuck by herself.

***

Bridget had been asleep for hours by the time I got home. Charli was in bed too, but still awake. She sat up as I walked in.

"Hi."

I leaned down and kissed her. "Hey. Sorry I'm late."

"Have you eaten?"

"I got something at the office."

"Bridget helped cook tonight," said Charli. "There's some funky-looking pasta in the fridge if you're interested."

I smiled. "Pass, thank you," I replied, dragging off my tie.

"It'll still be there in the morning," she pointed out. "She'll make you try it for breakfast."

I dropped my cufflinks into the glass dish on the dresser and turned back to face her. "I'm out early. A meeting at eight."

Charli groaned, a hint that the conversation was about to take an unpleasant turn. "It's Bridget's first ballet lesson tomorrow," she reminded me. "I was hoping you'd come."

"Why?" I asked thoughtlessly. "Do you need backup?"

Her face dropped. "That was unkind."

"It was," I agreed, feeling a total jerk. "I'm sorry."

Charli shuffled across the bed. I didn't move. "Please ditch your meeting."

"No."

"Why not?"

"It's my job, Charlotte."

"Get a new job, Adam." If looks could kill, I would've been dead.

I grinned at her. "You're so pretty when you're mad."

Lightening the conversation was the best I could do. Charli was very tolerant when it came to the outrageously long hours I worked, but occasionally she needed to vent. It was always in my best interest to shut up and let her do it.

"You're on the wrong path, Adam," she muttered.

I wanted to tell her we both were lately, but I didn't. I defended my choice of career as if I believed in it. "As long as we're in New York, this is my path," I told her. "It's what I do."

"But why?" she asked. "You hate it. I know you do."

I unbuttoned my shirt while I pondered her question. "I studied for years to do this. It seems like less of a waste of time if I actually make use of my degree."

Her ire slipped as curiosity set in. "Why do you hate it so much?"

I almost laughed. I'd spent three years tearing up boats for a living. Entire days were spent hanging out on the beach with our kid. Going from that to wearing a suit and working horrendous hours in an office was never going to be a good transition.

"It's not my bliss," I said simply.

"Quit." She shrugged as if it was no big deal. "Take on the renovations at the club. You'd be perfect for the job."

I screwed up my shirt and threw it at the chair. "Maybe."

She groaned. "Why won't you just do it?"

I wasn't ready to give her the truthful answer. A change in vocation wasn't going to fix things. A change in scenery was what I was hoping for, and now that Olivia was on the scene, the urge to grab my family and run was at an all-time high.

"Did you pick up the dry-cleaning?" I asked, changing the subject. She shook her head. "I need it, Charli. I told you this morning that I needed it."

"And I told you I'd pick it up," she replied.

I was confused. "So you did pick it up?"

"No." She grinned. "I forgot."

"Perfect," I muttered.

"You have ten million shirts in there." She flapped her hand at the closet. "Find one."

I angrily swept the hangers across the rail. "I don't need this at midnight. Seriously."

"Probably not," she agreed. "You know what you need?"

"No, tell me."

"A distraction."

I turned back to her. She'd managed to get undressed in three seconds flat. I was impressed – and successfully distracted.

"How did you do that so fast?"

Her smile was the best kind of wicked. "Ever tried getting into a wetsuit while naked on a public beach?"

"No, but I'm assuming you have."

"Once or twice."

I grinned. "You're dangerous, Charlotte."

"Are you still thinking about the dry-cleaning, Adam?"

Our room wasn't exactly large. Three steps were all it took before she was pinned beneath me on the bed. I answered her by kissing the wry smile off her face.

My next move was quickly halted by a little voice behind me.

"Hi Daddy."

Charli made a grab for the bedding. I made a dash for the little girl in the doorway.

"Hi, baby." I scooped her off the floor and kissed her. "It's really late. I'll take you back to bed," I offered.

"I'm not tired."

She didn't sound tired either. I glanced back at Charli, who was pretending to be asleep. I tried using it to my advantage. "Look, Mom's asleep."

Bridget leaned forward for a closer look. "No she's not," she told me. "She's still breathing."

I shook my head, trying to clear it of Bridget logic. "It's bed time."

The kid didn't skip a beat. "We can make a deal, Daddy," she said sweetly. Clearly she'd been spending too much time with Ryan. I was never going to win now. "What did you have in mind?"

She pointed at my nightstand. "I could look in there for something."

That was the moment Charli's sleeping act fell apart. She laughed, gaining the instant attention of the junior negotiator in my arms. "Hi, Mummy."

"Hi, Bridge," she replied, still giggling.

I lowered Bridget to her feet and she headed for the nightstand. I let her rummage around for half a minute before ordering her to make a decision. She pulled out a packet of mints.

"I really love these," she declared, waving them at me.

"That's great, but you're not having them."

"You won't like them," warned Charli. "They're hot."

Bridget dropped them back in the drawer and tried again. "How about these?" she asked.

No matter how eager I was to get her out of the room, sending her back to bed with a handful of coins wasn't going to happen. "No money."

"I really love money, Daddy."

"Give her paper money." Charli's suggestion was hardly going to win us any parenting awards, but I was beyond arguing. I puffed out a long breath of frustration and pulled my wallet out. "All I have is a fifty."

"I love fifties," beamed Bridget.

"Just do it, Adam," ordered Charli.

I reluctantly handed the bill to my daughter. "You're an extortionist," I told her. "*Fait accompli*, okay?"

She nodded as if she had a half a clue what I meant. "Tuck me in, please," she demanded. "And Mum too."

I scooped her up. "I've been trying to tuck your mama up for half an hour."

"Bye Mum," Bridget called over my shoulder.

"Good night, Bridge," she replied, giggling again.

I turned back to Charli as we got to the door. "Don't you dare fall asleep before I get back," I warned.

"Of course not," she replied. "Fifty bucks buys the whole night."

39. DANCING FEET

Charli

Despite the peak hour traffic, the cab ride downtown didn't take as long as expected. We arrived at the studio fifteen minutes early.

I breathed a sigh of relief to find the front door unlocked. Bridget probably would've smashed her way in if she'd been denied entry. She pointed to a doorway on her left. "I can dance in that room," she informed me. "But I have to use walking feet in here."

I smiled at her. "I'm glad you listened to the rules, Bridge."

"Me too," she crowed. "I have lovely ears."

The girl behind the desk introduced herself. "I'm Erin, the dance co-ordinator."

I wondered what that meant, but didn't embarrass myself by asking. I tried introducing Bridget, but she cut me off to explain that they'd already met. "You can go through." She pointed to the same doorway Bridget had. "Olivia is expecting you."

I hadn't seen Olivia in ballerina mode before. Not only did she look different with her long dark hair pulled back into a tight chignon, she walked differently.

She practically floated across the floor to greet us. I glanced at my little girl doing her monkey dance and thumping her feet on the floor, and wondered how both of us could've missed the elegance gene.

"I'm thrilled you made it," she beamed.

"Dancing feet in here!" squealed Bridget.

Olivia put her finger to her lips. "Shush," she murmured. "Quiet voice in here."

Bridget nodded. I doubted the silence would hold for long.

"You need to take your boots off and put your ballet slippers on," instructed Olivia.

I'd smuggled the demon slippers into the lesson in my handbag, not confident that she'd entertain the idea of wearing them.

"No thank you," said Bridget. "I'm wearing boots."

At least she'd been polite about it.

"Charli." Olivia dragged her gaze from Bridget to frown at me. "Can I speak to you in private, please?"

I wanted to say no, but Bridget dropped her my hand and took off. With her busy making faces in front of the mirror, I had no choice but to hear her out.

Olivia's standards were high, which Ella had warned us about. Galoshes weren't going to cut it. Her bottom line was clear and simple. The boots went or Bridget did.

"It's for her own good," she said gently.

My eyes drifted to my daughter. "She's worn boots every day since she learned to walk."

"How bizarre," she replied.

I tried not to glower when I looked at her. "It's not bizarre. It's just Bridget," I explained. "It's just a quirk."

The look on Olivia's face was on of pure pity. "You know, Alex's mother had funny habits. At first I used to think she was just quirky, but it was more than that." She glanced back at Bridget. "She was barmy. Utterly mad."

"She was also a drunk," I snapped.

Olivia gave me a tight smile. "If she wants to dance, the boots must go," she insisted. "Why don't you let me have a word with her? Maybe I can convince her?"

All I ever wanted was to do right by my daughter, but it was much easier in theory than practice. I wanted to encourage her individuality, but protect her from being considered weird because of it. I didn't know how to win.

"I'm not sure she's ready," I mumbled.

"You're not ready," she corrected. "You coddle her too much."

I could feel the tension spreading across my chest. What would Olivia know about coddling a child? The notion was laughable, but she seemed to miss the irony.

"Adam handles Bridget differently, you know," she told me. "But I suppose that's to be expected. They're closer, aren't they?"

Bridget had been Daddy's girl since the day she was born. To me, it seemed like a natural choice. Adam had it all together. I still had days when I felt like a scattered mess. I couldn't even make the call as to whether I should enforce the no-boots rule. But it hurt to have it brought to my attention.

"They are close," I conceded. "I like it that way."

Olivia smiled again, but it was still wrong. "Pull yourself together, Charli. She won't move forward without encouragement."

She was pushing me to consent to something that my heart was fighting against, and when the other little dancers filed into the room, the pressure intensified. She wasn't going to bend the rules and let her dance with boots on. Against my better judgement, I told her to go ahead and have a crack at changing Bridget's mind.

Olivia looked smug, like she'd just stolen something from me. Perhaps she had and I just hadn't realised it yet. "She'll be fine, Charli."

***

As in Ella's class, the parents didn't hang around. I couldn't have left if I'd wanted to. I wasn't ready to leave my little girl in a group she wasn't familiar with, but Bridget wasn't showing any hint of feeling the same way. I stood at the back of the class, silently willing her to turn around and look for me, like she did with her dad. When she didn't, I tried not to feel hurt by it.

"Okay, class," announced Olivia clapping her hands together. "I have something to share."

This group was completely different to Ella's motley crew. Each of the five girls in the class stood in front of her as if they were standing to attention. Even Bridget followed protocol.

Olivia slipped out of view, returning a minute later with a beautiful ballet costume in hand. The sparkly sage green getup floated behind her as she trailed the coat hanger through the air and hung it on the mirror in front of her.

She turned back to face her class, shushing the excited little squeaks that escaped them. "We have a concert coming up soon," she announced. "Everyone will be wearing one of these costumes."

She didn't shush them this time, allowing them the simple pleasure of being excited, but then did something that completely and utterly broke my heart.

"Do you like it, Maddy?" she asked, addressing the first little girl in line.

"Yes!" she replied.

Olivia continued down the line, garnering the same response from each girl.

Then it was Bridget's turn. "I just love it!" she beamed.

"It's a shame you won't be wearing one." Olivia's tone was confusingly gentle. "You won't take off the boots." She pointed at Bridget's feet. "Ballerinas don't wear boots."

My only saving grace was that Bridget's back was to me. I imagine she looked devastated.

"I love boots," she defended in a voice smaller than her.

Olivia shook her head. "Not in this class. You need to take them off now, or go home."

The little girl standing next to her leaned down and spoke. "Just take them off. You won't be able to go to the concert with them."

"But I don't want to," replied Bridget.

I could only assume she knew that I'd failed her miserably. Not once did she turn around to look at me.

"Last warning, Bridget," demanded Olivia. "Throw the boots away or get out."

Her tone was getting rougher and so were her words. Clearly it wasn't about encouraging Bridget to broaden her horizons. She was making an example of her.

My child stood firm until the very last minute. When she finally made her decision, I watched as she crouched down and pulled off her boots, painfully slowly just to make her point.

"I will throw them away," she muttered, finally standing up.

Even from a distance, Olivia's expression was smug. She'd probably anticipated the win. It's not hard to get one over on a tiny little girl. But what she wouldn't have been expecting was the unceremonious way that Bridget discarded her boots.

Every girl took a giant step back as both galoshes bounced off the mirrored wall. I expected it to shatter, but fortunately, after a long moment of wobbling, it held.

Olivia looked furious. I couldn't see Bridget, but could tell by her posture that she wasn't the least bit penitent.

"You're very lucky that didn't break," she hissed. "I'm sure your daddy wouldn't be pleased with having to pay for a new mirror."

"*Tête de guimauve,*" Bridget replied.

When she finally turned around to look for me, I wished she hadn't. She looked devastated, with good reason. Thanks to the ballet teacher from hell, my daughter was under the impression that I'd just sold her out. I'd promised her she could keep the boots, but that option had been ripped from her, and I'd stood by and let it happen.

***

I was hurt, angry, and certain that I was the worst mother in the world, excluding my own. I wasn't up to confronting Olivia. The second she dismissed the class, I grabbed Bridget and left. I didn't give a damn about my mother. All I cared about was making sure the damage she'd done to my kid wasn't permanent.

Bridget didn't say a word as I hurriedly marched her along the sidewalk – even to complain that I was walking too fast.

We rounded the first corner we came to. I pulled her aside and crouched in front of her. "I'm so sorry." I hugged her hard. "I don't know what just happened in there but I promise it'll never happen again."

"You said I could choose," she said flatly.

I pulled her in close again and hugged her much too tightly. "I know. I'm sorry," I mumbled, kissing the top of her head over and over. "I won't take you there again. You can wear your boots all day long."

Her voice was muffled against my chest. "No more dancing?" she asked.

I released her from my hold and leaned back to look at her. "No," I assured her.

"But I threw away my boots!" she growled. "She said I could stay now."

If I was out of my depth before, I was positively drowning now. I had no clue what to say. "You want to go back?"

"Daddy will take me," she insisted. "Okay?"

I wasn't quite sure what I was agreeing to, but one thing was for certain. If Adam had been there to witness Olivia's treatment of his daughter, there's no way it would've escalated past the first harsh word.

I was the one who was too inept to stand up for her. I was the coward who stood back and watched it play out. And I was the one who'd probably never recover from it.

40. MERMAID HELL

Adam

Stepping out of the elevator to find Bridget sitting outside our front door was a first. She didn't look worried, so I tried not to be.

"Hi, baby," I greeted. "You're on the wrong side of the door."

"It's locked," she said as if it was no big deal.

"Why are you out here? Where's Mom?"

Bridget gave me the rundown while I fumbled for my key. While Charli's back was turned, she'd decided to check out life on the other side of the door, managing to lock herself out in the process.

"Now I can't get back in." She threw her arms wide, emphasizing how much she'd been inconvenienced.

I wasn't buying her claim that she'd been sitting there for three days, but anything longer than three seconds was unacceptable. I ushered Bridget inside and began calling Charli's name before I'd even closed the door.

"I'm here," she replied, rounding the doorway to the hallway. "What's the matter?"

I chewed my bottom lip, trying to work out if I was angry or concerned. "Bridget was sitting outside the door when I got home," I replied. "Where were you?"

"I'm here, Adam," she muttered, pushing past me. "She could only have been out there for a minute."

"I was stuck for three days," Bridget interjected. "I'm very tired and hungry now."

Both of us ignored her for obvious reasons.

"What's going on, Charlotte?"

After diverting Bridget's attention by turning on her mermaid movie, she walked through to the kitchen, grabbed an apple out of the fruit bowl and began cutting it up. "We went to dance class," she replied roughly. "Need I say more?"

The sad truth was that I didn't want to hear more. I was so tired of hearing the tale of Olivia's heartless wrongdoings, mainly because of Charli's frustrating habit of repeatedly forgiving her. I decided not to ask questions and stuck to the more important issue at hand. I pointed at the front door. "Make sure that stays locked from now on," I muttered. "Anything could've happened."

When faced with the choice of throwing the apple or the knife, my wife loved me enough to throw the apple. It wasn't a perfect shot. I turned in time to deflect it with my arm.

"You're an arse," she growled, pushing past me again. The bedroom door slammed a few seconds later and she was gone.

I sat on the couch with Bridget and suffered through fifteen minutes of mermaid hell while I pondered my next move. In that time, Little Miss Obvious reminded me four times that I was in trouble.

"Yes, I realise that. Thank you."

"Big trouble," she taunted, singing the words.

"I know."

"Huge trouble," she whispered.

"Bridget Décarie, shut up and eat your apple."

***

Charli isn't a brooder. She began her explanation for the fruit assault the second I opened the bedroom door. "Don't tell me how to look after my kid," she ranted. "Even when I get it wrong."

"Okay." I put both hands up in surrender. "I won't."

"I didn't get it wrong!" she yelled. "I felt as bullied as Bridget did. It wasn't my idea to single her out and force her to ditch the bloody boots!"

At the risk of being killed for it, I had to confess that I had no idea what she was talking about. From what I could tell, it had nothing to do with Bridget's solo excursion into the foyer.

Charli slumped on the edge of the bed. "I don't even want to tell you about it."

I sat down beside her. "Would it make me a really bad father if I said I didn't want to hear about it?"

She let out a quiet laugh. "No."

"That's a relief."

Charli looked across at me. "How was your meeting?"

I tucked her hair behind her ear. "Nothing that couldn't be handled in an email."

She nodded. "A crappy day all round then."

"It's going to get worse, Coccinelle," I warned. "We're due at my parents' place for dinner."

***

I wasn't exaggerating when I claimed the day would get rougher. Ryan and Bente's so-called surprise engagement announcement was overshadowed by Charli's dark mood and my father's decision to kick her while she was down. The digs started the minute we arrived, and by the time we sat down to dinner, protecting her had become impossible.

Freedom of speech was seriously lacking when Charli was in the king's company. When she dared to give a La La explanation of why Bente's engagement ring contained exactly fifty-eight facets, things got ugly. My first reaction was to get Bridget out of the room. I sent her out to find her boots.

It wasn't honest of Dad to tear shreds off Charli. His real gripe was with my brother, namely his decision to propose to Bente before working out the details of a pre-nup. Charli realised it too, which is probably why she tried to divert the subject by telling her fairy-tale in the first place.

"I'm not listening to this any more," he snapped.

"Don't cut her off," I chided. "Don't ever do that."

Dad glared at me. "The minute your wife contributes something worth listening to, I will hear her out."

I knew the only option I had was to get us out of there. If we stayed, there was no telling how much further civility would slide. I grabbed Charli's hand and pulled her to her feet. "That's it," I declared. "We're done."

Bridget came running into the room, waving a boot in each hand. "Help me please, Daddy."

I crouched and helped her pull them on.

"Stay," my mother pleaded. "This is supposed to be Ryan and Bente's evening."

"It still is, Mom," I assured her.

"Yes," said Charli, turning her attention to Bente and Ryan. "Congratulations again. I'm really happy for both of you."

"So am I," I agreed. "Just make sure you get that pre-nup wrapped up nice and tight, Ryan." It was an unnecessary jibe that felt remarkably good, especially when I noticed the pissed off look on Dad's face. "Bente will have half a chance of being accepted into the fold if there's no danger of her ripping you off in the divorce." Even my mother's gasp of horror wasn't enough to shut me up. "And if you can make sure she keeps her opinions to herself, that'll score points too," I added.

Ryan let me have my moment and said nothing, but my father accused me of being ridiculous. By that point he was probably right, but I ignored his demand to sit back down. Instead, I made my point louder by sticking to my guns and leaving.

***

Bridget and I milled on the sidewalk like a couple of lost puppies while we waited for Charli to walk out. I was dreading having to go back in there and get her. But like a true team player, she eventually appeared.

"Your father would like me to let you know that he doesn't appreciate your attitude, monsieur," she stated, slowly making her way down the front steps.

"I'll take it under advisement," I replied, smiling at her.

She stepped off the stoop and linked her arms around my neck. "I kind of like it when you're naughty," she teased.

"I can be naughty," offered Bridget, wedging herself between us. "It's easy."

"No one doubts your talent, Bridge." I put my hand on her head. "Just stick with being nice for now."

"Let's go home." Charli grabbed my hand. "We could walk. It's a nice night."

I reached for Bridget with my free hand and looked up at the sky. There wasn't a cloud in it and the stars were bright. For a short minute I managed to pretend we were somewhere else.

"It's the same sky, wherever you're watching from, Adam," Charli murmured.

I gave her fingers a gentle squeeze. "It's what underneath that counts." When I cut in front of her path by stepping in front of her, Bridget skipped forward to keep up. "Let's not go home," I suggested. "Where do you want to go?"

At that moment, she looked so beautiful that I would've taken her to the moon if she'd asked.

"Can we go swimming?" asked Bridget tugging on my hand. "That would be a lovely adventure at night time."

It was an impossible suggestion at eight o'clock on a Tuesday night, but I was a long time supporter of all things La La. I picked Bridget up and made a promise I wasn't sure I could keep. "Yes," I said, tickling her belly. "Let's do it. A swimming adventure sounds perfect."

My daughter's witchy little cackle was the best sound I'd heard all day.

Charli hooked her arm through mine. "How are you going to pull this one off, Boy Wonder?"

"I'm not sure yet."

"Winging it again?" she asked.

I wiggled my eyebrows at her. "You can't fly without wings, Coccinelle."

***

Fortunately, a plan came together quickly. Bridget wasn't happy about heading home, or the notion of waiting in the cab while I ran up to the apartment to get what we needed.

"Just wait with Mommy," I told her. "I'll be back in a minute."

"Bring Treasure too, please," she demanded.

I closed the door before she could add anything else to her list of requests and hurried inside. I packed a bag of clothes, threw in the ghastly Treasure and made a few necessary phone calls. I returned to the waiting cab feeling slightly more confident of pulling off the adventure Bridget was seeking.

"The Castlereagh Hotel, please," I instructed the driver.

"A hotel pool?" asked Charli.

Bridget clambered onto my lap. I sat her back down on her seat and buckled her seat belt. "Wait and see," I said vaguely.

Charli turned her head, smiling out the window. "Far from what we once were, but not yet who we're going to be," she mumbled.

I slipped my arm behind Bridget to run my hand through her mama's hair. "What does that mean?" I asked.

"It means we're going swimming!" Bridget's shrill squeal made the driver wince. "For all of the night time."

I was hopeful that she wouldn't last that long. I had big plans for her mother.

The Castlereagh Hotel wasn't somewhere any of us had visited before. Considering it was barely six blocks from our apartment, we had no need to. It wasn't a random choice of hotel, which became clear to Charli when my co-conspirator met us in the lobby. She let out a small groan of disapproval and dropped her hold on my hand. "Still winging it, Adam?" she whispered as we approached.

"No, Charlotte," I murmured in reply. "All part of my plan."

41. ADVENTURES

Charli

I'd stumbled across Whitney Vaughn only once since being back in New York – at a bakery, of all places. It was strange and uncomfortable. I complimented her dress, and she complimented the cannoli I'd just bought.

Our second meeting was likely to be just as tiresome once the fake compliments started flowing, so I kept my mouth shut and let Adam do the talking. "I really appreciate this, Whit," he said, kissing both her cheeks.

"No problem. Just make sure you leave these at reception," she replied, dropping a small bunch of keys into his palm.

I was keen to know what was going on, and was pretty sure I looked odd because of it. Luckily, Bridget stole Whitney's attention away from my puzzled expression. "Hi, girl," she beamed. "I'm going swimming."

Whitney smiled down at her. "That's lovely."

"A lovely adventure at night time," Bridget elaborated.

I pulled her back toward me. "How are you, Whitney?" I asked politely.

"Fine, thank you." I couldn't find any hint of strain in her smile.

The scandalous crime of stealing her boyfriend seemed to have reduced to a misdemeanour over time, but we were never going to be friends. Whitney clearly felt the same way. She didn't try making small talk. After giving Adam a few instructions that I couldn't quite catch, she left.

***

After checking in and declining the offer of being escorted to our room, we made our way over to the elevator.

Adam's plan for the evening must've been a good one. I studied him closely in the black reflective door as we took the ride to the twelfth floor. He looked too smug for a man who claimed to be winging it.

I opened the brochure I'd picked up at the reception desk. "It says they have no pool, Adam."

"No pool?" asked Bridget, yanking on his shirt.

Adam hitched her higher on his hip. "Really?" His surprised tone wasn't the least bit believable. "Maybe it's a secret pool."

Bridget turned her head, granting me the widest dimpled grin her little face could make. "I just love secret pools." She'd tried to whisper but excitement got the better of her. "There might be magic in it."

No matter how big the dramas in our life became, we could always whittle our world back down to being no bigger than the three of us. That in itself was a piece of pure magic.

The door slid open. Adam carried our overnight bag and our kid. I carried nothing more than the hotel brochure and the card to get us into the room.

Before I even opened the door I knew it would be grand. What I wasn't expecting was a massive two-bedroom suite. As soon as Adam lowered Bridget to her feet, she made a beeline for the bed. I didn't scold her for bouncing. I was too preoccupied with checking out the view of Times Square from the window.

Adam unzipped the bag he'd packed and unceremoniously dumped everything onto the bed. Our kid was now dodging toothbrushes, underwear and Treasure, but still bouncing. He slowed her down by demanding that she put her swimsuit on. Mine was draped over my shoulder a few seconds later with the same order.

"I thought I'd swim naked," I teased, turning back to face him.

His dimpled smile was wide. "I won't stop you."

***

The cloak-and-dagger performance that Adam put on as we made our way to the ground floor was a perfect reminder that there wasn't anything he wouldn't do for us. I could practically hear Bridget's heart thumping as he held her back and pretended to check around doorways. "The coast is clear," he announced. "Just play it cool, baby."

"I'm cool," replied Bridget in a loud whisper. "So is Treasure."

I lagged behind, mainly so she wouldn't hear me giggle. When I caught up to them, they were standing at the entrance to the hotel spa.

"We're going in here?" I asked, peering through the blackened window of the door.

"The most secret pool in New York," Adam proclaimed, putting his finger to his lips. "Nobody knows it's here."

According to the small plaque mounted on the wall beside the door, everybody knew it was there between the hours of nine and six – when it was open for business.

"We have secret keys to get in," he continued, jingling them in front of his wide-eyed daughter.

"Whitney works here?" I murmured.

He shook his head but kept jingling the keys. "Owns it," he corrected. "Three of them, I think."

Letting us gatecrash after hours was a remarkable gesture, all things considered. Whitney Vaughn didn't trust me as far as she could throw me, but her respect for Adam ran deep.

"Can we go in now?" asked Bridget, bouncing on the spot. Treasure bounced too, at painful-looking angles as her head flopped around.

Before he could answer, an elderly couple rounded the corner and began making their way up the corridor.

Adam straightened up and Bridget followed suit as if it was the most important mission of her life. Her little body was so rigid that her shoulders almost touched her ears. "Play it cool, Daddy," she whispered.

It took an eternity for the couple to reach us, and when they finally did, Adam nodded his head and said good evening.

As anticlimactic as it was, Bridget waited until they passed and let out a hugely exaggerated sigh of relief. "That was close," she said seriously.

"Too close," agreed Adam, winking at me. "Let's hurry up and get inside."

***

The spa was in darkness, and judging by the way Adam went about fixing that problem, the parting instructions Whitney gave him were all lighting related. After working the necessary switches, he led us past the small reception area and down a short corridor. There was a salon to our left and a few private rooms on the right. I paid little attention to them. My focus was on the enchanted child in her rock star father's arms.

When we reached the door at the end, Adam lowered Bridget to the floor and told her to wait. "I need to make sure the coast is clear. If anyone comes, whistle."

Bridget nodded wildly and grabbed my hand. "I will," she promised, clutching Treasure tighter.

Adam disappeared. Bridget stepped so close to me that one of her feet was on mine. "Mummy," she murmured. "I don't know how to whistle."

"No worries, Bridge," I replied, trying not to laugh. "I do."

***

The few minutes of waiting while Adam set the scene were well worth it. When the door opened, he ushered us through to a setting I didn't even imagine existed in Manhattan.

The pool area was modern, but Roman in design. Faux limestone columns lined the long narrow pool and old-fashioned coach lights were expertly dimmed to set the scene. The brightest light in the room came from the bluer than blue water.

Bridget dumped Treasure on a chair and made a beeline for it. "I just love it in here." Her tiny voice carried, thanks to the acoustics of the room.

"We should stay a while then," replied her father from the other side of the pool.

I looked across at him. Every now and then I'd catch a glimpse of the Adam who'd lived on the beach. That bloke was free and never stressed. New York Adam was nothing like that man. He was constantly tired and battling hard to keep everyone happy. I wondered if he knew he was doing a stellar job.

"You make me happy," I called impulsively.

Adam threw his arms wide. "Then I have the whole world," he beamed.

42. PLAYING IT COOL

Adam

Bridget was a competent swimmer by the age of two, and the skill of being a fish isn't one that diminishes after time on dry land. She jumped into the water and flapped around as if she was drowning. Neither of us moved to save her because we knew differently.

My attention was only half reserved for the girl-fish. The other half was for her mother, the original girl-fish. As soon as Charli swam within reach, I grabbed her, pulling her close. The water was cool, but her back felt warm against me. "You're beautiful," I murmured against her neck.

"Thank you." I could hear the smile in her voice. "So are you."

I pushed off the edge of the pool with my foot, propelling us closer to Bridget. "Not such a bad night after all," I told her.

Charli twisted to look at me. "It's perfect," she replied. "I'm glad you thought of it."

"It was Bridge's idea."

"Not really." She lightly kissed me. "You brought the magic tonight."

Charli had magic running through her veins. She was brilliant storyteller with an imagination to match. My thoughts turned to Bridget's compass. I'd given it to her, but the magic she associated with it had come from her own mind. She'd been putting Ryan through the wringer for weeks looking for his so-called secret place. He hung in there with her because he was hopeful she'd find it. If it had the power to make a believer out of him, anything was possible. Bringing Bridget to a deserted swimming pool late at night was mysterious and sneaky and fun, but the magic had again come from her. It's fair to say that the bright blue water wasn't caused by an infusion of butterfly juice, but that was her take on it.

I was sure my mind had never been that free, and I told Charli so.

"Of course it was," she insisted. "You just don't remember it any more."

"You think so?"

Her brown eyes lit up – a telltale sign that I was going to enjoy her answer. "On these magic shores children are forever beaching their coracles," she recited. "We too have been there; we can still hear the sound of the surf, though we shall land no more."

"Charlotte," I moaned. "You know all the pretty words."

Her laugh touched my lips, which threatened the possibility of a total loss of control. Perhaps sensing the line of decency was blurring, she held me back. "You think *Peter Pan* is pretty?" she teased.

"I think you're pretty," I clarified, making her smile.

I pulled my arms through the water, putting me in a better position to see Bridget, who was up the other end chatting with the princess fish she was diving for.

"What are princess fish anyway?" I asked.

"I'm not exactly sure."

"Do you think they're any relation to sea dogs?"

"Totally different, Adam," she laughed. "Don't you know anything?"

"No," I replied, focusing on her mouth. "I land there no more."

Charli wrapped her legs around my waist, which was more dangerous than the pout she gave me. "I still land there."

"I know. It's who you are." Reminding her of it felt like the biggest coup of the evening.

I had no idea what had gone on that morning at Bridget's dance class, but it didn't take a genius to work out that Olivia had upset her again. The war that raged within Charli wasn't complex. She didn't like the woman, and was struggling with the notion of being her daughter. But no matter how hard Olivia tried, she would never overcome the fact that Charli was a hundred per cent Blake.

"I know who I am, Adam," she said quietly. "How about you? Any idea who you are?"

My hands settled on her hips. "I know who I am."

"You should be him, then," she whispered, "and stop pretending to be a hard-arse lawyer."

I might've agreed if I'd had a chance. A squeal from the other end of the pool put a stop to the conversation. "Treasure can't swim!" yelled Bridget.

It was worse than that. Treasure couldn't even float. Bridget stood at the edge of the pool, pointing into the water. "Get her, Daddy. Quick!"

I had no choice but to save the thing on the bottom of the pool. I dragged the waterlogged doll up and dumped it on the edge. "Is she dead?" asked Bridget.

I had no freaking clue. I looked back at Charli for an answer, which was pointless. She shrugged.

I was contemplating calling the time of death and sending Bridget flowers when out of the blue, she picked Treasure up and gave her a shake. "Oh, she's not dead," she said casually. "She's just playing it cool."

"Well, that's a relief," I muttered.

Charli could barely speak for laughing. "I think we need to go now," she suggested. "Dad can't handle any more drama and I can't carry him if he passes out."

***

My plans for a quiet night differed a little from Bridget's. There was a reason I booked a two-room suite, and it wasn't so Treasure could have her own bed.

The king size bed swallowed Bridget whole, but that's where she ended up, settled between the two of us as if that's where she belonged.

Conversation was nonsensical, and got worse as she grew tireder. Charli was spared most of it. Bridget jabbered in French until her words ran out and she finally fell asleep.

I wasn't in any hurry to move her. She did belong there, no matter how much I pretended to be inconvenienced by it. "Tonight was good," I said quietly. "We should do it more often."

Laying her arm across Bridget, Charli reached for me. "Imagine what it'll be like with two kids." She smiled. "We'll need a bigger bed."

"I'll build us a bigger bed," I pledged.

"Excellent." She giggled. "That's what you do."

Time alone with Charli and Bridget never failed to remind me that no matter what was going on around us, we were okay. Our plans still stood. We were going to get over the bumps in the road caused by family, location and work, and make more babies.

"I'm sorry I beat you up today," Charli said randomly. "I shouldn't have done that."

I reached across Bridget, catching them both in my hold as I rested my hand on Charli's hip. "Beat me up?" I asked, smiling. "A slight embellishment."

"Mmm. Perhaps."

"You'll need lessons from Bente if you want to learn how to cause real damage," I teased. "Bagels are where the action is."

Her quiet laugh wrapped around me. "Ryan has his work cut out then, huh?"

"And I haven't?" I moved my hand, trailing my fingers across her body. "You're a complete and utter nightmare to deal with."

"Like Olivia," she said.

The mention of her name was like fingernails down a blackboard. It irked me that she'd crept into an otherwise perfect conversation.

"Nothing like her."

She laced her fingers through mine. "You said I was looking for the good in her," she mumbled. "I can't find any, and yet I keep trying. Why do you suppose that is?"

I didn't have an answer. As far as I was concerned, the better option would've been to cut her loose and forget they'd ever met.

"My dad's no picnic either, Charlotte."

The hardest line my father ever took paled in comparison to Olivia's poison, but it was the best I could come up with.

"You keep going back for more too."

"Because he's my father."

Charli stared across at me for an eternity. Even when Bridget stirred, she didn't break eye contact. She just gently patted her back and continued her thoughtful stare. "You're still trying to please him," she said finally. "That's why you're sticking your job out."

"We're not talking about me."

"But I'm right, aren't I?"

It was a hard truth to admit to. I was a grown man with a family of my own, but the pull of conforming and making my father proud was still there.

"It's probably part of it, Charli," I conceded.

She placed her hand on my cheek. "You're good, Adam," she whispered. "And he is proud."

I turned my head and kissed her palm. "This thing with Olivia – it's not the same. You owe her nothing."

"I feel like I owe her the opportunity to know me."

I couldn't grasp why. She'd brought nothing but trouble, and hadn't shown Charli an ounce of anything other than drama and fakery.

"Everything happens for a reason," she added. "There are eight million people in this city, and we found each other. It might be magic."

"It's not magic. You were never lost, Charlotte," I told her, rolling to stare at the ceiling. "She could've made contact at any time."

"She keeps telling me how it broke her heart to give me up and that she's never gotten over it," she replied. "Maybe she thought I'd reject her."

"Then why does she treat you the way she does?" I turned back to her. "Conning you into buying her designer bags and being a bitch aren't the acts of someone who's trying to win you over."

I never intended to upset her. I couldn't even move to comfort her when she began to cry. Our kid was between us, sleeping like the dead.

"Don't move, okay?" I didn't wait for an answer. I got out of bed, picked Bridget up and carried her to the room next door. The only movement came from Treasure who thudded against the floor when I dumped her out of bed. Bridget didn't stir. I swept her hair off her face, covered her and slipped out of the room.

Charli's position hadn't changed. I climbed back into bed and wrapped my arms around her. It was the best way I knew to comfort her. Words weren't working out so well.

"When I was fifteen, I had a hundred and four things on my never-done list," she said randomly.

"How many do you have now?"

"Ninety-one."

I'd first learned of Charli's never-done list just days after meeting her. It was probably my first hint that I'd stumbled across a girl who saw the world differently from most – the first of a million things that made her special.

"You're on target then?"

Her body moved against mine as she laughed. It wasn't a complete triumph; I could feel her tears against my chest. My hand moved to her back, drawing invisible circles on her skin while I waited for her to speak again.

"She's not on my list, Adam." Her whisper was barely audible, but the meaning behind them was loud and clear. "I have a list of ninety-one things that I've never done. Meeting my mother didn't rate highly enough for me to want to strike it off. I feel guilty about that."

Of all the emotions that could've come with being reunited with her mother, guilt should not have been one of them.

"It's not a reason to keep her around," I told her. "Having her in your life is not supposed to make you unhappy. Being your mother is not a licence for her to hurt you."

"Why do you think she keeps hurting me?" she asked quietly.

I sighed. "Don't ask me, Charli. Ask yourself why you keep letting her."

She lifted her head, resting her chin on my chest. Her gorgeous face was stained with tears but she was calm. "She might come good," she said hopefully.

"Why are you so willing to give her the chance?"

After a long pause, she finally replied. "Because you used to hurt my heart all the time. Imagine if I hadn't given you the chance to change your ways."

It didn't bear thinking about. Her willingness to forgive me time and time again was the sole reason I led the charmed life I was living. I'd done my fair share of lying and manipulating to get what I wanted, but the difference between Olivia and I was clear. All I ever wanted was Charlotte. Olivia didn't want her when she was born, and nothing convinced me that anything had changed.

43. TEN MORE BRIDGETS

Charli

One night of dealing with nothing but the chaos we created ourselves was all it took to bring our little universe back into alignment.

Predictably, Adam never made good on his threat of taking the next day off work, but he wasn't in any hurry to get there on time. We ordered room service for breakfast, packed up our still-wet swimming gear and checked out a little after nine.

It was business as usual. Adam left for the office, Mrs Brown arrived to watch Bridget, and I headed to the gallery.

We'd had such a good night that I was determined not to let anything darken my mood. Even Bronson's disappearing act the second I walked in the door didn't faze me.

"Things to do, my darling," he called, brushing past me at the door.

"Have a nice day, Bronson."

"Bound to," he replied. "The sun is shining and I look fabulous."

I wasn't going to argue. Any man brave enough to wear a pastel print smock and cheesecloth pants deserved the title of fabulous.

***

In an unusual move, I closed the gallery for an hour while I took a lunch break. I wasn't feeling particularly good about the way Fiona's dinner party had been cut short the night before, so in an attempt to make amends, I decided to take the short walk across to Fifth Avenue and pay her a visit.

Fiona made us lunch, which was an inadvertently hostile act. There was no way I could bluff my way through eating one round of cucumber sandwiches, let alone the four she placed in front of me.

"I'm sorry about last night," I began. "Things got a little heated."

Her smile was tiny. "We're not a perfect family, are we?" she asked quietly. "Poor Bente must think she's marrying into a pack of wild animals."

I pursed my lips and dropped my head as thoughts turned to Malibu and Fabergé. Anything the Décaries dished out was amateur compared to the Denison family dynamics.

Fiona leaned across the table, resting her hand on top of mine. "Is something troubling Adam, darling?" she asked gently. "He's not usually so confrontational."

Her obliviousness had always been a major gripe of mine. Fiona saw only what she wanted to, and then had the audacity to claim she was kept in the dark.

"Adam doesn't like the way Jean-Luc speaks to me," I said bluntly. "He can be very rude."

She smiled, but had trouble looking at me. "Jean-Luc is very fond of you, Charli."

For reasons I'd never been able to explain, even to myself, I was fond of him too. But I wasn't about to admit it to her. "You asked me why Adam was upset," I said. "That's why he was upset."

The queen slid the plate of sandwiches closer to me. "Is everything else alright?"

For a quick moment I contemplated telling her the extraordinary news that I'd reconnected with my mother. Then I remembered that there wasn't anything positive to say about it. "Everything is fine," I said. "We're very busy, but that's nothing new."

"I wish you'd share more of your lives with me. The most information I get these days is from my granddaughter."

I picked up a quarter of a sandwich and took a tiny bite, buying some time while I thought of something to tell her. "I've been meaning to ask you a favour actually," I said finally.

Her reply came at warp speed. "Anything, darling."

"Do you know Olivia Kara?" The question was redundant but necessary.

Clearly disappointed by my question, Fiona's shoulders slumped. "We've attended a few of the same charity events in the past."

"She's hosting one of her own in a few weeks," I explained. "I was hoping you'd rally your troops and support her cause."

She laughed humourlessly. "I have no troops, darling. That implies khaki slacks and war paint. I only know one woman who dresses like that."

"Who?" I asked.

"Regina Barclay." She returned my sly smile with one of her own. "Wretch of a woman. Last time she was here she stole the soaps from the downstairs bathroom."

We both burst into giggles, and it was a long time before we returned to the subject of Olivia's charity event.

"It's a luncheon, I think," I said vaguely.

"Are you helping her?" Fiona frowned as she asked the question. I prayed that was because she was appalled, not suspicious.

"No," I replied. "She's Bridget's ballet teacher, that's all. I'd just like to support her."

After the way Olivia had treated Bridget the day before, I shouldn't have even entertained the idea of helping her. Perhaps I was trying to prove a point. I was true to my word. I was good and honourable and giving – all the qualities that my mother seemed to lack.

After a long moment of deliberation, Fiona smiled. "I shall rally my troops," she announced. "If it's important to you, I'll support it."

I leaned across and hugged her. "Thank you."

Fiona leaned back, picking at my hair like a mother hen. "Of course, darling. You look precious today," she said. "Relaxed and happy."

I picked up a sandwich I didn't want. "I am happy. We had a wonderful night once we left here. Adam took us swimming."

When she asked for details, I told her everything except Treasure's unfortunate accident. "Bridget thought we'd snuck in," I explained. "She was running on pure adrenaline."

Even her soft laugh sounded English. "Bless her little heart. I wish we had ten more just like her."

"Ten more Bridgets?" That was a concept and a half.

"I always found it terribly sad being an only child," she said seriously. "I don't want that for her."

Given the queen's tendency to overreact, I rarely gave her information willingly. News that we were trying for a baby would probably result in cringeworthy advice and premature shopping sprees, but I was in a giving mood. "It's just an idea at this stage," I stressed. "So please keep it to yourself."

The woman was in danger of combusting. She flapped her hands in front of her face to stop the threat of tears. "Oh, Charli," she cooed. "A New York baby would be wonderful."

I felt tremendous guilt that the Décaries had missed so much time with Bridget while she was little, but I just couldn't commit to raising the new baby in New York. "We'll see what happens," I said vaguely. "I'm not even pregnant yet."

She patted my hand. "It means the world that you told me."

The queen thought I'd told her a secret, but if word got out I wouldn't blame her. Ryan had cornered me to tease me about it the night before, which meant Adam's mouth was bigger than mine.

After consuming more cucumber sandwiches than I ever hoped to see again, I headed back to work feeling infinitely better.

Fiona wasn't a complicated woman. She lived for her family, wanting nothing more than to see her boys settled and happy. She'd been worried about Adam when I arrived. My good news story put her completely at ease. For once, I was the bearer of joy instead of drama.

44. STRANGE AND ANTISOCIAL

Adam

Charli's decision not to attend Bridget's next dance lesson wasn't entirely her own. From what I could gather from Junior, her Mom wasn't invited.

"Just us, Daddy," she pleaded. "Okay?"

The kid was crafty. Her favourite MO when pinning me down with tricky conversations was to wait until I was in the shower. I ran my hand over the glass, clearing a patch on the screen. Bridget was sitting on her little pink footstool patiently awaiting my answer.

"When is it on?"

I was merely buying time. I knew the twelve o'clock lesson time was a standing arrangement.

"Sixty o'clock," she replied immediately.

"I'll think about it, okay?"

"Okay."

The lull in conversation lasted all of ten seconds.

"Did you think about it, Daddy?"

One day my daughter was going to come to me with something so outrageous that I'd have to shut her down purely to save her from herself. But today wasn't that day. She wasn't asking to go clubbing. She wanted me to take her to a ballet lesson during my lunch hour. It was a no-brainer.

"Yes, Bridge," I replied. "I'll take you."

***

Thanks to my decision not to ask for the details of the last run-in with the ballerina, I had no idea what I'd signed on for. Charli's parting instruction was to keep a close eye on Bridget.

"Don't let Olivia single her out," she warned. "And don't make her take her boots off."

Madame Kara wasn't in a position to be making any sort of demands. If she dared to create drama, I was prepared to bring a little of my own to the party. I had no qualms about sharing what I knew with her if the opportunity arose.

Despite her mother's reservations, Bridget had no problem ditching her boots in favour of the ballet slippers Charli had packed into her backpack. It was the strangest turnaround I'd ever seen the kid make.

"These are the shoes for dancing," Bridget explained knowingly. I offered to help her put them on but she wouldn't let me near them. "No, I can do it," she replied, shuffling along the floor in case I made a grab for her.

Olivia's class was much smaller than Ella's, and much better behaved. The atmosphere was calm and controlled, which did remarkable things to Bridget. I stood near the doorway and observed my usually scattered girl paying absolute attention to her teacher. When she wasn't doing that, she was watching and copying the other girls.

Olivia noticed too and praised her. "Wonderful, Bridget."

She'd singled her out, but not in the way Charli was worried about. I couldn't deny that it felt good, but I didn't entirely trust it.

As the other girls filed out at the end of class, Olivia approached. Bridget was sitting on the floor taking her shoes off.

"I have a present for you," said Olivia, crouching down beside her. Whatever it was was hidden behind her back.

"I just love presents," beamed Bridget.

Olivia brought her hand to her front, presenting her with a pair of little satin ballet slippers. "They're much better than the ones you have," she explained. "Kinder to your feet." She looked up at me. "They're softer. She's not used to wearing them so they'll help her adjust."

Bridget didn't give a damn about comfort. The thing she was most impressed by was the colour. "They're purple!" she announced, excitedly waving them at me. "Not pink ones."

In a fluid move only a dancer could make, Olivia stood. "I thought it might be nice to retain a little individuality. I know it's important to her mother."

"Thank you." The smile I gave her felt completely false. "It's appreciated."

That was the moment she struck – with the unerring accuracy of a cobra. I didn't even see it coming, and I certainly wasn't expecting it to be aimed at Charli.

"Bridget performs much better when her mother isn't here, Adam," she declared. "Charli holds her back."

It might not have angered me as much if she'd said it in private, but Bridget was hanging on every word, which I suspect was her intention. "We can talk about this later." My voice was quiet but forceful. "Now isn't the time." I quickly helped Bridget pull on her boots. Her slippers were roughly shoved into her backpack and I grabbed her hand.

Olivia continued as if I hadn't spoken. "Charli should be encouraging Bridget to be independent, not strange and antisocial."

"Let's go, baby," I told my daughter.

I had a hundred things to say, and couldn't mention a single one. The presence of Bridget forced me to keep my mouth shut – at least for the time being.

We were halfway across the room when Olivia delivered her final blow. I ignored her when she called to Bridget, keeping a firm hold on her hand as we walked toward the door, but Bridget turned her head at the sound of her name.

"Don't do anything silly – like leave my class." Olivia's voice was sickly sweet. "It would be a terrible shame if you missed out on wearing one of those pretty costumes at the concert."

Pushed by pure loathing, I dropped my hold on Bridget's hand and took a few steps back toward Olivia. "What is your game, lady?"

"Teaching ballet." She raised an eyebrow.

"Because those who can't do, teach, right?"

It was as close as I could come to mentioning her phony credentials without inciting war, but it wasn't enough to rattle her.

"You pay me to teach."

"An oversight on my part," I replied. "I'd pay you to go away now. It might be cheaper in the long run."

"I'll go when I'm ready, Adam." The only thing colder than her words was her expression.

There was no way of censoring what I wanted to say. I walked back to Bridget, grabbed her hand and got the hell out of there.

***

I could only assume that Bridget knew her ballet career was over. As soon as we got outside, she burst into tears. I scooped her up but didn't slow my walk, determined to put distance between us and the bitch ballerina.

"Don't cry, Bridge." I kissed the top of her head. "We're done. You're not going back there."

"No!" she wailed, clinging to my shirt. "Please let me go some more. I want to go to the concert," she said desperately. "Please Daddy."

Bridget was completely distraught for all the wrong reasons. She didn't have a clue that Olivia was toying with us. All she was worried about was that I wasn't going to let her go back to class. I could barely think straight, so I didn't give her an answer. I told her we'd work it out later, which was encouraging enough to calm her down.

Nothing was going to calm me down. I had no idea how we were supposed to handle things from there. All I knew for certain was that Olivia was rotten to the core, and one way or another I was going to shut her down.

***

Bridget was a different kid when I arrived home that night. She was happy, calm and pleased to see me. Her mother was pleased to see me too. That could only mean that Bridget hadn't told her about the drama that went down at ballet.

We had dinner together, which had become a rare treat lately. Bridget told us all about her afternoon with Ryan, and Charli shared the news that she'd had lunch with my mother.

"Cucumber sandwiches." She pulled a face, making Bridget giggle.

"Mamie is not a good cook," said Bridget waving her fork in the air. "I just hate it all."

It wasn't exactly riveting conversation, but it was light and happy – right up until Charli asked her about ballet. Our kid looked across at me, paused for thought and then burst into tears again. It was a dizzying shift, and a reminder of what an ordeal the whole saga was for her.

Charli wrapped her up in a hug. "What's the matter?"

Bridget's answer wasn't exactly detailed. In a staccato rasp, she begged Charli to let her go back to ballet classes. "I want to go to the concert," she pleaded.

Charlotte glared at me.

"Don't look at me." I put both hands in the air. "It's your call."

"What happened?" she asked.

Everything hinged on my answer. I could either tell the truth or lie, and neither option was particularly appealing. The devastated look on my daughter's face tipped the scale in favour of lying.

"Nothing," I muttered unwillingly. "It went well. Olivia was full of praise for Bridget."

Charli loosened her hold on Bridget to look at her. "She was?"

"And she gave me some purple shoes," said Bridget, pulling in a few shallow breaths between words. "I really love them."

Charli swept her hair off her forehead. "You like Olivia's class, don't you?"

Bridget nodded. "Yes I do."

When Charli looked across at me, I could almost read her thoughts – possibly because they matched my own. As long as Bridget had her heart set on attending the wicked witchs classes, we were stuck.

45. NIPPY CHIHUAHUAS

Charli

I managed not to ask another Olivia-related question until we went to bed, and the speed with which Adam answered me led me to think he'd been using the three hours since dinner to prepare for it.

"I don't like her, Charli," he grumbled, throwing back the covers on his side. "I'm sorry. I think she's nasty and I don't want anything to do with her."

I didn't ask why because I was afraid of the answer. If his ballet experience had been anything like mine, his reasons were more than valid.

As soon as he lay down, I laid my head on his shoulder. "You told Bridget she wasn't going back, didn't you?" I asked bleakly. "That's why she's freaking out."

"Yes. She didn't take it well."

"I told her the same thing the other day," I replied. "That's why she wanted you to take her."

His arm curled around me. "So what do we do about it?"

I didn't think we had a choice. For reasons I'd probably never understand, Bridget loved Olivia's class. Neither of us would be forgiven if we pulled the pin.

"I think we have to let her stay." The words were so impossibly hard to say. "What do you think?"

His hold on me tightened. "I think it's time that I had a little chat with your mother."

As loaded as his words were, I couldn't deny that I felt an element of relief. I couldn't handle Olivia on my best day. There was a cutting side to her personality that was far beyond the scope of anything I could deal with, but I still felt like I needed to try. If Adam could get through to her, maybe she'd change her ways.

I wasn't ready to give up on her. She was my mother – a woman who was once so loved by Alex that he made a baby with her. I had to believe it counted for something.

***

We put a quick end to Bridget's panic the next morning. Over cereal and toast, Adam assured her that we wouldn't pull her from Olivia's class.

"I'll come with you," he promised.

"Every day?" she asked hopefully.

"Three days a week." He managed to reply without grimacing. "Mrs Brown will drop you at my office, we'll go to ballet, and Ryan will pick you up from my office. Okay?"

The nervous tension she'd been plagued by disappeared in an instant. "Yes!" she squealed. "I love that deal."

"Good." Adam kissed the top of her head. "Because we love you and we want you to be happy."

It was a plan we hadn't discussed, and it was far more one-sided than I expected. He barely got a lunchbreak most days. Committing to three days a week of ballet was ludicrous. "I can take her," I offered.

Adam stood up and carried his bowl to the sink. "No," he replied. "I've got this."

My propensity for overlooking Olivia's bad behaviour wasn't something Adam understood, but he never interfered. Such a lax approach was never going to apply to Bridget. The only way he was ever going to be able to deal with her being in Olivia's class was if he was there to keep an eye on her.

He knew it and I knew it. We didn't need to talk about it.

***

When it came to juggling my hectic schedule, spending time at Billet-doux was on the bottom of my list. According to Ryan, the longer I stayed away, the better business partner I became.

Noelle, the front of house manager, also preferred it when I wasn't there. "You shouldn't be in Ryan's office when he's not around," she scolded.

I didn't even slow my walk. "It's my office too, Noelle."

Like a snippy little Chihuahua, she chased me. "Why are you even here?"

I stopped walking and turned around. Noelle skidded to a stop. "Performance appraisals," I lied. "How'd you do this month?"

Her expression was strange, as if she'd managed to take offense and panic at the same time. "I work super hard all the time," she snapped in her trademark high pitched voice. "Always."

Noelle took her job very seriously. She also took Ryan very seriously, but nippy Chihuahuas had never been his type. She was an exemplary employee and Ryan paid her accordingly – just not in the way she wanted him to.

"Then you have nothing to worry about," I said, opening the office door.

"Ryan will be here any minute," she warned.

"Fabulous." I inched the door shut. "When he gets here, show him to my office."

"It's Ryan's office," she squeaked through the door.

***

Ryan's office was nothing like Adam's. Adam's was like a fancy hotel room with a glorious cityscape view. Everything was perfectly co-ordinated and chic to match the job description of a hard-arse lawyer.

Ryan's office was more like a dungeon. His desk was covered with junk and the drawers of the old filing cabinet were rusted shut. The one and only time I'd ever seen a hint of nostalgia from the man was when I suggested that we get rid of it. "It came with the building," he protested. "Imagine the stories that thing could tell."

Despite the mayhem caused by the overload of paperwork, he knew where every single thing was. Ryan could always tell when I'd been in there, so Noelle's threat of telling him was a waste of time.

I'd only been at the desk for a few minutes when the door flew open. "Good morning, fairy pants," he drawled. "Get off my chair."

"Good morning Ryan," I replied. "It's my chair too."

Perhaps he knew I wasn't going to move. He sat on the other chair. "I have stuff to do."

"Do you really?" I asked sceptically.

"No," he confessed. "I'm just hiding from Noelle until it's time to pick Bridget up." His expression remained completely stone-faced. "How about you?"

I shrugged. "Well, I'm supposed to be at work but Bronson told me to get out and enjoy the sunshine."

Ryan looked confused. "Why?"

I could feel the smile creeping across my face. "Because winter is coming."

He shook his head as if trying to dislodge the illogical workings of my boss's mind. It was a pointless exercise. Not even I could work Bronson out. "So we're both free for a few hours?"

"I told him I'd go back to the gallery at twelve." I glanced at the time on the computer screen. "When my vitamin D levels were acceptable."

Ryan chuckled blackly. "Maybe you could spend the morning with me."

My eyes darted around the dungeon. "Here?" I inquired. "We'd kill each other."

"Not here," he replied. "I've got to go and buy a suit."

"Why? The six hundred you already have aren't obnoxious enough?"

"A suit to get married in," he clarified. "I'd like your opinion."

Never before had Ryan sought my opinion on anything. "Really?" I sounded far too excited. "You want my advice?"

He flashed me his usual superior smile. "No, Tinker Bell. You can just stand there and tell me how good I look."

46. CLEARING THE AIR

Adam

My day started off perfectly. I got out of the cab a few blocks early, grabbed coffee along the way and still made it to work on time. Then I stepped out of the elevator on the forty-third floor and everything went to hell.

Olivia was sitting in the reception area, presumably waiting for me.

"I told her to make an appointment," whispered Tennille as I passed the reception desk.

Olivia swanned toward me with poise. "I told her you'd make an exception."

Coffee in hand, I pointed toward my office. "I make a lot of exceptions for you, Olivia."

The woman sauntered down the corridor as if she knew where she was going. I turned to Tennille. "Can you hold my calls please?"

She looked as if she'd just tasted something sour. "If you're not out in an hour, I'll presume she's beaten you up and left you for dead."

I couldn't help grinning at her. "Pleasant, huh?"

Her long nails began tapping away at her keyboard. "I've dealt with worse," she muttered.

I took my time walking to my office, realising the only joy I was going to have that morning was leaving Olivia standing without purpose in the corridor while I leisurely finished my coffee.

The passive aggressive approach was wasted on her. She only responded to aggressive. "This had better be quick," I told her, opening my door and ushering her through. "Some of us have real jobs."

Olivia walked to the window. When she set her red purse on the couch, I wondered if it was the one I'd paid for.

"I think it's time you and I cleared the air," she said.

I sat and opened my laptop. "What do you want, Olivia?" I asked. "That's all I need to know."

It was all I'd wanted to know from the very beginning.

She slowly turned to face me, frowning. "I don't want anything. That's the point."

I was sick and tired of playing games. I told her to clarify her statement or get out.

"You started this, Adam." She folded her arms. "If I'd wanted Charli in my life, don't you think I would've done something about it years ago?"

I swallowed hard, trying to quell the disgust rising in my throat. "So why didn't you just leave it alone?"

She shrugged. "I realised that she's useful to me."

"How?"

The smile that crossed her face was ice cold. "She's a Décarie now."

47. PECAN PIE

Charli

Ryan was my kind of shopper. He didn't dally. We grabbed a cab, headed to his favourite tailor and began the short but particular task of choosing a suit.

"What colour?" he asked me, wandering around the small exclusive store. "Charcoal or black?"

"White," I replied. "With wide lapels."

"If you're not going to take this seriously, you're of no use to me."

"Ryan, you're not going to pay any attention to my opinion anyway," I said pointedly. "Just pick whatever you like."

"You're absolutely right." He began eyeing off the small number of suits on display. "Sit down and be quiet while I choose."

I'd been to some upmarket stores in my time, but none that served tea and cake. I sat in a small lounge area while a man with a tape measure around his neck and a mouthful of pins fussed with Ryan's pant leg.

"We should come back here again, Ryan," I teased. "Free snacks."

He glanced at me. "You can take the girl out of the boondocks...."

"I like the boondocks." Being in snooty boutiques that served morning tea reminded me of just how much.

"You're going back, aren't you?" he asked seriously. "To the Cove."

"Why do you ask?"

"Because you all belong there," he said simply. "I'm surprised you've stuck it out here as long as you have."

245

Jean-Luc referred to my job as an art adventure. Truthfully, our whole existence in New York was an adventure. Adam got to test the waters of a career in law, Bridget got to experience life in a big city, and I found my feet with a career I loved – and then completely lost my footing by stumbling upon my mother. Home was starting to call to me, and thoughts of packing it in and jumping ship were growing stronger by the day.

"You'll miss us when we're gone," I teased.

His reply astounded me. "I will."

I took a sip of tea, purely as a distraction. I wasn't quite sure how to continue the conversation, or even if I wanted to. Taking Bridget away from Ryan was going to be impossibly hard on my heart. They were close, and both were going to feel the loss.

"I won't miss all of you," he added. "That repulsive doll your kid drags around needs to be put out of its misery."

I smiled. He'd dug us out of a serious conversation that I wasn't up to having. "Treasure's a delight," I insisted.

"Every time I see it, it's uglier," he returned. "First she drew on its face so it looked like an accident victim and now it's warped like its been firebombed." He twisted his arms and cocked his head, pulling off an awesome Treasure impersonation.

"She got a bit waterlogged," I explained. "She drowned in a pool."

The man pinning the cuff of Ryan's jacket whipped his head up.

"Oh, she's fine now," I said, waving a hand at him. "Nothing to worry about."

Ryan let out a dark laugh. "You're a fruitcake."

I set my cup down. "Will you miss me when I go home?"

"Like a hole in the head," he muttered.

"You'll be preoccupied anyway. A married man," I announced with reverence. "Imagine that."

He glanced at me again, grinning like a big kid. "She's amazing, Charli."

"Chocolate cake is always amazing."

"She's pecan pie," he corrected.

"Whatever floats your boat, Ryan."

"And not crazy," he proudly added. "Unlike my little brother, I found a normal girl. We're going to have normal children who play normally with normal dolls."

I was still giggling when some prospective customers walked in. The middle-aged pair seemed to object to laughing in public. The woman looked at me as if I was something she'd scraped off her shoe. The man nudged her to keep moving forward. Ryan stared at me through the mirror. When I rolled my eyes at him, he winked.

Some of the best mischief I'd ever undertaken involved Ryan. Adam didn't have wicked tendencies. He was good and law abiding; his brother, however, could be as crooked as a bent stick.

"Remember a few weeks ago when we stole that bloke's wallet?" I spoke as if it was the most casual question on earth.

The woman spun around so quickly the oversized string of pearls on her neck rattled.

"Yes." Ryan chuckled. "Good times."

"And that time we conned a hundred bucks out of that shady waitress?"

His laugh grew louder. "Of course."

From the corner of my eye, I saw the woman clutch her handbag a little tighter. Her husband seemed to be covertly surveying the exits. The only one who didn't look concerned was the tailor, who'd probably heard enough nonsense in the past half hour to last him a lifetime. He kept pinning away as if nothing out of the ordinary had been said.

"Those are the things I'll miss most about you when I'm gone."

His smile through the mirror was minuscule, but it was there.

"When are you leaving?" asked the tailor, speaking for the first time.

I couldn't answer. Nothing had been decided. Adam and I had barely discussed it. Ryan answered instead, with words designed purely to rattle the shoppers on my left.

"Her lawyer thinks it could be as early as next week," he loudly announced. "Not going to get off with probation this time around are you, princess?"

The woman gasped, which was all the encouragement Ryan needed to continue. "A long stretch," he drawled, putting the weirdest spin on his accent I'd ever heard. "At least I've got a nice suit to wear to court. Wait 'til the judge sees. He's bound to go easy." He brushed his shoulder as if dusting it off. The tailor tapped his leg, signalling for him to step off the podium. "Now we've just got to figure out how we're going to pay for it."

The appalled couple were hanging on every word. When Ryan slowly turned to face them, the man grabbed his wife by the elbow and rushed her out the door.

It was the tailor who spoke first. We were too busy laughing. "I think you just lost me a sale," he said dryly.

"I suspect you might be right," replied Ryan.

48. VULNERABILITY

Adam

Olivia wasn't big on small talk unless she was trying to win Charli and Bridget over before brutally turning on them. She sat on the chair opposite my desk and got down to business. Her posture was rigid and straight, just like her words. "Charli is hell-bent on making this work out. She has an idealistic view that we'll eventually build a relationship befitting a mother and daughter."

Unfortunately, she wasn't too far off the mark. Charli wasn't prepared to accept that running into her mother was nothing more than dumb luck. She was convinced there was an element of magic in it.

"It's never going to happen," I said bluntly. "You know nothing about being a mother."

"Nor do I have any desire to," she replied. "Playing happy families was never my forte."

"No one says you have to love her, Olivia," I snapped. "But you don't need to hurt her. What do you get out of doing that?"

The corner of her mouth lifted, and at that moment, I'd never felt more hatred for anyone in my life.

"I enjoy the game," she said simply. "She'll forgive anything I do because she's desperate to make it work. I've proven that."

After weeks of trying to figure it out, the big ugly picture was suddenly crystal clear. Olivia's games were nothing more than research – testing just how far she could push before Charli called it quits. Clearly she'd moved onto to phase two, safe in the knowledge that Charlotte was no quitter.

"I could drag this out indefinitely, you know," she threatened.

"Over my dead body," I told her. "This ends today."

"I was hoping you'd see it that way," she replied. "I have a proposition for you."

I leaned back in my chair and listened as she spelled out what she wanted. Not a word of it took me by surprise.

"You said you were prepared to pay me to go away," she reminded me. "I'm open to that idea."

Given her penchant for head games, I felt it necessary to ask for clarification. "Are you telling me that I could cut you a cheque right now and you'd walk away?"

She didn't pause. "Yes."

"And if I don't?"

Her shoulders lifted. "Then I'm going to enjoy getting to know my daughter, and the benefits associated with that."

The thought of Olivia being a permanent fixture in our lives made me feel sick. There was no way I'd subject Charli to that kind of damage.

"Life as a washed-up ballerina must be tough," I mused. "I guess you've got to do what you can to get ahead."

Her blue eyes flashed with anger, but she kept herself in check. "Don't pretend to know me, Adam."

"But I do know you." I grabbed her prospectus from my top drawer. "Remember this?"

The only hint that her demeanour was slipping was the way she wrung her hands in her lap. Her expression remained flat, even after I spent the next few minutes calling her out on her fake credentials.

"Not one thing is true," I concluded. "You started as a fraud, and you're still a fraud. I could expose you and you'd be finished." I dropped the folder down in front of her. Olivia didn't even look at it. Her glare was reserved entirely for me.

"You could," she agreed. "But in turn, I could finish you."

"My qualifications are good." I laughed. "They gave me a certificate and everything."

"Everything you think you have could disappear in a flash, Adam." Her monotone voice was completely void of any emotion. "Poor Charli's very vulnerable."

I wasn't the least bit intimidated. I knew what I had – I'd spent seven years building it. "Give it your best shot." I leaned forward and lowered my tone. "I dare you."

"I'm not talking about you, specifically. It's evident that the silly girl's more than content to live the life of a wealthy society wife."

That comment alone proved how little she knew Charli. It was almost heartening that she had her pegged so wrong.

Olivia stood up and stalked back to the window, staring at the view for a long time before speaking again. "I could never turn her against you." She glanced back at me. "Believe me, I tried."

Leading Charli to believe that I'd refused to let her make contact with her mother had been a hard blow to deflect, but we got through it because we were absolutely tight.

"You're not that powerful, Olivia," I said strongly. "And Charli's not the least bit vulnerable."

When she slowly turned to face me, I was hit with the sinking feeling that my upper hand was gone.

"She's very insecure when it comes to dealing with Bridget, isn't she?" she asked. "That's natural considering she had no mother of her own – no experience to draw on." I could think of a hundred ways of describing Olivia, but stupid wasn't one of them. Charli's confidence wasn't always high where Bridget was concerned, and she'd picked up on it. "Bridget doesn't enjoy being let down by her mother," she added. "It seems to happen a lot in my presence. Poor Charli doesn't do well when faced with parental challenges."

"You're twisted," I spat. "You need help."

"No, what I need is financial incentive to leave," she replied calmly. "If I don't get it, little Bridget's relationship with her mother might take a turn for the worse."

I didn't doubt for a second that she could do it. She'd already backed us into a corner where Bridget was concerned, which is why she was still attending her stupid dance studio.

"You were hoping Charli would pull her out of class, weren't you?" I asked.

Her laugh was as cold as the rest of her. "It would've broken Bridget's heart," she said. "And it would've all been Charli's fault."

I shook my head, trying to shake free of the bigger picture coming to mind. "This is about more than money," I realised. "You're going out of your way to hurt Charli. What did she do to you?"

Olivia turned back to the window. "Plenty," she said sourly. "I'll enjoy returning the favour."

My first inclination was to pay the hateful woman off and get her the hell out of our lives. My second was to dig a little deeper. "What could she possibly have taken from you?" I demanded. "You gave her up at birth and got on with your life. She never sought you out – neither did Alex."

She turned to face me again, looking far less smug than before. "Charli told me she has little to do with her father," she said curiously. "I don't believe her."

If that was the line Charli had gone with, I wasn't about to enlighten her.

"What do you care?"

She almost smiled. "I've always cared for Alex," she replied.

My mind kept rejecting the picture I was trying to build of the two of them together. It was impossible to imagine. Alex was the most decent person I'd ever known. Olivia was the most twisted.

"He chose Charli over you, didn't he?" I guessed. "You lost the lot because he fell in love with his daughter."

"Just write me the cheque, Adam," she instructed, sounding totally bored and disinterested. "And then we're done."

Perhaps I wasn't feeling charitable, or maybe I knew that no amount of money was going to stop her coming back for more. I walked to the door and held it open. "I'm not giving you a cent. We're done here."

Olivia picked up her bag. "I'm sorry you feel that way," she said.

"Just get out."

The smile she gave me as she passed was every shade of vile. As soon as she was clear of the door, I slammed it shut.

49. LULU

Charli

Ryan wasn't the only one being measured up for wedding attire that day. Bridget had an appointment with Ivy late that afternoon at their apartment, which meant Adam and I were free and easy for a few hours. I expected him to take advantage by suggesting a quiet few hours at home, but he had different plans.

He met me at the gallery at exactly five, which meant he'd skipped out of work hours earlier than he should have. If he was worried about being dragged over the coals for it, he wasn't letting on. "Ready to go?"

"I've just got to lock up first." I set the alarm, followed him outside and pulled the door shut. Turning the key in the door was a process that took too long for Adam. He ended up taking them from me and locking it himself.

"All done?" he asked, giving the handle a rattle.

My eyes narrowed with suspicion. "What's your hurry, Boy Wonder?"

"No hurry." He handed me the keys. "I'm just excited to have you to myself for a while."

"Where are we going?"

Adam led me toward the waiting cab. "A special place," he replied.

I didn't ask any more questions. I opted to spend the cab ride thinking about the possibilities instead. Adam seemed preoccupied too. His hand never left my knee, and his eyes never left the window. He finally turned to me and began fussing with the frill on the hem of my skirt. "This is pretty."

I smiled. "Thank you."

He lightly kissed me. "Thank you," he said quietly. "For being gorgeous."

I dropped my head to his shoulder and breathed him in. "You know all the lovely words."

He replied with a gentle squeeze of my knee, his gaze returned to the window, and not another word was said.

***

The special place he wanted to show me was a decrepit old building on West 52nd – the club he and Ryan had bought.

I stood on the sidewalk, gazing up at the peeling window frames, half expecting to see something otherworldly staring back. "Is it abandoned?"

"Not quite." Adam grabbed my hand and pulled me toward the steps. "I told you about Tiger, right?"

The vague narrative he'd given when describing his new business partner didn't do him justice. The old man met us at the door, grumbling. "You said six, kid."

Adam glanced at his watch. "We're half an hour early."

Tiger grunted, but moved on. "Who's the broad?"

Adam didn't bat an eyelid at his crass question. I could only assume he was used to it. "This is my wife, Charlotte," he replied.

Tiger took a fat cigar out of his pocket and sniffed it. "I knew Baby Bardot's mother would be a looker."

Adam interpreted. "Tiger and Bridget are friends."

"She's a little French princess," Tiger declared.

Bridget had mentioned visiting the club with Ryan a few times. The most information she'd given me about Tiger was that he was funny and could take his teeth out. The only thing comical about him was his loud Hawaiian print shirt, and I had no intention of asking if the teeth trick was true.

"I brought Charli here to have a look around," said Adam, moving up a step.

Tiger leaned out and looked up and down the street. "When is he getting here?" he asked. "I'm busy."

Adam lifted his hand, raising mine with it. "This is Charli."

With his fat cigar clamped between his teeth, the old man smiled at me. "That's what they call you?" he asked. "Did your mother not like you?"

"No, as it happens." I grinned. "But my father took a shine to me."

Tiger threw his head back and roared with laughter. Adam didn't wait for him to compose himself. With a firm hold on my hand, he led me into the lobby of the most neglected building in Manhattan.

Tiger didn't follow us when we headed into the large main room at the back. I heard his feet clomping on the wooden steps as he trudged upstairs.

"He lives up there," explained Adam.

"Have you ever been up there?"

He shook his head. "Never."

I hadn't decided whether Tiger's story was a sad one or not. While I conceded that living alone in a run down old club was a depressing notion, there was clearly magic about the place.

I walked to the centre of the room and took a long look around. Paint peeled from every wall, and the flecks that had fallen to the floor looked like they'd been there for years. Using the toe of my shoe, I cleared a line along the dusty floor. The decorative parquetry underneath was intricate, badly worn, and in need of a lot of TLC, just like the rest of the place.

Adam didn't look the least bit daunted by the mammoth task. I could tell by his expression that his mind was spinning with ideas. Enthusiasm was a good look for him.

"This is wonderful," I declared, turning a full circle.

"Imagine how amazing this place would've been in its heyday."

I walked to the bar on the far side of the room, drawing a long line in the dust on the wooden counter. "I can almost hear it," I told him. "A band playing on the stage, the chinking glasses, the hopeful young lovers getting to know each other over a few drinks."

I moved to the business side of the bar. Glasses still lined the shelves, but most of the bottles on display were empty. Everything was where it should've been, which was eerie. For whatever reason, one night long ago, the club just stopped dead.

"Do you think we would've come here?" he asked.

"No, not your scene at all, monsieur," I purred.

Adam folded his arms. "How about you, Charlotte?" he asked. "Would it have been your scene?"

I picked up a silver drinks tray from beneath the counter and set two glasses down on it. "Totally my scene. I reckon I would've been Lulu the cocktail waitress in a past life."

His laugh was just dark enough to get my heart racing. "I'm sure I would've frequented this place just to hang out with Lulu."

"You might've tried," I replied. "But she would've been way out of your league."

"You think so?"

"Oh, I know so," I drawled. "She was no floozy."

As I continued looking around, I spotted something so out of place under the counter that I couldn't possibly help touching it. It was as if Lulu the cocktail waitress had planted the gold sequined headband there herself. I dusted off the long white feather at the top and placed it on my head. "What do you think?"

His stare was more thoughtful now. Perhaps I looked more ridiculous than I thought. "I think you've no idea how lovely you truly are," he said finally.

I felt a flash of heat in my cheeks. "Why, thank you, kind sir," I teased, dipping my head. "But I'm not done yet."

He groaned out my name, which was Adam-speak for stop what you're doing and behave. I ignored him and continued my transformation from art gallery curator to Lulu.

In a move I hadn't made since high school, I rolled the waistband of my skirt, shortening it just enough to make the height of my heels an obscene match.

"What are you doing, Charlotte?"

"Lulu would've shown some leg," I replied.

As hard as he might've tried fighting against it, the dimpled smile won out. "I can't see your legs from here."

I straightened my headband, picked up my tray and stepped out from behind the bar. I hadn't carried a tray since my waitressing days at Nellie's. My skills were non-existent then, and nothing had changed. My sexy-fifties-cocktail-waitress walk needed work too, but it had the desired effect. Adam met me half way, and took the tray. "You're dangerous, Charli." His eyes flitted from my eyes to my lips.

"Lulu," I corrected. He hooked his finger into the waistband of my skirt and drew me forward. His arms wrapped around me, his lips landed on mine and Lulu was a goner.

***

When it came to his gallery, Bronson was a neat freak. I arrived the next morning to find him polishing the leaves on the pot plant near the door.

"Shiny plants are happy plants, darling," he explained.

"What are you using to clean them with?"

He held up the spray can and read the label. "Pledge."

"I'm pretty sure that will hurt the plant, Bronson."

He waved the cloth in his hand. "Beauty is pain."

I sat at my desk, chuckling at the strange man who paid my wages. A day in Bronson's head would be like an overseas holiday. Spending time with him at the gallery wasn't that different to occupying Bridget. As long as he was busy, he was happy. For that reason, I wasn't going to separate him from his can of plant-killing Pledge.

I diverted my attention to the invoices on my desk. Bronson bought art like Fiona bought shoes. No expense was spared if something took his fancy, and like Fiona he had a great eye for a good deal. His gallery was hugely successful, and I was proud to be a part of it. When he was in the mood, he was a good salesman. Today was one of those days. He abandoned the can of furniture polish when the first customer walked in, and promptly sold her a twelve thousand dollar painting.

After praising the woman's eye for detail and her knowledge of the arts, he arranged delivery and sent her on her way as only Bronson could. "All done now, darling," he crowed, flapping his hands at her. "Shoo, shoo."

The customer didn't take offense. No one ever did. She skipped out the door twelve grand lighter with a huge smile on her face. Bronson shuffled over and slumped down on the chair opposite my desk. "I'm exhausted, Charlotte," he complained. The gallery had been open for business less than an hour.

"Can I get you something?"

"Yes." He slapped both hands on his knees. "Take care of the next client. Dazzle them with your charm and sell them something wonderful."

Ordinarily I might've given it a crack, but the next person through the door had never been remotely dazzled by me.

Olivia breezed in wearing a lovely summer dress and a bright smile. Politely, I would've described her as pretty, but it was a hard kind of pretty. I was glad I didn't look like her, but remembering the photo of her and Alex as teenagers reminded me that I used to. Somewhere along the line she'd lost the softness, and dealing with her made me feel like I was losing it too.

"Hello, Charli," she beamed.

I wanted to ask what she wanted, but managed to say hello instead.

Bronson levered himself to his feet. "Sell her something, darling," he instructed in a ridiculously indiscreet whisper.

"Actually, I am looking for a piece for the reception area of the studio," said Olivia, diverting her walk to check out the art hanging on the far wall.

Bronson clapped his hands. "Then this is where you belong today."

Choosing art is a process, whether the person selecting it realises it or not. When Jean-Luc bought his boat-on-the-beach picture, I watched it call to him for ten minutes before he knew he wanted it. His eyes kept darting toward it until he finally made the decision to buy.

Olivia didn't seem to go through any sort of process. She pointed out a large abstract piece that she'd hardly even looked at. "This would be perfect."

Photographs were my specialty, but she'd chosen a painting. Bronson took over the reins and revealed a whopping price tag, just shy of thirty thousand dollars.

I expected her to gracefully bow out of the deal, but she didn't. She cheekily asked him if he'd give her a month to pay for it.

Bronson wagged his finger at her, tutting like he was scolding a child. "It's not customary, darling," he said sternly. "My business doesn't operate that way." The relief I felt was immense. If the woman didn't have funds to buy a designer handbag, chances were that dropping thirty grand on art was beyond her means.

In an attempt to help her save face, I steered her in a different direction. "There are other pieces that are much cheaper," I offered, pointing toward the opposite wall. "Or a photograph. They're still exclusive, but generally not as expensive."

There was a sly edge to the smile she gave me. "I'm not interested in a silly photograph," she said bluntly. "I find no talent in clicking a camera."

It was another kick-in-the-face example of how little she knew me. Olivia never asked questions about my life. Conversations were always about her. She had no idea that I was a photographer who'd captured the twenty-four years of my life that she'd missed through the lens of a camera. I would've been offended by her ignorant comment if I wasn't concentrating so hard on trying to pre-empt her next move – and I knew there was one, because there was always a game in play where Olivia was concerned.

"Photography is a masterful craft," defended Bronson.

She unlocked me from her stare and turned to him. "Of course," she falsely agreed. "But I much prefer the intensity and depth of a painting."

Bronson bowed his head. "To each her own, darling."

He was accommodating because he thought he was about to make a huge sale. He would've agreed with anything at that point, thinking he was in control. I knew differently. Olivia was playing him like a fiddle; I just wasn't sure of the tune.

She turned back to the painting and sighed. "I truly adore it," she declared wistfully.

"I can hold it for a month," Bronson generously offered.

"That won't do." Olivia glanced at him. "I have a charity event coming up before then. I would like to have it on display."

My heart began thumping when she took a few slow steps toward me. "I'm not your average client." She spoke to him, but her eyes never left mine. "I'm hardly likely to stiff you considering my daughter works here."

I felt sick to my stomach. Olivia had publically claimed me as her daughter only twice, and she had been screwing me over both times.

Bronson started squealing like a little girl. "Why didn't you say so, darling?" he asked, waving both hands at me.

Words failed me. Olivia had no such problem. In two minutes flat, she'd arranged delivery and a fourteen-day account.

Bronson was kind and trusting. Perhaps that's why he dropped the ball. There was no contract signed, no conditions to be met. If the painting hadn't been so large, she could've carried it out there and then.

"Charli is a wonderful addition to my gallery," he prattled. "Her family is my family."

His experience with my family was limited to Ryan, who had no problem dropping a small fortune on artwork every time he walked through the door. The difference was, he could afford it.

"Are you sure about this, Bronson?" I asked in a small voice.

He took me by the shoulders and shook me. "Of course, darling," he crowed. "There is no risk to me. If your lovely mother skips the country, you can pay her bill."

He laughed, thinking he'd made a cheeky joke. The worst part was, Olivia laughed too.

I didn't trust my mother. I didn't respect her either. If Bronson had left the room, I might've finally told her so. But he didn't leave. He picked up his can of pledge and went back to polishing the leaves on his plant.

I walked back to my desk, despondent and worried. When I sat down, Olivia was right behind me.

"Did you have a chance to speak to Fiona?" she asked casually.

I frowned at her. "About what?"

"You offered to talk to her about attending my charity event," she reminded me.

The woman was relentless – always on the take. It was exhausting me, but in typical Olivia fashion she didn't notice.

"Yes," I replied quietly. "She said she'd love to support you."

She clasped her hands together, grinning broadly. "Wonderful. I'll send Erin back tomorrow with the official invitations. It's going to be fabulous."

I forced myself to smile at her. "No problem."

"I'm so happy, Charli," she beamed. "Things are working out beautifully."

***

The text message Adam sent me letting me know that he'd collect Bridget from Ryan's place after work couldn't have come on a better day. Needing time to clear my head, I decided to walk home. It wasn't necessarily the brightest move. My shoes weren't made for walking, so by the time I got there my feet ached as much as my head.

Adam's alarmed expression as I opened the door wasn't unexpected. Presumably I looked like something the cat had dragged in. At least he was polite enough not to mention it.

"Mama's home," he cheerily announced for Bridget's benefit.

They were both in the kitchen, cooking up a storm. Just by looking at the mess strewn across the counter I knew it was going to take me three days to clean up after them.

"Hi, lady." Bridget pointed a wooden spoon at me. "We're making dinner for you."

I hoped calling me lady was a one-off, but I could never be sure where Bridget was concerned. She'd recently ended a month-long phase of calling her father by name.

"That's wonderful," I praised. "Thank you."

I wasn't sure what I was thanking her for. While her dad's back was turned, she dumped an entire bunch of coriander into the pan.

Adam turned around but still didn't notice. His focus was on me. "Tired?" he asked quietly.

I grimaced. "I have a headache."

He picked Bridget up under her arms and transported her the short distance to the living room. It was a good move on his part. I suspect the bunch of parsley in her hand was seconds away from hitting the pan.

"But I'm cooking," she protested.

"And you're doing a good job, baby." He picked up the remote and pointed it at the TV. The cartoon mermaid lit the screen. "Take a break for a while."

Bridget handed Adam the parsley, grabbed Treasure off the coffee table and clambered onto the couch. He walked back to me and presented me with the bunch of parsley as if it was a posy of flowers.

"Thank you," I mumbled, taking it from his grasp. "It's lovely."

Adam took my face in his hands and tilted my head. I saw concern in his eyes. I wondered what he saw in mine. "What do you need?" he asked quietly.

Sleep was the only thing I could think of to remedy the ache in my head. Time away from the world to gather my thoughts would also be beneficial.

"Go to bed." He lightly pressed his lips to mine. "I'll bring you some dinner."

I smiled. "Don't threaten me, Adam," I whispered.

The little girl on the couch chimed in. "It's a lovely dinner, lady," she insisted. "I cooked it."

***

Our apartment was so small that private conversations were impossible. I lay in bed listening to my little family chatting over dinner in the next room.

"It's not right, Bridge," complained Adam. "What did you put in it?"

"Just weed," came the little reply. "I love weed."

Laughing made my head throb. I put my fingertips to my temples in a futile attempt to rub the pain away. Adam had a better remedy. As soon as Bridget was in bed, he came into the room carrying a big bowl and a glass of milk.

I shuffled to sit up. "Cereal?"

He balanced the bowl on my lap. "Only the best for you."

"How did you know which one I'd like?" It was a fair question. Our extensive cereal selection took up two shelves in the pantry.

"I chose the one with the lowest nutritional value." Adam poured the glass of milk into the bowl. "Like I said, only the best."

I smiled at the chocolaty bowl of breakfast junk food, quietly thrilled that he knew me so well.

He put his hand on my forehead. "How's the head?"

"Busy," I replied. "Olivia came to see me at work today."

I was used to the mention of her name inciting a look of distaste, but he gave me something different this time. Adam actually looked panicked. "What did she want?" He sounded panicked too. "Actually, don't answer that. Charli, we really need to talk."

He stood up and paced the small room, looking anywhere but at me. "Olivia came to see me too," he revealed. "I meant to tell you yesterday, but we had such a good afternoon and I didn't want to ruin it."

The bowl of cereal in my lap was suddenly unappetising. I leaned across and set it down on the bedside table.

Adam looked completely stricken, and I knew he would rather have been anywhere else on earth but in that room.

"You're about to break my heart, aren't you?" I asked weakly.

"I think so," he admitted.

I nodded, resigned. If Adam couldn't stop it from happening, no one could, and I got the distinct impression he'd been trying to save me for weeks. "Just tell me," I muttered.

I'd listened to some brutal truths in my time but nothing compared to hearing that my own mother was willing to get out of our lives in exchange for money. I wasn't even shocked. I wondered if that made me as hard as her.

Adam stopped pacing at the foot of the bed. "I told her she won't see a cent," he said strongly.

I looked up at him, slightly tortured by the notion that that might not necessarily be true. If Olivia reneged on her agreement to pay for the painting she'd all but conned out of Bronson, I was going to have to cover it.

I'd been trying to work out her latest scam all day, and given myself a migraine doing it. Everything was suddenly clear, including my head. One way or another, Olivia intended to get paid.

I reached for Adam but said nothing. He'd gone to great lengths to let her know that he wasn't going to pay her off. News of the shady art purchase would undo everything.

He didn't push me to talk. Perhaps he thought I needed time to come to terms with everything. Truthfully, I'd been suspicious since the first night I met her. If anything, he'd just validated my feelings of mistrust and unease.

The only confusing part centred on the fact that I was tied to the woman by blood. The only likeness I could find between us was that we were both determined to get what we wanted.

She was hell bent on getting my money.

And I was hell bent on making sure she paid dearly for it.

50. STARTING FIRES

Adam

Telling Charli about her mother's evil deeds came at the risk of having her doubt my truthfulness. That was the worst case scenario. If it had gone that way, I would've told her everything, starting with the phoney résumé and ending with Olivia's threat of turning Bridget against her.

Mercifully it never got that far. I gave her only the basics, hoping that I'd armed her with enough information to make her cut ties once and for all – right up until she pulled herself together and laid out a plan.

She dropped my hand. "Bridget's concert is in two weeks," she said. "I think we should keep quiet until then."

I was shaking my head before she'd even finished speaking. "I can't believe you're willing to leave the kid in her class, Charlotte. After all, she's –"

"For Bridget. No other reason."

I frowned, but didn't speak.

"I've also teed up your mum and a group of her friends to attend Olivia's charity luncheon at the studio. That's the week after."

"Then what? Christmas is coming up too. Perhaps you should keep her around until then."

Some kisses are designed to halt conversation, like the one she planted on me a few seconds later. I kissed her back – because I always kiss her back. She finally broke free to hit me with her next words of wisdom. "You want to know what your dad always says to me?"

I rested my forehead against hers. "Stop talking nonsense, Charlotte," I recited in a French laced whisper. "Stay home, raise my granddaughter and be a good wife to my son."

I felt her laugh. "Besides that."

"Enlighten me," I murmured.

"He says that in order to sell a bucket of water, you sometimes have to start a fire."

I groaned, seriously unhappy with the route she was preparing to take.

"Olivia is the fire, Charli," I warned. "She's no good."

"I'll make a deal with you, Adam," she offered.

"No."

She laid it out anyway, the same way our daughter did whenever I declined to negotiate. "I won't see her again. You take Bridget to dance lessons and that's it," she offered. "As soon as the concert is done, we'll walk away."

I knew there was more to it, but I couldn't bring myself to call her on it. All I cared about was keeping her away from her toxic mother. She was agreeing to do that so I had no reason to make waves.

"Just until the concert." I reiterated, raking both hands through her hair. "Promise?"

"I promise you."

It wasn't ideal, but for now it had to be enough.

51. BUSINESS AS USUAL

Charli

Avoiding Olivia wasn't going to be difficult. The only time I saw her was when she ambushed me at the gallery, and now that she owed Bronson money she was likely to steer clear.

The bad turn in weather kept everyone away that afternoon. Fall had arrived, and after a glorious summer, trees were starting to lose their leaves and the days were getting cooler.

Rain was added to the mix that day, but it wasn't enough to keep Olivia's sidekick Erin away. She waltzed into the gallery just before closing time. After collapsing her umbrella, she walked over and dropped a large envelope on my desk.

I looked up, studying her closely. Erin wasn't in ballet mode that day. She looked like any other teenage girl with a penchant for hoodies, jeans and Converse sneakers. And even though her long blonde hair was straggly and wet from the rain, it was still a better look than the too-tight bun she wore to work.

My gaze must've lingered too long. She fussed with her jacket, nervously zipping and then unzipping it. "These are the invitations to Olivia's charity thing." She pointed at the envelope. "I was told to bring them to you."

I opened the flap and peeked inside, surprised by the number of invitations in it. Obviously Olivia expected me to pull out all stops and rope Fiona into inviting half of Manhattan. "How many people are likely to attend?" I asked.

"Enough to pay the wages she owes me, hopefully," she muttered.

I looked up sharply, expecting to the see the expression of regret that usually comes after speaking before thinking. Clearly, Erin wasn't regretful at all. She remained completely straight-faced, which only added to her believability.

"She owes you money?" I asked.

"Olivia *always* owes me money," she replied, rolling her eyes. "Why do you think she runs these stupid events?"

I grabbed the chair from Bronson's desk. "Take a seat, Erin," I encouraged. "I'd really like to know more."

She hesitated, glancing at the chair. "What makes you think I'd tell you anything?"

I smoothed down the back of my dress and sat back down. "Because you're a decent kid, and it's the right thing to do."

Playing to her conscience was merely lip service. For all I knew, Erin was as shady as Olivia. The real reason I knew she was going to spill all was because she was angry.

After a moment of deliberation, she sat down. "What do you want to know?"

"How much of the donated funds does she siphon off for herself?"

Erin shook her head. "All of them," she scoffed. "There is no charity. Can you imagine Olivia helping disadvantaged children?"

"No," I conceded, slumping back in my chair. From what I'd seen, she had enough trouble helping out the privileged ones. I'd never seen a less compassionate teacher in all my life.

"Every few months she puts some stupid event together, cons spoiled rich women into supporting her fake cause, and makes off with enough money to keep the studio ticking over."

"Tuition costs a bomb," I pointed out. "Surely she makes good money."

Erin rolled her eyes again, an annoying but age-appropriate gesture for a disgruntled teenage girl. "She only runs two classes." She held two fingers in the air. "That's it."

"But why?"

She huffed out a hard laugh designed to make my question seem stupid. "Because she's awful. No one wants to be tutored by a class A bitch. It's only the diehards that stick around."

My daughter was one of the diehards. For some reason she loved the regimented structure and discipline of Olivia's class.

I held Erin's gaze for a long time, trying to take everything in. "Why do you stay?" I asked.

"I'm just waiting for my money," she replied. "As soon as I get it, I'm out."

"Sounds like a good plan."

She leaned forward, pushing the stack of invitations across the desk. "What about you, Mrs Décarie?" she asked. "Do you have a plan for dealing with this?"

No was the answer, but even if I'd come up with the most ingenious plan ever devised, I wouldn't have shared it with her. I picked up the envelope and sealed the flap. "No plan," I told her. "It's business as usual."

It had to be for now. Erin wasn't the only one who was owed money, and a few weeks of her wages didn't compare to the thirty grand she owed Bronson.

Erin stood, settling both hands in the front pocket of her hoodie. "You won't tell her I told you anything, right?" Her nervous tone was probably warranted. There was no telling what Olivia would do if she discovered she'd been sold out.

"Of course not." I smiled, trying to reassure her. "My mother and I aren't close."

"Your mother?" She gasped. "Olivia said she hardly knows you."

"She's right." I nodded. "She doesn't know me at all."

***

I'd been avoiding talking to my dad for weeks, worried that I might let slip that I was in contact with my mother. I wasn't sure why I was determined to keep it from him. Alex had never discouraged me from knowing Olivia, even offering to help me to find her at one point.

I couldn't imagine that she even vaguely resembled the fifteen-year-old girl he fell in love with all those years ago. In the few times we had discussed her over the years, he'd remembered Olivia fondly, filling my head with thoughts of a beautiful dancer who made the brave decision to give her baby up to follow her dreams. He'd portrayed himself as the selfish one who couldn't let me go.

It was so far from the truth that I was scared to tell him differently. I didn't give a damn about Olivia, but maybe after all these years, Alex still did.

In a flash of clarity, I realised why I was keeping him in the dark. With the very best of intentions, I was trying to protect him from finding out what she'd become.

52. WHINY DISPLAYS

Adam

It had been a good few weeks since Bridget had ventured over to the dark side. As much as I hated to admit it, the reason she was behaving was because she knew that stepping out of line would result in us cancelling her dance concert.

She hadn't completely reformed. I arrived home from work to find her standing at the sink with a carton of eggs.

"Good evening, Miss Décarie," I called.

The kid nearly jumped out of her skin. "Nothing," she replied.

Like a deer trapped in the headlights, she didn't move. I walked into the kitchen. "I didn't ask what you were doing."

She dropped the carton down on the counter. "I'm not doing nothing."

"Anything," I corrected.

"That's right."

I peered over the top of her, checking out the smashed eggs in the sink. "It doesn't look like nothing, Bridget."

When worked up, Bridget adopts her uncle's quirk of talking with her hands. She waved her arms as if she was drawing a picture in the air. "I was just seeing if all the eggs are the same inside."

I folded my arms. "And what did you conclude?"

Bridget didn't understand my question. She blinked a thousand times but said nothing.

"Are they all the same or not?" I rephrased.

"Yes they are." She reached into the front pocket of her dress. "But I have two more to check."

Determined not to smile, I bit my bottom lip and stalled my reply. "Don't you think that's wasteful?" I finally asked.

She stretched up on tiptoes to check the gloop in the sink. "I could make Treasure a cake with them," she offered. "A lovely one with sparkles." She took off to the pantry and pulled open the door. "We have sparkles in here."

I lifted her up and set her back near the sink. "You're not baking anything, Betty Crocker," I told her. "You are going to clean up this mess, though."

"Well, I think that's a little bit mean," she retorted with a swing of her hips.

"And I think you're a little bit naughty." I handed her the dishcloth. "Where's your mama?"

"In the shower," she muttered.

"Don't move until this is cleaned up," I ordered, pointing at her as I backed away. "I mean it, Bridget."

"I will try," she replied. "But I'm a very small girl."

"A small girl with a big cleanup job ahead of her," I called from the entry to the hallway. "Get cracking."

"Cracking eggs?" she asked hopefully.

I turned back to face her again. "How do you think a very small girl would handle being in very big trouble?"

Bridget swiped the cloth along the edge of the sink, pretending to be hard at work. "I would play it very cool," she mumbled.

***

My plan of surprising my wife in the shower didn't work out so well. Charli was in the bedroom dressed and good to go, which was a problem.

"No, no, no." I groaned out the words. "Where are you going?"

She twisted her hair into a knot and secured it at the top of her head. "To your parents' house for dinner. Get dressed."

I didn't want to get dressed. After a long and gruelling few days, I wanted to have an early night and get undressed. "No, Charlotte," I pleaded. "Call and cancel."

She pointed her hairbrush at me. "I will do no such thing. You have a chance to redeem yourself for misbehaving at the engagement dinner. Ryan and Bente will be there too."

I dropped to my knees and grabbed her hips. "Please stay home with me. I'm tired of people."

The whiny display had her in giggles. "They're not people, Adam. They're your family."

I pulled her forward, lifted her shirt and kissed her belly. "You don't understand, Charli," I mumbled. "I really need to get laid. I never, ever get laid."

She ran her hand through my hair. "You poor thing," she lamented.

"I know," I replied. "It's nothing short of tragic."

She took no pity on me. "We're still going to dinner."

"Did you not hear my plea, Charlotte?" I asked dramatically.

She stepped away breaking my hold. "Yes, I did," she confirmed. "You never, ever get laid."

"I really think we –"

"Shush," she demanded, swatting my shoulder.

I turned around to see Bridget at the door. "I cleaned up, Daddy," she grumbled.

"You're a good girl. Thank you." I didn't sound thankful. I sounded like I'd just been busted. "Are you ready to go to Mamie's?"

Charli didn't wait for Bridget to answer. She led her out of the room, mumbling something about getting her dressed.

I loosened my tie and pulled in a long breath. "We need a bigger apartment," I muttered to myself.

53. CAJUN RECIPES

Charli

Ryan and Bente's wedding preparations were in full swing, and the queen was excited. The minute we arrived, she bombarded me with every detail. We ended up chatting in the kitchen while she checked on dinner. To clarify, she chatted. I just nodded a lot and asked the occasional question in the hope of appearing interested.

"An ice sculpture?" I asked incredulously. "Whose idea was that?"

Fiona checked that the coast was clear before replying. "Ivy's," she whispered. "Dreadfully tacky – but you know me, darling. I'm very amenable."

I almost laughed but thought better of it.

"How about you, darling?" A plume of smoke rose from the oven when she opened the door, and then she quickly closed it as if it hadn't happened. "What have you been up to?"

"Just working," I replied.

Fiona glanced back at me, smiling widely. "Any news for me?"

Questions like that made me regret telling her about our baby plans, especially knowing she was probably going to ask me about it every single time I saw her.

"Not yet," I replied. "But you'll be the first to know."

Fiona pulled the oven mitt off her hands and cradled my cheeks. "I cannot wait, my darling. We have so many exciting things in the wings."

I smiled back. "Speaking of exciting things, I received the invitations for Olivia's charity luncheon today."

I surprised myself by sounding enthusiastic. In truth, the whole notion of helping Olivia commit fraud made my skin crawl, but until I could figure out a way of putting an end to her the best course of action was to contain her. For now, I was keeping her wicked deeds in-house.

Fiona picked up her mitt and opened the oven again, this time deciding to take the tray out. "Yes, fine," she replied. "Just let me know the details."

I cleared a space on the counter so she could set the tray down. "I had a quick look at the invitations," I said casually. "There are thirty tables available. Do you think your crowd could book them all?" My voice rose at the end, acutely aware that it was a cheeky request.

She glanced across at me. "Thirty?"

"Yes."

"She's really gone all out, hasn't she?" The sarcastic edge to her tone confused me so much that I lost my ability to keep bluffing my way through the conversation.

"Yes or no?" I asked, getting straight to the point.

Fiona studied her tray of burnt chicken. "Yes, darling. Anything for you."

Too relieved to pretend otherwise, I hugged her. "Thank you."

"Of course, Charli," she mumbled. "Now what are we going to do about this chicken?"

I looked at the smoking tray. "Tell them it's a Cajun recipe," I suggested.

"Good thinking, darling." She smiled. "That's exactly what I'll do."

***

Dinner wasn't a reprieve from the wedding talk. If anything, it was encouraged because it took the focus off the abominable food we'd been served.

The poor bride looked like she'd been put through the wringer lately, and a quick glance at Ryan showed that he wasn't faring much better. Not only were they dealing with Fiona's grandiose ideas: Ivy was in on the action.

Jean-Luc found the whole subject boring, and for the first time ever I was relieved when he cut in and changed the subject. He turned his attention to Bridget. "How are the ballet lessons going, my love?"

"I'm a lovely dancer," she informed him.

Ryan put his hand to his heart. "And so modest," he teased.

Bridget ignored him. "I have a concert soon – with lovely dresses and music for dancing."

"*Magnifique*." Jean-Luc spoke to Bridget, but looked at Adam. "Perhaps your father will take the day off work to accompany you."

Adam winked when I glanced at him. It was a comforting gesture he made often in the king's presence. It was code for 'take a deep breath and ignore him'. I tried to do just that. I also had a crack at changing the subject. "Dinner is lovely, Fiona," I falsely praised.

She beamed at me. "Thank you, darling. It's a Cajun recipe."

Ryan looked at his plate before scowling at me, "You are such a groveller."

"Ryan!" scolded his mother. "Apologise."

The notion was laughable. The man had never once apologised to me, even when I deserved it. I couldn't quite catch the mumble he came out with, but I'm certain it was no apology.

"It is lovely," agreed Bente, directing the compliment at her future mother-in-law. "I love Cajun food."

"How about burnt food, Bente?" teased Adam, avoiding my attempt at crushing his foot by shifting his leg. "Do you like burnt food?"

She didn't skip a beat. "I do if Fiona cooks it."

Adam laughed, and I tried not to. Even the King stifled a chuckle. But Ryan was overcome with something else – pure unadulterated admiration for the woman who was prepared to lie to keep his mother happy. "You're beautiful," he quietly told her. "I'm going to marry you."

Even Fiona smiled.

"I don't like black chicken, Mamie," said Bridget, trying to spear a piece with her fork. "But I will pretend."

"You're a class act, Bridge," joked Ryan.

"Yes I am." She pointed her fork at him. "A lovely one."

***

By the time dessert rolled around, conversation had returned to the wedding. I didn't think it had anything to do with the food. In a grand attempt at cutting us all a break, Ryan supplied dessert – a huge gateau from Billet-doux, which in turn inspired Fiona to voice her opinion on wedding cakes.

"Fruit cake is so traditional and classy." She lifted a piece of the gateau with a beautiful antique silver cake server, and dropped it into a plastic Smurf-themed bowl. The irony was not lost on me. "For you, my love," she said passing it to Bridget.

"I don't know much about cake," conceded Bente. "All I know is that I'd like it to have red roses to match the rest of the theme."

"Everything will match perfectly," declared Fiona. "I've even arranged a new carpet for the aisle of the church."

"A red one?" asked Ryan incredulously.

I wasn't the least bit surprised. Nothing was out of the realm of possibility when the queen was coordinating.

"Of course, Ryan." She passed a slice of cake to Bente. "The church is very welcoming of donations. They needed a new carpet along the aisle, and I wanted it red. It's being laid next week."

In one of the most embarrassing moments of my life, my daughter piped up. "My daddy never gets laid," she announced, waving her fork in the air.

I think I stopped breathing. Adam let out a strange sound that was one of total humiliation. Everyone else seemed frozen. No one moved. No one spoke.

Perhaps realising she was the reason for the stunned silence Bridget added to her comment. "Never, ever, ever," she mumbled.

Adam finally reacted. His hand flew over her mouth to stop her speaking. Ryan reacted too – by laughing so hard I thought he might burst. "Adam, you do remember the science of procreation, right?" The convoluted phrasing was designed to keep Bridget oblivious. "You're never going to expand the brood if you don't figure out how."

Adam released Bridget and sank down in his seat, gifting his brother a kick to the shins. Ryan didn't even care. He kept laughing.

I could feel my cheeks burning, and it only got worse when the one person I didn't want to make eye contact with ever again began to chuckle. "Out of the mouth of babes," said Jean-Luc.

"His only babe at this rate," added Ryan, making him chuckle harder.

Ignoring the idiocy, Bente leaned across the table. "Are you trying to have a baby, Charli?" she whispered.

"No," I replied, taking the plate that was frozen in my mother-in-law's stunned hands. "I'm just trying to have cake."

54. PIGEON WRANGLING

Adam

Bridget fell asleep on the couch right after dinner, looking too sweet to be the same girl who'd embarrassed the bejesus out of us earlier. As much as I wanted to call it a night and get out of there, I made better use of the quiet moment by grabbing Charli and sneaking out the door.

We hadn't been up to the rooftop garden in a long time. As soon as I pushed open the heavy steel door, I regretted not making better use of it over summer. It was the ultimate escape from the bustling city, and with a little effort I could make-believe we were somewhere else.

"It's so lovely up here," said Charli wandering to the edge to check out the night-time view.

However impressive the illuminated cityscape might've been, it was never going to be lovelier than her. It would've been grossly inadequate to say that there was just something about her because the attraction wasn't that random.

It was her unique mind and wild heart that kept me enchanted. Even after all this time, I wouldn't survive a day without a dose of either. But at that moment the attraction was much simpler – her smile as she glanced back at me is what made my heart start thumping. It was bright, warm and bewitching – the epitome of Charli and all that she meant to me.

I didn't want to tell her how lovely she looked. I wanted to tell her something more valuable. "I'm glad I married you."

The random declaration sounded odd, but not to Charlotte. She turned, resting her back against the guardrail. "Is the talk of weddings making you nostalgic, Adam?"

"No," I replied. "It's making me thankful that we eloped."

Charli pushed off the rail and ambled toward me. "Don't you ever wish we'd had a big wedding?"

As soon as she was near, I reached for her hand. "No, but I'll marry you again if you want a wedding."

"You would?" Her brown eyes widened. "Why?"

I raised her hand and slowly turned her around, pulling her back against my chest. "Because I don't want you to miss a single thing because you chose me," I whispered in her ear.

She ran her hand along my forearm. "What about the things you've missed?"

Her question was absurd. The only thing I was missing was the second-rate life of a second-rate man. I shuddered to think who I'd be without Charli and Bridget in my life.

"I haven't missed anything."

"Except getting laid," she murmured. "That never happens, right?"

I swept her hair across her shoulder and breathed the next words against her skin. "I've more than been punished for that slight embellishment, Charlotte."

"It's going to take a long time to live it down," she predicted. "And now they all know we're planning another baby."

"Ryan already knew," I confessed. "I told him. I'm sorry."

"No worries," she muttered. "I told your mother."

I stifled my laugh against her shoulder. "Well, that makes me feel a lot better."

Charli broke my hold. "Better about what?"

"I told my dad too," I admitted.

Her thumb found the dent in my cheek. "Quite the little family of over-sharers, aren't we?"

"It doesn't matter how many secrets we give away, Charli." My gaze wandered from her eyes to her mouth. "It's the ones we keep that count."

"Tell me a secret." Her soft voice held zero authority. "One full of lovely words and promises."

"Something no one else knows?"

"Just us."

I didn't speak again. I leaned, kissing her perfect lips. Her touch was gentle but the effect she had on me never was. The charge that passed between us was powerful enough to steal words from my mouth and thoughts from my head – and I'd experienced it enough times to know that it was never going to weaken or disappear.

It was the embodiment of us, and the whole explanation as to why we were the special two. That was the secret we were always going to keep.

***

The next week was strangely uneventful for us. Charli kept her promise and had no contact with her mother. Olivia's impromptu visits to the gallery stopped, but I suspect that was because for the time being, Charli was serving a purpose.

For reasons I'll never understand, Charli had roped my mother into supporting Olivia's upcoming charity event. I knew very little about it because I refused to hear the details. The whole notion was offensive, but a deal is a deal.

Upholding my end of the bargain meant accompanying Bridget to ballet lessons three days a week. My little girl's enthusiasm hadn't waned. If anything she was growing more excited by the prospect of dancing in the stupid concert.

Olivia did what she does best, elevating Bridget with high praise and fake promises, then waiting until she was out of earshot before reminding me that my daughter's self confidence was resting on a knife's edge.

"One of these days someone's going to break it to her that her co-ordination is non-existent," she warned. "Poor little mite." She cooed insincerely. "How will she cope?"

"I doubt we'll find out any time soon, Olivia," I replied, barely casting a glance her way. "We're both getting what we want at this stage of the game. Bridget's off-limits for now. We both know that."

Olivia had a lot riding on my mother's presence at her event. The only thing charitable about philanthropic ventures in Manhattan is the actual giving of money. Everything else that goes along with it is a big show of social standing and popularity – neither of which Olivia had. She needed Décarie support, and I needed to see my kid dance on a stage in a sparkly tutu. Once those two events played out, all bets were off.

"How are you going to break it to Bridget that she'll be leaving my class soon?" Olivia asked curiously. "I mean, you're going to remove her after the concert, aren't you?"

Ignoring the question, I looked past her and called out to Bridget, who was sitting on the floor of the studio struggling to put her boots back on. "I've got to get back to work, Bridge."

Her little backpack thumped against her back as she scurried over. "I'm ready now," she announced, leaping at me.

I fought the urge to slap Olivia's hand away when she reached out and stroked Bridget's hair. "Don't forget about the extra lessons leading up to the concert, will you?"

It was impossible to maintain a friendly tone, even for my daughter's benefit. "What extra lessons?" I snapped.

Her smile looked more like a smirk. "Starting tonight at six o'clock. Extra practice is important," she said. "Don't let Bridget down by keeping her away."

Bridget bunched up a fistful of my shirt in her hand. "Please, Daddy," she pleaded.

I glared at Olivia, so furious that I could feel my temples throbbing. "We'll be here."

There was no mistaking her smirk for a smile now. "Of course you will," she agreed.

***

If I could manage to turn up to a job I detested every single day, surely I could do the same for a few extra ballet lessons in the week leading up to the concert. At least, that was my rationale when trying to psyche myself into it. Having to deal with Olivia wasn't my only gripe. It was also the fact that it cut into valuable time that I just didn't have.

The sale of the club had finally gone through, and I'd managed to pull most of the permits together. Ryan and I were free to start renovations, which would've been great had I have had the time to do it.

He wasn't exactly free and easy either. The plans for the wedding of the century were now completely out of control. We stood on the steps outside the club while he explained the latest turn of events.

"Freaking doves, Adam," grumbled Ryan. "Ivy suggested releasing doves."

I couldn't help laughing, even at the risk of having him take a swing at me. "Why not just go to the park and wrangle some pigeons?" I handed him a roll of blueprints. "Or squirrels. Bridget knows a few. I'm sure she could hook you up."

"You are such a dick," he scolded – but he did smile.

I didn't venture much farther than the front steps that day. I quickly met with Tiger, then picked up a cab and went home to collect Bridget for her lesson.

"How come we didn't know about extra lessons?" quizzed Charli, trailing behind me as I carried Bridget to the door.

"Because I suspect it's a last-minute lesson plan designed to aggravate." I leaned down and chastely kissed her. "See you soon."

Charli nodded. "Have fun, baby."

Bridget looked over my shoulder. "Treasure will look after you," she said seriously. "But don't touch her, okay? Just look nicely at her."

"I'll do my best," muttered Charli.

55. DUMB LUCK

Charli

Bridget never knew how much her dad went over and above to make sure her little heart was happy. The last thing he had time for was trekking downtown for the second dance class of the day, but he did it without question.

I could feel the end in sight. All we had to do was hold out until the concert and then cut all ties with Olivia. Our plan was to tell Bridget that the concert was the big finale. Dance classes were ending and it was time to move on. It didn't even feel like a bad lie to tell. It was more like damage control, designed to stem the bleeding associated with having my mother in her life.

I hadn't had a thing to do with Olivia since Fiona sent confirmation that her party would book all thirty tables at the charity event. This was further affirmation that I was nothing more than a foot in the door to her.

Olivia meant nothing to me either. I was fast giving up the idea that there was an element of fate that brought her our way. Adam called it dumb luck, and after weeks of torment I finally found myself agreeing with him.

With that realisation, the determination to keep the news of Olivia from Alex was slipping. Curiosity was gnawing at me. I never felt like I got the truth from her, but he'd never told me anything at all.

In a move that took me fifteen minutes to work up to, I called him with the intention of asking why.

"My favourite daughter," he announced as soon as he picked up. "Where have you been?"

Just the sound of his voice took me to a place no one else could. It felt like home, no matter where in the world I was.

"It hasn't been that long," I defended with a smile. "I haven't heard from you either."

"I know." I could hear the regret in his voice. "Having a baby in the house lessens the number of hours in the day."

It was a fact I remembered well. I thought back to the times when I had to decide between eating and washing my hair because there wasn't time for both. For a split second it seemed crazy to want to do it all again, and then I remembered how much joy Bridget had brought us for no other reason than just being.

Alex was in that zone. He was smitten by all things Jack and Gabi, and rightly so. He was finally experiencing all the good that he deserved, and I quickly realised that now wasn't the time to taint it with pointless questions about his time with my mother. Alex Blake was no quitter. If he'd moved on from Olivia without ever looking back, it could only be because the past is where she belonged.

"How is Jack?" I asked. "Still cute?"

It was a redundant question. The pudgy little bundle was about as cute as a baby could be. I was merely trying to keep the conversation light.

"You were much cuter than your brother," he teased. "The kid has so much hair that he wakes up looking like he's licked a power socket."

I laughed, and when he did too, I laughed harder.

The next few minutes of conversation were just as easy and silly – a firm reminder that I shouldn't have avoided calling him for as long as I did. I was always going to need Alex, and he never failed to make me feel like he needed me in equal measure. It seemed criminal that I'd invested so much time in someone who was incapable of feeling that way.

"I miss you like sleep," he told me. "I'm hoping both come back to me soon."

"Soon," I said vaguely. "I think it's on the cards."

I didn't want to give him too much hope. Nothing had been decided. Nothing had even been discussed.

"Everything's alright though, right?" he asked quietly.

I pulled in a settling breath so that my reply would sound steady and true. "We're good, Dad," I assured. "I'm going to call you in a few days, okay?"

"You can call me every day if you want to," he replied. "Even when things aren't good."

What more did I need for crying out loud? I sat down on the edge of the bed feeling infinitely more at ease. "I love you, Alex," I said strongly. "And your Parisienne princess and your hairy baby."

***

I adored my job at the gallery, but life on the beach was beginning to beckon. I refused to mention it to Adam because I knew he'd have our bags packed before I got the words out.

My contract was up, and a tiny part of me was hoping that Bronson wouldn't renew it. I wouldn't have to decide then. My reason for staying in New York would be gone. I'd taken a ridiculous amount of time off during the weeks that Mrs Brown took a break, and was sure he'd take that into account when deciding, but I arrived at work the next morning to find a new contract sitting on my desk.

"Read through it and sign it, darling," he demanded. "Perhaps get your Wedgwood beauty to approve the terms."

"I will," I assured. "I'll let you know in a few days."

"Let me know what?" he asked. "Just sign it. You like my gallery and my gallery likes you."

Bronson Merriman was nothing if not idealistic. It made a nice change from the day-to-day tangles of my life. In all the time I'd known him, he'd never given me an ounce of grief – until that moment.

He swivelled his chair around and waved a piece of paper at me. "Your mother's account is past due," he said casually. "Be a love and fix it."

I almost stammered as I asked how, which was a silly reaction. There was nothing remotely shocking about finding out that Olivia had reneged on their agreement and made off with a thirty thousand dollar piece of artwork.

"Go and collect payment." His lax tone suggested it was no big deal. "Or pay it yourself. Call it an early Christmas present."

I'd given Olivia enough gifts lately, and planned to make sure she was long gone by Christmas. That would be her gift to me.

I grabbed my bag. "I'll go and see her now," I offered. "I'm sure it just slipped her mind."

I must've sounded believable; otherwise he would've held me down and forced me to write a cheque before leaving. As easy-going as Bronson was, he didn't play around when money was involved.

***

I spent the cab ride plotting my speech in my head. I'd simply imply that the thirty thousand dollar bill slipped her mind – and then try not to cringe as I said it.

I had no idea how it would play out, but I knew Olivia well enough to know that she wasn't going to apologise and cut me a cheque. What I wasn't expecting was a warm welcome at the door.

It wasn't my first rodeo when it came to deflecting disingenuous displays of affection. Fiona Décarie used to be the worst offender when it came to lacklustre hugs and cheek kisses that barely connected – and it never felt anywhere near as awkward as the hug Olivia gave me. My arms remained firmly at my sides as she wrapped me in her embrace. "I've missed you terribly in the last couple of weeks." The claim was as phony as her hug. "I've just been so busy. Bridget has been keeping me in the loop, though. She's quite the little chatterbox at ballet."

Ordinarily, a loaded statement like that would've rattled me, but I was determined to stay on task. "I understand you've been busy." I reached into my bag and pulled out the invoice. "I'm sure this slipped your mind, but it's past due. Bronson asked me to follow up on it."

Olivia took a step back, refusing to take the paper from me. "I'm mildly offended, Charli."

My heart began thudding at an alarming rate. Her words were innocuous, but they usually were before things took a turn for the nasty. I looked past her, glancing at the expensive piece of art taking pride of place above the reception desk. It was too big to grab and make a run for it. I was going to have to stay and duke it out.

"I don't want you to be offended," I said quietly. "I'd just like you to write me a cheque." I could barely look at her, but Olivia had no problem staring me down. "Then I'll let you get back to work. I can see you're busy."

I looked from left to right, emphasizing the fact that the place was completely void of anyone else besides us. It was a sly dig that rivalled hers. Perhaps it was finally a hint of proof that we truly were related.

Olivia walked to the reception desk, leaving me hanging with the invoice in my hand. "Perhaps you could cover it for me," she suggested. "Just for a few weeks."

Not so long ago, I would've done it. In the beginning I'd wanted her to like me, just as I'd tried desperately hard to like her. Those days were gone. She was never going to like me – no matter what I did for her.

"No, I don't think so." I didn't even sound regretful, and felt proud because of it. I waved the invoice at her. "I need this settled today."

Olivia sat down at her desk. "Well, that's probably not going to happen, and frankly, Charli, I'm surprised that you're taking it this far."

"It's a thirty thousand dollar painting," I brusquely reminded her. "The only reason Bronson let you walk out with it was –"

"Because you're my daughter," she interrupted. "I expected that to mean something to you."

As far as displays of fakery went, that was her grandest. For the first time ever, I called her out on it. "What does it mean to you, Olivia?" I edged closer to her desk. "Because to be honest, I'm not exactly feeling the connection."

Her shoulders dropped as she relaxed. It was the total opposite of how I was feeling. My chest was so tight it ached.

"The connection between a mother and daughter is more delicate than you think," she said quietly. "It's not always strong, Charli."

I wasn't buying her sad expression. She was talking in riddles, and it scared me.

"I have to get back to work." I dropped the invoice down on her desk. "Please take care of this by the end of the day."

If she said anything else, I didn't hear her. I hightailed it out the door as if I was being chased.

56. PURE ENCHANTMENT

Adam

Between ballet lessons and flower girl duties, Bridget's schedule was as busy as ours. Thanks to a last-minute dress fitting, she wasn't due home for dinner. The night was ours and we made the most of it by dining out.

The Blue Lark wasn't exactly upmarket but it had no children's menu, so to us it was haute cuisine. We found a booth in the corner, opting for privacy over a window view. Our decision to sit side by side wasn't exactly upmarket either, but without the distraction of our little person, I made the most of being able to sit next to Charli without interruption.

"It's odd without, Bridget isn't it?" she asked.

I put a hand on her thigh and reached for a menu with the other. "We can make it seem like she's here," I offered.

"How?"

I glanced at her, grinning. "Well, you can cut my food into small pieces, hand me a napkin every two minutes and keep reminding me that my fork is not a sword."

Charli lifted her menu to hide her giggle. "And you can ask me to take you to the bathroom the second our food arrives."

"She does do that."

"Every single time," she agreed. She put her hand on mine. "I'm actually glad it's just us tonight," she said quietly. "I need to talk to you about something."

I dropped the menu and angled toward her. "Are you pregnant?"

She managed to smile and cringe simultaneously. It made for an odd expression, but she still looked beautiful. "No."

"Well that's a relief." I reached into my pocket and grabbed the small box I'd been hiding from her. "Because that would totally kill the sentiment behind my present."

Her puzzled frown melted the instant she spied the box in my hand.

"Open it," I urged.

My eyes never left her face as she lifted the lid, searching for the look of wonderment that inevitably set in whenever magic took hold. She dangled the pink heart-shaped stone in the air by the chain. "Rose quartz," she mumbled, seemingly deep in thought.

If my wife had been the kind of woman who was dazzled by diamond rings and bouquets of flowers, life would've been much simpler. But she wasn't, which was partly why I adored her. Charli's tastes were much less ostentatious, but harder to cater to. I'd spent an hour in a new-age jewellery store that morning, listening to a bohemian woman named Azure rattle off the meaning of the rocks on display in her showcase.

Charlotte didn't exactly seem enamoured by the piece I'd chosen. It made me wonder if Azure's knowledge of gemmology was as sketchy as the gypsy headscarf she wore. "Do you know what it signifies, Coccinelle?" It was a stupid question but the only other one that came to mind involved asking if she liked it – and at that moment I was almost certain she didn't.

"It's a stone of the heart," she quietly replied. "It promotes self-nurturing, tending and reassurance if the wearer has lost their mother." She held the stone to her heart and looked straight at me. "It denotes empathy and sensitivity, and aids in the acceptance of change."

I'd inadvertently gifted her the most inappropriate present on the planet. At a time when Charlotte was gearing up to cut her mother loose, I'd given her a rock to help her get over it. When I made a grab for the necklace, she moved it out of reach. "Charlotte, please." I held out my hand. "Just give it back and I'll exchange it tomorrow."

"Not so fast, Boy Wonder," she replied. "Tell me your version."

"It's not my version," I grumbled. "I don't know rose quartz from a lump of marble. Azure, the hippie from a new-age store in the West Village told me it's supposed to aid in fertility. Clearly she has no idea." Left hanging with my arm outstretched, I wiggled my fingers. "Give it back."

"I don't want to."

"Please give it back," I repeated. "If you want, we'll go back to the store and throw it through the front window."

Charli laughed, which lessened my chagrin. "Some say it does boost fertility," she explained. "So Azure isn't a fraud."

"Truly?"

"Yes," she confirmed with a slight nod. "Others gems do too. Moonstone, black coral, pearls, red carnelian, turquoise –"

I didn't let her finish. I pressed my lips against hers, overtaken by nothing more complex than the feeling of pure enchantment. I was madly in love with a girl who could forget to pick up the dry-cleaning for three days on the run, but could recite the names of a hundred obscure gemstones on demand.

Charli finally broke away, which wasn't kind to either of us. "What was that for?" she asked.

"Because you know all the lovely words."

Charli turned her back. "Can you help me put it on, please?"

"Tell me what it means to you first."

I had to know which option she was running with. If it was the nurturing mother replacement I'd ask her to hang her keys on it and keep in her purse.

"I don't need help with fertility," she replied. "We're good at making babies when the time is right. It's only been three months, Adam."

"So it's a proxy hug from your loving mom?" I wiggled my eyebrows as I said it, leaving no doubt that I was joking.

"No." She laughed, but it was slightly off. "Remember, I said it denotes empathy and the acceptance of change. I think I'm going to need a big dose of that soon."

"Why, Charli?" She passed me the necklace. "What's happened?"

Her explanation wasn't short, but nor was the task of securing the necklace. I just managed to fix the clasp as she finished the tale of how Olivia had made off with a painting from Bronson's gallery without paying for it.

"Bronson sent me over to the studio this morning to chase it up." She turned back to face me. "I told her she had to come in and make payment by the end of the day."

I swept her hair off her shoulder. "And did she?"

Charli shook her head. "She doesn't have thirty grand, Adam. I don't think she has thirty cents."

Charli didn't know half of what I did. All she had to go on was suspicion. I had a folder in the drawer of my desk full of cold hard proof that the woman was a stone-broke fraud, but I would've felt no joy in enlightening her.

I studied her worried face carefully, quickly deciding that the universe had probably put an indefinite hold on our baby plans until we could get our act together. Charli was stressed to the point of snapping, and none it was her fault.

"Just pay it," I told her. "Write Bronson a cheque tomorrow."

"It's a lot of money," she mumbled.

"It is, but not to us, okay?" I kissed the back of her hand. "You work for Bronson. You can't have your mother indebted to him."

"So Olivia wins," she said sourly. "You wouldn't pay her off but she got your money anyway."

"She hasn't won anything, Charlotte," I explained. "I'm an attorney. One way or the other, I'm going to ruin her."

***

My father was usually unflappable, so when he stormed into my office early that morning, I knew something big was going down.

"The Dixon deal is falling apart." He'd made it sound like the sky was falling. "And if that happens, it's six months of work and countless millions down the drain."

It might've been his million-dollar fee at stake, but it was six months of my hard work that would all be for nothing if the deal collapsed. Strangely, I cared about that. "What is the problem, exactly?" I asked. "I had it all tied up as of last Wednesday. All they had to do was sign off on it."

Dad's frown intensified. "I've called a meeting. Cancel everything else," he ordered. "It's likely to take the rest of the day."

Corporate law is all about the meeting of minds. It was frustrating when we couldn't make it happen, but for it to happen on this day was nothing short of maddening. It was the day of Bridget's concert, which meant my troubles weren't limited to the collapse of a company merger. I had to decide which to deal with, and the seconds I spent doing it were long enough to rouse the suspicion of my father.

"Whatever else you have planned for today needs to come second." He lowered his tone, sounding more like my pissed off dad than my boss. "For once, Adam, make your job the priority."

Either way someone was going to be let down, and in a very rare moment of duty, I decided that it wouldn't be him. There was no reason why Charli couldn't take Bridget to the concert, but only I could deal with the problem my father was facing.

"I'll be at the meeting, Dad," I assured him.

His demeanour changed and he dropped his grip on the door handle. "Excellent," he replied. "Thank you."

I'd become so unreliable lately that he'd come into my office expecting me to let him down. It didn't feel good. Another thing that didn't feel good was calling Charli and explaining what had happened.

"It's no problem," she assured. "We'll handle it."

"Film it for me?" I asked. "I'll watch it with Bridget and make a big deal of it when I get home."

I really didn't need to see it. I'd been to so many practice sessions over the last few weeks that I knew the routine by heart, but I was going to pretend I didn't.

"Of course," she replied. "No worries."

I had plenty of worries about how that day was going to pan out; I just didn't want to tell her that. "Break a leg, Charlotte."

"Better than breaking hearts, right?" she quipped.

"Definitely," I replied. "No broken hearts today, please."

It wasn't her promise to make. It was all going to come down to the hateful ballerina and how twisted her play of the day was going to be.

I didn't want to tell Charli that either.

57. CONNECTIONS

Charli

To say that Bridget was disappointed that I was chaperoning her to the concert was an understatement. The kid lost the plot.

"My dad has to go," she demanded with a stamp of her foot. "You can't."

My feelings were hurt, but the last thing I wanted to do was let it show. I wasn't used to diva-like behaviour from Bridget, and I had no idea how to handle her.

"Daddy has to work," I explained, trying to keep my cool. "Either I take you or you don't go. Those are your choices."

Her crystalline eyes bored into me. "You'll appoint me," she complained after a long moment of deliberation. "And I'll be sad."

I frowned, unsure of what she meant. "What does that mean, Bridge?"

She threw out her arms, frustrated that she couldn't articulate her grievance properly. "Appoint me," she repeated.

On a hunch, I filled in the gap with a suggestion that hurt my heart. "Disappoint you?"

She nodded wildly. "Yes. It always makes me sad when you do that."

I was so crushed that every ounce of breath left my body. I took a step back, slumping onto the couch. Bridget wasn't in the habit of trying to use words she didn't understand. She'd been coached, and even though I knew exactly who'd done it, I asked anyway. "Who told you that?"

"Madame Kara," she said proudly.

"When?"

Her little shoulders lifted. "Sometimes."

My thoughts turned to the last conversation I'd had with Olivia. "The connection between a mother and daughter is more delicate than you think," she'd told me. She wasn't talking about my connection with her. We had no freaking connection. In the most abhorrent of moves, she'd been chipping away at my connection with my daughter.

"Find your bag of letters," I said weakly. "I'll put the word in your bag so you can remember it for next time."

Her little pink satchel of scrabble letters usually held fabulous words that I wanted her to know. Constellation and February had been the latest inclusions, and now I was gearing up to add a hideous word that my vile mother had seen fit to introduce.

Bridget returned to the room a short while later, excitedly rattling her bag of letters. I upended it on the coffee table, picked out the letters and pointed out the word as I choked on the pronunciation.

"I will get it right one day," she announced.

I kissed her cheek. "Me too, Bridge."

***

I knew something was amiss the second we walked through the front door of the studio. It was empty, which was impossible to accept because we were twenty minutes early.

With a firm hold on Bridget's hand, I marched through to the dance hall, and saw not a soul. My heart started hammering, already knowing we were in deep trouble.

"Where are they?" asked Bridget, clueless.

I unfairly shushed her, needing a minute to think. "Hello!" I called.

When I heard footsteps coming from the reception area, I scooped Bridget off her feet and rushed to find the source.

Erin met me at the doorway. "The concert," I blurted. "Where is everyone?"

She frowned at me. "At the Stafford Theatre," she replied. "Broadway and 8th."

It wasn't the most opportune time to be checking, but I was determined to know whose mistake it was. I lowered Bridget to her feet and reached for my phone. It was then that I noticed a text from Adam that I'd somehow missed in the commotion of getting Bridget ready.

– It's at the Stafford Theatre. You have to have her there by 2 p.m. Love you both.

I wanted to cry, and when I checked the time on my phone and saw that it was a quarter to two, I nearly did.

"Are you alright?" asked Erin.

I sniffed. "Perfect," I lied. "We're just running a little late." I picked Bridget up and ran for the door

"We can't be late," Bridget insisted. She put her hand to my cheek to ensure she had my full attention. "No one can be late."

"I'm going to get you there, baby," I promised. "Don't worry."

I stumbled as I stepped out onto the street, forcing Bridget to cling tighter. Adam and Ryan could carry her around for hours on end when the need arose, but I wasn't that strong. I lowered her to her feet and scanned from left to right in search of a cab.

For once, the universe took pity on me. Not only did a cab drive up, it actually stopped when I waved it down. I bundled Bridget inside, gave the driver curt and precise directions, and told him to hurry.

***

We arrived at the theatre fifteen minutes late. The backstage area was bedlam, but seeing so many amped-up ballerinas brought me hope. Olivia's girls weren't the only ones dancing, which meant there was a chance they hadn't performed yet.

When Bridget pointed out one of her friends to me, we followed her. The little girl wove through the crowd, leading us straight to Olivia and the rest of her posse.

From what I could tell, all the girls were there, each dressed in gorgeous sage green leotards with matching stiff tutus.

The mistake was mine, and I felt the need to greet Olivia with an apology. "I'm so sorry we're late."

She turned to face me, whacking me with a look of pure thunder. "I said no later than two."

"I know, but there was a mix-up of venues. We're here now."

"I'm going to dance soon," announced Bridget, maintaining her hold on my hand while she excitedly bounced on the spot.

I expected Olivia to point her in the direction of her costume and tell her to get dressed. There was no way I could've imagined it playing out any differently, which is why her next move paralysed me.

"I said two," she repeated before dropping her line of sight to Bridget. "There will be no dancing for you, Bridget. You can blame your mother for that. All she had to do was get you here on time."

"Please Olivia," I begged. "Don't do this to her."

I could feel Bridget's hand trembling in mine.

"You should've brought your daddy," she continued. "He's obviously the reliable one." Olivia glowered at me, and I knew in that instant she had no heart whatsoever. "Bridget will not be participating on stage. Feel free to watch from the audience if you'd like. There are probably some seats at the back."

The finality of her words hit Bridget like a freight train. She burst into tears. I wasn't faring much better, but it had little to do with her not dancing. My devastation came from the realisation that Olivia probably never had any intention of letting Bridget dance. Every single thing she'd put us through over the past few weeks had been designed to punish me, and me alone.

"Why are you doing this?" My voice was pathetically small, giving my daughter no confidence that I could remedy the situation.

"Leave, Charli," she said simply. "While your daughter still has a little bit of respect for you."

Using the last bit of strength I possessed, I picked Bridget up. She felt like a ragdoll in my arms, just as broken as I was. "Adam was right all along," I told her. "You are a hateful bitch."

Olivia smirked and pointed at the door. "Run along, darling," she mocked. "We have a dance to perform."

***

The cool air that hit my face as we pushed through the front door and exited onto the street was heavenly. I tilted my face to the sky, trying to soothe the burn in my cheeks. I couldn't ever remember feeling that level of rage before, and I wasn't the only one having trouble holding it together.

Bridget stopped crying once I got her outside. Devastation had given way to anger, and it took me less than a minute to work out that it was directed at me.

"You made me late." Her voice was small, but wild. "I said no one can be late."

"I know," I replied. "I'm so sorry."

To Bridget, my apology was baseless and empty. She turned around and stomped her little boots on the pavement as she stormed off. "I'm not talking to you ever again for nine weeks!"

She was too much like me to be able to follow through with dishing out the silent treatment, but enough like Adam to find a way around it. She continued her rant in French. Most of it escaped me, but a few familiar words jumped out. I grabbed her hand, pulling her to a stop.

"You listen to me, Bridget Décarie," I growled. "You can be as disappointed as you like, but if you call me a marshmallow head one more time there's going to be serious trouble."

Her pout could've cut glass, but she didn't speak again. It was a relief for the first few minutes, but showing will I didn't know she possessed, Bridget didn't utter another word to me for the rest of the afternoon.

58. EVERYTHING IS FIXABLE

Adam

My brother likes to think of himself as the ultimate alpha male, but he's not. Our father is. Dad commands attention and respect from everyone he deals with, and because he's charming and articulate, he gets it.

We spent seven hours glued to chairs in the boardroom as we tried our hardest to reel in a deal that was going south for no other reason than a clash of egos. For once, the ego wasn't Dad's. The deal had been mine from the beginning, and surprisingly, he took a back seat and let me handle it. After hours of renegotiation and a few alterations to the original contracts, a new deal was struck. The merger would go ahead as planned, and for now, both parties were happy.

It should've been the end of my working day, but my negotiation skills were in demand. Unable to check them earlier, I spent the cab ride home catching up on the million text messages Charli had sent me that afternoon. I hadn't really anticipated the concert going off without a hitch, but I wasn't expecting Olivia to sink as low as refusing to let Bridget participate.

It was her most vicious move to date. It destroyed Bridget, and judging by the play-by-play text updates her mama gave me, all blame was lumped squarely on Charli's shoulders.

I arrived home to World War Three. It wasn't playing out with weapons and screaming. Our apartment was deathly quiet, which was worse. Charli was in the kitchen, looking miserable and fed up. Bridget was nowhere to be seen.

"Where is she?" I asked.

"In her room," she muttered. "She won't come out and she won't talk to me." She slid a plate of cheese and crackers across the counter. "Can you please take this in to her? She's not eaten all day."

I picked up the plate. "I'll talk her round," I said gently. "I'll make her understand."

She shrugged. "I don't think it's fixable this time."

"Bridget's four, Charlotte," I reminded her. "Everything is fixable."

***

When we returned to New York and moved back into Gabrielle's apartment, we allocated the bigger bedroom to Bridget. The kid had more possessions than Charli and I put together, and putting it all into one room was the only hope we had of containing the clutter.

I inched open the door and took a good look around, searching for my wayward daughter. If I hadn't spotted two little feet poking out from under the bed, I might never have found her.

"Hello," I called. "Is anybody in here?"

"Nobody is in here," came a muffled reply.

I closed the door, shifted a piled of girls and sat on the floor beside her bed. "That's too bad," I lamented. "I brought snacks. I guess I'll have to eat them by myself."

It wasn't enough to coax her out, but when I set the plate down a little hand made a grab for a cracker.

"I'm very sorry that things didn't work out for you today, Bridge."

"We were late," she said simply.

It was important that I choose my words carefully. The point I wanted to get across was that Olivia was responsible for every ounce of disappointment she'd endured that day, not her mother.

"Baby, it wouldn't have mattered either way," I told her. "Olivia wasn't planning to let you dance today anyway."

Bridget was quiet for a long moment, and I worried that I'd been too truthful. Exposing her to a little more of the world wasn't supposed to include the introduction of hateful, twisted people.

"Why not?" she asked finally.

I censored my reply as best I could, giving her only the basics. Not everyone is nice. It was that simple – but a crushing piece of enlightenment to serve a small child nonetheless.

"Madame Kara is not a nice lady."

"Does she hate me?" She sounded worried by the prospect.

I shifted the plate of crackers aside and lay on the floor, needing to see her eyes. "She doesn't hate you," I assured her. "Olivia just doesn't realise how special you are."

"Malibu hates me," she retorted.

The conversation was now getting complicated. Malibu's problem with Bridget was that she *did* realise how special she was. I reached under the bed, sweeping her hair off her forehead. "No one hates you."

"Squirrels hate me."

"And what do you do about that, Bridge?"

"Oh, I stay away from them." Her face contorted into a grimace. "I say 'you're mean dudes, get out of here'."

I tried not to laugh, but failed. "Do you wish you were friends with the squirrels?"

"No," she drawled, as if it was a stupid question. "I hate them too. They're bad."

My daughter was born into wealth and privilege. There was nothing I couldn't buy for her and no place I couldn't take her, but all the money in the world counted for nothing when it came to protecting her from disappointment and hurt inflicted by others – even squirrels. All I could do was shelter her from it. I stared at the ceiling as I asked my next question. "So it's a good idea to stay away if you're not friends, right?"

"Yes it is."

I looked across at her again, silently willing her to understand the reasoning behind what I was about to tell her. "You're not going back to ballet any more."

"I know."

"Are you mad?"

"No." She sounded strong but looked devastated.

"I don't want you to be mad at your mom," I whispered. "She tried very hard for you today."

"Okay," she whispered back.

"And it'd be really nice if you apologised to her."

"I will," she assured me. "I will say 'sorry for being a mean dude'."

"That's all she needs to hear from you." I reached out and held her hand. "In English, Bridget, or it doesn't count."

59. SUNSHINE AND TEQUILA

Charli

Adam and I lay awake talking for hours that night. He was worried about me, and made me promise a hundred times to stay away from Olivia for good.

"Just let it go now," he urged. "She got what she wanted."

It wasn't until the moment she stomped on Bridget's concert plans that I wised up to what it was she did actually want from me. For some reason, Olivia's main objective had been to hurt me, and she'd cruelly carried it out via my daughter.

For Adam, it was reason enough to stay away, but I wasn't satisfied. I lied when I told him I'd let it go, and when I told him I had a meeting with a buyer the next morning, I was lying then too.

The only meeting I had planned for the day was at the Minuet Dance Studio. It was the day of Olivia's bogus charity luncheon, and judging by the glimpse I got of the inside of the dance hall as I passed the doorway, her plans were coming together nicely. Round tables and upholstered chairs had been brought in. There were masses of floral arrangements and rows of gift bags were lined up on a table in the reception area.

Olivia probably thought the details were classy and unique, but I'd attended enough functions to know that it was as stock standard and showy as any charity event – even the legitimate ones.

My lovely mother was nowhere to be seen, but Erin flew out from behind the reception desk as if I'd barged in waving a gun. "What are you doing here?" she hissed. "I don't think you're meant to be here."

I was certain of it.

"Where's Olivia?" My quiet tone matched hers, but void of panic. For the first time in weeks, I wasn't worried about a thing.

"She's in there." She pointed to the doorway of the dance hall. "Please, you have to go."

I peeked inside. Olivia was fussing with the table settings, probably mentally reckoning up her profit for the day ahead.

I grabbed Erin by the elbow and led her to the reception desk. "I have something for you." I reached into my bag, pulled out a cheque and handed it to her. "This will more than cover the money she owes you."

Her brown eyes bulged as she read the cheque. "You don't have to do this." She tried handing it back to me. "It's not right that I take it."

I pushed it back toward her. "It's conditional, Erin," I explained. "I need you to do something for me."

"Like what?"

"I want you to go in there right now and quit," I replied. "You don't have to say anything more. Just quit and leave."

"That's it?" she asked.

I reached into my bag again, this time pulling out a business card. "Call this lady. Her name is Ella Daniels. I mentioned that you're looking for a job, and she said she could use someone at her studio on a part-time basis."

Erin took the card and studied it. "Why would you do this for me?"

"Because you're a good kid," I replied. "So will you do it?"

She didn't answer, just walked into the hall and in a voice laced with both nerves and relief, announced that she was quitting.

I couldn't see Olivia from where I stood, but I had no problem hearing her. "You're needed here today," she barked. "I thought you wanted your money."

"No," replied Erin. "Keep it."

Poor Erin sounded nervous, which made me wonder what she thought Olivia could do to her. She wasted no time in finding out, hightailing it out of the room.

"Get back here!" screeched Olivia. "I'll get you your money!"

Erin didn't even hear. The front door swung shut and she was gone.

It was my turn to make a move. After a few steadying breaths, I stepped into the doorway. "I don't think she's coming back."

My mother's shoulders slumped as she breathed my name. "What are you doing here?"

I took a few steps into the room. "I thought you might need some help getting things ready."

Her look of suspicion was perfectly understandable. What I didn't understand was why it was so brief. "I'd appreciate a hand," she said politely. "And I want to apologise for yesterday. Recitals are very stressful events."

I swallowed hard, tried to suppress the urge to vomit. After all she'd put me through, she was still trying to play me. Olivia Kara thought I was an imbecile, or worse, some poor whipped puppy that she could beat and still expect loyalty from.

"What would you like me to do?" It took all I had to keep my tone polite, but I did it.

"We'll start with the cutlery." She pointed to a box on the table in front of me. "I'm sure you know how to set a lovely table."

I reached into the box and picked up a bunch of forks. "Yes, of course," I replied dryly. "The Décaries taught me lots of good manners."

"It's nice to see that things worked out for you, Charli," she said in her usual condescending tone.

I stopped what I was doing to glower at her.

"That rundown old hovel you lived in with your father was an abomination," she continued. "I felt sorry for both of you."

The bunch of forks in my hand crashed onto the table. She'd just added a new dimension to the drama, and I didn't doubt for a second that it was intentional.

"You've been to my house?"

"If you could call that shack a house." She laughed derisively. "It wasn't fit for farm animals."

My brain went into overdrive, trying to piece a timeline together in my mind. Alex's house was ramshackle when he first bought it. It took him years to repair it and make it the lovely little house it was today.

By my reckoning, I would've been three or four years old while it was in its worst shape. That meant Olivia hadn't walked away from me once, she'd done it twice. It also meant that Alex lied when he told me she'd never had anything to do with me.

Olivia remained ice cold, setting cutlery as if we were having a casual chat about the weather. "You're surprised," she said. "I can tell."

"Not really."

That was a lie. I desperately wanted to know why she'd been to our house, but there was no point asking. I'd save that question for my father.

I picked up the forks, busying myself while I thought things through, but Olivia kept chipping away.

"I feel nothing for you, you know," she said matter-of-factly. "I never have." It was almost a relief to hear her say it out loud, but it didn't make the blasé way she said it any less disturbing.

"It takes a cold woman to say that," I replied.

Olivia looked at me. "Did you think I'd fall in love with you and want to make up for all the time we missed?" she asked. "You're nothing more than something that once happened to me, Charli."

This woman didn't just dislike or resent me. She hated me with every fibre of her being, and even now I wasn't sure why.

"What did I ever do to you?" I asked calmly.

"I had a full scholarship lined up," she said irrelevantly. "The Australian Ballet Academy wooed me for a year. They even put my place on hold while I was pregnant."

"So what happened?" I managed to make it sound like I didn't care either way.

My indifference infuriated her. She thumped a stack of cutlery on the table. "Nerve damage from a poorly executed epidural," she said bitterly. "I never regained my strength and precision. They dismissed me two months into my scholarship. I was seventeen years old."

No wonder she despised me. I wasn't merely an inconvenience. I was a career-ending injury.

In the most bizarre of circumstances, she calmed herself down, I picked up a stack of napkins, and we continued setting tables. I knew before I arrived that this would be the last time I ever spoke to her. For that reason, I wanted to make sure nothing was left unsaid. "I wish I'd never found you," I told her.

"I'm sure you do, darling." She let out a sharp laugh. "But I, on the other hand did quite well out of our short-lived reunion."

I turned to the doorway, catching a glimpse of the hellishly expensive painting I'd forked out for hanging in the reception area. "I'm glad I was finally of some use to you," I said.

The nasty, soul-destroying conversation could've continued for the rest of the morning. Olivia had enough hatred built up to keep burning me for hours, but it was finally time to save myself.

"You're a sneaky, underhanded woman, Olivia," I announced making her laugh again. "My father is good to the core. You should know that."

She let out an exaggerated sigh. "He always was," she said pityingly. "Poor naïve, Alex."

"We butted heads a lot over the years," I revealed, fussing with the vase of pink roses in the centre of the table. "I'm not always good like him."

I could feel her steely glare demanding an explanation. After a long moment of keeping her hanging, I turned around to give her one. "I can be sneaky and underhanded when it comes to getting what I want. I must get that from my mother," I suggested. "I'm especially good at acts of revenge."

Sadly, I wasn't even lying. I'd been more than capable of bad behaviour in the past. None of my impious deeds came close to hers, but common sense dictated that the tinge of wicked in my soul was inherited from her. I was just thankful I'd almost grown out of it.

Olivia cackled as if I'd said something hilarious. "Forgive me," she said insincerely. "But a spoiled little Manhattan socialite trying to sound menacing is comical."

I shook my head, tutting. "You really should've taken the opportunity to get to know me better," I chided. "If you had, you'd know I'm the biggest misfit ever to hit the Upper East Side. There's a reason I don't fit in."

I might've sounded calm and collected, but my heart was hammering, still unsure if I'd be able to pull off my plan and escape with my wits about me. It wasn't my most well thought out idea, but I'd come too far to back down.

"Do tell." She sounded calm too, but wasn't.

"I'm trouble, Olivia," I declared. "You should've stayed away."

She threw her arms wide. "Look around, Charli. Reconnecting was a nice little earner for very little work. I got exactly what I wanted from you. As soon as I realised who you were married to, you became useful."

I glanced around the room, pretending to take it all in. "Oh, yes. I can see how well this worked for you."

Even if Erin hadn't told me that the charity event was a scam, I still would've worked it out. She was far too excited for someone so soulless. People like Olivia don't get keyed up over the success of charity endeavours unless there's something in it for them.

"Fiona booked all thirty tables," she said smugly. "Thousands of dollars in donations."

"Very profitable," I agreed. "It's a shame you won't see a cent of it."

I watched her closely, studying her reaction. Her expression remained straight, but both hands gripped the chair in front of her as if she wished it were my neck.

It was time to put her out of the misery she didn't even know she was in.

"I called in on Fiona this morning and told her to make sure not a single person turns up," I told her. "She stopped payment on the cheque she sent you. You've been left high and dry, lady."

That revelation hit with the force of a freight train. She staggered on to a chair. I mercilessly continued tormenting her.

"What did this charade set you back?" I wandered around the room. "A few thousand for the tables and chairs, another few thousand for the floral displays, and then of course there's the catering." I purposefully kept my tone upbeat. "I imagine you went with the theory that you have to spend money to make money, right?"

"You nasty piece of work," she hissed. "I've spent a fortune on this."

"I know." I smiled. "Maybe you can sell your new artwork to cover it."

"You bitch!" She cried out the insult, and ironically, it was the most emotion I'd ever seen from her.

"Today I am," I casually replied. "Today I am my mother's daughter, but you can rest assured it's a one-off."

"Just go," she yelled, pointing to the door. "Get out!"

I wanted to run but took my time, purely to aggravate. My time with my mother was about to come to a permanent end, and I'd never felt more relief in my life.

"Goodbye, Olivia."

Good riddance, Olivia.

***

When someone says they love you, you don't necessarily feel it. But when someone claims to outright hate you, you feel every damn ounce of it no matter how hard you try not to.

I couldn't face going to work. I didn't think I could face anything at that point. In the poorest of form, I texted Bronson and told him I wouldn't be in that day. His reply was quick, and on any other day it would've made me smile.

– You need sunshine and tequila in equal amounts.

I set off walking as if I had somewhere to be. I was desperate not to waste time analysing the past few weeks of my life. I didn't want to deal with the knowledge that I was one half Alex, one half psychotic bitch.

The only thing I wanted to feel was anger. My life had been interrupted by a woman I'd had no desire to connect with in the first place, and not one skerrick of good had come out of it.

She'd shamelessly ripped off my boss, forcing me to cover her bill. She'd driven a wedge between Bridget and I that I didn't know how to fix, and she'd made me worry that my dad was as much of a liar as she was.

I should've been brutally furious, but the rage just wasn't there. Somewhere along the line I'd given her the power to hurt me, which was the most pitiful feeling on earth. I felt wounded and weak, and no amount of power walking in high-heeled shoes and a tight skirt was going to take it away.

I went with wallowing instead. I walked into the first café I came across, ordered tea and a big slab of chocolate cake, and hid myself away for the rest of the morning.

60. UNDERLYING TENSION

Adam

Bridget apologised to Charli just as I asked her to do, but it wasn't exactly heartfelt. Her timing was good – we were sitting at the table eating breakfast – but she lost all credibility because of phrasing issues.

"Daddy said to say sorry for being mean," she announced.

It was impossible not to see the flash of hurt in Charli's eyes when she glanced at me. "Apology accepted," she mumbled. "Thank you."

It didn't feel right. There was underlying tension that neither of them seemed to understand, but the picture I had was crystal clear. Olivia had played on Charli's insecurity, which was masterful because she only had one. The only thing Charli ever second-guessed was the way she sometimes handled Bridget.

It was a cruel move to pit daughter against mother, but everything about Olivia was cruel. Our only saving grace was that we all knew it, including Bridget on a basic level.

Madame Kara was not worth the effort it took to worry about it. In time, the storm she'd created would blow over, the girls would forget about her and we would go back to being the tight-knit little family we were less than a month ago.

***

The real troubles in life are not the day-to-day struggles of being stuck in a job you hate or dealing with people you don't like. Real trouble is the phone call you get in the middle of the day that you never saw coming – the one that changes your life in an instant.

I was in my father's office at the time, discussing the merger we'd brokered the day before. If there was one thing my father detested, it was being interrupted by inane phone calls. I silenced Ryan's call twice before giving in and answering it. One phone call was a lipstick-on-the-face emergency. Two calls probably meant something more serious.

Ryan didn't give me a chance to utter a word beyond hello.

"Adam, there's been an accident," he blurted. "Bridget fell off the climbing thing at the park. We're at the hospital."

Fraught with worry, my mind went into autopilot. I managed to ask which hospital they were at. That was the only thing I asked, too worried that he'd overload me with information. Until I got there there was nothing I could do, and there's no worse feeling than hopelessness.

I shoved my phone into my pocket and jumped to my feet. I was almost to the door before I offered my father an explanation for my quick exit. "Bridget's been in an accident." The horrible words swelled in my chest. "I have to go."

"I'll call for a car," he replied. "It'll be faster than a cab." With the phone balanced between ear and shoulder, my father prompted me along. "Go, Adam," he urged. "Everything will be fine."

***

Charli's phone kept diverting to voicemail. I left her a message, doing my level best to play things down despite the ugly thoughts spinning through my mind.

By the time I made it outside a car was waiting for me, and less than half an hour later I was barrelling through the front doors of the emergency department demanding to see my daughter.

A polite but slow-moving nurse buzzed me through the double doors and escorted me along the corridor. I didn't ask her anything and she didn't speak until we reached a room at the end. "In there," she said quietly.

I swiped back the curtain.

Bridget looked tiny, swallowed up by the big hospital bed. I pulled her into my arms, utterly relieved that all the worst-case scenarios I'd been conjuring up in my mind weren't even close to being true. There was no blood, and no broken bones. She was crying, but she sounded more scared than hurt.

I lifted my head and noticed a nurse at the foot of the bed. I asked her what was going on; rewording the question a few times to make sure I was understood.

"A doctor will be in shortly," she replied, still writing notes on her clipboard. "He'll explain everything."

Her reply fell short. I wanted to know exactly what was going on, and if she wasn't able to explain it she was useless to me.

"Get someone in here now," I demanded. "If you can't tell me what I need to know then get someone who can."

"Let her do her job, Adam," came a voice behind me.

I turned around and noticed Ryan for the first time. He was leaning against the wall, looking more worried that I'd ever seen him. "What the hell happened?" I choked.

He didn't get a chance to reply. Bridget's head fell forward and she vomited straight down the front of my shirt. She was beyond hysterical now, which meant calming her down took precedence over dealing with the foul ordeal of having her lunch seeping through to my skin.

Ryan handed me a wad of paper towels. "Thank you," I muttered, pointlessly dabbing at my shirt.

My brother opted to wait outside after that. I understood why. I didn't want to be there either, but I wasn't going anywhere without my kid. As he left, he offered to keep trying to get hold of Charli. It shifted Bridget's focus from the horror of throwing up to the worry of not having her mom there with her.

"Ry's going to call her now," I assured her. "She'll be here soon."

Her tiny voice came in staccato rasps. "I want Mummy."

I wished Charlotte had been there to hear her plea. It would've gone a long way to mending both of them. I held Bridget a little bit tighter. "Soon, baby."

Once I calmed her down, I asked what had happened. Her answer took some deciphering. It was fair to say that her claim of being pressured into flying off the climbing frame by a pack of wild squirrels wasn't quite true, but the end result of a crash landing was.

"The mean one said 'just fly off here'," she dramatically explained. "But I fell down."

More tears came. All I could do was hold her. Until Charli arrived, it was just Bridget, vomit and tears.

61. NO GIRLS CAN FLY

Charli

I didn't touch the chocolate cake, which could only mean I was in a really bad way. I allowed myself two hours of wallowing. Anything beyond that was pathetic, and Olivia wasn't remotely important enough to affect me long-term.

After my third cup of tea I came up with a plan for the rest of the afternoon. I'd pick Bridget up from Ryan's and we'd head to the park. We had some serious ground to make up, and there was no better way to do it than with a bit of playground therapy.

The instant I switched my phone on, my grand plan fell apart. The screen lit up with a slew of missed calls and messages that had all come in the last hour.

I didn't need to listen to more than the first. Nothing could describe the horror of hearing Adam tell me that Bridget was hurt. I could barely think straight, and had to replay the message to find out which hospital to go to.

Pulling myself together as best I could, I found some money to pay my bill and dropped it on the table.

A waitress was by my side before I stood. "Everything okay?"

I slung my bag over my shoulder, gearing up to run. "Fine, thank you." I declined her offer of waiting for my change. I just wanted to get out of there.

"Awesome," she crowed, waving the fifty dollar bill. "You've just made my day."

Something about her happy demeanour brought me one step closer to despair. Forcing a smile, I hurried out the door. I did an okay job of holding myself together, managing to hail a cab on the street for the second time in two days. Maybe looking desperate was the trick.

Tears eluded me for the entire cab ride. My daughter was lying injured in a hospital bed and I wasn't crying. I'd wasted so much valuable emotion on my wretched mother that I hadn't saved enough to deal with the situation at hand. Perhaps I really was an awful, dreadful mother, just like my own.

**

When we pulled up outside the emergency department, I fell out of the taxi – literally. My heel got caught on something, possibly my conscience. I landed awkwardly on one knee, letting out yelp reminiscent of a wounded dog.

The cab driver jumped out and rushed to help me to my feet. "I'm fine," I insisted, shrugging him away. "Thank you."

He pointed down at my knee. "You might want to get that looked at, Miss."

Playing down the embarrassment and the pain, I straightened my skirt and pulled myself together as best I could. "I guess I'm at the right place then," I mumbled.

With an awkward smile and a nod, he told me to take care and left me to it. Once he drove off, I surveyed the damage I'd done to my knee. It was a mess, and the blood running down my shin reminded me that it was just as painful as it looked.

I took off my shoes and limped toward the door. I didn't make it past the waiting area. Ryan collared me, grabbing my elbow as I passed.

"Where is she?" I demanded.

"Adam's with her," he replied. "She's okay."

Hearing that brought me relief, but I was having trouble stringing the words together to say so. I stared at him, trying to decipher the reason for his quizzical frown. I must've looked like hell, and the first words out of my mouth were a strange attempt at explaining why. "I fell off my shoes."

Ryan nodded, but the frown remained. "Do you want me to get someone to have a look at your knee?"

"No. Where's Bridget?"

"I'll take you to her," he offered.

When we passed through the doors of the waiting room, panic finally set in. My recent experience with hospitals hadn't exactly been positive, and just being there threw me straight back to the endless days I'd spent holed up with Jack and Alex while Gabi was ill.

Along with panic came urgency. I didn't even realise I'd started running until Ryan ordered me to slow down. "You don't know where you're going."

He was right. I had no idea where I was going or what I was doing. I rarely did, and on days like this it was to Bridget's detriment.

***

The walls of the room closed in on me the second I walked through the door. Bridget lay on the bed and Adam sat beside her, looking far more damaged than our daughter.

"She was sick?" I asked, staring at the stain on his shirt.

Adam let go of Bridget's hand and stood, frowning at me. "Yeah. Are you alright?"

There had to be an element of shock screwing with my thought processes. I couldn't seem to find the right words, and everything I said came out wrong. It wasn't appropriate to lead with a vomit-related question. I should've been taking my daughter in my arms and demanding to know if she was okay.

Instead, I stood by the door as if she was contagious.

"Sit," Adam ordered. I did as I was told, grateful for the instruction.

"You hurt your leg, Mama?" asked Bridget.

I reached for her hand and told her it was no big deal, but she knew I was lying. It's hard to downplay blood. Adam grabbed some paper towels from a dispenser on the wall and pressed them against my knee. "What happened?"

"I fell," I replied before turning to Bridget. "You had a crash too?"

"It was very dangerous," she explained. "It knocked me up."

"Knocked you out," corrected Adam with a smile.

"She was out?" Finally, my voice sounded appropriately concerned. "For how long?"

"Three days," replied Bridget.

Adam's answer was more accurate. "Just a minute or two. They're going to do a CT scan as a precaution."

Bridget must've concluded that a scan was a surgical procedure. She burst into a flood of tears and begged us to take her home.

I didn't know how to settle her. It was the exact same feeling of hopelessness that used to plague me when she was a baby. Adam always knew what to do, which was a double-edged sword. On one hand, he could calm her. On the other, it highlighted the fact that he was almost always the more capable parent.

I took the towels off my knee and stood, moving aside so he could comfort her. "We can't go home just yet," he explained, cradling her as best he could without letting her near his shirt. "But it won't be long now."

The whimper that escaped my lips as I began to cry was unintentional. Adam looked at me. I didn't want attention. I just wanted Bridget to be alright, and at that point he was the only one who could reassure her that she was.

Maintaining his hold on our daughter, he held out his hand to me. "We're okay," he assured us both. "We're all here, and we're okay."

***

I accompanied Bridget to her scan, giving Adam an opportunity to get cleaned up. Bridget didn't take kindly to the procedure, but fatigue was getting the better of her. Hysterics gave way to shallow whimpering, and the lack of complaining on her part made the process run much smoother.

The ordeal was over in a few minutes, and they returned us downstairs to a room on a ward.

It was a lot more comfortable than the emergency room, and the lights had been dimmed, casting a warm glow that put us both at ease. It wasn't ideal, but it was doable.

Bridget finally settled, too tired to protest any more. I sat beside her, stroking her hair. I was weary too. The whole day had been nothing more than a giant sapping of self-worth, energy and confidence

"No girls can fly," she mumbled.

I smiled at her. "*Peter Pan* might disagree, baby."

Her dark blue eyes were heavy, threatening sleep at any moment. "No magic, Mama. It's not real."

I wondered if the bump on her head had brought on her new non-believer status. I wasn't about to demand an explanation, but I was curious. "Who told you that, Bridge?" I whispered.

"Ry," she whispered back.

I pulled the covers a little higher. "Go to sleep," I urged. "I love you."

"I need my daddy to come back."

"He'll be here in a minute," I promised.

"I need him."

"I know." I tucked her hair behind her ear. "Just go to sleep."

Adam's connection to Bridget was hard to define. It was a complex web of a hundred little things that made her see him in a perfect light. Unlike me, he was never indecisive or worried about letting her down – because he never did. I always felt like I stood on much shakier ground. I wasn't often her first choice as the go-to parent, and most of the time I was content with that. I was the one who fired up her imagination with fairy-tales, increased her vocabulary by putting scrabble letters in a bag, and encouraged her stubborn fascination with wearing gumboots – and then panicked that I was making her weird because of it.

Adam gave Bridget stability and I gave her magic. If Ryan had taken that from me, I was lost.

62. BACK TO BASICS

Adam

Light bulb moments usually hit when you least expect them. Bridget's playground mishap forced me to re-evaluate things. After months and months of procrastinating, everything suddenly became clear.

The way I divided my time between my family and my job was grossly unbalanced. Too many hours were spent cooped in an office working a job I hated while my brother hung out at the park with my daughter.

I didn't resent Ryan. I was hugely grateful that he was prepared to give up his afternoons to help us out. If anything I was jealous, which was ridiculous considering I'd had the power to change the situation all along.

There was no need to for me keep my job on the pretence that it was temporary. If Charli decided to renew her contract at the gallery, life in New York could be ongoing for a while. And if that was to happen, I was determined to make sure I was the one who'd be spending afternoons in the park with my kid.

I laid out my plans of quitting to Ryan over a cup of bad coffee in the waiting area. I expected him to be surprised, but he wasn't.

"Because of today?" he asked.

"Partly. It was a wake-up call."

"Just take a bit of time off," he suggested. "You might want to go back to it later."

"No, I won't."

"How do you know?"

"Because I'm not a lawyer, Ryan." I stared at the floor. "I just pretend to be. I freaking hate the job. I hate everything about it." When he asked if I'd consider taking on the work at the club, I told him I'd think about it. The prospect of overseeing the renovations had been tempting me for a while. I just wasn't prepared to commit to anything that night.

First and foremost I needed to make sure Bridget was okay, and then I needed to talk to Charli – something we hadn't really done for a while.

There's nothing sadder than missing someone you see every day. Little more than a month ago, the most important thing we had on our agenda was making a baby – and then Olivia's poison trickled in. All talk of future babies and nonsensical conversations about sea dogs took a back seat.

It was time to get back to basics.

***

Bridget had been moved to a ward. I spoke to a doctor in the corridor, who gave me the good news that she was okay. "There's a mild concussion, but there's no reason why she can't go home tomorrow," he explained. I was so relieved that my voice faltered as I thanked him. He smiled and pointed toward the door. "Your family are waiting for you."

Walking into that room was the calmest moment I'd had all day. Bridget was asleep, and the room was so quiet that I when I leaned down to kiss her, I could hear her breathing.

In an odd move that made no sense, Charli stood up and offered me her chair. I took her hand and pulled her back down. She lifted her head, looking up at me through weary brown eyes. "She's been asking for you."

I crouched in front of her. "I'm here now," I replied. "And someone's going to be in shortly to have a look at your knee."

Charli outstretched her leg, checking out her bloody knee. "Impressive, right?"

"I'm not sure." I grinned. "Was a scraped knee on your never-done list?" She shook her head.

I planted a kiss just above the scrape. "I love you, Charlotte," I declared. "Just in case I haven't told you that today."

Charli broke, throwing her arms around me with such force that I fell to my knees. I wasn't trying to incite tears, but there was no consoling her. I asked her a hundred times what was wrong before she finally offered an explanation.

"I didn't have a meeting this morning." Her voice was hoarse and small in my ear. "I lied to you."

I leaned back. "Where did you go?"

It was a pointless question. Her distraught mood told me it had to have something to do with her mother.

"I went to see Olivia. Please don't be mad."

I brushed tears from her cheeks with my thumbs. "I thought we agreed that it was done."

"It's definitely done now." She sniffled. "I made sure of it."

I should've known that Charli wasn't going to take Olivia's treatment of Bridget lying down. But what I wasn't expecting was such an elaborate act of settling the score.

"I went to your mum this morning and asked her not to show up," she explained. "I think she was relieved."

Even without knowing the family connection, my mother disliked Olivia. Any dealings she had with her would only ever have been as a favour to Charli.

"The whole event was a sham," she continued. "The only cause Olivia has is herself. She runs these bogus events and makes off with enough money to keep her non-existent ballet school ticking over until the next one. I shut her down."

Nothing about the revelation shocked me, but I was surprised that Charli had managed to keep it to herself for as long as she had.

"Why didn't you tell me earlier?"

"Because I wanted to deal with it and I knew you'd try talking me out of it."

I wanted to yell at her, but I wanted to kiss her more. I leaned, tasting her tears as I pressed my lips against hers. "Please tell me it's finished now," I murmured.

"I couldn't take another second of knowing her," she quietly replied. "Every dealing I've had with her has left me more beaten up than the last."

I kissed her again, utterly relieved.

"She hates me, Adam." I could feel her hands trembling on my neck. "Honestly despises me."

I wasn't going to lie and tell her otherwise. I'd known it for a while. "It doesn't matter," I replied strongly. "Your dad picked up her slack. He loves you enough for both of them."

She hugged me even tighter. "I'm scared that I'm like her," she whispered in my ear. "She's a terrible mother."

"You're nothing like her." It frustrated me that she was even making the comparison. "And she's no mother. There's not a damn thing she could teach you about how to raise your daughter."

63. INVINCIBLE

Charli

I had a tendency to paint over the ugly parts where Olivia was concerned, but for the first time ever, I told Adam everything – including my concern over the damage she'd done to my relationship with Bridget.

He didn't seem surprised, which led me to think he already knew. "We're going to get back on track, Charli," he assured me.

I nodded, which is where the lines of honesty blurred slightly. Getting back on track was going to be hard if we had a little non-believer in the mix. Whether he meant to or not, Ryan had snapped my strongest connection to my daughter. Without magic, I wasn't sure where I stood.

"I'm going to quit my job," he said out of the blue.

A sudden pain shot through my knee as I twisted to hold him tighter. It wasn't up to Adam to fix the whole world, but giving up the things that made him unhappy was a great start. "What are you going to do instead?"

He shrugged. "There's a lot of work at the club to be done."

"Until the beach beckons," I hinted.

I wasn't quite ready to throw in the towel and go home, but the reasons why were no longer work-related. Going home meant confronting Alex, and I had no plan for dealing with that just yet.

Adam smiled. "Do you hear it, Coccinelle?"

I shifted my hands to his face, settling my thumb in his dimpled cheek. "Today I do," I whispered.

***

I was tired, but Adam looked shattered. At least he was clean now. In an unexpected act of kindness, Ryan had swapped shirts with his brother. When I offered to find a cup of coffee, he didn't protest. I left him sitting beside our little girl, patting her back the same way he used to when she was a baby. It was an absent gesture brought on by total exhaustion, just like old times.

I ended up at a vending machine in the emergency waiting room. As soon as the cup started filling with coffee, I knew it wouldn't be good. Just the smell of it reminded me of burnt wood. I forced a lid on it and picked it up anyway, unwilling to head back empty-handed.

"Might I offer a better suggestion?" came a voice from behind.

Of all the crazy events that day, seeing Jean-Luc standing in front of me when I turned around was the most shocking.

"What are you doing here?"

"I heard they're keeping my granddaughter overnight," he replied. "I thought I'd stop by and check on her."

He hadn't arrived empty-handed. In a gesture almost as grand as swapping shirts, he'd brought coffee.

"Adam will be so thankful." I pointed at his tray. "He's getting all jittery from the withdrawals."

"I'm pleased to be of help." He motioned to a row of chairs. "Can we sit for a minute?"

I dumped the burnt wood coffee in a nearby bin and sat down. It was then that Jean-Luc noticed the cut on my knee. "Charli, what on earth happened?" He sounded aghast.

"I fell over," I replied, looking down at my knee. "That's the last time I hit the bar in my lunch hour."

"I want it seen to," he demanded, setting the Starbucks tray down on the empty seat beside him. "It looks painful."

I didn't argue when he made his way to the triage desk. It made me feel special, and I was rarely made to feel special by the king. I didn't hear the conversation, but when he turned and pointed at me, I figured he was making demands for band-aids and antiseptic.

He wandered back. "They're busy tonight," he explained. "I told them we'd wait."

"Adam's waiting for me."

"Adam can wait a bit longer."

I didn't argue with that either. He was probably asleep in the chair anyway.

Jean-Luc handed me a cup. "Earl Grey," he announced.

"You remembered I drink tea?" The only thing more embarrassing than my small voice was the fact that my eyes started welling with tears. It was such a simple detail, but at that moment it meant everything. My own mother didn't know I liked tea. She'd never taken the time to learn a single thing about me.

Tears didn't rattle the king as much as I expected they would. He reached into his top pocket and handed me a handkerchief.

"I'm sorry," I mumbled.

"It's been a hellacious day, Charlotte," he replied. "There's no need to put on a brave front."

I held my cup up to him. "Thanks for the tea."

"You're welcome, my love."

I wasn't just thanking him for the tea. In a rare moment, I was grateful for his company. Jean-Luc Décarie was everything you'd expect the patriarch an obscenely wealthy family to be. He was tough, rigid and extraordinarily unforgiving of anything he deemed unbecoming to his family. But very occasionally he'd do something nice, reminding me that he considered me part of the family he so fiercely protected.

Tonight's effort didn't stop with tea. A woman sitting on the row of chairs in front of us took exception when a nurse approached us to tend to my knee. She turned around and let loose. "We've been here four hours," she barked, pointing at the kid beside her.

The nurse replied in a calm voice that probably took years to master, "Someone will be with you shortly, ma'am." She turned back to me. "We'll get this cleaned up."

Jean-Luc replied for me. "Thank you. We appreciate it."

"My child has been waiting for four hours," interjected the furious woman.

The nurse ignored her. "I'll be back in a moment with a dressing," she said, already walking away.

Jean-Luc was having a harder time ignoring the woman, but I could tell he was trying. I almost felt sorry for her. She had no idea who she was up against. Her rude comments wouldn't even come close to matching Jean-Luc's if he decided to unload on her.

"This is ridiculous," she complained to no one in particular. The boy sitting beside her sank down in his chair, obviously wishing he was anywhere but there – sick or not.

"Madam," said Jean-Luc quietly. "I find you exceptionally rude."

She whipped her head around to glower at him. "I saw you arrive," she accused, looking him up and down. "With your designer suit and your fancy schmancy coffee. You only just got here."

"Is it the suit or the beverages that bother you the most?" he asked calmly.

"It's the preferential treatment!" She pointed at her kid again. "My boy has been sitting here for hours."

"So you keep telling me," he murmured, brushing invisible lint off the leg of his pants.

It wasn't the wait that was infuriating her now. It was the king's tone.

Her child let out a hacking cough that reminded me of a choking baby seal. Her response was to thump him on the back until he nearly coughed up a lung.

"My child is coughing," she snapped.

Jean-Luc leaned forward, resting his elbows on his knees. He spoke in a low and menacing voice befitting the king of Décarie land. "And my child is bleeding," he retorted. "Now turn around and wait your turn."

I wasn't surprised when she did as she was told, nor was I embarrassed by the obnoxious stand he'd taken. On a day when I was feeling most vulnerable, he'd stood up for me, protected me and reminded me that despite everything, I was the princess of his youngest prince.

***

Bridget woke just before six. Her mood was questionable, but her physical state was good. As soon as we could find someone prepared to discharge her, we bolted.

Her cranky mood was a strong sign that she needed more sleep, and because we got home before the sun was up, it was easy to trick her into going back to bed. I tucked her in while Adam searched for Treasure. Once reunited with the doll, Bridget gave up complaining and fell asleep.

A hot shower trumped sleep for Adam. He'd been dreaming of it since the night before. I snuck into the bathroom and watched him like a creeper for a long time before saying anything. Oblivious, he stood letting hot water run over his head.

"You remind me of a boy I used to know," I said finally.

Adam smiled but didn't speak.

"He was the first boy I ever saw naked," I continued. "Well, the first that counted."

His lovely dark laugh echoed in the small room. "Lucky guy."

"I was the lucky one," I corrected, keeping my eyes locked on his as I unbuttoned my top.

"So what happened to him?"

I shrugged off my shirt, letting it hit the wet floor. "I broke his heart," I said casually. "Then he broke mine – a few times."

I must've been moving too slowly. Adam's wet hands spun me around and unzipped my skirt.

"He sounds like a dick," he mused.

"He used to be," I agreed, kicking my skirt aside. "But he grew up, stopped breaking my heart and let me love him." My whole body shuddered as a wet hand swept my hair out of the way and unhooked my bra. "And he's very good with his hands."

His lips pressed against my shoulder – a move that changed the tempo of my breathing. "And his mouth?" he mumbled.

"Very good with his mouth," I confirmed shakily.

I shimmied out of my underwear, stepped into the shower and melted into his waiting arms.

Adam brushed the back of his hand down my cheek. "You kind of look like a girl I used to know too." He frowned. "She was young – only seventeen – mad as a hatter."

I pretended to push him away. He held me tighter. "But she was special," he said laughing. "Like no one I'd ever met before."

"Did you keep her?"

He dipped his head, chasing my lips. "Of course I did," he murmured against my mouth. "She loved me when I least deserved it."

We'd always belonged to each other, even when we couldn't find a way to be together. There were no obstacles now. We were open, complete and ready for whatever the world threw at us, and after what we'd endured that day I knew there was nothing we couldn't handle. Together we were invincible.

I put my hands to his cheeks, inching his head back. Water streamed down, making him blink.

"I've loved you my whole life," I declared.

His next words were said with his lips. My body was burning, and it had nothing to do with the temperature of the water. The blood coursing through my body was a fiery combination of true love and absolute desire.

I broke free to whisper in his ear. "We have to get out."

"Why, Charlotte?" In a move that made my legs shaky, he touched his lips to the side of my neck. "The water's hot. You're hot. What more do we need?"

I put both hands on his chest to keep him at bay and looked at my knee. "I wasn't supposed to get the dressing wet."

"Well, rebel, we can't have you breaking the rules."

Changing my mind would've been simple, but Adam didn't try. Before I knew it, I was bundled up in a towel and being carried across the hall.

***

A morning in bed together was my plan but Adam had other ideas. I sat up, tucking the sheet under my arms. "You're not seriously going to the office?" I grumbled. "Please come back to bed."

He continued raking through the closet looking for something to wear. "I won't be gone long," he promised. "I'm going to try and catch Dad at home before he leaves for work."

As much as I wished he'd take some time to sleep, I understood his mindset. Wanting to get the task of resigning over and done with quickly made sense.

"Don't let him change your mind," I coached.

Adam pulled on jeans and a T-shirt. "I won't."

"And don't take anything he says to heart," I added. "He's thoughtless when he's angry."

He walked back to the bed, leaned down and kissed me. "Don't worry about a thing. I can handle him."

I wished I'd warned Jean-Luc the night before. Perhaps with a little time to think things through, he'd be less likely to explode. As things stood, I had no choice but to stand back, let Adam walk out the door and wait for the fallout.

64. HOBBY

Adam

I was relieved not to have to explain my early morning visit to my mother. Mrs Brown met me at the door. Her smile was wide, but nothing compared to the grin she gave me when I told her we didn't need her babysitting prowess any more. She reached up and pinched my cheeks. "Wonderful, wonderful boy," she exclaimed. "I'm delighted."

I couldn't blame her. She'd been hoping for redundancy for a while. I thanked her again, making sure she understood how appreciative we were of all she'd done for us.

It earned me a harder pinch. "My pleasure, young man. Who is my replacement?"

I grinned at her. "I am."

Mrs Brown dropped her hold on me and frowned. "Does your father know?"

"No; that's why I'm here."

"He's in his office," she said quietly. "I wish you luck."

"Thanks," I replied, winking. "I might need it."

Mrs Brown had been working for my family since Ryan was little. Better than anyone, she knew the dynamics. Dad was going to be pissed at the news and there was no point pretending otherwise. My heart thumped as I climbed the stairs, which was a pathetic reaction that annoyed me. No matter how many times I reminded myself that I was grown, confronting my father always reduced me to feeling like a ten-year-old kid in trouble – especially if it went down in his home office.

The big arched windows facing Fifth Avenue boasted a gorgeous view of the park, but it was lost on Dad. His desk was positioned so his back was to the window. He couldn't see the park, but he had a stellar view of anyone walking into the room.

When I rounded the doorway he closed his laptop, giving me his full attention. "Adam. How is my granddaughter this morning?"

We were not off to a good start.

"Bridget, you mean?"

He motioned to the chair in front of his desk. "Of course I mean Bridget. How many granddaughters do I have?"

I sat down. "Just one, unless the rumours about Ryan are true."

He laughed, and for a moment the tension slipped.

"Bridget's fine," I confirmed. "We brought her home this morning."

"I think you should take a few days off to spend with her."

For a split second, the coward in me contemplated agreeing to it, but I knew all it would achieve was a few more days of stewing.

"Dad, I have something more permanent in mind," I hinted.

His shoulders fell, but he was far from relaxed. I didn't need to elaborate. He knew what was coming.

"If you walk away now, everything you've worked for has been for nothing," he said bitterly.

"It will always count for something," I insisted. "It's just not what I want to do."

He shook his head, looking bewildered. "I don't understand you. Life is not a free ride, no matter the circumstances."

"I'm not planning to do nothing," I snapped. "I'm going to oversee the renovation work at the club we've just bought."

Dad groaned as if it was the most ridiculous suggestion on earth. "A waste of a good mind," he barked in French.

I wished I'd been strong enough to speak up for myself when I was younger. If I had, studying for a law degree might never have come into play. I'd spent years believing that it was my calling, but looking back I realised that it was my father's dream, and had been all along.

"I'm not a lawyer," I said strongly.

"If you abandon your career, you'll be nothing." The harsh expression on his face told me that he truly believed it. "A construction worker at best."

My dad had no clue of the work I liked to do, and perhaps that wasn't his fault. Enlightening him was probably pointless, but I wanted to try.

"Construction doesn't interest me," I told him. "I like breathing new life into old things – buildings, boats, furniture."

The home I grew up in was a veritable storage locker of antique furniture. The desk he was sitting at was well over a hundred years old. That alone meant that he should've had an appreciation for the craft I was so passionate about, but I was struggling to make him understand.

"It's a hobby," he replied. "And it should remain that way."

"My daughter isn't a hobby," I retorted. "I want to free up more time to spend with her too. It's not right that Ryan sees her more than I do."

"Her mother should be spending time with her." He raised his voice for the first time. "Have Charli quit her job and tend to your daughter. That's how it should be done."

"Yes, Dad," I replied dryly, "if we were living in 1950."

"Meeting that girl was your undoing, Adam," he claimed, drumming his forefinger on his desk. "Your whole life went to hell after that."

Letting a comment like that go was never going to happen. I leaned forward, looking him dead in the eye. "I don't even know who I was before Charli, but I do know I wasn't particularly good. Would you rather I be a one-track asshole attorney or a good father and husband?" I asked. "Because past history shows that I can't be both."

"Find balance," he demanded.

The leather chair squeaked as I straightened up. "A righteous pose," I returned sarcastically. "You're asking me to do something you never could."

I hadn't intended to attack him, but I could tell that I had. Apologising wouldn't help. He wasn't in a forgiving mood.

"Get something to me in writing," he ordered in his best business-like voice. "I want a formal letter of resignation."

I stood to leave. "I'll do that," I assured him.

Dad opened his laptop and stared at the screen, despite that fact that it hadn't fired up yet. "Deliver your keys to the front desk," he instructed. "I'll have Tennille box up your belongings and clean out your desk."

I'd left the realm of errant son. I'd now become nothing more than an ex-employee, and it hurt far more than I expected it would.

"You're not going to let me back in?"

He stared straight at me. "You've made your decision. At least have the fortitude to stick by it."

"And what about you, Dad?" I asked bitterly. "What are you going to do?"

He didn't hesitate. "I'm going to stick by mine too."

Utterly destroyed but trying not to let it show, I shoved the chair back into position. "I guess that's it then." I pointed to the new picture hanging on the side wall. "Nice photo, by the way. I didn't think artistic nautical shots were to your taste. Perhaps a scene depicting an epic battle or a public hanging would've been more fitting for this room."

He turned to the photo on the wall. "Your wife introduced me to it," he replied. "Perhaps that's why you like it."

"I'm sure it is," I muttered. "What's your excuse?"

Dad slid his chair back and wandered over to the picture. "It reminds me of when I used to take my boys sailing on the river." He glanced at me. "Do you remember?"

"Every Saturday," I confirmed.

"Ryan never showed a lot of interest," he continued. "But you were a different story."

My brother's fascination only held as long as Dad let him steer. The rest of the time was spent complaining about having to wear a lifejacket or worrying that Jaws was going to rise up and eat him. But I loved it. There was nothing not to love about a little wooden boat being powered through the water by nothing more than the wind.

"It's a shame you lost interest," he added.

His recollection of that time was wildly different from mine. I could feel the ire bubbling in my gut. "We didn't lose interest," I snapped. "When I turned ten you hired a tutor. Saturday mornings on the Hudson gave way to extra homework sessions."

He didn't turn around. "I only ever wanted the best for you both," he replied. "I still do."

My mother's timing that morning was impeccable. She waltzed into the room rattling off a round of breakfast options to my father, then caught sight of me. "Adam, darling," she said, surprised. "You're here early. How is Bridget?"

"She's fine," I replied, leaning to kiss her. "We brought her home this morning."

"Wonderful," she beamed. "So what are you doing here then?"

I didn't answer. I was more interested in hearing my father's reply. Unfortunately, he wasn't quick to volunteer an explanation either.

"Well?" she demanded. "What's going on?"

"Everything is fine, Fi," Dad insisted.

Nothing was fine. I groaned, annoyed that he couldn't be truthful. My mother considered that a hostile act. She grabbed a fistful of my T-shirt. "You listen to me," she demanded. "We have a wedding in two weeks. There will be no discord between now and then. Do you understand?"

Ignoring the fact that she was doing her best to shake me like a ragdoll, I kept my focus firmly on my father. "I understand perfectly."

She let me go and set her sights on her husband. "And you!" She whacked his arm. "Why must you antagonise?"

Dad dared to smile at her. "I am doing no such thing."

She whacked him again.

Dad stepped forward and pulled her into his arms. "You truly are beautiful, Fiona Rose," he murmured.

There had never been a better cue to leave. Some things can never be unseen. I quickly said goodbye and made a dash for the door.

***

Whatever went on after I left obviously didn't last long. I'd only been home an hour when Mom showed up armed with enough supplies to bake us into the next millennium.

"I thought Bridget might like to help bake some cookies." She held a bag of groceries out to me. "It might cheer her up."

I put my finger to my lips. "They're sleeping, Mom."

I took the bag and motioned toward my sleeping girls in the living room. After Bridget woke, Charli lay with her on the couch for some mermaid therapy. Both of them were asleep in minutes, and until my mother showed up I'd been hopeful of following suit.

"Say no more," she whispered, pushing past me. "I'll make a start on them by myself."

Mom wasn't the only visitor that morning. When Ryan turned up and suggested we go out for coffee, I jumped at the chance. The smell of burning cookies was starting to filter through the apartment and Mom was driving me crazy.

One of the things I liked best about living in New York was the convenience of having everything on our doorstep. We walked no further than the café at the end of the block. "This is handy," noted Ryan.

"It is," I agreed. "As soon as Charli lets me, I'm going to train Bridget to run down here and buy me coffee."

He laughed, but barely sounded like himself. We hadn't been seated long before he confessed why.

The fall from the top of the climbing frame hadn't been the biggest crash to happen the day before. The first wreck happened when he took it upon himself to inform my daughter that there was no such thing as magic.

I was furious with him, but needed to handle it properly. Getting angry wasn't going to help anyone. "Why would you do that?" I asked. "She's four years old, Ryan."

"And I want her to live to see five," he replied. "You can't have her jumping –"

"It's not even about the jumping." Cutting him off was the best I could do. What I really wanted to do was lean across the table and punch him, but I was too exhausted to make a fist. "Why didn't you go the whole hog and enlighten her about Santa and the Easter Bunny while you were at it?"

"I know I shouldn't have said anything. It was a mistake."

As remorseful as he was, Ryan couldn't grasp the damage he'd done. This was going to destroy Charlotte, and in turn, Charlotte was probably going to destroy him. It seemed fair to warn him.

A worried frown set in. "Do you think I should tell Charli?" he asked. "I will if you want me to."

It was a gallant offer, all things considered. "No. She has enough to deal with at the moment. Just wait and see what happens."

"Is there something going on that I should know about?"

For a moment I considered telling him everything, but the story of Olivia wasn't mine to tell. "No," I replied. "Everything is fine."

65. DAMAGE

Charli

We had a tendency to close ranks when times got tough, and we'd never faced anything more brutal than the wringer the three of us had been put through over the past month.

The tough front Adam put up was purely for Bridget and I. He was hurting. As expected, his father hadn't taken the news of his resignation well. He'd resorted to his usual repertoire of cutting remarks and insults. It wasn't the first time, but unless they could work it out it was going to be the last. Adam's usual routine of giving Jean-Luc a few days to calm down didn't apply any more. He was done, and devastated because of it.

Bridget's bump on the head was cured by a few lazy days at home and chicken nuggets for dinner two nights on the run. In a sure-fire sign that she was feeling better, the tale of her death-defying leap from the playground equipment had grown to epic proportions. When I heard her telling Alex about it on the phone, the timeline of events now included bullying squirrels and Treasure's inability to catch her at the bottom. "Her arms don't bend wide enough," she explained.

I let her have her moment, mainly because that was the only moment she had going on. Since Ryan's thoughtless no-magic lecture, we hadn't even been able to get her to sit down and read a book with us. Fairy-tales were off limits. Not even the picture book version of Ariel held her interest. "It's not real, Mum," she insisted, over and over. "And I don't love it."

I wasn't going to push the issue, but the issue was pushing me. I felt like something precious had been stolen from me, and I vowed that when I finally got around to confronting the thief, he'd be sure to know it.

We hadn't seen Ryan all week, and Bridget clearly missed him. When I mentioned heading to his apartment for a dress fitting, she jumped at the chance to see him. She took off to her room, returning in a little summer dress offset with the heavy tweed coat her grandmother had gifted her back in July.

"I thought you hated that coat," I said, looking her up and down.

"Not this coat," she replied sweetly. "I just love this coat."

Bridget's enthusiasm for visiting her uncle seemed to wane once we got to his place. When the door opened, she became incredibly quiet and withdrawn, and I quickly realised it was because she was nervous. Ryan seemed anxious too, but it would've taken a cold soul not to notice how genuinely happy he was to have her back.

Thanks to Ivy's eagerness to get out of the apartment, the dress fitting was over and done with fairly quickly. Perhaps she knew a showdown was imminent. Bente picked up on the tension too, but found a way around it by removing Bridget from the room. "We'll go for a walk," she suggested, taking her by the hand.

I wanted to go with them. Being left alone with the object of my wrath was borderline awkward. I sat at the counter while Ryan made coffee I didn't want.

I wasn't sure what to say to him at first, but he made it easy for me by ridiculously asking if I was mad at him.

"You know I am."

"I wasn't trying to cause trouble, Charli," he explained. "Honestly."

I believed him a hundred percent, but it didn't lessen the damage he'd caused. I was tired of being undermined by Décaries. Jean-Luc and Fiona did it by way of outrageously expensive presents and money, and now Ryan had thrown his hat into the ring by vetoing magic.

"You stole something from me," I told him. "And for the life of me, I don't know how to get it back."

As expected, Ryan had no clue what I was talking about. Explaining it to him wasn't difficult. It was a conversation I'd rehearsed in my head for days, and getting rid of it was bliss.

I broke it down for him as simply as I could. The confidence I possessed when it came to parenting my daughter wasn't always high.

"You're a good mom, Charli," he assured me.

"Some days I am," I agreed. "And some days I have no clue what I'm doing. You want to know why I think that is?"

He looked at me but didn't answer, which was probably one of his wiser decisions of late.

"I had no mother, Ryan. How am I supposed to know what the hell I'm doing?"

I'd done a lot of soul searching over the last few days, and that was finally the conclusion I'd come to. After weeks of trying to find something to align myself to Olivia, I realised that looks and mannerisms were unimportant. I looked like my father, and that was that. No part of me wanted to resemble a vicious half-starved ballerina anyway.

The bigger worry was what she *hadn't* given me. Adam was right. There was nothing Olivia could teach me about being a good mother to my child. For me, doing right by my kid was always going to be trial and error.

"My connection to Bridget isn't going to the park or speaking French or reading books," I explained. "It's the stories that my dad gave me. That's how I connect with her, and that's how he connected with me." Winging it with tales of La La Land wasn't a new concept. By all accounts, Alex's mother had been no prize either.

Although he'd graciously heard me out, Ryan wasn't quite ready to forfeit. "She knocked herself out trying to fly, Charli," he pointed out. "You can't possibly think that's okay."

My palms were starting to sweat. I pressed them flat on the counter, appreciating the cool granite. "Perhaps if you hadn't stolen her wings she might've done it."

"Wings?" he asked incredulously. "You think I stole her wings?"

"We all lose them eventually, Ryan," I said quietly. "The moment you doubt whether you can fly, you cease forever to be able to do it."

My hothead brother-in-law's calm façade finally cracked. He demanded that I stop preaching nonsense – something he'd done a million times before.

"It's from *Peter Pan*, idiot."

"That doesn't make it any more credible."

Pure frustration escaped me in the form of an angry groan. "You just don't get it. I'm not crazy. I know the difference between a fairy-tale and real life, but what if there's the tiniest ring of truth to it?"

He deliberated for a long time, making me hopeful that he trying to understand the stand I was taking. "Impossible," he finally concluded, shutting me down the same way his father always did.

"Deny it all you want to, Ryan, but one day something extraordinary is going to happen and you're not going to be able to explain it away," I insisted. "You won't think it's impossible then. You're going to think it's magic. I just hope I'm around to see it."

I left Ryan's apartment on a promise that day. After a lot of bickering and the occasional round of raised voices, he surprised me with an extraordinary offer.

"I'll make it up to her, Charli," he vowed. "I don't know how, but I will."

I believed him, and the reason why was simple. Sometimes the only person with the power to make things right is the person who hurt you in the first place. The best we can hope for is that they're decent enough to try.

66. A HIT OF MAGIC

Adam

Charli was infinitely more productive than I was that week. She actually made it to work each morning, but then, she had a job to go to. I was content to take time out and hang out with my kid.

After days of radio silence, Ryan called me two days before the wedding and asked that we bring Bridget to the club.

"It's important," he said seriously. "I wouldn't ask if it wasn't."

I didn't make life difficult by protesting. Ryan had enough on his plate with out-of-control wedding plans. I was also keen to check out the ceiling, which had been stripped back and painted the week before, so a trip to the club was actually appealing.

***

We were the last to arrive. Ryan and Bente were standing in the main room, checking out something on the stage. My focus was entirely on the ceiling. The shabby, peeling paint was gone. It was now bright white, perfectly showcasing the flowery pattern pressed into the tin.

"Ceiling looks good," I commented.

"Yeah," agreed Ryan, sounding as if he didn't care either way.

Bridget was far more enthusiastic, but it probably had nothing to do with the ceiling. Breaking the hold I had on her, she scooted across the floor, throwing herself at Ryan.

He caught her, proving that despite everything he really was a good uncle. "I have something to show you," he told her.

Bridget squashed his cheeks between her hands. "Really? A surprise?"

Ryan turned around to speak to Charli. "You were right," he said vaguely.

"I'm always right," she muttered, unfazed by his comment.

"I'm sorry I stole from you. I'm going to give everything back to you today."

I had no idea what he was talking about, but Charlotte clearly did. She hooked her arm through mine and held tight, either anticipating something really good or expecting something dreadful. I couldn't decide which.

Ryan lowered Bridget to her feet. She took off running around the stage as if making up for the stage debut that had never happened.

"I love it up here," she announced. "Really love it."

Ryan slipped behind the velvet curtain and Bente edged toward us, looking as nervous as Charli. I was seconds away from demanding an explanation when Ryan reappeared carrying a pair of sparkly wings that told me all I needed to know. He was about to give my daughter a much-needed hit of magic.

67. CHECKED BOXES

Charli

When money is no object, the smallest of gestures is still grand. The wealth of my family had never impressed me, but I wasn't arrogant enough to claim that our lives weren't positively affected because of it. It afforded us the freedom of a gypsy lifestyle. Nowhere was off limits if the urge to wander beckoned.

Ryan's use of his wealth was a little more traditional. He lived an extravagant life, so the plans he came up with were always grand. Giving Bridget her wings back involved an elaborate set-up of cables and trickery designed to make her believe she was flying.

There weren't words to describe how it felt to see my little girl on stage, waving her arms and kicking her legs as she swung through the air. She was no Madam Butterfly, but there still seemed to be structure to her clumsy flailing.

I tore my eyes from her to glance at Adam. "Is she dancing?" I queried.

He leaned down and whispered in my ear. "That's the routine she was supposed to do at the recital."

He would know. Adam had suffered through a million hours of practice, and many of them had taken place on the sidewalk as they trekked back to his office after ballet lessons.

Bridget had worked tirelessly for weeks to learn the routine and had been excited by the prospect of showing it off on stage, only to have it ripped away by Olivia. Bridget might not have been Prima Ballerina material, but she was our Prima, and when I looked back up at the stage, she suddenly didn't seem so clumsy any more.

Ryan had inadvertently given her much more than he'd taken. As well as returning her wings, he'd also managed to fill the massive void left in her heart by my mother's wicked deeds.

All of Bridget's boxes were checked. She was on the stage and dancing in front of an audience in a beautiful sparkly costume.

***

Historically, your wedding day is supposed to be one of the happiest days of your life. Adam and I weren't exactly on board with the hoopla surrounding Ryan and Bente's wedding, but we were trying to be.

I'd endured my fair share of coffee dates with the queen, discussing nothing more riveting than guest lists and fruitcake, and always tried to appear interested. Wedding conversations with Bente were much more subdued, and as the day drew closer I got the impression that she was having some serious doubts about what she'd signed on for. Ryan wasn't faring much better. Adam had told me weeks ago that he was over it, and had no more input than the promise of turning up on the day.

The whole production was a powder keg threatening to blow at any minute, and in the worst timing imaginable, that minute came two hours before they were due at the church.

Bente was teary and bereft, unable to deal with the stress. Not only was she trying to come to grips with her parents' thoughtless decision to stay on vacation rather than attend her wedding, her sister and nieces had been struck down by a bad bout of food poisoning.

"None of my family will be there," she sobbed.

I didn't think that was the worst of her problems. I was having trouble getting past her appearance. Her dress had Ivy stamped all over it. It also had about six million beads and diamantes. It was a visual example of how Bente's simple, elegant ideas had been trampled on and ramped up to showgirl level – just like the rest of the arrangements.

I wasn't the only one who recognised she was out of her depth. After a long few hours of soul searching, the bride realised it too, and in the ultimate attempt at regaining control of the way her wedding played out, she called the whole thing off.

68. RING-INS

Adam

Breaking the news to my brother that his wedding had been called off was one of the more difficult things I'd had to do in my life. Convincing him that he hadn't been jilted was harder. Charli made it very clear when she called and told me the news. Bente had cancelled the wedding, not Ryan.

He sat on the couch looking every bit the dejected groom. "I can't deal with this, Adam," he moaned.

I grabbed his arm and forced him to stand. "You have to," I demanded. "Some things don't go according to plan, Ryan. Just change course and get back on track."

"How?"

I was the master of making the best of a bad situation. I had no idea how we were going to sort it out, but was confident we'd come up with something. "I'm not sure," I admitted. "Let's just get over there and figure something out."

***

I tried hard not to look shocked by Bente's appearance when we arrived at our apartment. Her face was stained with streaks of black makeup, and she'd been crying so hard that her cheeks were as puffy as her dress. Ordinarily Bente was a pretty girl, but at that moment Treasure looked more attractive.

Ignoring the ambience, Bridget was happy to see me. "Look at my dress, Daddy," she ordered. "I'm still very clean."

"Nice work, baby." I wasn't sure if Ryan and Bente needed a moment alone or a referee, but I was keen to escape the room. I picked up my very clean kid and headed down the hall. "We'll leave you two to talk," I offered.

I found Charli in the bedroom, but unlike me, she wasn't trying to find a safe haven. She was plotting a way of dragging the day back from the brink of disaster.

I dropped Bridget on the bed, making no attempt to rebuke her when she started bouncing. My concentration was entirely on my wife, who was standing by the closet half wearing a dress I hadn't seen in years.

"It's not customary to wear a wedding dress to someone else's wedding, Coccinelle," I teased. "You might upstage the bride." It wouldn't have been hard at that point. The bride was looking a little worse for wear.

"Shut up and help me," she replied laughing. "Please."

I took my time, trying to figure out what she had planned. I came up with only one scenario, and if I was right, it was going to be on par with the Cossack trouser debacle.

"You want us to stand in for them, don't you?"

Charli scraped her hair into a pile on top of her head, giving me access to the row of buttons down the back of her dress. "It's all I could come up with," she replied. "It's too late to cancel. Your mum will be a wreck." One by one I fastened the fiddly little buttons while she laid out her plan in its entirety. "Most of the guests are friends of your parents. They won't even know that we're ring-ins," she pointed out. "And your mum is desperate to see one of her sons get married. It won't kill us to give that to her."

I turned her to face me. "You want to get married again?"

Her gorgeous smile hit my heart. "Yes I do," she replied. "I just love marrying you."

I was too thankful for that admission to protest. I'd vowed a long time ago to give her anything she wanted – even if it was a big church wedding in front of hundreds of people we didn't know.

My hand slipped across the soft fabric of her dress as I pulled her in close. "I guess we're getting married then."

69. GRAND FINALE

Charli

Ryan once travelled all the way across town to settle a restaurant tab that I couldn't cover. It happened at a time when relations between the queen and I were at an all-time low, and even now I counted it as one of the most hopeless situations I'd ever been in. He swooped in and saved the day without hesitation – and I wanted to return the favour.

My wedding dress had been hanging in the closet for years, and until Adam fastened the last button I was nervous about getting into it. Pre-Bridget I was athletic and girlish, but I was softer now and somewhere along the line I'd achieved the impossible and grown some boobs.

I smoothed my hands across my stomach and studied my reflection. "Do you think it looks okay?" I asked.

Adam tugged at the bow on the back of my dress. "Is that a trick question?" he asked. "You're beautiful."

No life could be better than the one I'd found with him. We'd met at a time when I was utterly unlikable – even to myself. Adam was a boy I'd considered to be so far out of my league that believing that he loved me took effort.

Over time, the pedestal I'd placed him on moved to lower ground, allowing us to meet somewhere in the middle. Adam Décarie wasn't a perfect man, and once he stopped pretending to be, I loved him a whole lot more.

I studied him through the mirror, making no secret of it. Adam stared straight back.

"I couldn't have gotten through the last month without you," I said finally.

"You don't have to get through a single minute without me."

And that was the beauty of finding my other half. No matter how turbulent our lives could be at times, we were constant and united.

The subject of returning to Australia had only been mentioned in passing, but I'd woken that morning with the unyielding urge to pull the pin and do it. A wedding seemed like the perfect grand finale to our New York life.

"Today will be special," I whispered. "A new chapter."

"Same book though, right?"

"Yes." I laughed. "You signed on for the extended version."

70. BLOOD AND BANDAGES

Adam

Somewhere along the line I learned to be adaptable, which probably explained why sitting in a limo on the way to my second wedding didn't faze me. The company was stellar. Neither of my girls caught me staring, and if they had it wouldn't have bothered them. They were used to it.

"Why are you breaking it, Mummy?" asked Bridget, trying to make a grab for Charli's bouquet.

"I'm not breaking it." Charli shifted it out of her reach while she looked it over. "I'm fixing it." She plucked a red rose out of the mix and handed it to Bridget. "Do you like the red or white roses best?"

Our little girl pulled her best pouty face and deliberated. "The white ones."

Charli handed her another red rose. "Me too."

"What's the matter with it?" I asked curiously.

My gorgeous bride lifted her head. "Red and white flowers should never be put in the same bouquet. It's extremely bad luck," she explained. "I did warn Fiona."

I tutted in mock outrage. "The nerve of the woman."

Her smile was stunning. "Are you doubting the legend, Boy Wonder?"

"Never." I held my hand to my heart. "I wouldn't dare."

"Some believe that red and white roses represent blood and bandages during wartime. They don't go together." She twisted the bouquet, looking it over. "Maybe blood and bandages played a part in the wedding plans coming unstuck."

"Maybe you should've told Ryan that story."

She shook her head. "He's not superstitious."

"I'm superlicious!" squealed Bridget.

Charlotte handed her another red rose. "You are," she agreed laughing..

"Why do we have to marry Daddy today?"

Charli locked her warm brown eyes on mine. "Because we love him."

Bridget dropped the flowers on her lap and sank down in her seat, stretching her legs as far as she could in a bid to reach me. Her little booted feet rested on my knees. "We really love you, Daddy."

I grabbed her feet. "How lucky am I?"

"Very lucky," she replied. "So much lucky."

***

The ride to the church didn't take as long as we'd anticipated. I don't pretend to know much about wedding etiquette, but something told me that turning up half an hour before the ceremony wasn't the done thing.

"We could wait in the car for a while," I suggested.

"I'm on to you, Adam." Charli grinned. "We're going to have to face your parents some time."

"I'll hold your hand, Dad," Bridget offered.

If Bridget thought I needed support, I must've really looked nervous.

"You have to, baby," I replied, forcing a smile. "You're my best girl." For the first time that afternoon, I was feeling inconvenienced. Pulling Ryan out of the line of fire meant putting ourselves there instead. I had trouble dealing with my mother at the best of times, and this was not going to be one of them. Dealing with my father was worse. We hadn't spoken to him in days, and I was enjoying the respite.

The break in drama was effectively over the second we got out of the car. Bridget chose that moment to make a life-altering decision. "I really don't like boots," she announced.

The shocked look on Charli's face was warranted. It was a move neither of us had seen coming. Trying to convince Bridget to keep them on was pointless – she'd already kicked them off.

I leaned down and picked them up. "What are you going to wear when you walk down the aisle?" I asked.

"Just toes and feet."

I handed her the boots and scooped her up. "Right then. Toes and feet it is."

"Can I tell you something?" asked Charli in a tiny voice.

"Of course," I replied. "As long as it's true."

"I don't like my shoes either." She lifted the hem of her dress and looked at her feet. "I want to take them off."

I felt a slow smile creep across my face. "It's your day," I reasoned. "I'm pretty sure you can do whatever you want."

Charli shifted her bouquet to her other hand and pulled off her heels. Bridget found the move hysterical, giggling so hard that keeping a grip on her took work. I hitched her higher on my hip. "Are we good to go now, ladies?"

"Can I tell you something else?" Charli asked.

"Anything."

She rested her hand on Bridget's back and whispered in my ear. "I want to go home to the beach."

I'd been waiting to hear those words for months. I wasn't sure what had brought it on, but I wasn't going to question it. Downplaying my joy was impossible but I tried, masking my smile with a kiss. "I love you so very much," I whispered, resting my forehead against hers.

"Daddy, Mamie's coming," announced Bridget, tugging on my jacket.

I straightened up to see my mother barrelling along the sidewalk. "No, no, no!" she cried. "Where's your brother?"

I glanced at Charli before replying. "There's been a change of plans, Ma."

She stood in front us, looking Charli up and down. There was no need to explain. The wedding dress clued her in quickly. "You're getting married?" she asked shakily.

"We're the understudies." Charlotte passed her bouquet to me and grabbed Mom's hands.

I'd been trying to pre-empt the queen's reaction for hours. I expected wailing. What I didn't expect was the unladylike swearing that accompanied it.

"What's wrong with you boys?" she growled. "Why can't you just be normal? I raised imbeciles!"

Charli gallantly braved the outburst by holding her hands tighter. "Everything is fine," she assured her. "There will be a wedding today. We hope you'll be a part of it."

Mom snatched her hands free. "Of course I will." She smoothed the sides of her pale blue dress. "I've waited long enough for this, don't you think?"

"You look lovely, Mamie." Bridget's comment came at just the right time.

Mom softened in an instant. "Thank you, darling," she beamed, reaching to pinch her cheeks. "You do too. Where are your boots?"

Bridget twisted in my arms, lifting her foot. "I took them off. I really hate boots."

Dumbstruck, Mom glanced at me, then Charli.

"We're moving on to a new phase, Mamie," beamed Charlotte.

That might've been an opportune time to mention that we were flying the coop again, but neither of us did.

Mom began fussing with Charli's hair. "You look beautiful, darling," she praised. "But you always do."

Charlotte tugged at her dress, probably making sure her feet were hidden. Mom would've rescinded the compliment if she'd known she'd ditched her shoes.

"Is Ryan alright?" asked Mom, turning to me.

Jumping to the conclusion that my brother had been jilted at the altar was a reasonable leap. The real story was far less believable.

"He's fine," I assured her. "Bente got a little overwhelmed. They opted for a civil service."

She nodded, resigned. "I just want them to be happy," she said solemnly.

"I'm happy, Mamie," interjected Bridget cheerily. "I'm getting married to my Daddy today."

"Yes, my darling," she replied, perking up in an instant. "You are."

"I'm the best girl."

Mom took a moment to think things through. Over the years she'd become adaptable too. A four-year-old best girl wasn't too hard to come to terms with. "I think you and I should head inside," she suggested, opening her arms. Bridget leaned forward, falling into them. After fussing with her hair, Mom lowered Bridget to her feet and straightened her dress. "Quick, darling." She took her hand. "It's too cold out here for little girls."

Neither of us said a word as we watched them disappear through the front doors of the church, heading into the great unknown. I had no idea what sort of production we were about to take part in, but I knew it was huge.

Guests started filing through the doors, and the only person I recognised was Mrs Brown. She gave us a wave and we both waved back.

I leaned toward Charli. "Do you want to make a run for it?"

"No," she replied firmly. "We can do this."

I slipped my arm around her waist. "You really do look beautiful in that dress."

"Despite the bare feet?"

"I like you barefoot." I dipped my head, chasing her lips. "Although I'd prefer you barefoot and pregnant – in our little cottage on the beach."

She smiled slyly. "You've got it all worked out, haven't you?"

"I know when it's time to change course, Charlotte." I breathed the words into her hair. "It's been a tough few months for us. We deserve better times."

"Regrets?"

I tilted my head, half shrugging. "No, just an overwhelming desire to get back to normal. Our normal isn't in New York."

71. BACKUP PLAN

Charli

We hadn't seen Jean-Luc in days, and there would be no escaping him today. Adam's hackles went up the instant he spotted him. I wasn't quite so tense.

"My children and their stupid schemes," he announced, throwing his arms wide as he walked toward us. I was actually glad that was his opening remark. It meant the queen had clued him in and we didn't have to explain.

"This is a happy day, Dad," Adam grumbled. "Don't make a scene."

"I have no intention of doing any such thing." Jean-Luc stopped in front of us and folded his arms. "Am I still giving the bride away?"

"Of course," I replied. "I'm not walking that big aisle by myself."

Adam wasn't thrilled to be handing me over. Hearing him lay down the law wasn't unexpected. It was a given. "If you so much as insult a hair on her head –"

"You should go inside, Adam," Jean-Luc interrupted. "Bridget was dismantling the flower arrangements on the altar when I left."

I didn't doubt for a second it was true. "Adam, go," I urged, shooing him away with my bouquet. "I'll see you in a minute."

He nodded stiffly, looking torn. "Don't be too long."

I wondered what he thought was going to happen.

Jean-Luc waited until Adam began walking away, and called him back. His constant need to get the last word in infuriated me, but I held my tongue and waited for him to speak. So did Adam.

"You must take her rings," he said. "It won't be a proper ceremony without an exchange of rings."

He was right. I tucked my bouquet under my arm and slipped them off my finger. "Don't let Bridget hold them," I warned, handing them to Adam.

"I won't." He finally smiled. "She's got nowhere to stash them now that she's ditched the boots."

***

I didn't complain when Jean-Luc suggested we wait a few more minutes before heading inside. I was hardly an excited bride. Adam and I had no interest in walking down the aisle. We were merely taking one for the team – a notion that the king quickly picked up on.

"This is not really your scene is it, Charli?" he asked.

"The wedding or New York in general?"

He dropped his head, but I still saw his smile. "I think you've adapted remarkably well this time around, unlike Adam."

"We're leaving, you know," I warned. "I'm going to steal your precious boy away again."

Jean-Luc didn't seem alarmed. He probably knew it was on the cards when Adam quit his job.

"He hasn't been ours for years, Charlotte," he replied dryly. "Time away will do you good. I think you probably need it after the events of the past few months."

It wasn't an answer I was expecting, but he was right – I did need it. And the only way he could've known was if he'd been told. "You know that I found my mother?"

Jean-Luc nodded. "Life is full of defining moments," he said gently. "I hope you don't count that as one of yours."

I scowled. "I don't want to talk about this with you." I was too busy plotting what I was going to do to my bigmouth husband when I got hold of him.

"No; perhaps *your* father might be the better option," he said awkwardly.

My father-in-law wasn't renowned for heartfelt pep talks, so this rare moment was gauche and uncomfortable. Jean-Luc glanced across at the huge church and wisely changed the subject. "I wasn't joking about Bridget and the flowers," he said. "She was stripping red roses from the floral arrangements. I can only assume she knows something we don't."

"Bridget knows a lot of things you don't," I declared. "I made her that way."

"She's part Décarie," he insisted.

"Only the good parts." My catty comment didn't faze him at all. He would've expected no less from me.

"I heard that Ryan reinstated her wings," he commented. "I'm pleased."

He must've been lying. The king was the biggest opponent of all things La La.

"You and I don't fluff around and pretend to be polite to each other, Jean-Luc," I reminded him. "It's one of the things I like best about you. Please don't ruin it."

"I'm not trying to be polite. I admire Bridget's desire to fly. I always encourage ambition."

I couldn't argue. It was the only thing he did encourage. We were quiet for a long moment. I had nothing more to say, but Jean-Luc seemed to be working up to something else. I shuffled from foot to foot, trying to find relief from the freezing pavement while I waited.

"When Adam was young, he was a terribly restless sleeper," he said finally. "He'd throw himself out of bed some nights. It used to terrify his mother."

I couldn't help smiling. "He didn't grow out of it until Bridget was born," I told him. "He hasn't been restless in a while."

"He used to dream he was chasing something," he continued. "We asked him time and time again what it was, but he didn't know. Quite odd, don't you think?"

"Why would it be odd?"

"Well, it would've made more sense if something was chasing him."

I shook my head, suddenly seeing the much deeper picture. Adam had been running for most of his life, always trying to catch up to the life his parents had mapped out for him. He only stopped running when his daughter was born.

"Every night I'd line a stack of pillows on the floor next to his bed. Running while sleeping is only foolhardy if you have no backup plan. I assume the same rules apply to flying, – at least, that's what I told Bridget."

I dropped my line of sight to the pavement, unable to look at him. "I can't imagine you telling her any such thing."

"I have never clipped her wings, Charli," he said seriously. "Who do you think taught her to stack cushions on the floor?"

My head snapped up at the question. "You taught her that?"

He shrugged. "I encourage ambition, but a backup plan is important."

His admission floored me. I had no idea how to reply. "We should go," I told him, walking away. "Everyone will be waiting."

Jean-Luc called me back, just as he always does.

I groaned. "Don't ruin it." I spun around so fast that the bottom of my dress flared. "You and I just had a moment. Don't ruin it by saying something mean."

"You think I'm hard, don't you?"

Inconsistent was a better description. He *was* hard on me, but every now and then he'd show me glimpses of a much kinder man. I'd never fully managed to crack his tough exterior, and probably never would. Perhaps that's why I elected to agree with him. "Brutally hard at times," I agreed. "I hope you'll treat Bente differently."

"I expect I will. We don't share the same rapport."

Ignoring the fact that I'd begun shivering, I paced back to him. "Say something nice about me." I thrust my bouquet at him as if I was casting a spell. "I dare you."

He lifted his head. The smirk was gone. "You've been a wonderful, fiery addition to my family and I adore you." His low tone was as serious as the look on his handsome face.

I was so shocked I couldn't speak, which was a good thing. It saved me from killing the compliment with a smartarse comment. I mustered a rigid nod and walked away again.

"The loss wasn't yours, Charlotte," he called. "It was entirely your mother's." I stopped walking but didn't turn back. "You'll do well to remember that."

I swallowed hard to clear the lump from my throat. Then I walked back to him again and took his arm. "Hurry up and walk me down the aisle. Just to piss you off, I'm going to marry your son again."

72. THE MAGIC STICK

Adam

Despite the earlier drama of the day, our second wedding went off without a hitch. Both of us struggled to get through the stiflingly traditional ceremony, but we managed. Charli even managed to promise to love, honour and obey me without laughing. The inclusion of that vow proved how just little attention Ryan and Bente had paid to the planning of their nuptials.

By the end of the night, their reasons for bailing were obvious. It was hardly a romantic or intimate affair – more a well orchestrated production designed to showcase wealth and social pedigree. We endured walking up the aisle, cutting a six-layer cake and slow dancing – and had our photo taken a million times to prove it.

Any favour I owed my brother, dating back to the day I was born, had now been repaid.

***

Our first day of remarried life was good. For the first time since Bridget's fall we ventured back to the park. I expected her to hesitate, but she didn't show a hint of trepidation as she cut across the lawn and headed for the playground.

"She's fearless," I muttered under my breath.

"She has fear," amended Charli. "She just understands her limitations a little better now."

I stood on the edge of the path for a long time keeping an eye on Bridget. She flitted from one piece of equipment to another, steering clear of the climbing frame. "This is the beginning, isn't it?" I asked Charli.

She clenched her fists together and blew a warming breath into her hands. "Of what?"

"A few weeks ago she thought she could jump off that frame and fly," I replied. "She knows she can't now. Eventually she'll land there no more."

It was the only part of the *Peter Pan* quote I could remember, but the meaning was firmly in my mind.

Charli patted the seat beside her. "She still believes." As soon as I sat down, she cuddled against me in a ploy to get warm. "And if she stops, we'll show her more magic."

Keeping half an eye on Bridget I murmured against her cold cheek, "You sound mighty sure of yourself, Coccinelle."

She laughed quietly. "If I can make a believer out of her uncle, I can make anyone believe."

Not even Ryan could find an explanation for the discovery he'd made in Tiger's upstairs apartment a few days earlier. The horse he claimed to have almost won the Kentucky Derby with back in the sixties was named Secret North – the coordinate on Bridget's compass that they'd spent weeks tirelessly searching for.

I'd given up looking for logical explanations a long time ago. I'd been hit with the magic stick too many times.

"I'm going to convert your father next," she claimed.

It wasn't one of her better ideas. He wasn't the most open-minded man to begin with, and he'd become impossible to deal with lately. I refused to try any more.

The final straw was when he made good on his promise of having someone clear out my desk at the office. Nothing could describe the hurt of having my belongings delivered to our door as if it was trash he was putting out. Charli did her best to play it down, urging me to forgive and move on.

But I wasn't interested in making peace this time round –I'd done it too many times before. All I was interested in was getting back to the beach and kick-starting the life we should've been living.

"I think you should just steer clear of my father," I suggested.

Charli slipped a hand inside my coat. "I'm sorry, Boy Wonder," she explained, "but yesterday when I agreed to obey you, my fingers were crossed."

***

A firm plan for getting out of the country was hatched over the dinner table that night. I had no reason to stay in New York a minute longer. My job was gone, and now that the all the permits were approved, Ryan was overseeing the club renovations perfectly well by himself.

"You want to go next week?" Charli choked. "I can't wrap everything up in a week. I haven't even quit my job yet."

"I could go before you," I offered. "It'll give me a chance to make sure everything is perfect for when you get there."

Her stare was so intense that I had trouble maintaining eye contact. I focused on Bridget instead, who was doing her usual routine of pushing her food around her plate. I straightened her chair and pulled it closer to the table. "Eat something, please," I ordered.

"I am," she insisted. "You just can't see me."

Charli's mind was still on the subject of moving. "I'll need at least two weeks," she insisted.

"No problem," I replied. "It'll take me a week to get everything sorted at the cottage."

Her eyes drifted to our daughter. "And what about Bridge?" she asked. "Who will she travel with?"

I shrugged. "Let's ask her."

It was a risky move. Charli's confidence in the parenting department had taken a battering lately, and Bridget inadvertently had the power to knock her down even lower.

In a few short sentences I laid out the options to Bridget. She could either come to Australia with me or hang out in New York for an extra few weeks with her mama.

The kid barely thought about it. "I have to stay with my mum." She pointed her fork at Charli. "I need her."

My relief was nothing compared to the jolt that hit Charli. "You need me?" she asked in a tiny voice.

Bridget answered as if it was a silly question. "Yes," she replied. "All the time."

I leaned across and kissed the top of her head. She had no idea that she'd patched up her mother's heart with a few simple words, and that was how it was supposed to be.

"You're beautiful," I told her. "And I love you."

"Good," she replied. "Then I don't have to eat more dinner."

73. WILD ANIMALS

Charli

Quitting my job was like a bad break up. There were tears, and the 'it's not you, it's me' line was used more than once. Mercifully, Bronson didn't need much recovery time. After a cup of tea and a handful of tissues, he pulled himself together and went back to polishing the leaves on his potted plants.

"I'll be fine, darling." He took a step back and looked up at the top branches of his ficus. "Maybe I'll find someone taller next time." He was clearly over me. I, however, would never be over him.

I agreed to work until the end of the week, to make sure everything was up to date. I spent the rest of that morning cataloguing new pieces that Bronson had just picked up on a four-day buying spree. Everything was just about in order when something caught my eye.

"Bronson, what do you know about this?" I waved the piece of paper at him. "This painting was sold weeks ago."

He set his can of Pledge down and snatched the paper. "Oh, yes," he crowed, barely glancing at it. "It was returned. Your mother brought it back."

Olivia's audacity astounded me. I wasn't expecting her to take up my suggestion of returning the work to cover the costs of her failed charity scam, but she had.

"Did she say why?"

"She said she couldn't bear looking at it," he replied. "Apparently it reminds her of something ghastly – a time in her life that she doesn't wish to be reminded of."

The hateful words sank in. A few weeks ago they would've wrecked me, but as I sat absently clicking my pen, I realised something huge. I wasn't hurt. I wasn't even remotely affected. The storm caused by the introduction of my mother into my life had passed, and I'd survived.

"Did you refund her money?"

"Of course." Bronson picked up his can, grinning like a Cheshire cat. "I told her I'd send a cheque in the post – which I did – to the person who paid for it in the first place."

Nothing could dull my smile. "Adam?"

Bronson sighed wistfully. "Oh Adam, my Wedgwood-blue-eyed beauty," he crooned, flapping his dusting cloth at me. "Tell him to buy you something nice with the money. Cocktails and shoes."

I laughed. "I will."

"Good," he replied, walking away. "Karma has no menu, darling. You get served what you deserve."

***

We were experts when it came to packing up a household, mainly because we never really did. Jumping from country to country involved little more than a few pieces of excess luggage.

"One of these days we're going to buy a house, Charlotte," Adam declared, dragging the last of his suitcases into the living room. "And maybe some furniture to put in it."

I couldn't help laughing. The only stick of furniture we'd ever bought was a bed for our kid. Everything else was either stolen from Ryan or was already in whichever property we were squatting in at the time.

"Maybe we could look at it down the track," I replied. "When we're grown up and responsible."

"It'll happen one day." He kissed the top of my head. "But for now, we're gypsies with a lot of luggage."

"And a little bit of baggage," I hinted.

He leaned back, frowning. "Meaning?"

"Meaning, I want you to sort things out with your dad before you go."

Time was running out. Adam's flight was booked for the next afternoon. It wasn't the first spat the stubborn Décarie men had ever had, but something about this one felt different. If they couldn't find a way past it, I feared the damage might become permanent.

"Maybe you could go and see him in the morning," I suggested. "Call a truce and –"

"I have no intention of going over there, Charlotte," he interrupted. "I've done nothing wrong. I'm not the one who needs to apologise."

I shrugged. There was no point discussing it further. Adam wasn't going to budge. All I could do was cross my fingers and hope I had better luck with his equally stubborn father.

***

Bridget didn't quite grasp the concept that we'd only be apart from her dad for a week. Breakfast conversation the next morning was a little stranger than usual. "Don't forget who I am and don't find another kid," she ordered. "That would be bad."

Adam hid his smile behind his coffee mug. "I'll try not to."

"And please look after Treasure," she instructed. "You can't touch her. Just look nicely at her."

Adam blinked. "I'm taking Treasure?"

I pointed to one of the suitcases. "She's already packed," I said sheepishly. "I hope you get her through customs okay."

He groaned, making both of us giggle. "Just what I need," he grumbled.

I picked up my bowl and kissed his cheek. "Well, I hope you enjoy your last day in the Big Apple."

"We're going to the park," announced Bridget.

"Fabulous."

"To play with wild animals," she added.

Me too, I didn't reply. Trying to talk sense into Jean-Luc probably wasn't going to work, but I was going to give it a crack.

***

An hour before I was due at work, Fiona met me at the palace door armed with a tight hug and a few instructions. "Do not let him kick you out until you make him see sense."

It was hardly encouraging advice.

"You're married to the big lug," I reminded her. "And the other fool is your son. Why can't *you* force them to kiss and make up?"

She pouted, and annoyingly began fussing with my hair. "You're so much better at handling drama, darling."

"No promises."

Fiona looked at the package in my hand. "You brought him a present? That's a lovely idea."

"I didn't bring him a present," I corrected. "I brought him magic."

I doubt she believed me, but she was desperate. With a firm hand on my back, she pushed me to the stairs and sent me on my way. "Go, darling. Work your magic."

I trudged up the curved staircase as if headed to my own execution. The sour look on the king's face as I walked into his study did nothing to make me think differently.

He glanced up briefly. "To what do I owe this pleasure, Charlotte?" he asked formally.

He hadn't invited me in, but I took up residence on the chair opposite his desk anyway, leaning my parcel against his desk. "I wanted to talk to you about something."

Jean-Luc lifted his wrist, checking the time. "I have half an hour."

"You're all heart," I muttered.

Perhaps realising he was being an epic jerk, he set his pen down. "You have my full attention."

"Adam leaves tonight," I stated.

"So I heard."

"You're going to let him go without an apology?"

He frowned. "And what do you think I should be apologising for?"

"Adam worked incredibly hard for you," I reminded him. "Why won't you cut him some slack?"

His steely stare remained fixed on me. I was getting nowhere. "I don't agree with my son's choices of late."

"You can't make him be who you want him to be," I said roughly. "Just be happy that you've had a hand in who he is."

Jean-Luc leaned back but refused to unlock me from his gaze. "I have had no hand in this ridiculous newfound affinity to carpentry," he snapped. "That's your influence. Mine was forking out for the best education money could buy and a position in my law firm."

I was shaking my head before he'd even finished. "The wood thing is nothing to do with me. He's been that way inclined for years, and I find it sad that you didn't see it."

When he slammed his fist on his desk and ordered me out, I stood as if I was doing as I was told for once. Instead, I walked over to the photo he'd bought from the gallery.

"Tell me again why you like this so much?"

"We've been through this," he grumbled. "It's getting tiresome."

I turned back to him. "But you never gave me a straight answer. I've never made four thousand dollars on a picture before. I'd like to know why it's so special."

His eyes widened. "You took that picture?"

I nodded.

"Why didn't you tell me?"

"You didn't ask."

And for that reason, I'd never been forthcoming with the history of it – until then. I went back to his desk and picked up the package I'd brought with me. "I thought you'd like to see what the boat looked like when it was finished."

I tore the paper off and leaned the frame against my chest, holding it up to him. "Adam started working on it the day after Bridget turned one," I told him. "He finished a week before her second birthday."

The king didn't say a word. I was thrilled: if I'd rendered him speechless, I was getting somewhere.

"It was derelict when he found it." I motioned to the before picture with a nod. "It was delivered to his shed in two pieces and most of it was rotten, but he had to have it."

"Why?" The word seemed to hitch in his throat.

"He said it reminded him of the boat you used to take him sailing on when he was young. I guess it left an impression on him."

And if my hunch was right, it had left an indelible mark on Jean-Luc as well. "Is that why you like it too?"

The king's eyes darted between the picture on the wall and the one I was holding, finally settling on the overhauled yacht. "Adam did that?"

"All by himself," I proudly confirmed. "It wasn't very profitable, though. It's the only project he's undertaken that he didn't make any money on."

"Where's the boat now?" he asked curiously.

"We still have it." I smiled at the picture in my hands. "I don't think he tried too hard to sell it. This one's special."

"I'd like to see it one day," he choked.

"Well, it's funny you should mention that," I said wryly. "I was going to suggest that you come to the Cove for Christmas. Maybe you could check it out then."

The wounds Adam and Jean-Luc had inflicted on each other in the past few weeks ran a little too deep to be patched with a simple apology. Baby steps was my plan. All Adam hoped for was understanding. If I could get his father to the Cove, he'd see what kind of talents his son possessed – starting with the bank building and ending with the boat projects he'd taken on since then.

He didn't exactly jump at my suggestion. His mind was elsewhere. "Where did he learn to do work like this?" he asked.

"A lot of it was trial and error." I shrugged. "He got a lot of advice from contractors, and my dad. Alex is pretty handy."

He nodded, still staring at the picture. "It is extraordinary."

"I'm not surprised that you like it so much," I teased. "This boat is French."

Jean-Luc's laugh was a welcome break in the serious conversation. "How could you know that?"

"Well, when all the paint was scraped off, we found a brass nameplate on the stern. It was a French name."

"What was it?"

Knowing I'd botch the pronunciation, I wasn't even going to attempt it. I nodded at the frame on the wall. "I wrote it on the back of the picture."

Jean-Luc walked over and took it down. "*Dénouement*," he announced with reverence. "Do you know what that means?"

"No clue."

"It is the final part of a story or a play," he explained. "When all the complications and drama of the plot are resolved, the tale wraps up leaving no loose ends. Puzzle pieces fall into place and everything becomes clear."

I wondered if he understood the nuance of magic behind the words he'd just spoken. Then he surprised me by proving he did.

He held the picture up to me. "A spider web, you think?"

I wanted to cry – I was that elated.

"Yes," I confirmed in a shaky voice. "It's all about spider webs. Fate and spider webs."

He smiled at me. "Do you think there's a lesson in this for me?"

"I think it's proof that we're all where we're meant to be, and following the path we're supposed to," I replied.

Jean-Luc replaced the picture and sat back at his desk. "How do you explain the web connecting you to your mother, Charli?" he asked. "Surely that was a connection you could have done without."

We were getting a little off track. I'd never discussed Olivia with anyone other than Adam. I didn't know how to give an impartial account of what reuniting with her meant to me – or if I wanted to.

"I don't regret meeting her," I said quietly. "I told her I do, but I don't. It taught me that sometimes the best option is to walk away." I added, "And it was remarkably easy to do it."

"Why is that, do you think?"

"Because she didn't contribute a thing to who I am," I replied strongly. "She doesn't get to take any credit."

"I'm glad you recognise it," he told me. "And I'm glad you're not hurt by her failings."

I couldn't claim to be completely unscathed. I had a lot of questions for my father, and it terrified me to think he wasn't going to be able to give me the answers I needed – but that was a problem for another day.

"Your sons are good men," I told him. "You made them that way."

He smiled in a way that reminded me of Ryan.

"I cut the tie to my mother," I told him. "Your boys will never do that to you as long as you let them drift a little."

Jean-Luc frowned, and I worried that I was losing him. "They're always going to be tied to you, but they need room to move," I explained. "They're Money Spiders."

He threw his head back and laughed. "How apt."

"You've heard of money spiders before, right?" I asked, catching his infectious laugh. "They're not keen on sticking to one thing. They like to balloon. They attach themselves to a dragline of web and let the wind carry them – just like your boys do."

Jean-Luc's smile was as strong as I'd ever seen. "And why are they called Money Spiders?"

"Well, legend has it that if a money spider lands on you, he's come to spin you new clothes, which back in the day would've changed your fortune."

After a long moment of thought, he shook his head. "You're quite extraordinary at times." I wasn't sure if that was an insult or a compliment, so I kept my mouth shut on the off-chance he was being nice. The king walked to the huge bookshelf. "I suppose you're now going to claim that you've shown me magic?"

"Not at all." I wasn't that hopeful. "I'd be happy knowing I'd at least made you think outside the box a little bit."

After a moment of searching, Jean-Luc pulled a small black book from the shelves and made his way back to his desk. "When I was courting my wife, she used to go to extraordinary lengths to better her French," he told me. "When she worked at the Odeon, she used to sneak into the movies."

I laughed, trying to imagine my mother-in-law carrying out such a crime in her theatre-issued silk tights.

"Fiona has no patience." He smiled. "She never sat through a whole film – to this day I'm not sure that she ever has."

I looked at the book he'd set on the desk. When I realised it was a notebook, curiosity began to bubble. I pointed at it, to hurry him along.

"She used to sneak in half-way through the screenings," he said, patting the book. "And then she'd summarise the ending in French in this notebook." His line of sight dropped to the book in front of him. "To this day, I find it incredibly endearing."

I had no idea why he was sharing the story with me, but I was glad he had. It proved that he knew how it felt to be besotted and in love. It also went a long way to explaining why Lord Muck had chosen Fiona over all others.

"Is it a good read?"

Jean-Luc thumbed the pages. "The last half hour of hundreds of films are summarised in here. Her French at that time was appalling," he said with a chuckle. "But you might think it's magic."

"Why?"

He flipped back to the first page and turned the book to face me, tapping his index finger on the handwritten title on the first page. "*Dénouement*," he announced. "More spider webs, you think?"

"Yes!" I rushed out the word in absolute shock. "Totally magic."

He slid the book over to me. "I'm inclined to agree with you," he replied. "And because of that, I will no longer doubt the existence of Charlotte's web."

74. BARISTA EXTRAORDINAIRE

Adam

Absence makes the heart grow fonder. I'd missed the life we'd created in Australia, but I had no idea how much until I went back.

Getting into the laidback swing of things was as easy as dusting off the furniture and moving into the cottage. By the time Charli and Bridget arrived a week later, things were so close to the way they used to be it was as if we'd never left.

I didn't regret our time in New York. My daughter now had an understanding of how I'd grown up, and had spent time forming a tight bond with her grandparents and uncle.

My bond with my father wasn't anywhere near as tight as it should've been, but putting some distance between us had dulled my ire significantly – to the point where Mom and Dad were making plans to visit over Christmas.

Even after two months of planning, we weren't ready for them, which was unfortunate because they were due to arrive the next day.

Charli stood on the veranda, gazing at the lawn. "We could pitch a tent," she suggested. "Can you imagine your mother in a tent?"

I was having trouble imagining my mother in Pipers Cove. The lack of hotel accommodation was going to be the least of her gripes. "We'll just have to sort the spare room out," I replied. "Or they can bunk in with Bridget."

Her sly giggle wasn't so sly any more. It was more like a sinister cackle, which quickly gained the attention of one of our neighbours.

"G'day, Charli," crowed a voice from the fence line. Tyler was the eldest of Flynn Davis's stepsons. At ten years old, he was crooked, mouthy and completely and utterly in love with my wife.

"Hi Ty," Charli waved. "What are you up to today?"

He shrugged. "Just hanging out."

"How about you hang out on your side of the fence?" That suggestion earned me a stiff elbow to the ribs.

"Well, have fun," called Charli, ignoring my pained groan. "Maybe I'll see you later."

Predictably, Tyler missed his cue to leave. I took Charli by the hand and led her toward the door instead. "Jealous, Adam?" she mumbled.

As soon as we were inside, I kissed her for all I was worth. "I can never compete with what he can give you," I announced, breaking the embrace. "Perhaps you should go. If you love him, be free."

"Well, he does have a kick-arse mountain bike," she giggled. "All you have is a shed full of bits of broken boats."

My shed *was* full of boat pieces, but they only belonged to one boat. Within a week of being home, I had snagged my next project from a salvage yard in Hobart; after a long hiatus I was back in business. It was probably going to take me the best part of a year to restore, and I didn't care. I had the rest of my life to get it done.

"It's going to be an awesome vessel, Charlotte," I gloated. "Perhaps then you'll realise what a good catch I am."

"Maybe," she casually agreed. "No promises, though."

***

Bridget and Alex had been making up for lost time. He'd cut back his hours at the café significantly since Jack was born, and the time he did spend there almost always included his little blonde sidekick. When I arrived to pick her up that afternoon, she was less than pleased to see me. "I haven't finished working yet," she complained. "I need to stay."

Somewhere along the line, my daughter's aversion to a hard day's work had given way to playing the part of barista extraordinaire. I wasn't sure how Alex occupied her while she was there, but was certain brewing coffee wasn't in her job description.

"Pull up a chair," said Alex. "Bridget hasn't clocked off yet."

I sat at the counter, eye-to-eye with my kid. "What's the pay like?" I asked, making Alex smile.

Bridget leaned towards me. "Very bad," she whispered loudly. "But I get cake sometimes."

After a few minutes of banter while he brewed coffee, Alex slid a cup across the counter. Bridget went to work, grabbing a napkin and placing it beside my coffee.

"*Monsieur, une serviette pour vous,*" she announced, hamming it up.

"French waitresses now?" I asked, glancing at Alex. "This place is becoming a really classy joint."

"Mamie will like it," said Bridget.

"Your parents arrive tomorrow, right?" asked Alex. "Gabi's looking forward to seeing them."

I had to admit that I was too, and it was good to know that if drama took hold, I could send them Gabrielle's way for a while. "They're coming in on the four o'clock flight," I replied. "It's going to be an interesting few weeks."

"I'm sure they'll adjust."

"You're not supposed to smirk when you say that."

Alex laughed. "Come on Boy Wonder, how bad could it be?"

75. SPECIAL AGENTS

Charli

Pipers Cove was never going to be Fiona Décarie's scene. When we heard their car pull onto the driveway, we stepped out on to the veranda to greet them. Adam's arm slipped around my waist, and he held Bridget's hand. Suddenly we were models for a Hallmark card.

The king and queen weren't quite so well put together. Jean-Luc looked tired, but still managed to catch Bridget when she broke free of Adam and bolted across the lawn to leap at him. I couldn't understand the French that passed between them, but could tell the reunion was a happy one.

Fiona looked like she'd jogged all the way from Hobart. "Oh, darlings," she cried, arms outstretched as she staggered up the cobbled path in four-inch heels. "Travelling is such an ordeal."

"Maybe they ran out of champagne in first class," I muttered to Adam from the corner of my mouth. "She should try flying on an domestic African airline with caged chickens in the aisle."

He tried shushing me, but it got caught in a laugh. He covered by stepping down to greet her. I followed, and it was double cheek kisses all round.

"This is lovely, darling," she carolled, looking in every direction.

She could only have been telling the truth. It was perfect for a royal visit. The day was bright and reasonably warm, and the afternoon sun glinted off the ocean below the cliffs, highlighting the beautiful coastline we called home.

"You'll love it here," I assured her. "It'll be the perfect break for you."

"Are there snakes, Charli?" she asked, looking down at the ground. "Ryan told me there are snakes."

"Only little ones," I replied, making Jean-Luc laugh. "Tiny bites – more annoying than painful."

Fiona suddenly looked terrified, and when something hard pinged off the shed behind her, she ducked as if we were under attack.

Unfortunately we were, and I knew exactly who'd declared war on our visitors. I marched over to the centre of the yard and demanded that The Lost Boys come out of hiding.

"Right now!" I yelled.

Too young to know that staying put was the better option, five-year-old Mason appeared first, scrambling out of a bush near the fence. Sean and Tyler took a bit longer, but eventually surrendered.

"Who's got the slingshot?" I barked. Sean waved it half-heartedly. "Hand it over."

Tyler took it from his brother, opting to take the walk of shame himself. I stayed put and waited for him to reach me.

"We weren't trying to hit anyone," he muttered, dropping the slingshot into my hand. "Honest."

"Way to make a good impression, Ty," I scolded quietly. "Do you know who these people are?" I glanced over my shoulder at them. "French diplomats," I lied. "You should be protecting them, not waging war."

Tyler leaned past to get a closer look. "You're lying."

"I am not."

"Prove it."

"Mate," I scoffed with an upward nod, "check out the car. French Secret Service."

The Décarie's decision to opt for a chauffeured car at the airport helped me immensely. Combined with the power of a ten-year-old's imagination, the black sedan with tinted windows totally looked legitimate. Even better, the driver chose that moment to get out of the car and collect the luggage from the boot. His dark suit was a little on the cheap side, but he wore sunglasses and a surly frown – the perfect look for a French Secret Serviceman.

Chauffeured cars were a touch of grandeur that Tyler Davis had never been exposed to before. From that point, selling the lie was a breeze.

"Whoa," he mumbled, eyes wide.

I thrust the slingshot back at him. "No more weaponry while they're here," I ordered. "They've got men all over the place. Hostile acts like that will get you killed."

Glancing around in search of hidden agents, he nodded rapidly. "Understood."

"Good."

"We'll help protect them too," he offered.

"You do that, Ty," I agreed. "But keep your distance."

The Davis boys were mildly annoying and constantly intrusive. I smiled to myself as I walked back to my family. As long as the royals were in town, the miniature warriors next door would be keeping a safe distance.

***

That Christmas was one of the best I ever remembered having. Two families from totally different walks of life managed to gel enough to make a wonderful day.

It was give and take on both sides. It was fair to assume that Fiona wasn't being truthful when she described Floss's vegan Christmas menu as 'delightfully non-traditional'. And poor Alex looked flummoxed when he unwrapped his gift from the queen.

"It's a letter opener," she explained, noticing his confusion.

"Oh," he replied, examining it closely. "I thought it was a dagger. A nice silver dagger."

The queen sat on Floss's big red recliner, gently bouncing Jack on her knee. She looked mortified, but Gabrielle smoothed things over. "He's joking, tante Fiona," she explained, giving my father a hard elbow. "He knows what it is."

"Of course I do." Alex grinned at Fiona. "I'll keep it on my desk … in my shed."

Jean-Luc was the first to crack, laughing loud enough to match Floss's wild guffaw. He'd chilled out a lot in the two weeks since he'd arrived. All it took for him to soften up and pull his son back into the fold was to see the work Adam had abandoned his law career for.

The first place Adam took him to was the bank building. I'd been slowly getting the gallery back in order, but wasn't in a hurry to open for business. As a result it probably wasn't looking its best, but Jean-Luc was in awe. After years of complaining about Adam's useless hobby, he was now claiming bragging rights. "It's a fine example of Décarie craftsmanship," he declared to anyone who'd listen.

The refurbished boats were just as captivating, particularly *La Dénouement*. It had been dry-docked for as long as we'd owned it, but Jean-Luc demanded that they test it on water. Father and son were the only crew on the maiden voyage, and that was exactly how it was supposed to play out. They'd both felt an unexplainable attachment to the old sloop, and now that it was restored to its former glory, their attachment was to each other and to the memories it reminded them both of.

I'd had no idea Jean-Luc was an accomplished sailor. On a cloudy morning with very little wind, he successfully manoeuvred the boat out to sea, chasing the light breeze. Fiona and I sat on the beach and watched until it turned and disappeared around the jutting cliffs, and then her interest waned.

"Take me home, darling," she said, hooking her arm through mine. "All this sand is ruining my pedicure."

***

My kid had an uncanny knack for biding her time and picking her moment. It was a talent inherited from me. Picking my moments *and* my battles was my forte, but the problem I had faced since returning the Cove was that they were one and the same.

In the two months since we'd been home, I still hadn't raised the topic of Olivia with my father, which meant I was no longer biding my time – I was procrastinating. Adam never pushed me. The mere mention of Olivia's name still riled him. In the end Jean-Luc was the one who mentioned it.

I was on the veranda at the time, enjoying a few minutes of cool night air and peace.

"Are you in need of an escape, Charli?" He came and stood beside me.

I leaned both hands on the railing. "Is it that obvious?" I asked. "Whose bright idea was it to get Bridget a piano for Christmas?"

He chuckled. "It's a pretend one."

The sound that came out of it wasn't pretend, and I'd had a constant headache since Christmas morning because of it.

"Treasure plays too, you know." I grinned. "She's her support act."

Jean-Luc laughed. "That child is my joy." Perhaps realising his formal vernacular grated on me, he amended his comment with a smile. "*Bridget* is my joy."

In a sense the village was raising Bridget, and I'd realised only lately that it was for the best. Adam constantly bucked against his father's rigid style of parenting, but even he had to concede that he wasn't always wrong. We were always going to encourage her whimsical and imaginative side, but she'd recently shown us a new side that needed nurturing too. As dreadful as her ballet experience was, she'd thrived with direction and discipline, just as her grandfather predicted she would.

In turn, Jean-Luc finally opened his mind enough to realise that ambition and drive wasn't the be-all and end-all. You have to save some room for bliss, whether it's bashing away on a toy piano or tearing up boats.

I looked out at the night sky. "It's funny how things work out, don't you think?"

"Nothing surprises me any more," he replied.

Lots of things surprised me, namely the way he went on to thank me for suggesting they make the trip out here. "I feel like I'm back on sturdy ground with my son," he explained. "You're responsible for that."

My heart nearly burst out of my chest, which wasn't easy to hide. Somehow, I kept my cool. "You would've gotten there in the end."

Jean-Luc pulled in a long breath. "A fine *dénouement*, wouldn't you say?"

I glanced across. "Yes, I think so."

The king leaned forward, resting his elbows on the railing. "Do you still have the book I gave you?"

"Of course."

"If you could read French, you'd see that there is lots of inspiration in there. Plenty of tying of loose ends."

I frowned at him. "Are you having a dig at me?" I asked. "If I haven't learned your language after seven years of knowing your son, it's safe to say I'm never going to."

He laughed. "No, I'm past trying to broaden your mind with language. I'm trying something new."

"Well, I'm not getting it. You'll have to spell it out for me."

He smiled, but it wasn't right. "Give me the definition of *dénouement*," he ordered, putting extra French spin on the word.

"A final act of a book or a play where all loose ends are tied," I recited. "All puzzle pieces fit together."

"Correct," he announced.

It only took a second to work out where he was headed. "You're talking about the Olivia thing, aren't you?"

"It troubles me that you haven't spoken with your father about it," he replied. "Alex seems like a forthcoming and reasonable man."

"He is."

"So do it, Charli," he urged. "Pen your own *dénouement*."

76. THE BOONDOCKS

Adam

Despite the glorious cottage garden setting, my mother wasn't keen on spending any time outside, even when Bridget was with her. "I feel like we're being watched, darling," she complained.

I didn't have the heart to tell her that the Lost Boys – acting on Charli's instruction – were carrying out surveillance.

"It's the dumb boys in the trees," yelled Bridget. "I see you, dumb Mason."

"No you don't," came a muffled reply from the hedge near the fence.

Bridget's problem with the littlest Lost Boy dated to her first day back in town. Mason made the mistake of telling her how ugly Treasure was – an unforgivable faux pas in Bridget's book.

My mother glared at me, alarmed by the notion of boys spying from the trees. "What on earth is going on?"

I grinned. "Welcome to the boondocks, Ma."

***

As if being under surveillance wasn't strange enough, Charli was in a weird mood too. She'd been fidgety and restless all day, and couldn't settle when we went to bed that night. I asked her a hundred times what the problem was, and her answer never changed.

"Nothing. I'm fine."

I slipped my hand underneath her thin top. "I could calm you down," I offered.

"Oh nice plan, Adam," she replied, pushing my hand away. "I'd love to get it on while your parents are in the next room."

My laugh bounced off the skin of her shoulder. "We made a baby in their bathroom while they were in the next room," I reminded her.

Even in the darkness, I saw her smile. "It's not the same thing."

"It's exactly the same thing."

Her hand moved to my face. "I'm glad you sorted out your differences with your dad," she whispered.

I kissed her. "Me too, but I don't want to talk about my dad."

"How about my dad? Can we talk about him?"

"Why? What's going on?"

Her explanation was short, but a long time coming. "I'm going to see him tomorrow," she replied. "I'm going to tell Alex about Olivia."

I kissed her again, more out of support than anything. "I think it's time," I told her. "And I think it'll give you the closure you need."

"What if he tells me something that ruins everything?" Her voice was barely there. "I couldn't stand it."

I wasn't sure what to say to allay her fears, and everything I came up with would've sounded untrue. Charli pressed her cheek to my chest as I pulled her in closer. "Whatever will be, will be, Charlotte," I whispered.

77. STARS

Charli

Gabrielle had no plans to return to teaching, but she couldn't completely let go of her schoolmarm tendencies. When Jack was a few months old, she returned to giving weekly art classes in the town hall. I knew she wouldn't be home when I arrived at the house, which was a prime example of me picking my moment.

I didn't have Alex's complete attention. When I walked into the kitchen, he was deep in conversation with my brother and tinkering with engine parts on the table. Jack was in his swing beside him, looking laidback and carefree as always.

"You have to pull out the float pin," he told him. "Needle nose pliers work best."

"Gabi would skin you alive if she saw you working on car parts in the house."

Alex jumped at the sound of my voice. Jack did not.

He pulled a face at me. "It's off the lawnmower, so it doesn't count."

I walked to Jack and kissed his little head. In return, he grabbed a clump of my hair and refused to let go. "Ow. Help me," I pleaded.

Alex was no help. "Just give his hair a pull," he advised unsympathetically. "He's got enough of it."

Something about my laugh amused Jack. He let out the cutest little chuckle I'd ever heard, which only ended once I managed to free myself. Sensing tears were on the way, I handed him a rattly toy.

"Dad, I was hoping we could talk for a minute," I said, pulling out a chair.

He smiled across at me. "We can talk for hours if you want to."

I was hoping it wouldn't take that long. I wanted the story of Olivia to be short and painless, but that was never going to happen because I also wanted every last detail. I must've looked troubled because of it.

"What's wrong?" he asked.

I wasn't sure where to begin so I dug into my pocket and dragged out something I hoped would make him start the conversation. I set the ugly locket down on the table and pushed it toward him.

Alex wiped his hands on a rag and then picked it up. "What's this?"

I studied his face, seeing no hint of anything other than bewilderment. He had no clue what he was looking at.

"You haven't seen it before?" I asked in a small voice.

He slid it back to me. "Never."

In my heart of hearts, I had known it was a lie. Alex would never have gifted something so gaudy and cheap – even to Olivia. I had one last thing to show him. I passed him the wooden box.

He didn't look baffled this time. I could tell by his expression that he knew exactly what it was. He took it when I held it out to him. "I gave this to your mother." I'd never heard his voice sound so small. "Where did you get it?"

After months of planning the conversation in my head, none of it came out as I hoped it would. But the story was complete, and just as ugly as when it had played out for real.

After a long moment, he finally spoke. "Love affairs at seventeen are about intensity, not longevity."

I couldn't stop the pissed-off groan that escaped me. I didn't want the romantic spiel he'd given me in the past. Protecting my feelings wasn't an issue any more, and I told him so.

He nodded, resigned to the fact that he was going to have to be truthful with me. "Olivia wasn't always cold, Charli," he said. "I adored her at one time – completely loved her."

I shook my head, unable to believe him. "That's not the woman I met. The woman I met was an utter bitch."

His eyes drifted to the box in his hand. "She never used to be," he said quietly. "Things changed once she fell pregnant. She was so focused on her ballet that not even a baby in her belly slowed her down. It was a nightmare."

Tears started rolling down my cheeks the instant his voice got shaky. I was forcing him to revisit a place he'd left a long time ago, but he did it.

According to Alex, she wasn't prepared to give up nine months of her life to have a baby, but had no choice because abortion was out of the question. "She was too far along when we found out," he explained. "So Olivia decided adoption was the best option. She came up with the not-so-brilliant plan of carrying on as if she wasn't pregnant."

"It's hard to hide a bump in your belly," I pointed out.

He looked across at me. "Not if you don't eat."

I suddenly felt ill, but swallowed hard and kept it together.

"I spent months and months doing all I could just to get my daughter here safely." He choked out the words. "She wouldn't eat and she wouldn't stop her gruelling dance sessions. She didn't make a single concession for the little life struggling to grow inside her."

I dabbed my eyes with my fingertips, futilely attempting to stem the crying. Alex's eyes never left mine, but he no longer seemed to be looking at me.

"There was nothing I could do, Charli," he said weakly. "I loved her, and then I resented her, and then I lost respect for her." He brought his forearm to his face, swiping his sleeve across his eyes. "And in the end, I felt nothing for her."

I infinitesimally nodded. "I get it."

"Are you sure you get it?" he asked, regaining the strength in his voice. "Be sure you get it, Charlotte," he demanded. "Be sure that you understand how hard I fought for you. Be sure you know about the times I got down on my knees and begged her to eat something, or pleaded with her to stop training for hours on end."

"I get it, Alex," I cried. "I know."

If he'd left it there I wouldn't have argued, but I'd opened a floodgate and my father wasn't finished talking.

"One day she told me that she didn't care whether you lived or died," he remembered. "That was it for me."

"Olivia said there were complications, and that she was advised against having more children."

He gave a hard, humourless laugh. "The only complication Olivia had was you. And the only person who told her not to have more children was me," he growled. "Probably while I was trying to force feed her a bowl of cereal."

I frowned at him. "Cereal?"

"It's the only thing I could get her to eat. It's no wonder you like it so much."

I had no control over the giggle that crossed my lips. I'd spent weeks searching for some minute detail to align myself to her, and he'd given it to me. We both liked cereal.

"She hates me, Alex," I said, quickly composing myself. "She blames me for her life going wrong."

With his free hand, he reached across the table. "You listen to me," he ordered. "I couldn't care less how Olivia feels about you. You were never hers. You were mine all along."

The hole in my heart that had been plaguing me since the first night I'd met my mother healed in an instant. The man who'd protected me and loved me my whole life had fought for me even before I was born. That was all I need to know about the story of me.

I felt exhausted, but had one more burning question. "She knew we lived here," I blurted. "Did she come here?"

He grimaced. "She really went to town on you, didn't she?"

"Yeah." And he'd never know the half of it.

Alex reached across to Jack and smoothed his hair. "Olivia showed up here the day after my mother's funeral. You were three."

The story got worse. At a time when Alex was most vulnerable, she weaselled her way back in. "I'd just lost my mother, I was alone with this little kid and Olivia came knocking." He sounded annoyed with himself, as if being gullible was a crime. "I think she was in a bad place, too. Perhaps she thought I could do something about that."

Olivia was an opportunist. It didn't surprise me that she'd run to Alex when the chips were down. I wondered how long she stuck around once she worked out he had nothing to give her.

"Did she stay long?"

"Two days." He shook his head. "Nothing had changed. She barely even spoke to you, and when she did it was awkward. I told her to leave and never come back – and she never did."

"Just like that?"

"Not exactly like that," he conceded. "She let fly at me first, accusing me of being a terrible father, a good-for-nothing failure and every other nasty thing she could think of." That was the venom-tongued Olivia I knew. It was almost a relief to hear him say it. "That's when I decided to stick with the lie that my mother had started," he said bleakly. "I figured I couldn't fail you as badly if you didn't know I was your dad. The whole world was saved from knowing what a dud hand you'd been dealt in the parenting department."

"I never felt that way." I drummed my finger on the table with every word spoken, making sure he understood. "Never."

"Things were very different in the beginning, Charli. You were made out of love. It wasn't some casual –"

I cut him off, unwilling to let him finish the ugly sentence. "I know."

"How do you know?" he asked. "It doesn't sound like she painted a very pretty picture."

I flipped open the locket, showing him the picture inside. "You can't fake that," I told him. "The kids in that picture are happy."

He snapped the locket closed and finally smiled. "I really did love her," he declared. "But I loved you more."

I smiled back. "Will you tell me about the box?"

Alex picked it up and opened the lid, chuckling as he grabbed the typed card. "I typed this on my mum's typewriter. My handwriting sucked, even then." He raised the card to his face and read it out. "They're always close. All you have to do it look for them."

"She said it was about stars," I prompted.

"I used to promise her things," he explained. "Anything to get her to fly right and look after the baby in her belly."

His story didn't vary much from hers, but the meaning behind it was very different. "I'd already worked out by that point that there was no future for us, but I still held the tiniest amount of hope that she'd sort herself out and come good." I almost laughed at the irony. I'd spent weeks doing the same thing. "I told her that stars were promises wrapped up in light, and that they'd always remain and stay true," he explained. "All she had to do was look for them."

"Do you think she did?" I asked.

Alex flipped the box over, studying the back of it. "No, she had no magic in her heart," he replied. "Olivia wasn't into looking for stars. She was too busy trying to be one." He looked up at me, half-smiling. "She must've spent all these years thinking I gave her an empty box."

I frowned. "You did."

Using both hands and some effort, he pulled the back panel off the box. As it broke open, something flew out and tumbled across the table. Before I saw what it was, Alex picked it up. It was a charm bracelet, and every charm on it was a star.

"I never lied to her," he said, dangling it in front of me. "I gave her stars. All she had to do was care enough to look for them."

78. LOVELY

Adam

My parents returned home in the early New Year, which meant The Lost Boys were out of a job. With no French diplomats to protect, hiding out in the bushes gave way to much less covert forms of surveillance. Their constant presence annoyed me, but it infuriated my daughter.

An afternoon tea party at the beach should've been an escape, but Mason appeared at the base of the walking trail shortly after we arrived. Bridget was sitting a short distance from us, pouring pretend cups of tea for her heinous guest of honour, Treasure.

She jumped to her feet when she spotted him. "You can't play here," she scolded.

The littlest Lost Boy bravely continued his slow wander toward her. "Are you having a party?"

Bridget glanced down at the spread in front of her. "Yes," she confirmed. "A lovely one."

Charli hooked her arm through mine and leaned in close. "This is how it starts, Adam," she murmured from the corner of her mouth. "Your daughter is being wooed."

"Tell him to leave my girl alone, Charlotte."

"I think you have a few years before you need to start panicking," she replied.

She was probably right. Bridget wasn't exactly welcoming him with open arms. She sat down and continued pouring tea, leaving Mason hanging at the edge of the blanket.

"Do you like cake, Mason?" she asked irrelevantly.

"Yes," he replied. "Do you like pterodactyls?"

Her shoulders lifted. "I haven't tasted any before."

Mason laughed so hard that he clutched his belly and dropped to the sand. "You can't eat them, silly. They're distinct."

Charli glanced at me, grinning.

I smiled back. "He truly is related to Wade."

"He's five, Adam," she replied laughing. "Cut him some slack."

Bridget was forgiving too. After testing the friendship waters with a few more inane questions, she finally gave Mason permission to join her tea party.

Bridget passed him a cup.

"It's pink," he complained.

"Pink is lovely," she retorted.

"Why do you always say lovely?"

With a teacup in each hand, Bridget threw out her arms. "Because the whole world is lovely," she announced theatrically. "Look at it."

In that moment, I realised everything was golden. We'd endured a hellish last few months in New York – and my kid had come out of it still maintaining that the whole world was lovely.

"You are a bit crazy, Bridget," concluded Mason.

She thrust her cup forward as if making a toast. "Yes I am," she agreed. "Crazy lovely."

***

Determined to make the most of the summer months, entire afternoons were whittled away at the beach. Most of the time it was quiet and relaxing, but this day was shaping up to be a little different, and it had nothing to do with the arrival of Mason.

Charli and I both turned at the sound of a blood-curdling shriek coming from further up the beach. A few seconds later, Nancy, the butt-ugly Pomeranian came scurrying into view, with Jasmine Davis in hot pursuit.

"Stop her!" she screamed. "Her leash broke."

The kindest thing would've been to let the dog go. By my reckoning, Nancy had to be pushing three hundred in dog years. If she'd waited all that time to make a run for it, she deserved to be free.

I leaned closer to Charli. "Furry mutiny," I mumbled, making her giggle.

Nancy ran out of steam just as she reached us, panting like she was about to keel over. Her owner caught up a minute later, acting exactly the same way.

"Don't move," Jasmine ordered, arms outstretched.

I didn't like her chances of cornering her dog. Nancy was weighing up her options, and from where we sat, an ocean escape looked likely.

"Daddy," called Bridget, pointing. "Look at that lovely dog wearing a dress."

Clothes really did make the man – or in this case, the mutt. The ridiculous pink hoodie was designed to hide the fact that most of its fur was missing.

"I hate that ugly dog," grumbled Mason. "It really stinks."

Perhaps offended, Nancy got her second wind and took off running again.

"Mason, help aunty Jasmine," she cried, darting after her. "We have to catch her."

Called to duty, the Lost Boy jumped up and gave chase. Bridget abandoned her tea party, wandered over to us and piled on to my lap. "They won't catch that dog," she insisted.

"She'll slow down eventually," Charli assured her.

"No Mama." Bridget shook her head. "She's a sea dog."

As if on cue, Nancy proved her right by running into the low breaking waves. Jasmine must've really wanted her back. After warning Mason to stand back, she jumped in after her.

"You wouldn't see that in Manhattan," announced Charli in between giggles.

Jasmine eventually staggered out of the surf with her mangy mutt in her arms. She was spluttering, Nancy was exhausted and both of them looked like bedraggled monsters.

Bridget saw fit to welcome them back with cheers and a round of applause. "Happy, happy day for the sea hag!" she yelled.

It wasn't the first time I'd put my hand over my daughter's mouth to stop her speaking, but it was the first time I'd ever stifled a laugh while doing it. Charli wasn't as polite. She laid back in the sand, giving in to a fit of hysterics.

"Welcome to your new perfect life, Adam," she said, barely composing herself. "Never a dull moment."

Despite the madness, life *was* perfect. We were finally on track, and none of us were interested in looking back.

79. DÉNOUEMENT

Charli

Chances are, Jean-Luc wasn't speaking literally when he encouraged me to pen my own *dénouement*, but six months after returning to the Cove, I decided to write one in the notebook, and return it to its rightful owner.

I added my entry while standing at the counter of the post office with Bridget at my feet. Her constant bumping meant my handwriting wasn't as neat as it could've been, but the story was spectacular:

> *Charlotte and Adam – a dénouement*
> *Far from what they once were, but not yet what they're going to be.*

It was the closest I hoped we'd ever get to an ending. I wanted our story to continue forever, and as straight-laced as Jean-Luc was, I knew he'd appreciate the deeper meaning behind the words.

I sealed the parcel and handed it to postmistress Val. She glanced down at my belly. "How much longer do you have to go now, Charli?"

Bridget chimed in. "Three days."

"Not quite," I corrected with a smile. "Ten weeks."

"It's a girl baby," added Bridget.

"And how do you know?" asked Val, leaning over the counter to look at her.

Bridget cupped her hands to her mouth. "Magic," she whispered.

The uppity postmistress might not have been sold on her left-of-centre explanation, but I was.

Absolutely nothing is impossible to willing hearts.

THE END